J. ROZAN was born and raised in the Bronx and is a long-time
anhattan resident. An architect for many years, she is now a full-
me writer. Her critically acclaimed, award-winning novels and
ories have won most of crime fiction's greatest honours, including
e Edgar, Anthony, Shamus, Macavity and the Nero Award.

Praise for *Blood Rites*
(published in the US as *Reflecting the Sky*) and the
Bill Smith/Lydia Chin series:

"S.J. Rozan is one of my favourite crime writers. Intricate
plotting, great characters, smart, crisp writing. This is a
fantastic series – crime writing at its best" HARLAN COBEN

"With the Bill Smith and Lydia Chin mysteries,
S. J. Rozan has written the most consistently compelling series
of traditional detective novels published in this decade."
George Pelecanos

"This is a beautifully written book with a sophisticated plot,
rich in both action and atmosphere. . . ."
Publishers Weekly (starred review)

D0543608

Also by S.J. Rozan:

Trail of Blood
Blood Ties
Out for Blood

BLOOD RITES

S. J. ROZAN

EBURY
PRESS

1 3 5 7 9 10 8 6 4 2

Published in 2012 by Ebury Press, an imprint of Ebury Publishing
A Random House Group Company
First published in 2001 in the US by St Martins Press as *Reflecting the Sky*

The Random House Group Limited Reg. No. 954009

Addresses for companies within the Random House Group can be found at:
www.randomhouse.co.uk

A CIP catalogue record for this book is
available from the British Library

The Random House Group Limited supports The Forest Stewardship
Council (FSC®), the leading international forest certification organisation.
Our books carrying the FSC label are printed on FSC® certified paper.
FSC is the only forest certification scheme endorsed by the leading
environmental organisations, including Greenpeace.
Our paper procurement policy can be found at:
www.randomhouse.co.uk/environment

Printed and bound by CPI Group (UK) Ltd, Croydon, CR0 4YY

ISBN 9780091936341

To buy books by your favourite authors and register for offers visit
www.randomhouse.co.uk

Acknowledgments

Thank you to:

Steve Axelrod, my agent
Keith Kahla, my editor
who have no crows on their roofs

Susanna Bergtold, Nancy Ennis, Sui-Ling Tsang,
and Jill Weber
who were there in person

Richard (the Muse) Wilcox
who was there in spirit

Denise Bigo, John Douglas, Jennifer Jaffe, Tina Meyerhoff,
Larry Pontillo, and Tom Savage
who know the truth about swiftly running water

Charles Doherty
who is one of the gifts of Hong Kong

Steve Blier, Hillary Brown, Monty Freeman, Max Rudin,
Jim Russell, and Amy Schatz
who will take on any body of water

Betsy Harding, Royal Huber, Barbara Martin,
Jamie Scott, and Keith Snyder
who will take on any body of words

Doreen and Jonathan Chou,
Edna Quan and Anthony Siu,
Sandra Gong and Victor Sloan,
Howard and Marilyn Smith,
and the HKPD's Jean Chan Sui-mui
who could not have been more generous

and
hghnola and spencyr
who

Sadly,
for my mother

one

Damp, soupy heat washed over me as I pushed out through the revolving door. The bright morning glare was already hazed up by the shimmering exhaust of a river of cars, buses, and trucks. I looked left, looked right, got my bearings, and headed briskly down the sidewalk.

"Come *on*!" I turned to yell to my partner, Bill Smith, who still stood, looking a little groggy, his hands in his pockets, just gazing around. "Relive your misspent youth some other time! I don't want to be late."

With muttered words I was just as happy not to hear, he lurched down the sidewalk after me. Jostling, rushing pedestrians, many of them yelling into their cell phones, hurried past in both directions, making me feel like I had to work to keep my footing or I'd be tossed on their tide and swept away. Bill caught up to me as I stopped at the first corner, waiting with a crowd eight deep for the light to change.

"Late is extremely unlikely," he grumbled, taking advantage of the momentary halt in our forward charge to light a cigarette. "Impolitely early, maybe. We're twenty-five minutes ahead of even your obsessive-compulsive schedule. Will you slow down? And how do you know where you're going? I thought I was supposed to be your native guide."

"I don't know what you're supposed to be doing," I said as the light turned green and the crowd surged forward, "but it can't be guiding me around a place you haven't been in for twenty years."

A horn blasted as the last stragglers from our pedestrian stream leaped up onto the curb to avoid being mashed by a bus. The hiss and rumble of tires, the squeal of bus brakes, and the endless rattle of jackhammers from nearby construction made conversation difficult, but I was too keyed up to talk, anyway. The wind shifted, stirring the smells of diesel fuel and salt water into the scents of softened asphalt and frying pork already thick in the air. They were exciting smells, and it was an exciting morning, all the rushing, rumbling, surging, and yelling in the brightness. Though I didn't see, really, why I should be so affected by it. I've spent my entire life negotiating traffic, noise, glare, and sidewalks. I'm Lydia Chin, born and raised in Chinatown, a genuine native New Yorker.

Of course, this wasn't New York. This was Hong Kong, City of Life.

Life, pork, exhaust, and pedestrians. Bill matched his pace to mine and we hurried down the sidewalk in the sticky heat. Being from Chinatown, I was better at this business of threading through dense, moving crowds of Chinese people than he was, though the streams on the sidewalks of home had never flowed this fast. We kept being separated, coming together, getting pushed apart again. But we both knew where we were going—he because he had been here before, on R and R leaves in the navy; me because I had been studying maps for a week— and we ended up together and exactly where we wanted to be, at the turnstiles of the Star Ferry.

At which point I glanced at my watch, and then, because I know my watch, at his. "Wait," I said. "As you so accurately, although crabbily, pointed out, we're still early. The ferries run every eight minutes. Let's take the next one. I want to see."

He raised his eyebrows and sighed theatrically, but I didn't care. Leaving him to follow, I zipped past the English-language bookstore, the Japanese snack shop, the newspaper vendors and the public bathrooms. The ferry terminal buildings gave way to an open promenade with a railing, and suddenly there was the Hong Kong skyline shining across the harbor.

It was as though someone had unrolled New York, slapped it with dozens of huge, neon brand-name signs visible even in the hazy sunshine, and spread it against a backdrop of mountains along a waterfront so long I had to turn my head way to the left and then way to the right to see the ends of it. Water sparkled in the sun, lapping against the seawall we were standing on. The frothy wakes churned up by barges, fishing boats, great white yachts, and tiny green sampans heading both ways through the harbor criss-crossed the trails of ferries plowing back and forth across it, from Hong Kong Island, where we were going, to the tip of the Kowloon Peninsula, where we were. The ferry we'd almost taken tooted its horn as it nosed out of its berth, and from way off to the right came a much deeper sound, some other horn saying something in the universal language of ships.

"Close your mouth," Bill said. "People will know you're a tourist."

"I'm not a tourist. We're here on business. And why didn't you tell me it was this *huge*?"

He gazed across the harbor. "When I was here, it ended about there." He pointed with both hands at the limits of a much shorter waterfront. "And none of the biggest sky-scrapers were there, and neither was that." *That* was a low, swoopy building, all metallic curves and wings, shining in the sun, right in the center, right on the water. "But the impression was the same. I stood there with my mouth open, too."

"My mouth is not open. I'm Lydia Chin. Stuff like this doesn't impress me," I said, unable to take my eyes from the view across the water.

"I know," Bill said. "That's one of your best character-istics, how hard you are to impress." He looked at his watch. "Now we're right on schedule. We'd better go, or we actually will be late, and you'll blame me."

"Well, it'll be your fault," I said, tearing myself away from the skyline, turning to hurry back to the ferry. "You're the one with the good watch."

"Maybe that's why I'm here," Bill said as we dropped our ridged coins in the ferry turnstile and headed with the rest of the crowd up the stairs. "Because I have a watch that works."

"That's an expensive timekeeper." I trotted down the wooden ramp onto the boat and took a seat at the very front so I could see us sail across the harbor. "A business-class ticket and a week in a fancy hotel? It would have been cheaper for Grandfather Gao to buy me a Rolex."

"Or he could have put me in the same hotel room as you. That would have saved him a bundle. In fact, maybe we have a fiduciary duty to our client—"

I gave his fiduciary duty a dirty look and turned back to the opposite shore; we had started to move.

As the harbor breeze blew my hair around, I watched the edges of the skyline sharpen out of the haze. The buildings grew larger and Bill sat silent beside me, watching them too. It really wasn't clear to either of us why he was here. It wasn't, actually, clear to me why either of us was here.

What had seemed clear a week ago when I'd first heard this idea was that I was probably hallucinating and had lost my mind. Either that, or Grandfather Gao had lost his; but even suggesting that idea to myself made me so queasy from guilt that I had to calm myself with another sip of his tea.

I still couldn't believe it, though. "You want me to go to Hong Kong?" We were sitting at the low, lion-footed table in Grandfather Gao's Chinatown herb shop, surrounded by the dark wood cabinets with their small drawers, the brass urns and ceramic jars, the mingled smells of sweet incense and dried herbs that were as familiar to me as the flowered upholstery, family pictures, and spicy aroma of my mother's cooking in the Chinatown apartment where I grew up.

"With your partner," Grandfather Gao replied. His voice was its usual calm, somber self, but even in the shop's peaceful shadows I could see him smile at the excited squeak in my voice. He used to smile that same smile when

I was seven, when I made that same excited squeak.

I tried to control myself and act dignified. I liked to think I'd changed in the years since I used to come bouncing into the shop, interrupting Grandfather Gao in the middle of weighing out herbs for a customer or reading his Chinese newspaper, to tell him about some event or idea of enormous importance to a grade-school child. After all, I'm twenty-eight, a PI with her own practice, a licensed professional. Even if my license is in a profession my entire family abhors.

So I sipped my tea calmly and regarded my prospective client professionally. He wore a dark suit and tie, with a gloriously starched white shirt, as always. His thin black hair was combed straight back from his high forehead. He reached an age-spotted hand to the teapot and poured for me, and it suddenly occurred to me that maybe I'd changed in all these years, but Grandfather Gao hadn't, not one bit.

"I hope this is a convenient time for this journey, Ling Wan-Ju," he went on, as though this were a normal conversation. Because we spoke in Cantonese, as we always did, he used my Chinese name, as he always had. "Your partner also, I hope he is free?"

By my partner, he meant Bill Smith. Although, unlike my family, Grandfather Gao does not regard Bill as the human equivalent of the primrose path to hell, it was still a shock to hear him suggest that Bill accompany me to the other side of the world.

Nevertheless, resolving to regain my cool professional demeanor, as befits a private investigator about to be sent overseas, I said, "Grandfather, of course I'll do anything you ask. But you know I've never traveled. I may not be the right choice to perform this task for you, whatever it is." It was killing me to say this, since I was already seeing myself in a window seat on the New York–Hong Kong flight, but it was always best to come clean with Grandfather Gao.

"Your partner has traveled," he answered, unperturbed. "I have considered this carefully, Ling Wan-Ju. A stream undisturbed flows easily to the sea, but a stream can be diverted, set on another course. You are a person in whose ability to find the correct course I have a great deal of confidence."

I blushed from my toes to the roots of my hair. Grandfather Gao did nothing but sit in his chair and sip tea. I sipped tea, too, and tried to act as though people who meant to me what Grandfather Gao did said things to me like he'd just said every day of the week. When I found my voice, I said, "Thank you, Grandfather. What is the task?"

He didn't speak right away, but looked into the shadows of his shop. Behind him, tendrils of smoke wandered into the air from the three sticks of incense burning at General Gung's shrine, high on the wall.

"When I was a boy in China," he said, bringing his eyes back to me, "two other boys in the village were as close to me as brothers. We were constant companions, inseparable. One of those boys was your grandfather."

I knew that. That was why, when my parents came to America, Grandfather Gao had looked out for them, finding them the apartment my mother and I still lived in, getting my mother her first sewing job, arranging for English lessons for my oldest brother, Ted, who, along with my next-oldest brother, Elliot, had been born in Hong Kong. That was why, along with lots of other Chinatown kids whose families had been split apart when some came to America and some stayed behind, though he wasn't really ours, we had always called him "Grandfather."

As though he were reading my mind—a sense I had with disconcerting frequency—Grandfather Gao said, "When we were fourteen, I left China in the company of Wei Yao-Shi, the third companion of our boyhood days. Your grandfather remained in the village. We never saw him again."

"My father always said grandfather couldn't bear the thought of living anywhere but where his family had always lived."

Grandfather Gao nodded. He paused, looking not at me and not, I thought, at the dark wood or the parchment scroll his eyes seemed to rest on. "I came immediately to America," he said. "Wei Yao-Shi remained in Hong Kong for some years. He brought his younger brother, Ang-Ran, out of China. The two established an import-export firm." Now he looked at me. "When your parents left China, it was Wei Yao-Shi who sponsored them in Hong Kong."

He stopped speaking; I waited, wondering about the slight note of worry I thought I heard behind his calm, decisive voice.

"When the Wei brothers' firm began to do business in America," he began again, "Wei Yao-Shi came here. He opened an office. He married. He did not live in Chinatown, but bought a house in Westchester. Though he continued to spend a good part of each year in Hong Kong, he became . . . quite American. When you were small, Ling Wan-Ju, you met my old friend Wei Yao-Shi. He, like I, followed the progress of your family, for the sake of our friend, your grandfather."

This was news to me. Seeing my expression, Grandfather Gao smiled. "His reports to your grandfather were quite satisfactory."

Well, good, I thought, not sure I was quite comfortable with being watched and reported on, even if the reports were satisfactory.

"Your grandfather died many years ago in China," Grandfather Gao said. "Now Wei Yao-Shi has died here in New York."

At General Gung's shrine the incense smoke seemed to shudder, as though a breeze had found a way into the shop's cool recesses. "I'm sorry, Grandfather."

"Thank you, Ling Wan-Ju. He was, of course, as I am, an old man."

I didn't at all like what that implied. "Grandfather—"

He silenced me with a look. "The seasons will change, Ling Wan-Ju. The leaves will fall."

I knew better than to get involved when the nature metaphors began. I sat in silence, waiting for him to go on.

"Wei Yao-Shi left me with a task to accomplish. A letter

to be given to his brother in Hong Kong. A keepsake to be delivered to his young grandson, also there. His own ashes, to be taken home for burial. I would like you, with your partner, to do these things for me."

We sat for some time in the quiet of the shop, drinking tea, as Grandfather Gao explained to me the specifics of the situation. The more I heard, the more I understood his thought that things were not simple. What was involved, though, still didn't seem like things you'd need a PI to accomplish, much less two, but I had voiced my opinion and Grandfather Gao seemed set on this path. I saw no reason to argue further.

When we were done I went home, took a deep breath, and explained my client's request to my mother.

"To Hong Kong?" She sat on our living room couch, me beside her. The sun poured in the window, sparkling off my father's collection of mud figures in their glass cabinet. The expression on my mother's face was the same as it would have been if I'd told her Grandfather Gao wanted me to fly up to heaven and bring him back one of the peaches of immortality. "Gao Mian-Liang wants you to go to Hong Kong? He has chosen you for this important task?"

"With Bill," I said. "He said Bill needs to come along."

I was as astounded as she was: she at what I had said, I because I had never before seen my mother at a loss for words.

I could understand her dilemma, though. On the one hand, she couldn't imagine I could go all the way to Hong Kong, a place on the other side of the world I knew nothing about—and where almost everyone is Chinese, a state of being that according to my mother I, an American born and raised, also knew nothing about—and not screw this up. On the other hand, there was no way she could contradict Grandfather Gao's decision in this or any other matter. And on the third hand, Bill was supposed to be going, too.

This last became her point of departure. "If you went alone," she said, "alone, with no distraction, possibly you could accomplish this task. Or—" her whole face brightened with inspiration and relief; she had found an answer, "—or, Ling Wan-Ju, if I were to go with you, I could guide you. I could help you. I could make sure you did not fail in this undertaking, so important to Grandfather Gao."

Oh boy, I thought. But I didn't stop her as she grabbed the red kitchen phone ("Red, most likely to bring good news") and dialed the number at Grandfather Gao's shop.

After that conversation, I called Bill.

"I'm coming over."

"Good," he said. "Why?"

"Just wait till you hear."

It took me, adrenaline-filled as I was, about six minutes to get from the apartment to his place above the bar on Laight Street. Generally, it's a ten-minute walk, but that's if you walk.

Bill was waiting for me at the top of the stairs, a fresh cup of coffee in his hand. He poured hot water into a teapot as I paced the living room, outlining the job we'd been offered.

"Grandfather Gao?" Bill said. "Can I call him that? And will you please sit down?"

"Yes. And no. I can't."

Neatly sidestepping me, he moved to the couch safely out of my path and put his coffee on the table beside him. "Your tea's ready. You want it to go?" I glared. He grinned. "Boy, I've never seen you like this."

"Grandfather Gao!" I said, striding by. "Grandfather Gao wants to hire *me*! Do you know who he is in Chinatown? Do you know what he's been in my life? Do you know what he is in the eyes of my *mother*?"

Bill did know, and I knew he did, but he asked, "What?"

"Respectability itself! The Man Who! Even my mother can't object to my working for Grandfather Gao. I mean, she does on principle because she hates this profession. But she's secretly thrilled that *Grandfather Gao* thinks a worthless girl like me can be some use to him."

"If it's a secret how do you know?"

"She's my mother. And Grandfather Gao—" I turned and strode the other way, "Grandfather Gao could get anybody he wanted to work for him! But he thinks *I'm* the one who can help him out. Me! Little Ling Wan-Ju. That tomboy. That misguided problem child. And—!"

Bill waited, patience itself. Finally, after I'd done another lap, he said, "And what?"

"*And* he wants to send us to Hong Kong! The other side of the *planet*! Ted and Elliot were born there. My parents used to live there."

"And Suzie Wong."

"Hong Kong! It's almost China."

"It is China, now."

"You know what I mean! I've hardly ever been anywhere in my whole life, and now I have a client offering me business-class tickets and a week in a hotel in Hong Kong. How can you just sit there like that?"

He picked up his coffee. "Okay, tell me again."

"Thursday," I said, telling him the important part. "Can you do it? Can you come?"

"He really wants me to? Why?"

I stopped pacing and just stood for a moment, looking at him. "I don't know," I confessed. "What he wants us to do seems pretty simple, not something a paying client might think he needs two people for. But it was his idea. He said, 'Neither the little bird nor the water buffalo, different though they are, can do its work alone.' "

"And I suppose you would be the little bird?"

I didn't answer, because it seemed obvious. Bill sipped his coffee. "You know, of course, that the bird sits up there on the water buffalo's rump and eats his fleas?"

I detoured into the kitchen and picked up the tea he'd fixed for me. "If you have fleas, you're sitting in coach."

The tea was jasmine, one of my favorite kinds, and I had to admit that over the four or so years we'd known each other Bill had learned to make a not bad cup of tea.

But all I could think as I sipped it was, I wonder if they drink jasmine tea in Hong Kong.

"And what are we supposed to do in Hong Kong?" Bill asked.

"Bring a bequest to a seven-year-old boy."

"Any particular seven-year-old boy, or do we get to choose?"

"Harry," I said impatiently, starting to pace again. "The grandson of Wei Yao-Shi. Didn't I tell you that already?"

"You haven't actually said anything coherent since you got here. I think it would help if you sat down."

"It wouldn't. I told you, I can't." He was following me with his head as though I were a one-woman tennis match. "Now listen: This little boy—his Chinese name is Wei Hao-Han, by the way—his grandfather, Wei Yao-Shi, just died. Mr. Wei and *my* grandfather and Grandfather Gao were inseparable buddies in the home village in China."

"Used to hang out on street corners together, whistle at girls, stuff like that?"

"Certainly not. The home village didn't have streets, just dirt paths. Can you hang out on a dirt path corner?"

"Depends on whether that's where the girls go by."

"Oh, of course. Anyway, my grandfather stayed there, but Mr. Wei and Grandfather Gao left to come to America when they were fourteen."

"Looking for street corners."

"No doubt."

I told Bill about Mr. Wei's younger brother, the import-export firm, the office Mr. Wei came to New York to establish, his marriage, his traveling back and forth, and the house in the suburbs.

"Now," I said, "a month ago Mr. Wei died and left this thing with Grandfather Gao with instructions to give it to his grandson Harry and a letter to his brother at the same time and Grandfather Gao wants you and me to go to Hong Kong to deliver them. How hard is that?"

"To understand, or to do? Or to say in one breath the way you did? Because I don't think I could do that."

"You could if you didn't smoke."

"You pace. I smoke." He struck a match and lit a cigarette, maybe to illustrate the point. I picked up pacing speed, to keep up my side.

"I understand it," he said, dropping the match in an ashtray. "Mostly. But I do have one question. No, two."

"Shoot."

"You say Mr. Wei came here and married. How come he has a seven-year-old grandson in Hong Kong? Did his kids move back there?"

"Ah. I was afraid you'd ask that."

Bill raised his eyebrows and I prepared to tell him the rest of the situation, the part that made the thing not simple. "Mr. Wei's American son, Franklin, lives here in New York. But apparently about a year after Mr. Wei got married here he got married in Hong Kong."

"Hmmm. Short-lived marriage, the one here."

"Actually, no."

"Say what?"

I took a defensive sip of tea. "Now don't go getting all superior and moral. It's the traditional Chinese way. A man is entitled to as many wives as he can support."

"He is? You mean still? Today? They still do that?"

"Well, no," I conceded. "By my parents' time they'd pretty much stopped, and of course Mao stamped that sort of thing right out. But men of Mr. Wei's generation—well, it happened."

"It happened." He was grinning. No one could ever say Bill was a handsome man, but when he grins this particular grin I sometimes have trouble staying as dignified as I like to be. "You mean, like an accident? Stumble into the church, wedding going on, you find out it's yours? Had one already, but what the hell?"

"We don't get married in church."

"You're grasping at straws. And you approve of that kind of behavior?"

"I can see certain merits," I said airily. "The more wives

there are, the less time each one has to spend with the husband."

"A good point. I'll remember that after you marry me. Did Mr. Wei's wives approve?"

"At least you'll have something to remember. They didn't know."

Bill pulled on his cigarette. "Now that's not a sign of a man with a clear conscience. When did they find out?"

"The wives? Both dead, long since, and it seems they never did know. The people who were surprised were the sons, on both sides of the planet, when the will was read. Grandfather Gao knew all along, and the younger brother in Hong Kong, but no one else did."

"How many sons? And did Grandfather Gao approve?"

"Two: one here, one there. And when did you get to be such a puritan?"

"Hey, you're the one who doesn't drink, smoke, or swear. Who'd have thought that when it came right down to it you were as twisted as the next guy? Wei was supporting both families the whole time?"

"Better," I said, leaving the next guy out of it. "He was living with both. According to Grandfather Gao, each family thought it was just an unfortunate necessity of business that he had to keep going back and forth to the other side of the world."

"This is great. But what if they needed to talk to him when he was on the other side of the world? Wouldn't the jig be up as soon as someone made a phone call?"

"He told both families he was staying in hotels and to contact him at work if they needed to. In Hong Kong that was the firm's office. That's why the brother had to know. In New York he used Grandfather Gao's number at the shop."

"And that worked all these years?"

"Seems to have."

Bill finished his coffee and set his mug down. "Okay. Intriguing as Mr. Wei's lifestyle is, let me ask my other question. Why us? This seems like a fairly straightforward job, delivering a legacy to a kid. You don't need an investigator to do this. What is it, by the way?"

"Jade. Some valuable piece, something Mr. Wei got in China on one of his buying trips and used to wear around his neck."

"Oh-ho, so he made buying trips to China? How do we know he hasn't got another three dozen wives over there?"

"Why do I get the feeling you're not taking this seriously?"

He gave me a look over his coffee that almost made me laugh. But someone around here needed to act like a grown-up, and neither Bill nor, I had to admit, old Mr. Wei seemed willing to play that role.

"Anyway," I said professionally, "he didn't go there that often. It was usually the brother who did the China trips. And to answer your question—assuming you still care about the answer—"

"Oh, I do, deeply."

"—Grandfather Gao says he's hiring us because he wants someone he can depend on, partly because of the other piece."

"The other piece of jade?"

"The other piece of the job. Delivering the bequest and the letter is only half of it. We also have to deliver Mr. Wei."

"You're kidding."

"He wants—wanted—to be buried in Hong Kong. Next to his second wife. In a mausoleum in Sha Tin on a windy mountain with a view of the hills and the water—" I broke off and looked at Bill, who was grinning yet again. "*What*?"

"You mean we're taking the old two-timer with us? Carrying his cheatin' heart home? Laying dem double-crossing bones to rest?"

"Ashes. And show some respect."

"You misread me. I have nothing but respect for your Mr. Wei. What a guy. Maybe just by being in the presence of his mortal remains, I can learn something."

"You," I said with all the dignity I could collect, "will

never learn anything. Anyway, the ceremony should be interesting. The half-brother will be there."

"What, from New York?"

"Dr. Franklin Wei. He's an orthopedist, in case you get your foot stuck in your mouth. Grandfather Gao says he's planning to go to the funeral."

"This is getting better and better. Why doesn't he take the jade? And the letter? And the ashes?"

"According to Grandfather Gao he's a little irresponsible. Married and divorced three times. Sequentially, not simultaneously."

"I was about to ask."

"I know you were. A wild and crazy guy."

"Me?"

"Dr. Franklin Wei. New girlfriend every six weeks. Known at all the best clubs and hot spots. Cancels office hours to go to the ball game. May or may not actually show up in Hong Kong. Grandfather Gao didn't want to risk it. Besides, it seems a little weird for him to be the one responsible for taking his father's jade to the son of his father's other son, under these circumstances."

"I think this whole thing is a going to be a little weird."

"Are you telling me you're coming?"

He pulled on the cigarette again. "You remember, of course, that the last time we left town together you got hurt?"

"So did you."

"Not as badly as you."

"Whose fault was that?"

"Mine, no doubt."

"If that's an apology," I said, "I accept."

"I just wanted you to know what you're getting into."

"I'll sign a waiver. So you'll come?"

"Well, I'd still like to know why he wants me to. Besides the water buffalo thing."

I gave him a look a little more serious than the ones I'd been giving him. "You're thinking he's expecting some kind of trouble?"

"The thought had crossed my mind."

"Mine, too," I said. "I tried to ask him. I said whatever small skills you and I might have, we were honored to put them at his disposal. I said we would exercise all our powers to accomplish the task he was setting us, and I was sure we could be most successful on his behalf if he were to tell us about any special concerns he had so we could prepare ourselves to meet them."

"Elegant, setting aside the *small*. And?"

I shook my head. "He said, 'Ling Wan-Ju, storm clouds often pass without rain, just as a dam can fail and flood a village on a clear, fine day.' "

"Well, that clears that up."

"You know Grandfather Gao never actually says everything he means. He thinks it works better if people find things out for themselves. And when he does talk," I admitted, "half the time it's in nature metaphors like that that I never understand."

"And that's why you're so crazy about him?"

"I'm crazy about him, as you so delicately put it, because he's wise, and kind, and fair. And he's a wonderful herbalist, and he makes great tea, and he never treated me like a dumb kid, even when I was one. And you," I told him, "should consider this: He's the only Chinese person of my acquaintance, with the possible exceptions of my brother Andrew and my best and oldest friend Mary, who would consider giving you the time of day."

"Well, you said he was wise." He squashed his cigarette out. "You don't think he could be setting us up?"

I was appalled. "Absolutely not! Grandfather Gao would never do anything to hurt me! If he's expecting trouble, and he wants to hire us, it's because he thinks we can handle whatever it's going to be. Which is another reason I *have* to take this job. I can't let him down if he's thinking like that."

Bill met my eyes and held them without speaking for almost longer than I could stand it. Then he looked back down and did some more cigarette-squashing. "When does he want us to leave?"

"Thursday! Thursday Thursday Thursday! *Well?*"

"What does your mother have to say? Not about the job, but about me going?"

"My mother?" I was surprised at the question, but I answered it with the truth. "You can't expect her to feel anything but pure horror at the idea of me flying to the other side of the world with you."

"I suppose not."

"On the other hand, like I told you, she secretly thinks working for Grandfather Gao will keep me out of trouble for a while, and she's always wanted me to go to Hong Kong. She says if I saw Hong Kong maybe I would understand better."

"Understand what?"

"She never says. But I'm sure it has something to do with my shortcomings as a Chinese daughter."

"So she approves?"

"She would walk off a cliff if Grandfather Gao suggested it, especially if it was for the good of her children. But she still doesn't like the idea of me going alone with you. She had a solution."

"Which was?"

"For her to come."

I enjoyed the expression on his face when I said that almost as much as I like his grin.

"Oh, my God. What did you say?"

"What could I say? She's my mother. But luckily Grandfather Gao said no."

"You said yes?"

"She's my mother."

He stared. "And I thought I knew you. My God, a guy's friends can turn on him."

"Besides, I wasn't sure you were coming."

"I'm not sure I should. You might be lying. We'll get to the airport, and there'll be your mother, with her shopping bags and that flowered umbrella to hit me over the head with—"

"I'm going to hit you over the head myself unless you tell me whether you're coming."

I stopped pacing and stood in front of him, resisting the urge to stamp my foot.

"Well," he said at last, "it's certainly tempting. The other side of the world on someone's else's nickel? A chance to spend a week in a hotel with you?"

"Separate rooms."

"A city where everyone smokes, where the weather's tropical, where I can relive some of the high points of my misspent youth?"

"On separate floors."

"Where the girls in the tight cheongsams sip mai-tais in booths in dim smoky bars until the Mama-sans call them over for you?"

"Separate hotels."

"Where the Tsingtao flows like water and every other basement's an opium den?"

"Separate land masses. Me on the Hong Kong side, you in Kowloon."

"Well, when you put it that way," he said, "how could I possibly turn it down?"

two

He hadn't turned it down, and neither had I. At the crack of dawn Thursday we were on a plane, and after thirteen hours in the leather upholstered, private-video-screened, nearly flat-reclining business-class seats Grandfather Gao had provided for us, we were in Tokyo. We had a two-hour layover, during which I sipped green tea and tried to look dignified while fighting a combination of excitement and exhaustion, and Bill drank beer and wandered off to the smoking lounge to sit puffing with the Japanese businessmen. Then another four-hour flight, and then, sometime near midnight, we came roaring in over all those skyscrapers and neon and landed on Lantau Island, in the shiny new Hong Kong airport. A car, also arranged by Grandfather Gao, met us and took us to the Hong Kong Hotel on the Kowloon side, where we spent the night in different rooms on separate floors. And now, after a breakfast of waffles and bacon for Bill and congee with pickled vegetables and preserved eggs for me—when in Rome, after all—here we were on the Star Ferry, about to dock.

The ferry creaked and rocked and was hauled in and tied by weathered Chinese men in uniforms that looked like the sailor suits an uncle had once given my brothers. My mother hadn't liked those suits—"Pah. Dress little boys like soldiers."—but my father had said that since Ted, Elliot, Andrew, and Tim were nothing alike in any other way, it was good occasionally to see them dressed alike. There was no sailor suit for me, of course.

Bill and I hurried along with the rest of the crowd, down the wooden ramp, up the concrete one, and onto the side-walk outside the terminal. I tried not to gape at the rickshaw men, as leathery and wrinkled as their rickshaws were red and gleaming. Now, they were just another tourist attrac-tion, the tips for posing for photos their only income, because now it was illegal to pull rickshaws in Hong Kong. But I thought of them, younger, stronger, just as poor, trotting through exhaust-spewing traffic yoked to their two-wheeled carts in heat like this. I looked at Bill and couldn't help asking, "Were they still pulling rickshaws when you were here before?"

"They weren't illegal yet. But I never took one."

"I thought that was the kind of thing American sailors did on leave."

"American sailors on leave have more . . . urgent . . . things to do. Come on, here's a cab."

We were taking a cab to the Weis' apartment, although on the map it looked like just the kind of long walk I love, especially in a city I'm new to. But both Bill and the guidebooks I'd been reading like crazy over the last week said Hong Kong, especially the Hong Kong Island side, was not made for the convenience of pedestrians. Our plan was to meet the Wei family and their attorney at the apartment, give Harry his jade and Mr. Wei's brother his letter, and arrange a date for the ceremony involved with placing Mr. Wei's ashes at the mausoleum. It wasn't much of a job, but it was what we'd been sent all the way here by Grandfather Gao to do, and I didn't want to screw it up in any way. There'd be plenty of time for exploring later, and plenty of exploring I wanted to do.

I gave the cab driver the Weis' address and settled back to watch the city go by. It was a little unnerving to watch it go by on the wrong side of the road, because Hong Kong people were taught to drive by the British; but everyone here seemed to have the hang of it, so I relaxed.

Our cab left the skyscraper-crowded Central district and started to work its way uphill. Hong Kong Island is basically a mountain rising out of the sea, and according to the guidebooks, the more money you have, the higher up you live. The Weis—the Hong Kong Weis, anyhow—lived in a high-up, high-rise neighborhood called Midlevels, where, especially in the newer buildings, money started to show.

The New York Wei, Dr. Franklin Wei, lived on Park and Seventy-first. Money showed there, too.

The road curved and twisted as it climbed, snaking through banyan, palm, and banana trees that shaded people, most of them Chinese, trudging the steep streets. The shadowed alleys and open windows of the older neighborhoods hunched between the impossibly tall, slender buildings that grew more numerous as we approached the address we were headed for. When we finally got there, to No. 10 Robinson Road, there was almost nothing anymore but towering apartment houses, taller and slimmer than I'd ever seen, white concrete or tan or pink with window glass tinted brown or blue against the sun.

We paid the cab and stood to look around a minute before we went in, because as Bill pointed out, we were still early. Well, he was the one with the dependable watch.

"Look how skinny these buildings are," I said, raising my voice over the jackhammers that were hard at work on this side of the harbor, too. "And they have pipes on the outside. We don't do that in New York, do we?"

"Plumbing doesn't freeze here," Bill said. "If you run the pipes up outside, the walls inside can be thinner and there's more space in the apartments."

I looked at the pipes, slim tubes grouped in rows of four or six, fastened back to the building wall every story or so, and thought about how crowded life would have to be, to make you care about another four inches inside your apartment.

We went into the glassed-in, air-conditioned lobby through a door opened for us by a uniformed doorman who didn't seem at all impressed by my gray linen slacks and blouse or Bill's navy blue suit. Ha, I thought, what you don't know. The security man at the curved granite desk—different from the security man who stood discreetly by the bronze-doored elevators—phoned up to the Wei apartment to say we were coming. Then the elevator security man took over, turning a key to send us to the twenty-sixth floor. The elevator whooshed us up silently, barely giving us time to admire the polished granite cab walls with the number 10 chiseled into them.

At twenty-six we got off and turned right down the carpeted hallway. Framed prints of Hong Kong harbor from a century ago, when the bustle was just beginning, hung on the walls. Tiny junks and sampans in them slipped in and out among the anchored British navy ships and the merchant ships flying a dozen different flags, none of them Chinese. One of the prints showed a view of the harbor from the hill we were on, a view all the way across to Kowloon. I wondered how much of the harbor you could see from the Wei's apartment.

I got that answer as we approached the door to 26C. Through the foyer archway into the living room I could catch a glimpse of sliding doors with drapes half-closed against the morning sun, and a sliver of a harbor view glittering in the slot between two of No. 10's high-rise neighbors. I could see this because the apartment door was standing open.

Bill and I glanced at each other. I stepped up to the door and knocked. There was no response, so I knocked again. I called out "Yau mo yen ah?"—"Is anyone there?"—and then as an afterthought added "Hello!" but still nothing. I gave Bill another look, then stepped inside.

Bill came up close, to watch my back: That's how we do this wherever we do it, whoever's in front, whoever's behind. As my heart sped up and I stepped through the foyer into the Weis' living room I sensed rather than saw Bill's hand reach into his jacket just as mine moved toward my belt, but we both came up empty. American PIs, no matter how licensed you are, can't bring guns into Hong Kong. Last week, in between reading guidebooks and studying maps, I had checked on that. Bill and I had agreed that this didn't sound like a job that really needed an investigator; but on the other hand, that's what we were.

And besides, we might have been wrong. Hong Kong, New York, or Dnepropetrovsk, a room that's been tossed is a room that's been tossed. And this one had been.

Once through the foyer the living room revealed itself in all its messed-up glory. Pictures off the wall, sofa cushions strewn around, drawers opened and their contents dumped. A vase of hibiscus blossoms, formerly resident on the coffee table in the center of the room, lay in a puddle on the pale blue carpet.

My heart now pounding, I met Bill's eyes again. He nodded. Since I was closest to the sliding doors I edged over and inched back the drapes to see the full extent of the balcony outside. It was as wide as the living room and no one was on it. In fact it was a good bet no one was in the apartment—that is, no one who had done this—because if they were still in the middle of their work they wouldn't have left the door wide open. But someone might be here, someone scared or hurt. We could have backed out, gone downstairs, and called the police, but it would take them time to get here. We'd do that as soon as we had a quick look around.

The quick look revealed nothing. Three bedrooms and a dining room, a maid's room off the kitchen, all of them empty, all of them wrecked. Not much was broken, but breaking things makes noise. Everything had been opened, turned upside down, gone through. But no one was hiding under a bed or cowering in a closet, and, though I wouldn't have said I was expecting it, I found myself letting out a long breath when no one was found lifeless in a pool of blood, either.

Still watchful, having touched almost nothing, Bill and I moved back out into the hall.

"Well," I said, picturing Grandfather Gao glancing at his watch in the room behind the herb shop in Chinatown, sipping at his evening tea and imagining everything going well here, "I guess we'd better go learn how you call the Hong Kong police."

Bill was about to answer, but the discreet ring of the elevator chime made us both spin around. A roundheaded, open-faced man in his thirties and a gray-haired woman stepped into the hall, talking and heading our way. They saw us; the man smiled, shifting his briefcase to his left hand so he could thrust his right forward for a handshake. "Miss Chin and Mr. Smith?" He smiled. His English was accented but clear. "I was told you'd come up. I'm Steven Wei; I'm sorry to be late. Didn't—?" He stopped when he saw the open door, looked quizzically from Bill to me.

"Don't go in," I said. "There's a problem."

"A—what does that mean?" Steven Wei threw a glance at his own threshold, where Bill's arm across the doorway blocked his way.

"I'm sorry, Mr. Wei," I said. "Someone's been here. The apartment's been searched. No one's there now," I added. "But we'd better call the police."

"Searched? What do you mean no one's there? Where's Li-Ling? Where are Harry and Maria?" He pushed past Bill, who dropped his arm without protest. Steven Wei stopped two steps into the room. I couldn't see his face, but his body looked like he'd walked into a wall. "What happened here?"

"I don't know." I stepped in beside him. "The door was open when we got here. We knocked, no one answered, and we came in. It looked like this."

"How do you know no one's here? Li-Ling! Harry!" His voice held the rising tones of panic. He started toward the bedrooms.

I grabbed his arm. "We looked."

He stopped. "What?"

"In case someone was hurt, or—we looked. There's no one here. Mr. Wei, we'd better call the police."

"No. No police." That came not from Steven Wei, but from the woman he'd come off the elevator with. She was tiny, with large almond eyes behind delicate gold-rimmed glasses, and these were the first words she'd spoken. She couldn't have weighed more than eighty pounds, and although the wrinkles around her eyes and mouth put her age close to sixty, the gray in her short hair would have been the only thing to keep her from being mistaken, from the back, for a twelve-year-old girl. Her voice was soft but her words were peremptory. "We will go inside."

She stood waiting for Bill, not, it seemed to me, out of politeness, but to make sure he was going to do as she'd said. He gave me a quick look, read my eyes, and did it. She stepped in behind him and shut the door.

She glanced rapidly around the room and then, as though she didn't need to see any more, said, "Steven. Come, sit down." She indicated a carved wooden chair with an upholstered seat, as though Steven Wei needed instructions in his own living room, and then righted its mate for herself.

"Who are you?" I asked, not moving.

"Zhu Nai-Qian. Natalie Zhu. I am Steven's attorney. Sit down." Natalie Zhu's Chinese accent was much more pronounced than Steven Wei's, but it didn't keep me from understanding what she said, and what she meant by it: I'm In Charge Here.

Bill moved to the far wall and leaned casually beside the sliding doors. From there he could see the apartment door, plus both other ways into this room; so I perched on the edge of the cushionless couch. Natalie Zhu flicked her eyes from the cushions on the floor to me with a slight rise of her delicate eyebrows. Probably she would have slipped a cushion under her tiny behind before depositing it on a couch frame. But I was better padded, and I'd sat down already. I crossed my legs as though Lydia Chin sat around on cushionless couches all the time.

"I think we should call the police," I said again.

"No." Natalie Zhu dismissed that idea and, for the moment, me. "Steven, we were expecting to meet Li-Ling here? And Maria, with Harry?"

Steven Wei swallowed. "Ten o'clock." He reached into his pocket, pulled out a cell phone. "I'm going to call them." He punched in a set of numbers. After a few moments he swore in Cantonese, ended that call, and punched in another set. He listened, then lowered the phone, looking like he wanted to throw it through the window. "Li-Ling's said to leave a message. That probably means she hasn't got it with her. Maria's just rings and rings."

He stood abruptly, looked around, a man who wanted to take some action but didn't know what to do. "What . . . how could this have happened? The security men . . . Who let these people upstairs?" He stood and headed for the speaker by the front door.

"Steven." Natalie Zhu spoke calmly, but the tone of her voice stopped Steven Wei in his tracks. "There is no point in that at this moment. You will find your doorman was bribed, or one of your maintenance men was involved. What will this tell you? There will be time for that later. Sit down."

Steven Wei stood for a moment, his hand stopped in midreach for the speaker handset. He slowly turned and returned to his chair.

Li-Ling Wei was Steven's wife; Bill and I knew that. "Who's Maria?" I asked.

"Maria Quezon," Steven answered mechanically, a beat late, looking around as though he were unsure where the question had come from. "Harry's amah. She's Filipina."

"An au pair, you would call her," Natalie Zhu added.

I'd call her an amah, just like you do, I thought. What makes you think I don't know what *amah* means? And Bill, for your information, used to live in the Phillipines.

I took a deep, slow breath. Calm down, Lydia, I told myself. Don't take your adrenaline rush out on these people.

"And they're not here," I said. "And they don't answer their cell phones. And the apartment's been ransacked. The police—"

"Calling the police would be a mistake." Natalie Zhu looked right at me. "With respect, Ms. Chin, you are not from Hong Kong. You cannot be expected to know how to handle . . . situations . . . like this."

"I know that this house is torn apart and three people are missing," I retorted. "And I know kidnappings for ransom aren't uncommon here." There, I thought, let's get it on the table.

"True," Natalie Zhu agreed, unruffled. "And victims are

usually returned unharmed once the ransom is paid. Unless the families involve the police." Emphasis, it seemed to me, on the *unless*.

"But those families are rich." Steven Wei shook his head. "I'm not rich. Who—?" He lifted his hands, his words all tangled.

Natalie Zhu looked at him. The look may have been sympathetic, but her voice was sharp. "Someone with an exaggerated idea of your wealth. The death of your father was widely reported; Lion Rock is a respected, established firm. Also, the kidnapping may have been easy, which makes the risk less."

Steven Wei didn't answer, just looked at her, as though he hadn't understood a word she'd said.

"What do you mean, easy?" I asked.

Natalie Zhu turned to me. "If they had help."

"The amah?"

"It is possible."

"No," Steven said. "It's not. Maria—"

"Maria has been with you all of Harry's life, Maria loves Harry like her own son, yes, of course," Natalie Zhu said almost contemptuously. "Steven, she may have a brother in trouble, a sick mother at home—you have no idea, have you?"

Steven Wei looked a little sick himself.

"What are you suggesting?" I said. "We just sit here and wait?"

Natalie Zhu looked straight at me, then turned her head deliberately to Bill, so that we'd know she hadn't forgotten he was there, too. "Yes," she said.

We didn't wait long.

And we didn't wait silently. Natalie Zhu, turning back to me, said, "We have been assuming you are the emissaries sent from Gao Mian-Liang with Harry's jade. Is that correct? May I see some identification?"

"And we've been assuming you're Steven Wei and his lawyer," I said, handing her my passport. "But I suppose you might be impostors."

Bill caught my tone and gave me a glance as he handed her his passport, and Steven Wei's face reddened, but the corner of Natalie Zhu's mouth tugged upward and a quick look flashed in her eyes, something like approval, I thought. "Yes, we could." She snapped her briefcase open—she carried no handbag—and took out her identity card, motioning for Steven Wei to do the same.

"Natalie . . ." Steven Wei's protest flared and faded, a spark unable to set a fire.

"Steven, she is right." She flipped through my passport and handed it back. "She is also Lydia Chin. Thank you. I do not mean to offend, but of course, in a situation like this . . ."

"Of course."

She looked from me to Bill and back again. "Do you speak Chinese, or shall we continue in English?"

"English, if you don't mind," Bill said before I could answer. "Can I smoke?" No one said anything. "I guess that's a yes," Bill said. He bent down to pick something up off the floor. "Is this an ashtray?" It seemed to me that the object in question could be nothing else. Both Steven Wei and Natalie Zhu looked at it, Wei finally nodding.

"If we're not calling the police," I said, "maybe Mr. Wei could look through the apartment and see if anything is missing?"

Steven Wei, looking lost, cast a look at Natalie Zhu. She met his eyes; something unspoken passed between them. Natalie Zhu said, "A good idea," and stood. Wei looked anything but happy, but he stood, too. He gave one long look around the living room, then moved heavily toward the bedrooms.

I followed, saying nothing, but watching where he looked, where he searched. He opened certain drawers, certain jewelry boxes: In one bedroom, the one that held a large painted Chinese armoire and a carved teak bench, he moved a heavy camphorwood trunk away from the wall to reveal a safe. Spinning the combination, he looked inside, sifted through the contents, and closed the safe again.

"Nothing is missing," he finally said, standing in the hallway, looking around. "There's not much of great value, and nothing is gone." He met my eyes, looked away, looked back, as though it were important that I comprehend what he was about to tell me. "We live comfortably. But I'm not a wealthy man, nor was my father. I don't understand this."

I didn't know what he understood, or for that matter what I did. I opened my mouth to make an answer, but the phone rang.

It froze us all. Natalie Zhu thawed first. In two steps she reached it, grabbed it up, and demanded, *"Wai!"*— "Speak!" in Cantonese.

The caller evidently did, and then Natalie Zhu began again, still in Cantonese. Relief sounded in her voice, but it didn't last long. "This is Zhu Nai-Qian. Where are you?" Pause. "They are not with you?" Another pause. "No, we have not. Here, you had better speak to Wei Di-Fen." She lowered the phone, said, "It's Li-Ling," and handed the receiver to Steven Wei, who was already on his feet.

"Are you all right?" Steven Wei spoke quickly and low to his wife—also in Chinese—listened, spoke again. He turned to me and Bill when he hung up.

"They went out early," he said, switching back to English. "Li-Ling wanted to buy some sweets, to have with tea when you came." His look was accusatory, as though that made this our fault. "Maria and Harry went with her, and Maria took Harry to play in the park. He was too excited to stay up here, just waiting."

I had gathered most of this from Steven Wei's side of the Cantonese conversation, but I let him continue to tell it.

"Li-Ling went to the park to meet them, but they weren't there. She waited, then walked around to the church. Harry . . . he likes to climb on the rocks there. Then she went back to the park. Then she went back to the bakery, in case they'd gone to meet her. That's where she called from." He looked at each of us in turn, as though one of us could make something of what he'd said, find an answer in it. No one spoke.

"I told her to come home," he said.

Now there was silence for a time. Natalie Zhu returned to her straight-backed chair. Steven Wei paced, sat, stood, sat again.

Questions ran around in my mind, things I wanted to know; and I could see Bill had questions, too, because I know him well enough to see what he's thinking, sometimes, from the look in his eyes, the way he moves. But I kept my questions to myself, for now, and so did he.

As much to keep moving as to have another look around, I put the cushions back on the couch. If the cops weren't coming there was no point in leaving the place looking like a monsoon had hit it. I stood the furniture up, put the hibiscus blossoms back in their vase, and went and got more water for them. Two silver-framed photographs lay on the floor; as I came back from the kitchen with the flowers I saw Steven Wei bending over, picking them up, rubbing his thumb along the frame of one. Putting the vase down, I went over to look.

The smaller photo, with the soft-toned contrast and stiff formality of a studio portrait, showed a middle-aged man in a suit and a tie standing behind a seated woman with a toddler on her lap. The clothes dated the picture to about thirty years ago, and the faces of the child and the standing man were both Steven Wei's face.

The other picture was also a family grouping. Steven Wei, arms around his knees, was seated on a picnic blanket on a hilltop next to a pretty woman who wore a scarf to keep her hair from blowing in the breeze. The ocean sparkled in the distance. A little boy wearing a white kung fu *gi* and a big grin had thrown a kick and was holding the pose, probably hoping the photographer would get on with it before he fell over. Two old men also sat on the blanket, the one from the formal portrait and another, thinner but otherwise almost identical in looks. And the lawyer, Natalie Zhu, who sat a little ways apart. This picture was not more than a year or two old, and the little boy's face, like those in the other picture, was also Steven Wei's.

Bill had drifted over from the window to look over Steven's shoulder, too. I glanced at him; then Steven seemed to notice both of us. He straightened, set the photos on the sideboard, and walked stiffly back to his chair.

I was still watching Bill. He stood at the window and smoked, looking as though he were doing nothing in particular. Then, pressing out his cigarette, he said, "Can I ask you something?"

Steven Wei looked around and found the question addressed to no one else. "Yes?"

"Why did you go out this morning? You knew we were coming. Your wife went out shopping, and the amah took Harry out to play, but where did you go?"

Bill's tone was mild and conversational, but if I'd been Steven Wei, my own guilt at not having been here would have made me defensive and furious at the question. Steven Wei flushed crimson. "My uncle asked me yesterday to come to the warehouse early today, with Natalie," he said crisply. "To go over some bills of lading and other papers. There is a large shipment coming in from China tomorrow, and one going out to New York in a few days."

"Antique furniture, am I right?" Bill asked.

"Some antique, some new," Wei said, obviously not caring whether Bill had it right or not.

"And the paperwork couldn't wait, until this afternoon, say?"

Steven Wei had clearly been asking himself the same question since he'd seen his torn-apart living room. "The paperwork my father used to take care of will have to be done by someone else now. These are Lion Rock's first shipments since my father passed on. Uncle Ang-Ran apologized about the timing, but the ship for New York sails in two days whether the paperwork is right or not. He is not an expert at the regulations involved, and he doesn't speak English well."

"And you are an expert? You're an accountant—is this sort of thing your specialty?"

Steven Wei looked at Bill like you'd look at a gnat you'd been swatting at but hadn't managed to get rid of. "I'll learn. I've left my previous position to take over Father's duties. I've inherited most of his share of the firm."

Bill nodded, then asked, "Did you get done this morning what you went to do?"

After a long look, Steven Wei replied, "Not entirely. But Uncle Ang-Ran thought he could complete it and did not want us to be late to meet you."

I thought it might be time to step in here. "Your uncle?" I asked Steven Wei. "Your father's partner?"

"Wei Ang-Ran," he told me; and I could tell from his voice that he was struggling to even be civil. Under the circumstances, I couldn't blame him. "Father's younger brother."

"And what about your brother?" Bill asked.

The room resounded with a horrified silence. I wondered if you could be deported from Hong Kong for gaucheness.

"You mean my father's other son?" Steven Wei finally asked.

Bill, the broad-shouldered, slouching image of American laissez-faire, nodded. "I imagine it's a touchy subject," he said, vastly understating the glaringly obvious, "but I was just wondering. Is he taking over the New York end of the business?"

I kept my mouth shut, letting him play out the hand. Natalie Zhu, sharp-eyed, seemed to be doing the same.

Steven Wei slumped back in his chair, the fire gone out again. "I've never met him," he said. "He's two years older than I. A doctor, from what I understand. My father seems to have left him a small share of the business also." He glanced at Natalie Zhu, who, her mouth pursed in distaste, nodded but said nothing. "I understand he plans to come to Hong Kong for Father's funeral. I was hoping to talk to him then. To buy him out. My uncle is childless, and so, I understand, is this—is my brother." He clearly found the word difficult to say. "I had always planned that Harry would inherit Lion Rock Enterprises."

The room fell silent again; no one, it seemed, was willing to talk much about Harry's future, right now.

And in the silence the phone rang again.

This time it wasn't the ivory-colored telephone on the laquered desk. The rings, insistent and shrill, came from Steven Wei's pocket. He whipped out his cell phone, fumbled it open, and said, *"Wai! Wai!"* He listened, his face reddening. He started to speak, stopped abruptly, listened briefly again, then shouted, *"Wai!"* into the phone once more. He lowered it, staring at it as though it had done something unprecedented and traitorous.

He looked up at the rest of us. "They hung up," he said.

"Who was it? What did they say?" Natalie Zhu demanded.

Steven Wei paused a moment. "He said Harry and Maria were being . . . well taken care of. And if I did what I was told they'd be home soon."

"A man?" I asked.

"What did he tell you to do?" Natalie Zhu said, with a sharp glance at me.

Steven Wei looked at me, too, and for a moment didn't speak. Then he said, "At noon, at Wong Tai Sin. To be at the fortune-tellers' stalls. Alone."

"With the ransom?"

He shook his head. "He said I would receive instructions there."

Natalie Zhu frowned. Steven Wei said to no one in particular, "Why don't they just want the money now? Why prolong this?"

Nobody else answered, so I did. "It's standard. A dry run, to be sure you'll follow instructions. Alone, no cops, on time, everything. If you do it right, next time will be the real thing. This might indicate that they're pros, that they've done this sort of thing before."

Steven Wei just stared at me. So did Natalie Zhu.

With a quick look at Bill, I told them, "We're investigators. Private cops, you might say. We've dealt with things like this before."

Steven Wei and Natalie Zhu looked at each other. "Things like this?" Steven Wei repeated. "Kidnapping?"

"Dealing with this sort of thing is the kind of work we do."

The strict truth was, it was the kind of work Bill had done. I'd never handled a real kidnapping before. But we were partners now, so I was entitled to claim his experience. And it wasn't like I didn't have experience of my own to bring to this partnership. Like for example, I was the one who spoke Chinese.

Steven Wei, in Chinese, said something low and fast to Natalie Zhu.

She answered in English: "That's a good question." She turned to me. "Steven finds it an interesting coincidence, as I do, that you should happen to be here just now, if this is true. Why did Gao Mian-Liang send investigators?"

That wasn't exactly what Steven had said, but it was close enough. "I'm not sure what you mean," I said, though I was.

"She means," Bill said from his post by the window, "that we could have engineered this whole thing."

"I did not mean to suggest—"

"Sure you did, and I would, too, in your shoes," he said. "Gao Mian-Liang sends us to drop this jade thing off with Harry, and we see a chance to make a few bucks on the side. We pay the amah to take Harry to the movies, pay some hotel bellboy to phone in a ransom demand, and let on that we're experts in this kind of thing. But you don't want us involved, so you tell us to get lost. Which is what you're about to do, right?" He didn't wait for an answer. "You pay the ransom, we collect it, and then there's another phone call saying something went wrong. So Harry has to be rescued, and we do that heroically, and the grateful family lays another large sum on us. We split it with the bellboy and the amah, go home rich, and everyone's happy.

That's what they're thinking. If I were you," he turned to Steven Wei, "that's what I'd be thinking."

That was what Steven Wei was thinking, because that was more or less what he'd said in Chinese to Natalie Zhu. Being Chinese, and therefore congenitally reluctant to give direct offense, he started to deny it; but his words sounded just a bit pro forma, though he didn't get past, "I don't . . . There is not . . ."

"Mr. Wei," I said, "if that's what you're thinking, I can understand it. In fact I can see why you might hope it was true, because in that case there'd be no real danger. But it isn't. We don't know where Harry is. But," I said, trying to choose my words carefully, "we'd like to do anything we can to help get him back."

Maybe Steven Wei was about to answer, or maybe not, but the door flew open. We all turned to see the pretty woman from the photo on the desk, her expensive perm disheveled, her carefully made-up face flushed, standing in the doorway, looking at all of us. She was sweating heavily, possibly because the day's heat was hard enough to handle even if you weren't, as she was, obviously pregnant.

Steven Wei jumped up and went to her. "Li-Ling!"

"Is Hao-Han back?" Li-Ling Wei spoke in Chinese. Her eyes swept the room, looking for something she clearly did not find.

"No." Steven and Li-ling Wei stopped before each other. He took her hands in his. "A phone call came."

Steven Wei, in Chinese, told his wife about Wong Tai Sin, noon, the fortune-tellers.

Li-Ling Wei listened, her eyes widening. When Steven was through Li-Ling looked quickly at Natalie Zhu, who did not speak. Her eyes went back to her husband. Gripping his arm, as though for support, she looked at me and Bill. Clearly trying to compose herself, she spoke in English. "You're the Americans. With Harry's jade."

"Lydia Chin," I answered her. "This is my partner, Bill Smith. I'm very sorry about this situation, Mrs. Wei."

"Yes," she said, and then, "Thank you," as an afterthought. She looked around her, at the room I'd attempted to straighten, at the people in it. She seemed to have run out of words.

Natalie Zhu took up the slack. Looking pointedly at her watch, she said, "Steven will need to leave soon for Wong Tai Sin. Li-Ling, you will stay here with me." She turned to me. "Thank you for your offer of help. We will call you if we need you."

That was the "get lost" Bill had mentioned. I was of two minds about that, but Bill had made his up already. He offered Steven Wei his hand, said, "Anything we can do," nodded to Natalie Zhu and Li-Ling Wei, and walked through the room to the door.

"You'll let us know?" I asked. "As soon as something happens?"

Steven Wei just looked at me, then nodded. Natalie Zhu said, "We will call you. Thank you."

I felt her eyes on me until the door closed behind us.

As we stood waiting for the elevator among the prints of the harbor, I said to Bill, "I guess this is the dam flooding the village on a clear day."

"Or," he said, "it could be the storm cloud passing without rain."

"I'm not sure I understand that, but before the elevator comes, tell me this: Are you sure leaving there was the right thing to do?"

"Positive. And for the same reasons you do."

"Which are—?"

"Well, we couldn't have stayed anyway if they wanted us out, and insisting would only have made them distrust us more than they're already inclined to. I don't know what our role in this is supposed to be, but there's no point in alienating anyone without a good reason. And besides—"

"Besides," I said, "if we don't leave now we won't get to Wong Tai Sin before he does."

"Right." Bill and I exchanged a look, the elevator came, and we headed back to the tall stone-lined lobby, and Robinson Road.

Like most residential areas, Robinson Road wasn't a great place to catch a cab. It took us three blocks of rapid down-hill striding to find a small business district, and another half-block sprint to seize a cab someone else had just gotten out of. The back of my linen blouse was already damp when we climbed in. The air-conditioner in the cab was going full blast; it wasn't the freshest air in the world, but it was cool.

"Wong Tai Sin," I told the driver.

"What place in Wong Tai Sin?" he asked me in Can-tonese as he pulled away from the curb.

Steven Wei had been ordered to the fortune-tellers' stalls; that could only mean one thing. "The temple," I said.

I settled back against the cab seat and said to Bill, "That little boy. He's only seven. Do you suppose he's scared?"

"Yes," Bill said, and that was all he said.

Out the window, I could catch a glimpse of the harbor every now and then as our cab made sharp turns to switch-back down the hill. Well, if we were going to do anything for Harry, it could only be by doing our job.

"Thanks for that nonsense with the ashtray," I said. "That was to keep them from thinking about your answer to the English-or-Chinese question and whether it really went for both of us, right?"

"Right. And thanks for rearranging the furniture so I could watch them while they were watching you."

"You're welcome. Learn anything?"

"Well, you know these Chinese: inscrutable. How about you, when they were speaking Chinese? That's the kind of Chinese you speak, right?"

"Luckily, yes, in Hong Kong they speak Cantonese. On the mainland they speak Mandarin, and I'd be as ignorant as you."

"Never. So—?"

"Nothing, really. Everything they said in Chinese was pretty much what they translated for us. The bit about us being a little suspicious included a reference to Grandfather

Gao that was edited out of the English version."

"What about him?"

"About the Three Brothers tong. Some of the New York tongs are associated with Hong Kong triads. Kidnapping is apparently a triad industry here, so they were wondering if there was a connection."

"Is there?"

I turned to stare at him. "Between Grandfather Gao and this? Of course not."

"You sure?"

"Of course I'm sure! First of all, Three Brothers is sort of well known for refusing to connect with any of the triads. The Weis might not know that, but I do. Second and more important, old Mr. Wei was Grandfather Gao's oldest friend. There's no way Grandfather Gao would do anything to hurt him, even after he was dead. But . . ."

"But what?"

"I want to call him as soon as we can. We have to tell him what happened, for one thing. And I need to ask him if this is his storm cloud, or his flood, or whatever, or if this is a total surprise to him and he really just sent us here for our health."

"Maybe you're here for the water crisis, and *I'm* here for *your* health."

I scowled at this thought. "A bodyguard?"

"Don't get mad at me, I'm just following orders."

"Those weren't your orders."

"That you know of."

I shot him a look. "You didn't—"

"—talk to Grandfather Gao without you? No, of course not. But it makes sense."

"Does not."

"Does too. How about if we don't take the repeats?"

That effectively stopped my clever retort, so I turned to look out the window. We had come down the hill back to the commercial center of Hong Kong Island. Our cab slipped in and out of the swirling traffic, cutting off trams, buses, and other peoples' cabs. Large neon signs in Chinese and English hung overhead like the fruit of some rampant electrical vine at the height of its midsummer abundance.

Bill's hand went to the crank at his window, to let in some sticky hot air. Then he looked at me and gave up the idea.

"You like this weather, don't you?" I said as a peace offering. After all, if he really had been sent to watch over me, it wasn't his fault. Except that he took the job. Except that it was me who'd demanded, back in his apartment that night, that he agree to come.

He said, "It comes from being badly brought up."

"Or it's practice for where you're going in the next life."

"Saudi Arabia?"

"That's not what I meant, but close enough."

"Okay. Can we get back to work?"

"Well, all right."

"Good. Now answer me this: Steven Wei and Natalie Zhu. Why didn't they throw us out right away, as soon as they were sure we were who we said we were? We'd come to do a job, we couldn't do it, now they had problems. Why not kick us out, thank you, good-bye?"

"Oh, I think he wanted to. But she wanted to check us out. She was watching us, just like we were watching them."

"You suppose she found out any more than we did?"

I looked at him, wondering what there was to find out about us, and how you went about it.

"Okay," Bill said, moving on. "Tell me where we're going."

I did. "Wong Tai Sin."

"Which is obviously on the Kowloon side, because we're about to go into the tunnel. Is that all I get?"

"Wong Tai Sin," I told him, passing on some of my guidebook knowledge, "is one of the first new towns they built here, up by the border between Kowloon and the New Territories. There's a huge temple there, also known as Wong Tai Sin."

"Catchy. And we're going to the town, or the temple?"

"The temple. To watch Steven Wei at the fortune-tellers' stalls."

"They let fortune-tellers into the temple?"

"That's one of the reasons you go to the temple—to get your fortune told."

"Really? Where I come from, fortune-tellers get the evil eye from good, upright churchgoing folk."

"Where you come from, the unexplained occurrences of daily life are pretty much ignored in favor of a more abstract theology."

"Wordy but true. So as the expert on the unexplained, maybe you can enlighten me about a few more questions I have."

"Please let me try."

"One: If the object of kidnapping the kid was to kidnap the kid, who tossed the place and why?"

"I've been wondering that myself," I admitted. "Especially since nothing seems to be missing."

"According to Wei."

"According to Wei. So either they didn't find what they were looking for, or he didn't find that they found it. Or he was lying to us about nothing being missing."

"Or something else."

"What else?"

"Don't know."

"Great."

"Want to hear my next question?"

"Desperately."

"Were the kidnappers just waiting around outside, hoping the amah would bring the kid out sometime, or did they know something?"

"You don't buy this loves-him-like-her-own-son business?"

"Maybe I do; I'm just not sure what that kind of love means."

I looked at him, but I couldn't read his expression. That's more rare now than it used to be, but it still happens sometimes.

"And," he said, "If Steven Wei and Natalie Zhu were at the warehouse, and Li-Ling Wei, Maria, and Harry were out in the park, who told the guy at the desk to send us up?"

Some of Bill's questions were ones I had thought of, and some were new to me, and I had some of my own. We discussed them all the way to Wong Tai Sin.

The drive took us along expressways bordered by green hills with variously colored concrete buildings erupting from their slopes. Thin, sinuous roots of banyan trees reached over the rough mortar of concrete block retaining walls as though searching for a less precarious footing. Our discussion was underscored by the plaintive words and bubblegum tunes of Canto-pop from the driver's radio. Concrete and glass towers sped by on either side of the road, horns honked and the sun streamed through the haze, and finally the cab pulled up to a small, sloped plaza and let us out.

Soot-streaked pastel-green apartment buildings loomed above us, belligerently facing the white and pink ones across the road. People came and went through the plaza in all directions. Some just strolled and talked, some hurried to the street, some negotiated prices for incense and oranges and red paper prayers at a string of stalls leading up to a large carved temple gate. And some, like us, walked through the gate and into the temple of Wong Tai Sin.

"My God," said Bill as, through the gate, we climbed the steps and got a good look around. "This is as wild as a tent meeting."

"Is that a good thing or a bad thing?"

"Someday I'll take you to a tent meeting. Is this it? Where the action is?"

We had reached a large open courtyard in front of a huge painted and gilded pavilion. In the pavilion's dim and smoky depths I could just about make out the larger-than-life, or at least larger-than-human, carved wooden statues of Wong Tai Sin himself—who cures diseases, foretells the outcome of horse races, and is said to be very generous with his help if you're a follower of his—and half a dozen of his fellow gods. The midday sun pouring down met the incense smoke rising up, and this was definitely where the action was.

People crowded the stone courtyard, some alone, others in family groups, many kneeling on newspaper or mats they had brought. A few Westerners were scattered here and there—tourists watching the goings-on—but most of these people had come to do business. Bowing, waving incense sticks around, or just holding them out to their chosen gods, they murmured prayers of request or thanks. More incense smoldered in a giant bronze burner. A breeze pushed the sweet-smelling smoke this way and that; a cloud of it engulfed us and my eyes began to tear. Someone tapped a gong, the deep sound rising through the whine of the traffic from beyond the gates and the conversations, prayers, and rustling of paper as offerings were unwrapped.

Incense sticks in little cups on the paving flanked the offerings: piles of oranges or bottles of wine, here and there a roast chicken. Bill and I watched one young man and woman—newly married, perhaps, and hoping for children—as they knelt together on a mat. Before them, on a mat of its own, placed where the gods could appreciate the expense and effort, was a whole roast pig. The young man watched intently as the woman shook a wooden box of prayer sticks until one fell to the ground. He picked it up. They both studied the characters on its side, the young man copying them onto a scrap of paper; then he stood and hurried off through the crowd.

"Where's he going?" Bill asked.

"To see the fortune-teller." I glanced at my watch. "Okay. It's half past eleven. Steven Wei will be here soon, but he probably won't dare come too early, in case he's not supposed to. We have a little time. Let's do what we can."

We trotted back down the steps through the temple gate to the incense-sellers' stalls, and beyond them. I was taking a guess, but I was right. The incense and paper prayers gave way rather abruptly to tee shirts, plastic sandals, house-

wares, soft drinks, pots and pans. Bill took off his jacket
and tie and bought a cheap Adidas knock-off bag to stuff
them into. He slipped on his sunglasses and bought a new
black baseball cap that said HONG KONG in bright colors.
In the next stall he picked up a disposable camera on a
strap and hung it around his neck. That was about all we
could do for him. I bought a big straw hat and a loose blue
flowered shirt. A quick woman-to-woman conversation
with the stall's owner about the embarassing scent of sweat
on my linen blouse got me the chance to quick-change into
the shirt behind a rack of dresses in the back of the stall. I
chose a large straw carryall, dropped my shoulder bag and
blouse inside, put on my own sunglasses, and that was
about all we could do for me.

We hurried back up to the temple courtyard. "Okay," I
said, looking around. "He'll come in here, and the fortune-
tellers are over there." I pointed to another row of stalls,
permanent ones with the same metal roll-down doors merchants use to guard against evildoers in New York. At this
busy time of day, almost all the doors were up, the fortune-
tellers open for business. "You stay here and wait for him.
Try to look like just another pushy rude American tourist.
Think you can do that?"

"In my sleep," Bill said. "Where are you going?"

"To get my fortune told."

The fortune-tellers' stalls stretched out in a line along
the curving perimeter of the temple grounds, nestling
against the wall dividing the temple from the towering
apartment buildings that surrounded it. With their laundry
poles stuck at cocky angles beside their bathroom windows,
the apartment buildings seemed to be flying the banners of
a hundred different tribes.

I walked quickly down the avenue of stalls to my destination, the stall at the end. From there, because of the
curve, I would be able to see anyone who came into the
fortune-tellers' area, and anything that went on there.

About half the fortune-tellers had customers: middle-
aged women, young men, a mother and her children, all

bent intently over the charts or books the fortune-teller had
spread in front of them. Almost all the fortune-tellers, I
realized as I passed them, were men. Some of them included, on their signs, assurances in English that their English was good (TELL YOUR FORTUNE, ENGLISH OR
CHINESE), that they were not fly-by-night (TWENTY YEARS
SAME PLACE), and a few indicated that they were not merely
neutral passers-on of occult information, but active partners
in your hopes and dreams (FORTUNE TOLD HERE, ALWAYS
GOOD RESULT!). The Chinese was much the same, some of
the stall owners going so far as to have posted yellowing
newspaper articles about the time they had accurately pre-
dicted a winning lottery number or counseled against a marriage where the would-be groom had later been unmasked
as a notorious international cad and scoundrel.

The end-stall proprietor, however, was a purist. A
middle-aged man with glasses and thinning hair, his signs
were in Chinese only; and while his overhead banner de-
clared him to be Wang Wo, a practitioner of the numero-
logical method of divination—because at Wong Tai Sin
you got your choice, and the meaning of the characters on
your prayer stick could be different depending on the system of reading them—he made no claims of past accuracy
nor offered any guarantees of satisfaction.

I sat down before him with a smile and a nod. He nodded professionally back and stubbed out the hand-rolled
cigarette he'd been working on when I came over. He took
a battered book with rice-paper pages from a neat pile on
the folding table that served as his desk and held out his
hand for the paper with my copied prayer-stick characters.

"I'm not here to get my fortune told," I said in Cantonese.

Still looking at me, he slowly withdrew the hand that
was waiting for my paper. "Ah?"

"No. But I'll pay you three times the cost of telling my
fortune to let me sit here until I'm ready to leave."

Wang Wo regarded me. "The temple of Wong Tai Sin

has a beautiful garden with benches on paths, others in pavilions, for those who wish to sit."

"You can't see the fortune-tellers from there."

He smiled. "You find us so interesting?"

"Fascinating."

Crossing one leg over the other, he brought the book into his lap. "You will keep me from doing business."

"I'll pay for your lost business."

He pointed the book behind me. "There is a bench there, for customers waiting. You could sit for free."

"If you had no customer in the stall, it would appear strange for me to be sitting there."

"So. You want to watch the fortune-tellers, but you do not want to be watched."

"That's right."

Wang Wo continued to look at me. To avoid the rudeness of returning his look with a direct stare, I glanced up the line of stalls to check the action—of the kind I was interested in, there wasn't any—and then let my eyes travel over Wang Wo's own stall. I took in the incense wafting from the small shrine to Kuan Yin, Goddess of Mercy, the books and papers piled on gray metal shelves, and the gold and black characters on the red scrolls that hung on the walls.

Wang Wo spoke. "Perhaps, in that case, you should permit me to tell your fortune after all. That way you will appear to be a real customer."

That way I *would* be a real customer, I thought; but it wasn't a bad idea, and if it was what it took to get Wang Wo to let me sit here, why not? "Yes, all right," I said. I repositioned my chair to make viewing along the curve easier. "I don't have a prayer stick," I told Wang Wo.

"There are many ways to understand one's fate," he answered. He reached onto a shelf behind him for a complicated chart, divided into a lot of small segments, each filled with numbers and Chinese characters. Eyes on the chart, he asked me for my place of birth, and the date, including the exact hour which, because these things are important to my mother for this very reason, I happen to know. I gave him the answers, keeping an eye out for Steven Wei.

Wang Wo wrote a few things down while consulting the chart, then flipped open the battered book and wrote more things down from its pages. Then he looked up at me.

" 'Swiftly running water does not reflect the sky.' "

A Chinese nature metaphor. Swell. All the way to Hong Kong, and this is what I get. I glanced at Wang Wo, then went back to the Steven Wei watch. "What does it mean?" I asked.

"That is for you to discern, in regard to your own life. You can be guided by this fortune, or not, as you wish; its truth remains, regardless of whether you choose to understand it."

Boy, I thought, you sound like you went to the same Obscure Conversation Academy as Grandfather Gao. Then both Wang Wo and Grandfather Gao were pushed to the back of my mind by the sudden appearance on the scene of Steven Wei.

In monogrammed shirt and dress slacks but minus jacket and tie, Steven Wei had entered the fortune-tellers' area and stopped in front of the stalls at the end of the row. He shifted his weight from one foot to the other, wiped his brow with a handkerchief, looked left and right and left again, waiting for something to happen. I waited, too. I didn't see Bill, but he could easily have a fix on Wei from the temple courtyard, where he wouldn't be visible from here. I scanned the strollers, sitters, and customers in the fortuner-tellers' area, looking for the answer to the important question: Who else was watching Steven Wei?

Wei looked at his watch, wiped the sweat from the back of his neck, shifted some more. I could feel Wang Wo's eyes following mine to their target.

"You have found what you were watching for?"

"Yes."

"A nervous young man," he commented.

A bent old woman approached the nervous young man. She was selling paper prayers from a bamboo basket. Wei

shooed her away, but she didn't go. Holding out a folded
paper from her basket, she tapped him on the wrist with it
and spoke. At first he snapped at her impatiently. Then, in
what looked like midword, he stopped and snatched the
paper from her hands. He unfolded it quickly as the old
woman scolded him, her palm up, demanding payment.
Distractedly, reading his piece of paper, he thrust a bill at
her and she scurried away.

My eyes still on the far stalls, I reached into my own
pocket for my own bills. I glanced down, counted out three
times Wang Wo's usual fee, and placed it on his card-table
desk.

"You have seen all you needed to see?"

"No," I answered. "But I don't think the rest can be seen
from here. I have to move on now."

"As is often the case," Wang Wo replied. I suspected
that of being a nature metaphor, too, but this wasn't the
time to worry about it. Steven Wei turned to leave the area.
I stood to follow. Wang Wo handed me a piece of paper
with Chinese characters on it.

"What's this?"

"Your fortune," Wang Wo said. "It is not why you came
here, but our paths often lead us not where we meant to
go, but where we need to be."

I stuffed the paper in my pocket and hurried off to find
out where Steven Wei needed to be.

three

Steven Wei, with long quick steps, headed out of the temple grounds. The new instructions on the old lady's folded paper would tell him where and when to deliver the ransom, or maybe they just said to go home and wait for the next phone call. I didn't think I'd get very far following him, though I was certainly game to hail a taxi and try. What I really wanted to know was who else was interested in the movements of Steven Wei.

Because I hadn't seen anybody. Try as I might, from fortune-tellers to customers to skeptics just strolling down the path, no one but me and the old lady—and Bill, wherever he was—had seemed the least bit interested in Steven Wei.

That was strange. Why send him here if not to make sure he'd follow orders, be at the right place at the right time without cops on his tail, because that's what you want when the ransom is delivered? And how could you make sure of that if you weren't watching?

Well, there could be one other reason: not a dry run, but a wild goose chase. Something to keep Steven Wei occupied while something else was going on.

What else? Who knew? Standing on the temple steps above the sloped plaza, I watched Steven Wei whip the cell phone out of his pocket and shout briefly into it. He ended that call, then punched in another number and spoke some more, seeming frustrated and impatient as this second conversation went on. A gong from the temple rang slowly three times, underscoring the traffic and the hurrying and Steven Wei's impatience. Snapping the phone shut, Wei fidgeted at the curb until a cab swung around the corner. He stepped into the street, it screeched to a stop, and he was gone. I looked around for another one, but there weren't any. I had to content myself with recording the license number of the one that was driving Steven Wei off.

A muscular young man with sweat darkening his white tee shirt muttered a curse after that same cab, then turned and made for the subway entrance that was right there. If he'd been watching Steven Wei I hadn't seen him. Maybe he'd just been waiting a long time, only to have Steven Wei usurp his taxi. Maybe I should take the subway myself: I had a subway map, and obviously cabs were a little hard to come by up here at Wong Tai Sin. They must be hard to come by: Without acknowledging my existence at all, Bill, in his new Hong Kong baseball cap and his sunglasses, came striding fast across the plaza and disappeared into the subway entrance, too.

I stared after him. Now I had three choices: join Bill in whatever he was up to, go somewhere where I could make a phone call—which, according to the guidebook, was not all that easy in Hong Kong, public phones being almost nonexistent—or return to the temple to discuss paper prayers with an old lady.

Bill, I decided, could take care of himself and his business, though I was dying to know what it was and whether it had to do with the young man with the muscles. I wanted desperately to call the Weis, to find out if that's where Steven Wei had just called and if so what the new instructions were, but the find-a-phone project seemed Least Likely to Succeed and I had to admit there was no reason to expect them to tell me anything except "Go away." The old lady, on the other hand, was right here.

Except that she wasn't.

I made the rounds of the other old ladies with their bamboo baskets at the entrance to the fortune-tellers' area. The first one I talked to put a name to the lady I was looking for—Mo Ruo—after I'd described her, with her sleeveless print blouse, her loose black pants, her pointed straw hat to keep off the sun.

"Mo Ruo works over there," the old lady told me, gesturing toward a spot near her own. "Left side, second place in."

It was clear that these ladies had assigned themselves proprietary spots to do their business from, and also clear that they were more than willing to poach on each others' territory. I slipped a ten-dollar bill—Hong Kong dollars, worth not quite thirteen cents each, but ten of them would be about what one of these ladies made in an hour—into her basket, which bought me her conversation but not her undivided attention. She was wrinkled and bent but persistent, moving stubbornly into the path of anyone who crossed her radar, pushing her folded prayers at people who might need a little boost in their relationship with their chosen gods. "Usually she is here all day, until the temple closes," she told me about Mo Ruo. "Very eager to make money, always thinking this way." Unlike anyone else in Hong Kong, I thought, but I didn't say it.

"Where would she be now?" I asked. "Eating lunch?"

She gave me a contemptuous glance as she took off to chase down a customer. "Mo Ruo eats her lunch here," she said when I caught up with her. I looked where she pointed, to three other old ladies sitting on newspapers in the shade, their bamboo baskets by their sides, scooping chopsticks in and out of plastic containers of noodles or rice brought from home.

"Can you tell me where she might have gone?" I asked again.

She thrust her chin forward, the old-time Chinese substitute for a shrug.

Nuts to this. I took out a scrap of paper, scribbled my name and the hotel phone number in Chinese characters. "When you see her, will you tell her I want to talk to her?" I put the paper into her basket with another ten-dollar bill. She shoved the bill into a pocket. Then she folded the paper without looking at it and shoved it into another. That told me two things: one, she probably couldn't read. And two, because of my free ways with ten-dollar bills, she would keep the paper and have someone read it to her, or to Mo Ruo, whenever the time was right.

Okay, next things next. I wished for my cell phone, at

home in New York in the bureau drawer keeping my gun company. The gun would have worked in Hong Kong but I couldn't bring it; I could have brought the cell phone but it wouldn't have worked. But if I had a cell phone I could call the Weis, to try to find out what was going on. And Bill could call me, and tell me what was going on, if he had a cell phone, too.

I took myself down into the subway entrance and bought a ticket from a machine where you pressed your station on an electronic map and it told you how much money it wanted. I found the right platform—all the important signs were in both Chinese and English—and when the train came I got on it. I stood in the swaying car holding the metal pole and feeling very much at home. I could have been back in New York on the F train, I thought as I glanced around me, except for one thing: Everyone in this car looked like me.

The air-conditioning in the subway car, like all the air-conditioning I'd encountered in Hong Kong so far, was set about five degrees cooler than it needed to be. You didn't notice it at first—at first, all you did was offer a prayer of thanks to the god of subways, or taxis or hotel lobbies or wherever you were—but by the time you left and went back out into the heat you were, briefly, grateful for the sun on your back. I felt that gratitude on my walk from the subway stop to the hotel, but it didn't last. By the time I stepped into the hushed lobby the air-conditioning was once again a relief.

Hoping Bill had called, I stopped by the desk to see if I had any messages. I had, but not from Bill. The one message I had was from Steven Wei.

I ripped open the envelope. The message was, "Call immediately," and included Steven Wei's home and cell phone numbers.

"The gentleman left a message on your voice mail, also," the young desk clerk told me, seeming slightly disapproving. "He seemed most anxious to speak with you." Hurrying across the lobby to the elevator, I guessed that meant

Steven Wei had given the desk clerk a hard time.

The little red light on the phone was blinking as I entered my room. Picking up the phone to retrieve the message, I caught sight of myself in the mirror, in my new flowered blouse and my straw sunhat. My God, Lydia, I thought, you look positively Chinese.

The voice-mail message was substantially the same as the written one, and in the background, behind honking horns and the air brakes on buses, I heard the three rings of the temple gong. The second phone call Steven Wei had made from Wong Tai Sin, as I stood on the steps watching him, had been to me.

As Bill would say, ain't that a kick in the head?

Wondering just where Bill was, I called Steven Wei. I chose the home number, figuring he'd had time to get home in his cab while I was on the subway, but the voice that snapped, *"Wai!"* into the phone wasn't Steven Wei's, it was the voice of Natalie Zhu.

"Where have you been?" she demanded in English when I told her it was me.

"You told us to get lost," I said. "You didn't say to sit by the phone. In fact, I got the distinct impression you weren't going to call."

"You should have left your cell-phone number," she reprimanded, ignoring everything else I'd said.

"I don't have one. Is Steven Wei there? Why did he call me?"

Silently—possibly speechless at the thought of someone in Hong Kong without a cell phone—Natalie Zhu must have passed the phone to Steven Wei, because it was he who spoke next.

"You must come back here immediately," he said urgently, without greeting or preamble.

"Why?"

"The kidnappers want Harry's jade."

Harry's jade, his legacy from his grandfather? Was that what this was about?

"How do you know?"

"The instructions I received at Wong Tai Sin." Okay, Steven, just checking. "They will call here again at three o'clock. They want the jade."

I thought about this. "How do they know about the jade?" I asked.

He was briefly silent, as though he hadn't thought to ask that. "I don't know. Can that make a difference? You must bring it here immediately. Please!" The desperation in his voice made me want to reach through the phone and pat him on the back.

"Have you learned anything else? Has the amah come back?"

"No. Only this one demand. How soon can you be here?"

I checked the room clock. It wasn't one yet. "I'll come as soon as I can." Or almost. "I'll be there well before three."

"You cannot—" he was saying as I said good-bye.

I imagined Steven Wei's round face frowning into the phone in his apartment in the sky. I wondered if anyone had straightened things there, put everything back in its proper place. I felt bad about not rushing right over there, but it wouldn't have done any good except to reassure Steven Wei. And if I went there now, they'd take the jade from me, thank me very much, and throw me out again. If I timed this right and got there later, when the phone call came, maybe I might learn something.

And of course Lydia Chin's need to know everything superseded all.

But maybe this time it didn't. Maybe this time everything really would be better if I butted out.

Sitting on the bed, I took my bag out of the straw carryall and took a small velvet-covered box out of my bag. I opened the hinged lid and stared at the tiny, delicately carved laughing Buddha, apple-green jade against white silk. Then I picked up the phone again and dialed.

The rings stopped after the fifth one, and a voice said, *"Wai!"* as Natalie Zhu's had, but this voice was a man's and it was sleepy. Well, no wonder: Where Grandfather Gao was, it was one in the morning.

"Grandfather, this is Chin Ling Wan-Ju," I said in Cantonese. "I apologize for disturbing your rest."

"Ling Wan-Ju? What is wrong?" He was instantly awake, but calm and collected as usual. "You are all right, your partner all right also?"

"Yes, Grandfather, but there is a problem." I filled him in on the kidnapping, the searched apartment, the temple, and the demand for Harry's jade.

"Has the child been hurt?" This question, too, he asked in his usual calm manner; but something, maybe just a trick of the long-distance wires, made his voice a little less sure than I was used to hearing it.

"I don't know," I said, being honest. "But there's no reason at this point to think that he has."

"That is well." I thought I heard a small sigh of relief from the other side of the world.

"Grandfather," I said, trying to avoid the unforgivable rudeness of a direct accusatory question, "I am sorry for my lack of understanding. If your expectation that something like this would happen is the reason you sent us here instead of—of someone less professional, I did not comprehend that when we spoke."

There was a pause. I had offered him an opening; now it was up to him. "No, I did not expect it," he replied evenly. "The task seemed simple. I hoped for a smooth, harmonious result. But circumstances forced me to consider that the still surface of a glassy lake often conceals jagged rocks."

Oh, for Pete's sake. It's a good thing, I thought, that I love you as much as I do.

"If I understood fully the circumstances to which you refer, I'm sure I could be much more useful in this task."

"Ling Wan-Ju, I do not fully understand them myself." Grandfather Gao paused, and I waited. Once again his words filled the distance between us. "The task Wei Yao-Shi left to me, which I have sent you to fulfill, seemed simple. But I knew my old friend a very long time. Something was troubling him, though he would not speak of it. His manner led me to think it would be a wise precaution to entrust my interests, which in this case are his, to those in whose abilities I had the most complete confidence."

The most complete confidence. Hear that, Lydia?

"I'm grateful that, thinking that way, you chose me, Grandfather," I said, adding, "Bill feels the same." Might as well get Bill some good Chinese press while I had the chance. "I do wish I knew exactly what those interests are. It would help me know how to serve them best. Do you think Wei Yao-Shi was worried that something like this would happen?"

"As to Wei Yao-Shi, we can only speculate on his concerns. At this point I do not believe that would be profitable. But remember, Ling Wan-Ju, you have known me all your life. My own interests have not changed. Now tell me: What do you propose to do?"

Confused but dutiful, I answered, "I don't see that I have much choice. If the price of the child's return is Wei Yao-Shi's jade, what can I do but turn it over to them?"

"What, indeed?" Grandfather Gao responded. "The jade itself is of small consequence in this matter. But do you feel this action is sufficient?"

"Is there something else I should be doing?"

"You are the professional in these matters, Ling Wan-Ju."

Usually that's *my* line. And the way he said it—and the fact that I'd known him all my life—made me feel like there *was* something else to be done, if only Lydia Chin were bright enough to think of it.

So I thought. "Grandfather, tell me this: What is this jade worth?"

"We discussed that in New York, Ling Wan-Ju," he said, scolding me gently. "Perhaps twelve thousand dollars— American dollars. Fifteen, if the market is right."

"I just wanted to make sure I remembered correctly," I

said. "Because it doesn't seem like enough to risk a kidnapping for."

"No, it does not."

"Also, something else: How would anyone outside the family know about the jade? Wei Yao-Shi left it with you when he went into the hospital, to give to Harry if he died, but it isn't in his will or anything, isn't that right?"

"That is correct. The will names myself as responsible for distributing personal property possessed by Wei Yao-Shi at the time of his death, but does not list this property."

"Then it would seem that someone inside the family, or at least close to the family, would have to be involved in this."

"Yes." Go on, Ling Wan-Ju, you backward but hardworking child.

I suddenly decided not to go on. I loved Grandfather Gao and I trusted him, but I wanted to think on my own for a while. Actually, I wanted to think with Bill, but he wasn't here. And speaking of that, where was he? "Grandfather, there are some things I want to do," I said. "I will call you again as the situation develops." There, that's your last chance to tell me to mind my own business.

Another brief pause. "Please remember, Ling Wan-Ju, that the safety of the child must be your first concern," said Grandfather Gao, in a way that made me wonder if I'd somehow implied it was not. "Family was of the highest importance to Wei Yao-Shi."

Uh-huh, I thought. That must be why he had two of them.

But "mind your own business" was nowhere in sight.

"Yes, Grandfather. I will do my best."

"I am sure you will." I thought I could hear a smile in his voice as we hung up, and although it was a strange time to be smiling, the sound of it warmed me in my too-cool room in the Hong Kong Hotel.

I did want to think, but I was Lydia Chin: I could do two things at once. From the desk by the window I pulled out the hotel's directory of guest services and checked for

what I wanted. Of course, I found it. I wanted something
else, also, but I had no doubt a little looking downstairs
would find me that, too. I dialed Bill's room, but only got
his hotel voice mail. I left a message that I was in the hotel
but not in my room, and then I left my room so it would
be true.

The Hong Kong Hotel is at one end of one of the biggest,
classiest shopping malls in a city that, according to the
guidebook, prides itself on constantly redefining luxury
shopping. I checked the directory and headed to the third
floor, past Italian designer shoe stores, shops with brightly
colored bolts of liquidy silk in the windows, stores that sold
Qing dynasty bride's and groom's painted wedding chests
for use as armoires to put the TV in in the modern Hong
Kong apartment. As I scurried by I glanced at one shop
window where the linen suits and skimpy silk dresses displayed were, by my rough calculations, inexpensive enough
for me to consider. They were also, it seemed, shaped for
people who, like me and most Asians I know, are, by the
standards of American designers, undressably short.

The shop I was looking for was tiny but well located,
at a corner where two wide shopping boulevards converged.
Its windows were tiny, too, which suited the exquisite, glis-
tening jewels they displayed.

Behind the counter, an old man with wispy white hair
and a thick mustache looked up as I came in. He removed
the jeweler's loupe from his right eye, placed the gold chain
he'd been examining on a velvet tray, and said, "Good afternoon," in Cantonese.

"Good afternoon to you, uncle," I replied.

The courtesy of the old-fashioned reply must have
pleased him, because he smiled. "Such a warm day. Have
you had tea?" He beckoned to a young woman at the rear
of the shop, only about ten feet away.

"Thank you," I said, as she brought a pot and two tiny
cups over on a tray painted with cranes and willow trees.
I waited for her to pour for both the old man and me and

to replace the pot on the tray. I sipped at the tea, golden in the white porcelain cup. "Your tea is delicious," I told the old man. "So delicately flavored. The perfect refreshment among so many beautiful things."

He bowed his head to acknowledge the compliment. "I try in my shop to offer only those items which approach, in some small way, the beauty of their wearers."

Okay, I thought, enough of this, or I'll walk out of here with a diamond tennis bracelet it'll take me a decade to pay off.

"Uncle," I said, putting my teacup down, "I have a piece of jade whose value I am curious to know."

He nodded as though this were exactly what he'd been expecting. I got the feeling he'd have done that no matter what I said, because I was the customer, but that he probably felt a little pang as he saw the tennis bracelet fading from my wrist.

I took the little velvet box from my bag and opened it to show him Harry's jade.

He regarded it gravely. "May I?" he said, reaching for the box. He lifted the Buddha by its chain, letting it dangle from his hand. It sparkled in the bright lights. He put the loupe back into his eye and for the next minute or so, he didn't speak.

Finally he looked up, removed the loupe, and placed the Buddha back in its box.

"It is quite beautiful," he said. "The carver's hand was precise, but also playful. Do you wish to sell it?"

"Perhaps one day, uncle." It seemed rude to ask for a professional appraisal of the thing without offering him the hope of someday getting his hands on it. "Now I wish only to understand its true value."

"No," he corrected me mildly. "What you are asking is its price."

I felt myself blush. "Yes, uncle. What you say is true."

He smiled and looked again at the jade. "If you were interested in selling it, I would be prepared to offer one hundred twenty thousand dollars."

My heart jumped and I almost knocked my teacup over. Then I reminded myself: Hong Kong dollars. That was fifteen thousand, American. Which meant he probably thought he could sell it for twenty.

More than I had been told, but not enough to really notice.

"Uncle," I asked, "is there anything . . . unusual . . . about this jade?"

"In what way?"

"I don't know," I said. "Its color? Its age? Anything?"

"It appears to be approximately three hundred years old," he said, "from the late Ming or early Qing. The stone is good, a bright apple green much valued today, although this piece is streaked with paler veins. The jadecarver, as I have said, was precise, but he did not attempt any unusual or difficult details—for example, do you see here how the folds of the Buddha's robe are suggested, but not elaborated?" He shook his head. "No, it is fine piece, but there are others like it. In what way did you think it might be unusual?"

"Uncle, I don't know," I repeated. "Only that I have been offered for this piece a far greater price than you have told me it is worth." That wasn't the exact truth, but close enough. "Although I don't want to sell it, I wondered why the offer was so high."

He shook his head. "That I cannot tell you."

I looked again at the Buddha on its white silk bed. I thanked the old man and the young woman and took my leave of them and their tiny, sparkling store.

The next shop I was heading for was larger, more straightforward, and empty of other customers when I found it. I did my business, charging it on the American Express card, taking on faith my ability to explain the need for this to Grandfather Gao when it came time for him, the client, to cover the expenses of this job. I headed back to the hotel, shopping bag in hand.

In my room the little red message light on the phone

was blinking, and the message was from Bill. It said, "I'm in the bar."

My first thought was: Oh, surprise. My second was: Thank God. What, Lydia? I demanded, as I felt a flush of relief spread through me. Bill's a grown-up. He's been in this business for twenty years. Whatever he was up to, he can handle himself. This is a civilized city, it has cabs and subways and cops. Yes, I argued with myself, locking up my room and heading down the hall, but he's a foreigner here. The way things work in other places isn't necessarily the way they work here. He may not remember that, or know it when he sees it. I took the elevator to the shopping mall mezzanine and then floated down on the escalator to the lobby bar.

In the cool, high-ceilinged splendor of the bar it took me about three seconds to spot Bill. He sat at a table near the piano, his back to the low wall, with a view that took in the main lobby, the hotel entrance and the escalator. He raised his beer glass in greeting. I stopped by the desk to redirect any phone calls, then trotted across the marble floor.

"Such class, coming from you," I said as I deposited myself on the armchair across from Bill's at the low carved table. "You usually don't bother with a glass."

"If you took me to places like this more often, I might class up my act," he answered. "In fact, it might be your responsibility to do that. For the good of my immortal soul, or something."

"If the good of your immortal soul depends on the use of a beer glass, I'm afraid you're beyond my help." I was trying for a blasé air of moral superiority, but by accident our eyes met. I saw something in his that mirrored the relief I'd felt hearing his voice on my phone message, and he saw something in mine and grinned that grin again.

"I'm starving," I said, snatching up the menu card from the table and studying it intently.

"Before you bury yourself in food, tell me: Have you spoken to the Weis? Is there any news about the kid?"

I looked up at the tone in his voice. It struck me that he'd been trying for something, too, maybe simple cool professionalism, but where there's a kid involved, Bill can't really manage that. "Yes, in fact," I said, gently. "No real news, but we have to go up there soon."

"Why?"

I detailed my conversation with Steven Wei.

"The jade." Bill sipped some beer, watching tourists, travelers, businessmen coming and going in the high-ceilinged lobby. "I don't know about that."

"What don't you know?"

"A lot of things. Why anyone who knew we were bringing the jade today wouldn't just mug *us* on the way over. Or on the other hand, wait until the Weis had the jade for sure. How did they know we weren't just bringing papers to sign? The jade could even still be in New York, waiting for us to say it was okay to ship it over."

"Unless someone in the family was involved, who really knew what was going on."

"Or someone close to the family."

"The amah?"

"She knew," Bill said. "And it might be natural for her to think of using the kid."

She's been taking care of him since he was a baby, I thought: It doesn't seem natural to me.

A uniformed waiter approached our table and stood waiting, in case I wanted anything to go with Bill's beer. "Lemonade, please," I said. "And a chicken salad sandwich. And two steamed pork buns."

"Three," said Bill. The waiter bowed slightly and left. "In case you're really starving," Bill said. "To make sure there's something left for me."

"You think I don't think about you," I said, "but I do. For example, I have something in this bag for you. But you can't have it until you tell me where you've been."

"Am I sure I want it?" he asked dubiously, eyeing the shopping bag by my foot.

"I'm sure you don't. But you'll be glad to have it. Now

come on, talk. We have to be at the Weis' before three."

He shrugged and sipped his beer. "Just doing my job. There was a guy who seemed to care when Steven Wei came and went, so after Wei took off in a cab I followed him."

"Young guy? White tee shirt, black pants?"

"You saw him, too?"

"I followed Steven Wei back out to the plaza. I saw the guy cursing after the cab, but I wasn't sure."

"What happened in the fortune-tellers' place?"

I got a strange fortune, I suddenly thought, about swiftly running water; but that wasn't what he wanted to know. "An old woman prayer-seller gave Wei a paper prayer. He read it and then hightailed it back to the plaza. I followed in time to see him grab a cab, see your young guy, and then see you going into the subway. How did you know how the subway works, by the way?"

"I didn't. I figured I'd lose him, but I thought maybe I'd at least get to see which way he went. As it happened he needed a ticket, so I stood on line at the next machine and bought one to the same place he did."

"Where?"

"How do I know? Wait, I wrote it down." He searched the papers in his pocket for a scrap that he unfolded and read me. "Choi Hung."

"Where's that?"

"That way." He pointed vaguely north.

"Never mind, I'll look on the map later. Then what?"

"Then I followed the guy and put my ticket in the machine the same way he did. He taught me a lot, actually."

"You followed him all the way home?"

"Not home. He was going back to work."

"How do you know?"

"Because that's where he went. When we got off the subway he made a call from his cell phone, but he didn't stop walking while he talked. I wasn't nearly close enough to see the number, but he didn't seem happy. Then I followed him up a long, hot hill and down the other side, like the king of goddamn France. Then there we were at Thundering Mountain Film Studios. He's a stuntman."

"No kidding?" I pictured the kid's muscular arms and chest under his white tee shirt. "How do you know?"

"I waited until he'd gone in and asked the guard. I wasn't sure you'd want me to approach the kid myself, and I wasn't sure the guard would let me in anyway. So I told the guard the kid had been making eyes at my girlfriend, and I was pissed off, and who the hell was he?"

"What made you think the guard spoke English?"

"What did I have to lose if he didn't? And he did, some. Enough to practically laugh in my face. He said the kid's name is Iron Fist Chang, and not for nothing. He said ol' Iron Fist may not be the brightest bulb on the tree, but he's one of Thundering Mountain's lead stuntmen, a big-league kung fu expert. But, the guy said, I shouldn't worry about my girlfriend, because Chang's got a cute little Filipina girlfriend of his own. Plus of course he could have as many girls as he wanted, being a Thundering Mountain stuntman and all." He sipped his beer. "He sort of implied that any girl who'd fall for the likes of me was bound to be beneath the notice of a guy like Iron Fist anyway. I considered popping him one for insulting my girlfriend."

"You don't have a girlfriend."

"Lucky for him."

The waiter arrived and from his tray set down a bamboo steamer, a plate with a quartered sandwich, and a tall frosted glass of lemonade.

"All right," I said. "That's good. A name is much more than I thought we'd get. I just wish we knew a cop to give it to."

Bill nodded as he reached for some potato chips from my sandwich plate. "I don't like this," he said, more somberly. "We're working blind. Following Wei this morning was irresistible, but maybe we should back off."

"On principle I hate to back off, but you might be right."

"On principle you hate it when I'm right. But we don't even have a client."

"Disregarding the first part of that statement, let me correct you on the second part." I told him about my conversation with Grandfather Gao.

He sipped thoughtfully at his beer. "So that was authorization to proceed?"

"From him, yes, that's about as direct an order as we can expect to get. Though it isn't quite clear to me what we're supposed to proceed to do."

"Protect his interests."

"Name one."

"You're the one who's known him all your life."

"So it's my job to figure this out?"

"It seems only fair. You're the Chinese person in this situation."

"I'm the Chinese person in most situations. But I'll think about it." I drank some lemonade, wondering what genius had first thought up this tart, sweet, perfect drink.

Bill reached for a steamed pork bun. "I have to admit I feel a little stupid," he said. "There we are watching Steven Wei, and there he is calling you."

"How about that? Don't you just hate to miss those important calls?" I bit into a pork bun myself, tasted the sweet, spicy meat at the center of the warm bread. "Well," I said, "you won't have to worry about that any more." I lifted a box out of the shopping bag that was still sitting patiently at my feet. "This is for you."

He took the box, opened it, and held up the cell phone from it. "Hot damn."

"You don't have to pretend to be happy about it. I know you hate those things. But you really need one here."

"No, I love it. Now I can be like everyone else. I was beginning to feel different. Like I stuck out somehow."

"Oh, yes, well, this will be sure to cure that. The number's on it." He took the phone out of the plastic it was wrapped in. "Flip it open, press the red button, and dial 5786-2224." With a glance at me he did as I told him. He finished dialing and put the phone to his ear as my pocket began to chirp.

I whipped out the phone I'd gotten for myself. "Hello?"

"I guess it works," Bill said, both across the table and in my ear.

No one else in the bar so much as looked at us.

four

Our new subway expertise notwithstanding, we took the ferry to the Hong Kong side, to grab a cab up to the Weis'. The ferry ride was still breezy and beautiful, the sun still gleaming off the sharp edges of skyscrapers, though a thick gray fog now wrapped Victoria Peak at the top of the island, dulling the harbor water.

"The richest people in Hong Kong live up there," I told Bill, pointing at the hillside as it disappeared upward into the mist. "That's how you know you've arrived, when you can buy a house up there. And the guidebook says it's like that half the time, damp and yucky and no view at all."

The cab ride from the ferry dock was longer than the morning's ride because traffic was thicker, but we still got to the Weis by twenty to three. I had been in favor of taking a few minutes to question the desk man on the subject of just who had told him to let us up earlier, but Bill was against it.

"He may be in on it," he said, "and if we start spooking them with questions they may back off from making this trade. If we need to we can think about a way to approach him later. Right now we don't want to miss the phone call."

"When you're right, you're right," I grumbled. "And let the record show I said that."

But he wasn't all that right. When we got up to the Weis', it seemed we'd missed the phone call. Not the one we'd been expecting, but another one.

Li-Ling Wei, gray-faced and silent, let us in. The living room been straightened up, and a quick glance down the hall suggested that the other rooms had been, too. Well, it's what I would have done, something to keep busy, something to do. Someone had made tea, but according to the three half-full teacups, no one had really drunk it. Out the living-room window, here on the hillside on the twenty-sixth floor, the mist that shrouded the Peak was beginning to descend, torn shreds of clouds floating by, not quite transparent, not quite opaque.

Steven Wei was pacing, but he stopped to squeeze Li-Ling's hand as she returned from the front door. He led her solicitously back to an armchair which she looked at with fearful eyes, as if, in this world that had so radically changed, it might come to life and attack her. Natalie Zhu, across the room, sat composed and still, looking as though she hadn't moved since we'd left. Her face was an impassive mask carved from ice, but behind their delicate glasses her eyes took in every move Bill or I made.

"There's been a phone call," Steven Wei said, after we'd all spent a few seconds too long looking at each other, saying nothing. "With a demand."

"You told me that," I said. "The jade. We brought it. Though—"

"Not the jade. Half an hour ago. A different voice. Saying that Harry was all right but they wanted twenty million dollars for his return. They are giving me until tomorrow afternoon to raise the money."

"Twenty million dollars?" I stifled a gasp and did the quick arithmetic; that was two and a half million, American. "Do you have that kind of money?"

"No," Steven Wei said simply.

"What about the jade?"

"They said they didn't know what I was talking about."

I looked at Bill as the meaning of this sank in.

"Did you—?" Bill began.

"Ask for proof? They hung up too fast. I was too startled. No." The way Steven Wei's eyes dropped when he said this, and the look Natalie Zhu gave him, implied they'd been through this unpleasantness already.

"When the other call comes," Natalie Zhu said, a woman used to solving the problem at hand and not wasting time over earlier mistakes, "then we will ask."

"And if they refuse?" Steven looked up rapidly. "My son—"

"Steven. Why would they refuse? The people holding Harry will expect to have to give proof. The others will be unable. We will make no payment until we are sure."

We, I thought? He's not your son. I stole a look at Li-Ling Wei. She perched on the edge of the chair, her eyes wide and a little wild, staring at the floor. Her arms hugged herself over her round stomach. She seemed on the edge of tears. I wanted to go over there, put my arm around her, tell her it would be all right, but I wasn't sure that would be welcome.

And much as I hoped it would be all right, I wasn't sure about that, either.

I suddenly wasn't sure about anything: what to do, what to say, whether to give them the jade, whether Bill and I should be here at all. It was a dizzying, unmoored feeling, not helped by the view from the Weis' living-room window, which reminded me that I was high up in the air, in a pencil-slim building on the side of a mountain, floating over a harbor thousands of miles from home.

Bill moved into the room. His hand brushed mine lightly, casually, an accidental touch as he passed by. Some accident. The roughness of his fingers, the scent of his sweat, even the temperature of his skin were all completely familiar, exactly what I knew they'd be. They brought me back to solid ground.

I flushed. He carefully didn't look at me, which was a good thing. I wasn't sure how I felt about the fact that he could tell, without words, what I was feeling and, still without words, do something about it. Even if what he did about it made me feel better.

Well, I'd worry about that later; now, back to business. I opened my bag to take out the jade to show Steven and Li-Ling. They were both clearly having trouble keeping themselves together; the jade might reassure them a little. But before my hand closed on the box, the intercom at the front door buzzed.

Steven Wei threw a look at Natalie Zhu, then jumped up and grabbed the handset. Li-Ling rose awkwardly from her chair and stood with her hands pressed together. "Yes?" Steven barked in Cantonese. "What?"

The desk man spoke; Steven Wei seemed to be having trouble understanding him. "What?" he repeated. "Who?"

The answer came. Steven Wei lowered the handset, looked blankly around the room. Natalie Zhu began to stand, ready to take over and handle whatever situation this was. But Steven raised the handset again, spoke to the desk man, and hung up. He turned to face us.

"I told them to let him come up." He spoke woodenly, waiting for a response.

"Who, Steven?" Natalie Zhu said sharply.

Steven Wei looked at her as though her question were as incomprehensible to him as whatever it was the desk man had said. He gestured helplessly at the intercom and repeated what he'd been told. "It's Franklin Wei," he said. "From New York. My brother."

Bill lit a cigarette; otherwise, no one moved and not a word was said in the Wei apartment until the doorbell rang. When it did, I was the one standing closest to it, so I was the one who opened it.

A round-faced man stood in the hall wearing a Ralph Lauren polo shirt, khakis, and a tentative smile. My eyes widened before I could help it. Except for another inch in height and a pair of horn-rim glasses, I could have been looking at Steven Wei. The unlined face, the short, neat haircut, the way the smile lit up his face—a smile I had seen on Steven Wei just once, standing in this same hall— they were all the same.

"Hello," he said in Cantonese. "I'm Wei Fu-Ran. Franklin. Are you Li-Ling?" He held a large bunch of flowers and a box of chocolates; he offered me both.

"I'm Lydia Chin," I answered in English, not responding directly to anything he'd said in Chinese. "You'd better come in."

Franklin Wei's eyebrows came together as he heard my tone of voice. He waited politely for an explanation, but the smile remained. He entered the apartment and caught sight of his brother, Steven.

Under other circumstances, it could have been a funny moment. Two men, nearly identical, unaware of each other's existence until a month ago, one of them completely astounded by the other's unexpected arrival, the other about to be shocked by the situation he was walking into. This could make for a great Chinese comic opera setup, except a comic opera wouldn't center on a kidnapped seven-year-old boy.

Where to start? Well, there was the obvious. In English, I said, "Franklin Wei, this is Steven. Steven Wei, this is Franklin."

Franklin Wei shifted the chocolates to his left hand and held out his right. Steven Wei, on autopilot, put out his own hand, and they shook, brother to brother, man to man.

"I know. It's a shock," Franklin said to Steven, continuing in English. His English had the cadences of a native New Yorker's; his Chinese, like mine, had the ease of being raised among native speakers. Obviously neither language was a foreign one to him; I wondered which he thought in. "I called your office. When they told me you were home, I couldn't resist the surprise. Sorry." He grinned.

I wasn't sure, if things had been different, whether Steven would have enjoyed the joke, but he wasn't returning his brother's grin now. Franklin Wei glanced around the room, then back at Steven. "Did I interrupt something? Hey, I really am sorry. This was really rude of me, huh? I just thought it would be kind of a kick . . ." He trailed off in the silence.

This seemed manifestly unfair to Franklin. Here he was thinking that the frowns and the furrowed brows in this room were because he hadn't called before he came. Someone should clue him in. He was, after all, family.

"There's a problem, Dr. Wei," I said. "It has nothing to do with you."

Natalie Zhu stirred in her chair. I expected her to stand

up, stop me, to take charge and take over, but all she did was watch me, and wait.

So I went on. I introduced everyone in the room: Bill, Natalie Zhu (whom I called first by her Chinese name, and then Natalie), and the real Li-Ling. Then I said to Franklin, "We're in the middle of a bad situation."

"I'm sorry," he said again. "Did I screw something up?"

"No. But your arrival may be one more shock than anyone was ready for." I told him about the kidnapping, and the frightening complication of the new phone call. As I spoke I kept waiting for someone to stop me, to tell me this was not any of Franklin Wei's business and certainly none of mine. But Li-Ling Wei just stared at the floor, as though she was being forced to listen again to something she had not wanted to hear the first time; and Steven Wei, glancing occasionally at Natalie Zhu, saw that she was making no move to end my telling of the story and said nothing himself.

"Jesus," Franklin Wei said softly when I was through. "Damn." He looked at his brother. "I'm really sorry." There, I thought, how's that? You fly all the way to the other side of the world and wind up saying nothing but *I'm sorry*. "Is there anything I can do?"

Steven Wei shook his head. "There is . . . we're waiting for the next phone call. At three o'clock." He looked at his watch, as did everyone else, when he said that. "A few minutes," Steven Wei said unnecessarily.

Franklin Wei took a handkerchief from his back pocket to wipe sweat from his face. The movement rustled the paper around the bouquet of flowers he still held. Li-Ling Wei seemed to awaken at the sound. She stood and, moving slowly but steadily, took the flowers and chocolates from the man who looked so like her husband. Bowing in thanks, she carried them into the kitchen, returning with the flowers in a vase of water.

Franklin Wei looked at me. "I know who you are now," he said. "Grandfather Gao told me you'd be here. You brought Dad's jade. And the ashes."

"That's right," I said.

"Truth is," he said, "I was kind of surprised Dad wanted to be buried here. Not as amazed as when I found out about you guys—" Franklin turned to Steven, trying for a smile "—but the way Dad felt about the old traditions, the way he used to laugh at all that? It just surprised me, him wanting to come back here. So I thought I'd come along . . . well, hell, man. I wish it weren't like this."

Steven Wei obviously wished it weren't like this, too. I was a little thrown hearing Franklin Wei, high up here in the air above Hong Kong, refer to "Grandfather Gao," but I thought, why not? Given the longtime friendship between Grandfather Gao and old Mr. Wei, Grandfather Gao must have been a frequent visitor at the Weis' Westchester home. A lot of Chinatown kids used the honorific *Grandfather* for Gao Mian-Liang, so why not this sunny, suburban, all-American Chinese boy?

Steven Wei was thrown, too, but by something else. "Laugh at the old traditions?" he said. "Father?" As he spoke, my mind returned to this morning's search of the apartment, to the room with the wall safe. I saw the camphorwood trunk, the armoire, the teak bench so like the one in Grandfather Gao's shop. The bed had been narrow, piled with brocade bolsters between the curving head- and footboards, and on the deep red wall, next to a pair of painted scrolls, hung a small shrine to Tin Hua, goddess of the sea. The room was quiet, dark, full of the pull of years. It was of a different nature from the pale-blue-and-ivory sleekness of the rest of the apartment, and I had assumed it had belonged to old Mr. Wei. "My father loved the old ways," Steven was saying. "He was never so happy as when he was telling us stories about the home village or talking in the tearoom with his friends. He loved the old music, and the classic texts."

Franklin and Steven Wei looked at each other. And ending any immediate chance of either finding out more about the other's view of the man they both called father, the telephone rang.

This time, as in the morning, the shrill chirps came from the cell phone in Steven Wei's pocket. He whipped it out. *"Wai!"* As he listened to the response from the other end of the line, Natalie Zhu came and stood before him. She made no move to take the phone from him, but her presence seemed to challenge him into steeliness, and when he was through listening, his voice was controlled and calm.

"What proof do I have that you are holding my son?" he asked in Chinese. "Let me speak to him."

An answer; then, "No, that is not enough. I have gotten another call. Someone else also claiming to be holding my son and his amah." Pause. "With a—different demand. I will bring the jade wherever you like if you bring my son to me at the same place, but I will not turn the jade over to you before I see him."

Pause. "Yes, I have the jade. I can—No, it—" To whatever went on at the other end after that, Steven Wei managed only fragmented replies. Then suddenly he lost his composure and shouted, *"Wai! Wai!"* into the phone. He shouted once more, then stopped.

Face flushed, he lowered the phone and looked around the room. "He said if we don't give him the jade we'll be sorry. Then he hung up." Realizing he'd spoken in Chinese, he repeated himself in English.

"Did he offer proof?" That was Natalie Zhu, sticking to the important point.

Steven Wei shook his head. "He said he thought this was a transaction between gentlemen. That he'd been behaving as one, but if I chose not to do so, he could behave ... in other ways." He looked at Natalie Zhu. "Do you think that means—?"

"Did he say he would call again?" She cut him off.

"Yes."

Natalie Zhu, arms crossed over her silk blouse, kept her eyes on Steven Wei for a while. Then she turned deliberately to face me, Bill, and Franklin Wei.

"I'm sorry," she said, not particularly sounding it. "We must speak privately. Dr. Wei, it is unfortunate that your arrival has come at this bad time. The situation will no doubt be resolved soon. We will let you know as soon as there is happy news to report. Miss Chin, please leave the jade. We will call you."

So here we were, getting thrown out of the Weis' apartment again. I opened my mouth to object, though I wasn't sure on what grounds besides Lydia Chin's need to be in on everything. Then, meeting Natalie Zhu's eyes, I abruptly stopped. I did some quick mental flip-flops, then decided.

After all, Grandfather Gao had told me to do what I thought was right. And if none of this had ever happened and everything had been okay to begin with, Steven and Li-Ling Wei would be effectively in charge of this jade by now anyhow.

Taking the velvet box from my bag, I handed it, not to Natalie Zhu, but to Li-Ling Wei. One hand over her huge stomach, she opened it. Both Steven and Franklin Wei looked in at the laughing Buddha gleaming on his white silk.

Franklin smiled. "I remember when Dad got that," he said. "I must have been, I don't know, five. He brought me one, too, not a Buddha, just this thing." He reached under his shirt and pulled out a gold chain from which dangled a pointed jade amulet, faceted and about an inch long. "It was the only old-timey thing I ever saw him do. I haven't worn it since I was like twelve, just put it on when I decided to come here. Seemed like, I don't know, a cool thing to wear to Hong Kong."

Steven Wei slowly reached under his own shirt and pulled out an amulet exactly like it. "I don't remember a time when Father did not wear his jade," he said. "Or a time when I did not wear mine."

"I want to talk to you," I told Bill, standing on the sidewalk on Robinson Road, after, to the rattle of jackhammers in the swampy heat, we had put Franklin Wei in a taxi.

"I'm at the Peninsula," Franklin had said. "Will you call me? I mean, if anything happens?" Gesturing upward in the general direction of the twenty-sixth floor, he added, "They might not think of it." They might not, I thought; or they might, but that didn't mean they'd do it. We'd taken the hotel's phone number and given him our cell phone numbers in exchange. We'd given them to the Weis, too, Steven Wei nodding in distracted thanks, Natalie Zhu raising a barely discernible eyebrow as she found out we'd actually gone out and gotten cell phones since this morning.

Now, to me, Bill said, "Where?"

"How about the park? The scene of the crime."

"Maybe."

"Not the park? You want to go somewhere else?"

"No, the park's good. I meant maybe it's the scene of the crime."

"You really don't buy the idea that this is what it looks like?" I asked as we headed downhill to the little park that, according to Steven Wei, Maria Quezon and Harry went to all the time.

"What the hell does it even look like?" I raised my eyebrows at the short-tempered growl in his voice, but said nothing. He shook a cigarette out of the pack, lit a match as we passed under the fronds of a huge palm tree growing on a wall. "The kid grabbed the day—just about the hour—we show up from New York. Two ransom demands, one for more money than the family has, one for less than the risk is worth."

"You think that's true, that they don't have that much money?"

"Maybe it's not. Maybe they're not sure about us and he was being cagey. Shouldn't be hard to find out."

"All right," I said, "but if the first call was from phony kidnappers, what was the point of sending Steven Wei to Wong Tai Sin? If that was you, wouldn't you just want to get in and get what you could before the real guys call and Steven realizes he's been had?"

"Yes," he said shortly. "So, assuming that one of the calls is real and that's the one that sent Steven Wei to the temple, who made the other one, and how did they find out the kid was taken?"

"Assuming." I turned to look at him. "You think maybe neither is real?"

"I don't know what I think. If that was the real call, why wouldn't they prove they had the kid?"

"Maybe," I said slowly, "something's happened to the kid."

"I thought of that." Bill said, his voice lower. He gazed down the hill, across the harbor. "But even if the kid's already dead, they'd know what he was wearing. If he had birthmarks, they'd know that. Missing teeth, whatever. They could have tried to fake it."

"Maybe they don't think that fast. Maybe they're nervous. Maybe they're not pros." I stepped aside for a sweating woman pulling a grocery cart up the steep sidewalk.

Bill didn't answer me directly. He said, "There are a few other things I want to know. I still want to know why the apartment was wrecked."

"And who let us up."

"And who paid the old lady prayer-seller at Wong Tai Sin."

"And how your friend Iron Fist Chang fits in."

We walked between wooden gateposts holding up a red arch with the characters for "Kwong Hon Terrace Garden" painted on it in gold. The concrete-paved park nestled between low, old buildings, ran through the block and ended in another arched gateway to another street. Small children shrieked as they ran through sprays of water from the mouths of three bronze frogs. Half a dozen Filipina amahs shared sliced papaya and cans of coconut soda, giggled and gossiped, called to their charges. We sat on a concrete bench in the shade of a banana tree. I stared at the bananas, growing upside down just the way they're supposed to.

"Old Mr. Wei," Bill said. "I want to know what he was worried about. I want to know what we were sent here to do."

I looked at him, watched his eyes follow an amah as she

jumped up to comfort a toddler who had slipped in the bronze frogs' pool. She picked the child up, hugged and cajoled him, gave him a slice of papaya, and sent him, giggling, back to his friends. I touched Bill's arm. "I'm sorry," I said.

He turned to me, surprised. "About what?"

"This." I waved my arm around. "Everything's so—confusing. So illogical and unreasonable. So Chinese."

"Do you mean to tell me," he said, taking the cigarette from his mouth, "that when you're being confusing, illogical, and unreasonable, it's genetic?"

"You know what I mean."

He shook his head. "I don't. No offense, but you people are no different from anybody else. Everyone wants the same thing, in the end."

"Which is?"

"To protect what you love."

A trickle of sweat slid down my cheek. I wiped it away and asked, "That's what it's all about? Love?"

Bill didn't answer. I said, "What about greed? Revenge? Wanting to make someone suffer? Those things aren't about love."

"No," Bill said. "They're about protection."

The amahs talked and laughed in the shade and the children ran and splashed in the frog pool. Bill and I sat silently until his cigarette was done.

"Okay," I said, "suppose you're right. I'm dubious, but suppose. Who's protecting what around here?"

"I don't know," Bill said. "But I can think of a few people to ask. The uncle. The desk man. Iron Fist. The old lady."

As my cell phone rang, I added, "And the new client."

Bill's questioning look held me as I answered the phone in English with a businesslike "Lydia Chin speaking."

Natalie Zhu wasn't impressed.

"We can speak in English if you prefer it, Ms. Chin," she said dryly, in Cantonese. "Or perhaps you'd rather Chinese?"

Oh, all right, I thought. So I wasn't fooling you. Big deal. It was worth a try. "Let's stay in the habit of English," I said, as cool as she was. "For my partner."

"Fine," she agreed, switching languages. "Can you talk freely?"

"I'm in the park at Kwong Hon Terrace. No one's near but Bill. And you?"

Bill had his eyes on me, waiting to be filled in, so I mouthed "Natalie Zhu" for him and watched him raise his eyebrows.

"I am on the balcony," Natalie Zhu answered, and I had an image of her steely small form, cell phone pressed to her ear, standing in the hot breeze on the twenty-sixth floor, commanding the view over Robinson Road, the roofs of the Central skyscrapers, the harbor. "I told Steven I had to make some calls putting off other work in my office as long as this situation continues. You are not surprised at my calling you?"

"Did you expect me to be?"

"I had hoped you would not. I had hoped an understanding had passed between us."

I wouldn't exactly call it an understanding, I thought, just a direct look in the eye, just held an extra second, just a little more contact than was necessary if all you were really doing was throwing us out.

"I understood you would call," I told her. "I don't yet understand why."

"You are investigators," she said. "Sent by Gao Mian-Liang. Wei Yao-Shi"—Old Mr. Wei—"always spoke most highly of Gao Mian-Liang. Now tell me: Why did Gao Mian-Liang send you here?"

I answered honestly. "He told us it was to deliver the jade and a letter to Mr. Wei's brother, and to bring Mr. Wei's ashes."

"Pardon me, but that seems unlikely."

"To us, too. Earlier today I called and told him what had happened and asked him, in view of the situation, if there was anything further he could tell us. He said there wasn't, but that we should do whatever we felt needed to be done."

A pause as she digested the fact that I'd told Grandfather Gao that Harry had been kidnapped. She might have made an issue of it, but all she said was, "And what do you feel needs to be done?"

"I'm not sure. But I can't say, Ms. Zhu, that I think this is just a simple kidnapping, or that getting Harry back is going to be as easy as meeting a ransom demand."

"Nor do I."

Oh, really? "Well, then," I suggested, "why don't you tell me what you do think? And tell me why you're calling us in secret, instead of speaking to us in front of Steven and Li-Ling?"

"What I think, Ms. Chin, is that Maria Quezon is involved in this. I am speaking in secret because Steven would never permit me to ask that you make her the target of an investigation. But I believe if you find Maria, you will find the child."

Steven wouldn't permit it, I thought. Since when does Steven tell you what to do?

"You were the one opposed to calling the police," I said. "Your position was, play along and everything will be all right. Why have you changed your mind?"

"About the police, I have not. That would be dangerous. But I believe circumstances now warrant that some action be taken."

"Circumstances?"

"You would make a good attorney, Ms. Chin. You ask questions to which you very well know the answers in order to hear them from your opponent. Circumstances. Two ransom demands, a refusal to prove that the child is being held. You say you are now in Kwong Hon Terrace Garden. Tell me, do you think it would have been possible to abduct Harry and Maria by force from that park at nine o'clock in the morning without the police hearing about it even before we did?"

Filing away *opponent* for later, I had to admit as I looked around that that last question was a very good one. There were the amahs over by the frogs. There was a pair of Chinese grandmothers who had come in after we had, parking strollers beside a bench and fanning themselves with paper fans. There were three shirtless teenage boys doing chin-ups on the swing set, probably hoping some girls would happen by to impress. It was July; school was out; in the morning, before the day got really hot and most people retreated to air-conditioning, this park was probably even more crowded than this. No, it wasn't likely a kidnapping could have happened here, or on the crowded streets with their narrow sidewalks on the way to here, and go unnoticed and unreported.

"I have not changed my mind about the police," Natalie Zhu repeated. "They are not capable of finding Harry without taking action so obvious that the kidnappers will be alerted. But you are in a different position."

"What do you want us to do?"

"As I say: Find Maria Quezon. You are professionals, trusted by Gao Mian-Liang; that is a high recommendation for your abilities. Perhaps you can proceed without arousing suspicions. I am not familiar with your usual terms of employment, but whatever they are I will accept them. I would ask, however, that you report to me anything you find, however insignificant it seems. Nothing you do must endanger the child. Because you are not from Hong Kong, it is possible you may miss the implications of your actions. But as you say, I do not believe this is simple. Some action must be taken. Will you accept?"

Darn tootin', I wanted to answer, to balance Natalie Zhu's formal manner and the fact that I knew she was saying all this to me from three hundred feet in the sky; but I restrained myself. "Yes," I told her. "We'll take the job."

I asked for information on Maria Quezon; she gave me very little. Maria had lived with the Wei family for all of Harry's seven years, except for an annual two-week trip back to the Philippines, where she had family in the mountain village of Cabagan. She had come recommended by someone, but Natalie Zhu didn't know who; her sister also worked in Hong Kong, but Natalie Zhu didn't know where. She had a boyfriend, but Natalie Zhu didn't know him. She surely must have friends among the other amahs, although Natalie Zhu had no idea of how to go about finding them, since there were one hundred thousand Filipinas in Hong Kong looking after other people's children. Li-Ling Wei might possibly know, but again, she did not want Li-Ling or Steven to know what we were doing.

"Steven's strength is also his flaw," she said. "He is a devoted family man, very loyal. Harry, Li-Ling, and now the expected little one are central to his life. His loyalty extended, of course, to his father, and extends to his uncle. I am honored to say it extends also to myself; and after so many years, to Maria Quezon as well. He will not hear a bad word against any of us. Unfortunately, not everyone returns such devotion in kind."

Unfortunate indeed, I thought. "I'd like to look through her things," I said. "In her room. She's bound to have something that will give us a line on her boyfriend or her sister, something to start with."

"No," Natalie Zhu said calmly. "As I said, I cannot allow Steven or Li-Ling to know about this. I will look through her room myself, at the first opportunity. I will let you know what I find."

I didn't like that as much, but you don't argue with a door after it's slammed shut. "All right," I told Natalie Zhu. "Call us if you find anything. And if anything happens."

She gave me the number of her cell phone, the better for secret-keeping, and hung up. I flipped my phone closed and said to Bill, "We're hired."

"Well, I'm impressed," he said. "You really knew she was going to call?"

"From the look she gave me as she was throwing us out. I got the feeling she had something to say, and since she wasn't saying it there, I thought she'd try later."

"So what are we hired to do?"

"Find the amah." I gave him a rundown of Natalie Zhu's

request and her reasoning. "What do you think?" I asked when I was finished.

He lit another cigarette, looked across the park. Two of the amahs, chattering away, were packing up their diaper bags, strollers, and children. "I think it's bullshit," he said.

"Funny, I had that same thought. Which part?"

"All of it. Why she doesn't want Steven Wei to know what we're doing. Loyalty to the amah only goes so far, when your kid's at stake."

"Maybe she's afraid he thinks nothing should be done at all. Just to sit tight and follow directions."

"Did you get the feeling he did any thinking for himself when she was around?"

"No," I said. "And that's another thing. Sneaking out onto the balcony. Laying it on thick about how good we must be if Grandfather Gao sent us. What happened to the I-give-the-orders, this-is-how-it-is Natalie Zhu we used to know?"

"So what do you think the point is?"

"To use us find Maria Quezon for some other reason, something Steven Wei wouldn't like. Or—"

"—or to keep us busy. To get us out of the way."

The amahs pushed their strollers past us on their way out of the park. One of the toddlers, the one who'd fallen, was already asleep, cookie crumbs sticking to his round cheeks.

"And she thinks this will be sure to do it," I said. "Two Americans looking for a Filipina in Hong Kong. This could keep us *seriously* out of the way. Why would she want to do that?"

"So we won't interfere with whatever she's doing."

"Which would be what?"

"Or," he said, not answering my question, "there's another possibility. Maybe she's not trying to keep us from interfering with her. Maybe she's trying to interfere with us."

"With us, with what?"

"Whatever it is we were sent here to do." Bill mashed his cigarette on the side of the bench. "I wish to hell I knew what that was."

The cloud cover from the Peak had crept downhill while we'd been sitting here, making the air no cooler but even more unpleasantly sticky. Without the drama of strong sun and sharp shadows, the buildings surrounding the little park were revealed as neglected and shabby. I could see the rust on their metal windows and the cracks in their concrete. A truck straining up the hill left a bloom of exhaust to mix with the damp mist and drift in our direction.

"Grandfather Gao sent us," I said. "That's all she knows about us. If she's trying to distract us it must be because she thinks he had something more in mind than Harry's jade and old Mr. Wei's funeral arrangements. You don't suppose," a new thought hit me, "that all of this is for our benefit?"

Bill didn't answer right away. "No," he finally said. "Or: Maybe it is, but if it is, the parents aren't in on it. What they're going through, worrying about their kid, they're not faking that."

Well, I thought, you're more of an expert than I am. I suddenly wanted to take his hand, hold it just a minute; but I knew that was the last thing he'd want, so I pretended instead that I didn't see what was in his eyes and I said, "I'm calling Grandfather Gao."

Bill didn't answer. I took the cell phone out again, but before I tried to call New York on it I called the hotel, just to check, though I wasn't sure who besides Grandfather Gao himself would have called me.

Someone had, though. I scribbled down the number, thanked the desk clerk, pressed the OFF button, and turned to Bill.

"You'll never guess."

He waited, then decided to do it my way. "Steven Wei."

I shook my head. He went on guessing, and I went on shaking my head. "Li-Ling Wei. Franklin Wei. Iron Fist

Chang. The old lady, whatever her name was. The fortune-teller. That god from the temple, Wong Tai Sin. Sorry, wrong number."

He was out of guesses. I told him: "The police."

five

The Mandarin Oriental Hotel was just easing out of the afternoon tea business and into the cocktail hour when Bill and I arrived. As soon as we walked into the stately cool of the lobby, I wished I were back in one of my own sharply pressed linen shirts instead of this street-stall flowered blouse, and I wished Bill were still wearing a jacket and tie.

The Mandarin Oriental stood in placid peace on one of central Hong Kong's busiest avenues like a dowager duchess rising above the hysteria of her household staff. Outside, the building was serious-looking stone, and on the inside dark polished wood, beveled glass, and marble all exuded an air of outpost-of-empire that would take generations to wear away.

Bill and I were admitted by a white-gloved doorman and, when we asked our way to the Clipper Lounge, were gravely shown to a grand staircase by a lobby attendant who must have spent all his spare time shining the buttons on his uniform. The other women I saw, both Chinese and non, were all impeccably turned out, including the kind of high-heeled strappy sandals I would wear only in an emergency. The men, I was surprised to see, generally wore polo shirts—always with some recognizable logo—or dress shirts open at the neck. Few jackets, few ties. Considering it was about two hundred degrees outside, I guessed that made sense. I glanced at Bill. Maybe he didn't look so out of place, then. Maybe it was just me.

From the top of the stairs Bill and I turned right along a wide mezzanine. Our steps in the plush carpet made no sound to distract our attention from the elegant jewelry stores with diamonds and jade sparkling in their tiny show windows or the tailor's shops where you could choose a bolt of the finest cloth in the morning, have a fitting in the afternoon, and take your new handsewn suit home with you on the evening plane.

Thinking of the jewelry shop in the mall by the Hong Kong Hotel, I said to Bill, "Look at how those jewels glow and sparkle. They did that in the old man's shop, too. They sort of call to you, don't they? As though they were alive. As though they could tell you something, if you spoke the language."

He peered into the window of the shop we were passing. "High-intensity lighting," he said. "That high, that close, it would sparkle off tin."

I looked also, first at him, then at the little lights tucked up above the glass. Another time, I might have made some crack, maybe about the limitations of Western rational thought; and Bill would have come back with something equally silly, probably including a half-real pass at me. But there had been a few occasions for wisecracks and passes in the last few hours that Bill had uncharacteristically let slide. Uncharacteristic, but not completely surprising. Over the years I had seen him in these darker, distant moods more than once. These were the times when I was reminded why he lived alone, and why that was a good idea.

So we walked in silence to the end of this elegant alley and came to the Clipper Lounge. Large potted palms screened groups of low tables and chairs from the unwanted sight of one another and string quartet music was piped in at just the right volume to make conversation easy to hold but difficult to overhear. A stunningly beautiful Chinese woman, much younger than I, sipped a pink drink from a tall-stemmed glass as she sat with a silver-haired Westerner; they were speaking French. Three Japanese businessmen drank beer, ate peanuts, and enthusiastically talked, smoked, laughed, and interrupted each other. I wondered if Bill recognized them from the Tokyo airport smoking lounge, but I didn't get a chance to ask. A smiling man, polo-shirted under his pale linen jacket, was waving us over from behind a potted palm. We headed in his direction, me strolling nonchalantly as though street-stall blouses were quite the thing on the boulevards of Paris, where I normally frequented.

When we got there the smiling man held out his hand and said, "Lydia Chin? I'm Mark Quan." The potted palm said nothing.

I offered Mark Quan my hand, told him I was pleased to meet him, and introduced Bill. We shook, we smiled, and then Detective Sergeant Mark Quan of the Hong Kong Police Department Detective Bureau invited us to sit down.

"What can I get you?" he asked, waving a waiter over. He was speaking perfect American English; in fact, it seemed to me to have a tiny touch of Southern drawl.

"Can I still get tea?"

"This is the Mandarin Oriental." Mark Quan winked. "You can get anything you want."

He was a stocky man, sun-bronzed in his white Armani Xchange polo shirt, cream-colored linen jacket, and tan khakis. He looked in his early thirties, a little chubbier, maybe, than he ought to be, but with an ease to his movements that gave me the idea that thinking fat was the same as soft might in this case be a mistake. That idea was reinforced by the fact that his friendly smile was knocked a little cockeyed by the faded scar on his upper lip.

He ordered my tea and a gin and bitter lemon for himself. Bill ordered a beer.

"Did you have trouble finding the hotel?" Mark Quan asked when the waiter had marched solemnly away to fulfill his sworn duty to bring us our drinks or die. "You're new to Hong Kong, right?"

"No, the traffic was just heavy. It took a little longer than I thought," I answered, matching him small talk for small talk.

"I thought you might rather come here than to the Bureau office," he said. "It's comfortable here, and the refreshments are better." He smiled ruefully. "It's a little-known fact that the tea in Hong Kong police stations is as bad as the coffee in American ones." He settled back in his upholstered chair across the low table from us. The table was a wood-and-brass affair with hinges and handholds. It looked like something the English carried around to have tea on in the far-flung colonies. "So." Mark Quan smiled expectantly at me and Bill. "What can I do for you?"

I gave Bill a quick, confused glance. He raised an eyebrow, asking me if I wanted him to take the question so I could watch and listen, but I decided not to do it that way. I said to Mark Quan, "I don't understand. We're here because *you* called *us*."

"Well, sure," he said. "I was asked to extend you every courtesy. A drink at the Mandarin Oriental's a good beginning, but it can't be all you need. Life's never that easy."

"To extend us—Who asked you to do that?"

Mark Quan gave me an inquiring look; then his face relaxed into a smile. "I guess he didn't tell you he was calling me?"

"Whoever he is, no, he didn't."

"That's like him," Mark Quan said. "Never gives anything away. Doesn't tell you anything you don't need to know, or half of what you do. Kind of drives you crazy sometimes, doesn't it? But he's almost always right."

There was only one man I knew who fit that description, and he fit it perfectly. "Gao Mian-Liang? Gao Mian-Liang called you?"

"That's right," Mark Quan said. "Grandfather Gao."

Bill lit a cigarette. I felt like I needed one, too.

"I guess it's a lot less of a surprise to me than to you," Mark Quan went on.

Uh-huh, I thought, I guess.

Bill dropped the match into an ashtray, where it lay in the middle of the hotel's gilded logo. "He's called you before, then?" Bill asked, probably just to give me time to get used to this.

"He's been calling me like this for years," Mark Quan said. "Nothing for months, then just a suggestion: Pick up this pickpocket, look into that cash transfer. 'Although the crowing of the cock does not bring the sunrise, he fails in his duty if he remains asleep.' "

Clearly the same Grandfather Gao.

At that moment our intrepid waiter returned from his mission, discreetly triumphant. He set down a porcelain tea service, including tiny silver tongs to grab tiny sugar cubes with, and poured Bill's beer into a long thin glass. Mark Quan's drink came decorated with a sunburst of lemon. I poured myself some tea through a silver strainer that had a bowl of its own to sit in while it waited to be needed again. I sipped; the tea was keemun, strong and slightly sweet, so I added a slice of lemon from a fan of them on a plate. I must have been running on fumes, I realized, as I sipped again and felt every cell in my body perk up like plants that have been waiting desperately for the man with the watering can.

"Detective," I said, "can you explain this from a little closer to the beginning? How do you know Grandfather Gao, and why does he call you?"

Mark Quan sipped from the frosted glass. "He was friends with my dad in the States before we moved here."

"You're not from Hong Kong?"

He grinned. "Actually I was born here. My folks moved us to Birmingham, Alabama, when I was six months old. But my dad grew up here and always wanted to come back. I was just out of high school when he and Ma decided to make the big move, so I came along to see what it was all about."

"I guess you liked it."

"Well, you know." He shrugged. "I just never felt like I fit in Birmingham."

I was surprised to hear myself think, I do know. I drank some tea and asked, "And Grandfather Gao?"

"My dad's a Chinese doctor. In Birmingham he ran a grocery store; on the side, he treated practically every Chinese person in Alabama. He used to go up to New York to buy herbs from Grandfather Gao. A few times he took me with him. They'd drink tea and talk, and I'd sit there in the middle of all those jars and drawers feeling like I was on the moon. I never understood a word Grandfather Gao said.

It was all Chinese nature metaphors. But I liked the shop. It was quiet and it smelled good, and he always gave me tea, like I was a grown-up, too. And candy."

I found myself smiling, thinking about the dark shelves, the porcelain jars and the small wood drawers with red Chinese characters painted on them—and Grandfather Gao's nature metaphors. "I grew up around the corner from the shop. I used to go there all the time."

Mark Quan grinned. His eyes met mine; then his grew wide. "Wait," he said. "Wait, I remember you! You were that little kid!"

"What little kid?"

"That was you!" His smile expanded to light up his whole face. The scar on his lip, it seemed to me, became more obvious the bigger his smile grew. "We played chess. My dad and Grandfather Gao, and you and me. There was a blizzard and we couldn't go home. Remember?"

"The blizzard?" I said. "That big one? When I was seven?" My mind flew back, leaving the potted palms and string quartet music for the snow-silenced streets of Chinatown at twilight, twenty-odd years ago. "I stopped at Grandfather Gao's shop about five, on my way home from Chinese school." I looked from Mark Quan to Bill. "I was so excited. I wanted to tell him about the snow—the snowbanks were bigger than I was, and it was snowing so hard you could barely see the streetlights." I stared at Mark Quan. "And there was a man and a boy there, having tea and sweets. I was embarrassed, bursting in with all my noise, trailing snow into the shop. But Grandfather Gao seemed delighted and asked me to stay. He said his guests lived far away and couldn't leave because of the storm, and he'd be grateful if I would stay and help him entertain them. I felt so important. But then Grandfather Gao and the man started a game of Chinese chess, and he suggested I play chess with the boy. And I thought, oh, but this is a big boy like my brothers. He won't want to play chess with a little girl. I thought Grandfather Gao would be so disappointed in me, because I couldn't do what he wanted me to."

"But he wasn't," Mark Quan said.

"No." I smiled. "The boy took out the board and the pieces and played with me just as though playing chess with a seven-year-old girl was a normal thing for a big boy to do. That was *you*?"

"It was." Mark Quan, still grinning, took another drink. "I was eleven. And you beat me."

"You beat him?" Bill spoke for the first time in what seemed like ages. "Grandfather Gao's guest?"

"He was so nice!" I said. "He didn't treat me like an annoying pest or anything." As though it had just happened, I remembered the way my stomach had clenched when I thought I'd have to disappoint Grandfather Gao, and the gratitude I'd felt when the boy, without skipping a beat, agreed to play with me. "I wanted to play my best," I told Mark Quan. "To give you a real game. I didn't want you to think you were stuck playing with a baby."

"It was a good game," said Mark Quan. "I'm glad it didn't occur to you to let me win."

Bill said, "To her? It never does."

They gave each other a boys-only look. I shrugged and looked at the potted palm to see if it had anything to say.

"After chess, Grandfather Gao made us dinner," Mark Quan said. "In the little kitchen in the back of the shop. And we ate right there on the table with the carved lion's feet."

"Shrimp with water chestnuts!" I said. "I felt so grown up, a dinner guest."

I remembered that meal: Grandfather Gao calling my parents for permission for me to stay; the warmth of the shop and the aromas of food stir-frying in the wok while the blizzard blew outside; and later, getting bundled back into my winter jacket and boots so the two men and the boy could walk me home, the men talking quietly, the boy and I throwing snowballs, laughing and falling down in the deep, soft snow.

"That was a magical night," I said.

Mark Quan sat back and smiled. "Wow. So that was

you." He sipped his drink again as I pulled myself back from Pell Street to Hong Kong. "And now you work for him?"

"For Grandfather Gao?" I shook my head. "I'm a private investigator. Bill's my partner. We're working for Grandfather Gao on this case, but it's the first time."

"Private investigators. He didn't tell me that." Mark Quan's genial expression didn't change, but he said nothing for a few moments. Then he asked, "What's the case?"

"Well," I said, "we're not really sure."

He looked from me to Bill and nodded. "And you're not sure whether you should tell me, even if we did play chess?"

I flushed, but he was right. "Can you tell us a little more about why he called you? You said he's been calling you for years."

Mark Quan rested an ankle on his knee, settled back in his chair. "After I came back here and joined the Department, Grandfather Gao picked me as his contact. It didn't make some of the old-timers happy. I was the new kid, and an ex-pat besides. Even the idea of my being a cop got under their skin."

"It's not an obvious choice."

"It was for me. I wanted to be a cop since I was a kid, but in Birmingham I was short, fat, and Chinese. Here short and Chinese isn't a problem. And I speak both languages and three others besides, and I started studying kung fu when I was nine and I've never stopped, so that cancels out the weight problem." He patted his stomach and grinned again. I found myself thinking, I wouldn't really say fat. Solid, maybe. I mean, you wouldn't call a tree trunk *fat*.

"But they don't like me," he went on. "They don't trust me. They don't think I can think the way people do here. And I'm too much of an American, which means not enough of a team player. Anyone else, twelve years on the Department, my record, he'd be a Lieutenant. I'm lucky I made Sergeant. I'd never have gotten even this far without Grandfather Gao."

"Grandfather Gao has influence in the HKPD?"

"No, that's not what I mean. But because I'm his contact, whatever he gives us comes through me. Makes them think I'm indispensable."

"His contact for what?"

"Anything he thinks we should know over here. A man in his position hears things."

"What position?"

"Just the way he's situated in Chinatown. Respected elder, all that. Long-time merchant, senior member of the Three Brothers Association. That's his tong," he added, for Bill's benefit. Polite of him; but Bill already knew that.

"Last year he passed me something that helped us bust up a bookmaking operation the Strength and Harmony Association was running," Mark Quan said. "I should have gotten a promotion out of that, but at least I got a nice New Year's bonus."

"The Strength and Harmony Association?" asked Bill. This was one he didn't know. I knew what it was, but I waited for the answer.

"One of the triads." Mark Quan sounded surprised, as though everyone knew that. "They're a splinter off one of the Big Five, the 14K, from about thirty years ago. Their head guys thought the 14K was getting too sloppy, too loose. Too in tune with modern times. Strength and Harmony keeps up the old ways. Discipline, initiation ceremonies, rankings—Incense Masters, Red Poles, White Paper Fans—all that stuff." He added, "This wasn't the first time Grandfather Gao's messed up their plans."

"I didn't know the triads allowed splinter groups," Bill said.

"If they don't get in the way," Mark Quan said. "The triad thinking seems to be, the more distractions for the police, the better. The triads deny their own existence, anyway."

"Like the Mafia."

"Right. And the more of these ambiguous gangs there are, the harder it is for us to prove who's triad and who isn't. Like, any Italian in the States can surround himself with a bunch of bums and call himself the don of a Mafia family. That doesn't make him one, but it still makes him the boss of a gang. The cops will want to watch him. So we keep our eyes on the Big Five, and on the splinters, too."

The stunning young woman and her French-speaking companion stood and strolled away to the strains of the string quartet.

"What reason did Grandfather Gao give you when he told you to call us?" I asked.

"He said he'd sent you over here to do a job for him and you'd run into difficulties. And, um, wait, 'If you share the task, you may find joint effort results in mutual advantage.' "

"He didn't mention the little bird and the water buffalo, did he?" Bill asked.

"No," Mark Quan said. "What he said was that beasts of the same paws roam together, and that many jackals can bring down a tiger."

We spent the next half hour filling Mark Quan in on the job we'd been sent to do and what had happened since we'd come to do it. I asked to see his HKPD identification just to keep on the safe side; it seemed unnecessarily rude, however, to mention that the real reason we'd been late arriving was that we'd called the HKPD to check on him, after I'd returned the call he'd made to our hotel and he invited us to meet him here.

But there was one more thing I just had to do before spilling our guts to this almost-complete stranger. Maybe it was rude, too, though he didn't seem to think so. "Go ahead," he said. "I'd do it if I were you."

So, whipping out my cell phone, I called Grandfather Gao from the Mandarin Oriental Hotel.

It was about five in the morning in New York, but

Grandfather Gao sounded his usual calm self when he answered. I guessed he hadn't gone back to bed since he'd spoken to Mark Quan. Maybe even since, in the middle of that same New York night, he'd spoken to me.

I greeted him respectfully and then got down to business: I asked him whether he knew a Hong Kong policeman named Mark Quan.

"I have known him since he was a child," Grandfather Gao informed me. "Longer, Ling Wan-Ju, than I have known you, as he is four years your elder."

"I met him once, years ago, didn't I? In your shop, in that big blizzard."

I could almost hear him smile. "You have a fine memory."

"No. He remembered first. But I loved that night. I never forgot it."

"It was very pleasant. If my memory is correct, you won your game of Chinese chess."

"Correct as usual, Grandfather. Could you please describe Mark Quan to me?"

"A man of medium height, caring perhaps a bit too much for the pleasures of the table. This deceives many into thinking his will, also his body, are weak. A small scar on his lip, which to the wise will indicate the truth."

"Did you call him to tell him to contact us?"

"I did. I assume he has done so?"

"Yes. We're sitting with him now at the Mandarin Oriental Hotel."

"Then you will be able to judge whether his appearance is as I say."

"It is precisely, Grandfather."

"His trustworthiness is also. You may find his goals to be different from your own; but I believe he will prove a valuable ally to you in your work."

I considered for a moment and then took the plunge. At the risk of being rudely direct, I asked, "Do you think that what happened here might have involved any organized group?"

By that, of course, I meant a triad. He knew that, and he answered calmly. "It is possible, yes. If so, it is still more important that you and Quan Mai assist one another."

Well, now I knew Mark Quan's Chinese name, in case I was wondering. I asked, "Grandfather, why would such a group be interested in a little boy like Wei Hao-Han?"

Although I carefully had my eyes on a potted palm and not on Mark Quan, I could see him, and I saw his eyebrows go up. That told me two things: American born or not, he spoke Cantonese well enough to eavesdrop; and Grandfather Gao hadn't told him about Harry's kidnapping.

"I do not know," Grandfather Gao answered. "Nor would I hurry to the conclusion that they are directly responsible for what happened. Involvement, Ling Wan-Ju, can mean many things."

I braced myself for the inevitable nature metaphor, probably something about birds riding the wind but not bringing the clouds. Surprisingly, it didn't come.

"There has been," I told him, "a second ransom demand. For a lot of money. Not the jade."

"Ah? From the same party?"

"No."

A pause. "That is disturbing."

Personally, I thought, I find this whole thing disturbing.

"And Franklin Wei is here," I said.

"You knew he was planning to go to Hong Kong, Ling Wan-Ju."

"Yes, well," I said, "there's a little too much going on here for me."

"Then," said Grandfather Gao, "it would be well to continue your work. The spider takes the time she needs to spin her web, creating order in the midst of chaos. But she begins before she is hungry."

Sure, I thought, flipping my cell phone shut, and she spins it out of her own guts.

So the half hour we spent filling Mark Quan in was also occupied with other things. After the call to Grandfather

Gao there was one to the Weis, where Steven Wei, sounding ever more desperate, told me he had heard nothing more from either caller since we'd left.

"But," he mumbled, almost as an afterthought, "I have had a call from—from my brother."

"Franklin? Why did he call?"

"To offer me money."

"Excuse me?"

"If the second ransom demand turns out to be real. He has a small stock portfolio, perhaps two hundred thousand American dollars, and a flat in New York he believes is worth close to eight hundred thousand, American. He will call his bank in New York when it opens on Monday to find out how quickly they will give him a loan."

I wasn't sure what to say. "That's a million dollars. He didn't even know you existed until a few weeks ago."

"He has been married three times," Steven Wei offered by way of explanation. "But he has no children."

There was nothing else to be learned there, and no other messages left for us at our hotel. Over another round of drinks—coffee for Bill this time—we told Mark Quan about our day: the Weis, both Steven and Franklin, the temple, Natalie Zhu and Kwong Hon Terrace Garden. He frowned and nodded and asked questions, and at the end, leaning forward in his chair, his steepled fingers pressed to his lips, he sat silently in thought for a few minutes. Then he said, "I wish they'd report the damn thing. I want to bug that phone."

"Is that what you'd do if they had?"

He nodded. "The calls are probably coming from cell phones, but we might get lucky." He sighed and leaned back. "Their instinct not to report it isn't necessarily wrong. This sort of thing happens in Hong Kong more than we like to admit. It's a business: You pay, you get your kid back, your father, whoever it is. Keep it polite, no one gets hurt and the HKPD doesn't get involved. Cops hate it, but that's the best way to handle it from the family's point of view. Except for that first phone call, I'd say that was how to handle this one, too. But I don't like that call."

"I don't like either call," said Bill.

"No," Mark Quan agreed. "But if I had to choose one, my money's on the money, if you know what I mean."

"Steven Wei said he didn't have that much," I said.

"I can check on that."

"But you think the first call's the fake?"

"Yes. But I have no idea what's behind it. Well." He put his hands on his knees, looked at us. "There are a couple of things we could do now. One of them is: nothing. We could keep out of the way, wait and see what happens."

Bill shook his head. "If I thought this was just business, I'd be in favor of that. But those two phone calls . . . And Natalie Zhu: I think she was blowing smoke, but she's right about one thing. You couldn't grab anyone from that park, or the streets near it, without fifty people seeing you."

Mark Quan looked at me. I nodded agreement.

"Okay," he said. "Officially I can't act on the kidnapping because it hasn't been reported. You guys don't count. If I called the family and told them what you said, they'd deny it."

I said, "I'm sure that's true."

"But," he said, "I can sniff around and see if anyone knows anything they might want to tell me. I'll feel better if I check up on Natalie Zhu, just to make sure she's on the level. And I can see if the Department knows anything about Iron Fist Chang. Once I find out what his story is, I'll probably go over and see him myself."

To get that started, Mark Quan took his cell phone off the place on his belt where uniformed cops wear their guns—Mark Quan's gun was under his left arm, if the faint bulge in his linen jacket meant anything—and called HKPD HQ. He spoke in Cantonese, quick and assured, but, I noticed, American-accented.

"Okay," he said when the call was through. "They'll run him through the computer. If anything comes up I'll let you know."

"What about the amah?" I asked.

"I can try to check her out, but we won't get anywhere unless we get lucky. The problem with the Filipinas is that their lives are such open books."

"What do you mean?"

"They can't get into Hong Kong unless they have the right papers and mostly they live in with their employers. If they get in any kind of trouble they get shipped home. The PRC government doesn't want them here; there are thousands of Cantonese girls right over the border who'd love to have those jobs. That didn't bother the British, but it annoys the hell out of Beijing." Mark Quan grinned. "So, I guarantee all I'll find on Maria Quezon is her passport number and her address, which in this case will be the Weis'. But I'll look."

"What about the sister? Natalie Zhu thought her sister worked here, too. Can you find her?"

"I can look. But Quezon is like Smith." He switched the grin to Bill. "Of the hundred thousand amahs here, five thousand of them must be Quezons. And one or the other of them, or both, could be married and using the husband's name."

I thought for a minute. "Why do they call them amahs? That's not a Cantonese word. Is it from what they speak in the Philippines?"

Mark Quan looked blank.

Surprisingly, Bill took the question. "It's from the Portuguese," he said. "For *nurse*. The British picked it up in the glory days of Empire to refer to their native servants. First in India, then all over Asia."

"All servants from the inferior races being basically the same?" I asked.

"I think that's the general idea. In the Philippines they speak Tagalog," he added.

"You know," I said, "you're kind of handy to have around."

We left the Mandarin Oriental with Mark Quan, walking out into the steamy heat of early evening. I felt a warm damp film condense on my skin as soon as we stepped onto the sidewalk. The air was hazy, thick with humidity, car exhaust, and construction dust. Ignoring the honking, swirling traffic, an electric streetcar rattled to a halt down the block. People swarmed onto one end and off the other. Tugging on its overhead lines, the car started up again, carrying passengers from place to place on the route it was tethered to.

"I'll call you if I find anything," Mark Quan said. "And you'll call me if you hear from the family?"

We said we would, and then we said good-bye, watching him walk through the heat toward the building, a few blocks away, that held the headquarters of the HKPD.

"Your Grandfather Gao sure seems to get around." Bill lit a cigarette as we stood, an unmoving two-person island in a churning sea of people, on the sidewalk outside the hotel.

"He sure does." I turned to look at him. Our eyes met. "You look tired," I said.

"Only from the point of view of your boundless manic energy."

"No, from the point of view of anybody who can see you. Are you feeling jet-lagged?"

"I'm feeling suddenly totally beat, like I ran into a brick wall, which I think is the same thing. But if you're asking me if I want to pack it in for the day, the answer is no."

"Even if there's nothing else we can do?"

"But there is."

"What?"

"I don't know. But you have a plan."

"I do? How do you know?"

" 'Each water buffalo knows well the song of the little bird on his own rump.' "

I narrowed my eyes in suspicion. "Who told you that?"

"A water buffalo down at the Bronx Zoo. I met him one fine summer day. I asked him how his rump was, and we got to talking, about little birds, things like that . . ."

I threw him a look over my shoulder as I started to walk away. "Well, if you want to hear my song, hurry up," I said.

Because, of course, I did have a plan.

six

The plan involved a trip to the east end of Hong Kong Island, which, after a hard look at the traffic, we decided to make by subway as far as we could and by cab after that. As far as we could get by subway, according to my handy Laminated Detailed City Map of Hong Kong Island (companion piece to the Laminated Detailed City Map of Kowloon and the New Territories, also in my bag at the moment along with a few other potentially useful items) was the very last stop.

The Hong Kong subway was a quieter, smoother ride than the subways of home. The ads in the stations and the cars were in Chinese, and the smiling people in the ads were Chinese, as were the largely unsmiling people in the subway cars themselves. Students and grandmothers and office workers, shop girls and street sweepers, sat on stainless-steel benches or held on to poles with the same tired shoulders and empty stares as people on the IRT at the end of the day. Bill and I stood in the middle of the car, me indistinguishable from the rest of the crowd, Bill standing out because of his height and his features. There, I thought, now you know, and was immediately shocked at myself and pretended I'd never thought it.

We came up out of the subway into more soggy heat, grayer now that the low sun was behind the hills and the mist had thickened. The area we were in was grayer, too. Facing us was a park, largely concrete, where a group of teenage boys played hard, graceless basketball on one of a half-dozen courts. An asphalt soccer field was empty, climbing equipment for the little kids empty, too, at this dinner hour. Behind us to the right and left loomed residential high-rises displaying, even in the twilight, the same shabby concrete and fading paint as the buildings around Kwong Hon Terrace Garden, though these were obviously much newer. These huge housing projects—they called them *estates* here, but I knew a project when I saw one—had replaced a lot of buildings that had been here a lot longer, but some of the older structures still crouched among the project towers and filled the blocks from here to the harbor: three- and four-story factories, warehouses, industrial buildings of various grim and squat aspects. This was the working waterfront and this was its landscape.

It was not the greatest place in the world to get a cab. After ten minutes of standing around, watching no cabs whatever cruise by, I began to wonder just how lost we'd get if we tried to walk the mile or so to where we were going. But Bill had a much more brilliant idea.

"There's a bus depot over there," he said, pointing. "You can usually get a cab at a bus depot."

"How do you know that's a bus depot?" Here, well off the tourist or foreign-businessman track, almost no English was to be seen on street signs, store signs, or outdoor ads, except the occasional MARLBORO or CHIVAS floating among Chinese characters at stores whose window displays could have told you the same thing.

"A lot of buses turning that corner," Bill said. "With different route numbers on them."

Like most of the world, Hong Kong does its numbers the Western way.

Bill would have no idea where any of those buses were coming from, but he could see they were converging from a lot of different places. "Good old-fashioned detective work." I nodded approval. "Let's go."

It was a bus depot, and there were cabs there, and five minutes after getting in one we had reached our destination. Out of habit we went half a block beyond. I paid the driver, rounding up to the nearest Hong Kong dollar because I couldn't stand the idea of not tipping a cabbie at all, even though all the guidebooks said you don't in Hong Kong.

"This begs the question of how we're going to get back," Bill pointed out as the cab's red taillights drifted away down what I still thought of as the wrong side of the street.

"We can walk back," I said. "Now that we know the way."

"Uh-huh."

We backtracked down the sidewalk of Fung Yip Street until we reached the building we'd come to see, a flat-roofed, three-story structure of soot-covered brick that had probably once been red. Most of the windows in the nearby buildings were dark, but the windows of this one were shining a harsh fluorescent white. They provided enough light in the mist-soaked evening to illuminate the painted Chinese characters on the large wooden sign above the door and the smaller English words below them. They both read LION ROCK ENTERPRISES.

I tried the handle on the scarred wooden door; it turned and opened. Bill and I stepped into a small reception area, cooler than the steamy outdoors but not refrigerated like so many indoor Hong Kong spaces. A door in the mustard-yellow wall facing us led to the building's interior; that must be the Lion Rock warehouse itself. That door and a window and closed door into another office to our right were the only surfaces in this room not covered with pinned-up clipboards, charts, schedules, and calendars. At the center of this cramped, paper-covered space stood a battered steel desk holding a computer from which a young woman looked up, blinking in surprise. A nameplate on her desk read, NG JING-YI in Chinese. Below, in English, it said JEANETTE NG.

She looked at us and made her choice. "May I help you?" she asked, as Jeanette, in English.

So much for blending in. "Wei Ang-Ran, please," I answered.

"Your name?" She reached for the phone.

"Chin Ling Wan-Ju. This is Bill Smith." I added in Cantonese, "Wei Ang-Ran is not expecting us, but tell him we bring greetings from Gao Mian-Liang."

Jeanette/Jing-Yi raised an eyebrow at my switch in languages. She pressed a button on her phone. Through the window to our right I saw a thin old man pick up the phone on his desk. He looked up at us as Jing-Yi spoke: With him she used exclusively Cantonese. I gave him a quick bow of my head; he bowed back. Through the window I watched him hang up the phone, add fresh water from a steaming teakettle to the pot on his desk, and do a few other things in his office. Then the door opened and the thin old man came out.

"Ah! Chin Ling Wan-Ju. Mr. Smith." He greeted us with the resolutely polite air of a man caught at a bad time but determined to fulfill the requirements of hospitality. "Gao Mian-Liang told me I might expect you during your time in Hong Kong. Please come inside."

I nodded to Jeanette/Jing-Yi, and we followed him into his office.

The *Mr.* had been in English, but you'd have to have been listening hard to know that. Everything else was Cantonese, which he continued in as he closed the door behind us. "Have you had tea? Please." He pointed to two vinyl-covered chairs opposite his cluttered desk, so we sat as he added two small clay teacups from a bottom desk drawer to the cup and pot already in front of him. In here, as in the outer office, a door in the back wall led into the rest of the building. You couldn't see the warehouse floor right now, because that door was closed. But it hadn't been closed until Wei Ang-Ran had closed it just before he came out to greet us.

Wei Ang-Ran turned to Bill. "Very sorry," he said with an apologetic wave of the hand and an accent so thick it took me a second to realize he was speaking English. "My English, not so good. Not need speak, always too lazy learn."

"That's all right," Bill said. "I'm too tired to listen, anyway."

Wei Ang-Ran took that in with a courteous, blank look, so I translated. He nodded in polite appreciation and said in Cantonese, "Then you must have some tea." Since he was pouring steaming tea into the little clay cups as he said that and gesturing for Bill to take one, I didn't think that needed me.

"I wanted to convey greetings to you from Gao Mian-Liang without further delay," I told him, holding the clay cup in both hands and sipping from it. The tea was dark and aromatic, quite bracing as it flowed through my system. I wondered if it was helping Bill. "Also to bring you the letter your brother sent to you. Even though," I continued, "this is a difficult time for your family."

The old man's face clouded over. "Ah. You know about Hao-Han."

"We went to deliver your brother's bequest to the child this morning, as we were instructed. We were at the apartment when the first phone call came."

Wei Ang-Ran shook his head. "The death of my brother brought sadness to his son, but an old man's death is to be expected. For one's child to be in such danger . . . Still," he looked up, "we have every reason to hope that the situation will be resolved, the child returned without harm. Have we not?"

I wasn't sure what we had, but he was waiting for me to respond, so I agreed. From my bag I drew the fat brown envelope Grandfather Gao had given me, with Wei Ang-Ran's name in Chinese characters on it.

The old man looked at it without movement. I began to feel a little foolish just sitting there holding it out. With a start, as though he'd suddenly realized he'd made his guest uncomfortable, Wei Ang-Ran reached and took it from me. He held it in both hands as he stared at it.

"So thick," he said. "So much advice, so many things my brother has to say to me."

"I'm sure his words will be comforting," I said.

"Perhaps. But right now—no, I cannot read this now." He slipped open his desk drawer and placed the envelope in it. "I am now the head of this family. To accept advice or comfort from my brother after I have allowed such a thing to happen . . . Zhong xiao dao yi. You understand." He smiled sadly at me and shut the drawer.

I did understand. *"Zhong xiao dao yi,"* my mother's elder sister would say, scowling and wagging her finger, when I backtalked my mother or when my brothers fought. Once, memorably, I'd come home from the park with badly skinned knees and elbows and she'd used it on the brother who was supposed to have been watching me. *Country, family,* and *friends* is how it translates; what it means is "do the right thing." These are your obligations, it says, the threads of obedience and loyalty, protection and care that weave you into your place in the world. You give and are given to, you owe and are owed. Break one thread—through evil intent or casual carelessness, by deliberate action or mere inattention—and the whole fabric defining you will unravel.

These obligations do not change with death or circumstances. If your elder brother passes on, you nevertheless still owe him honor and deference. And if his grandson is kidnapped, you have failed utterly in your responsibilities in both directions.

That was about as Chinese as it got, and I had no answer to it. Briefly, we sipped our tea in silence. "You are a very diligent man," I finally observed. "Your staff also, most industrious. Your neighbors have closed for the day, yet you are still here, working so late."

His chin jutted forward, that Chinese shrug. "This becomes necessary at certain times. A shipment of furniture has just come in from China."

"Another goes out in a few days, is that correct? Wei Di-Fen"—Steven—"told us that. He said he came here this morning to examine some papers needed with the shipment."

"Yes." Wei Ang-Ran looked down into his teacup. "I wish I had not asked him. If he had been at home with his family this trouble could have been averted."

In the silence that followed the old man looked quite forlorn, so I answered him.

"This trouble was caused by someone's greed," I said. "Not by your diligence. The people responsible, if thwarted today, would have chosen another time. You cannot blame yourself."

Wei Ang-Ran did not seem convinced, and conversation once more came to an uncomfortable halt.

As the old man reached for the teapot to refill the cups, Bill turned to me. "Listen, tell Mr. Wei it's not him, it's jet lag, but I'm falling asleep here. I'm going to go out, have a cigarette, walk around the block. I'll be back in a minute."

"Are you sure?" I asked. "Do you want to go back to the hotel?"

"No, you stay and visit." He shrugged. "I can't understand a word you're saying anyway."

Wei Ang-Ran and I had been speaking Chinese, so I was sure that was true. Just as Bill and I were now speaking English, to the confusion of Wei Ang-Ran.

I explained the situation as Bill stood. Wei Ang-Ran stood also, bowing to Bill, who bowed back in a big, Western kind of way. He left the office, smiling at Jeanette Ng as he let himself out the heavy front door.

I turned back to the old man. "Permit me to express my condolences on the death of your brother. I imagine you were close, having worked together for so long."

He sighed. "I shall miss his conversation, his counsel. In a world of constant change he understood what was of lasting importance. Since childhood I have attempted to follow his lead. Now I must continue alone."

"It must be a difficult prospect, to run such a busy, prosperous business by yourself."

"Fortunately, it will not come to that. Wei Di-Fen has left his position to assume his father's responsibilities here. He is a serious young man, most assiduous."

"Will it be easy for him to take over his father's work?"

"His understanding grows daily. More important, his dedication is great. If not for this unfortunate situation, he would be here now. In fact, he offered to come tonight, as much must be done to prepare the shipment for New York. But his heart is clearly at home with his wife, waiting for word of his son. I would not allow him to come. But I assure you nothing less serious would have kept him away."

"You spoke to him recently? Is there news?"

"An hour ago. No, I am sorry to say there is not."

He lifted the teapot to refill the cups again. Probably, I thought, he can't wait until that pot is empty. That would be my signal to leave, courtesy on my side and hospitality on his having both been satisfied.

I murmured my thanks and lifted the cup to my lips. A sudden loud pounding on the back wall door almost made me spill tea all over my street-stall shirt.

Wei Ang-Ran seemed as startled as I was. "Yes?" he called in Cantonese. The flew door open and Bill stumbled in unceremoniously, shoved by a well-muscled, red-faced young man.

Bill turned to face the guy and I could see from the set of his shoulders that this was about to be trouble. "Hold on," I said quietly in English. "What happened?"

Wei Ang-Ran, on his feet, was asking the same question in Chinese. I stood, too, listening with one ear to the young man explaining in rapid and angry Chinese that he had caught this *gweilo* trespassing in the alley, spying through the windows, that if the *gweilo* hadn't repeated Wei Ang-Ran's name over and over as though he knew him he would right now be getting the beating he deserved, and if Wei Ang-Ran would deny knowing such a despicable person as was most surely the case, the beating would commence immediately. In my other ear was Bill, asking me in English to apologize to Wei Ang-Ran, saying that he hadn't intended to cause trouble, that he was just trying to satisfy a possibly rude but innocent curiousity.

"I used to be a longshoreman," he told me. "The logistics of an operation like this interest me. I wanted to see what was going on. I was really just looking for something to keep me awake."

I was attempting a simultaneous translation of Bill's apology for Wei Ang-Ran, so that made three of us talking at once in the small, cluttered office. That plus the hum of the air-conditioner and the shouts, thumps and occasional mechanical noises from the now-open warehouse door did nothing to calm the situation. Jeanette Ng was on her feet staring through the window.

Wei Ang-Ran looked from one of us to another, back and forth.

"I am very sorry," I repeated. "Especially at this time, it is unforgivable to have caused you any concern. My partner deeply regrets his error. He asks your forgiveness for the disturbance. His mistake was ignorant, not ill-intentioned. He regrets also taking this young man from his work. If the young man were to return now to the tasks he has so responsibly stayed late to perform, we will leave immediately, so as to cause you no further trouble."

Wei Ang-Ran nodded slowly. He listened to the young man—who apparently called himself Tony, which Wei Ang-Ran struggled manfully to pronounce—make angry accusations for another few minutes. Then he thanked him, rather formally, I thought, considering who was boss here, for his watchfulness and care, and instructed him to return to his duties. Tony shut his mouth and stood silently with his angry bulk in the doorway. After a long, contemptuous look at Bill, he gave a brief nod of the head—more agreement than obedience—to Wei Ang-Ran, turned, and pulled the warehouse door closed behind him.

"I am sorry," I said one final time. "We will leave immediately."

"There is no need," Wei Ang-Ran replied politely. "Mr. Smith clearly meant no harm. More tea?"

"Thank you, no," I said. "We have kept you from your work for too long." I stood, gathering my bag. "You are fortunate to have such dedicated employees."

The old man smiled, a bit sadly, it seemed to me, but didn't answer. "Please apologize to Mr. Smith if he was treated less than courteously. I hope he was not hurt?"

I did the translation for Bill, then Bill's answer for Wei Ang-Ran. "He says he was not, but that if he had been, he would have deserved it." Wei Ang-Ran smiled at that.

"Please once more accept our apologies," I said. "I hope we meet again soon under happier circumstances."

Wei Ang-Ran bowed, I bowed, Bill bowed. Wei Ang-Ran walked us to the heavy front door of Lion Rock Enterprises, and stood in the doorway watching us down the block. I wondered if that was politeness, or if he wanted to make sure we were really gone.

"Where are we going?" I asked Bill as he headed left from the door. Daylight was now completely vanished. The mist had turned to a very fine rain, clouding streetlights, polishing pavement. I felt the tiny drops falling on my shirt, but I didn't mind because it was just as hot out here in the dark as it had been in the sticky afternoon.

"You're the one who said we could walk back because now we knew the way." He kept going, not fast but steadily, his eyes searching the empty pavements ahead as though he expected something.

I hurried after him. "I also once tried to sell you the Brooklyn Bridge."

"Did I buy it?"

"No, you were smarter then. And speaking of the past, you were never a longshoreman."

"I was a sailor," he offered as our footsteps fell into their usual rhythm.

"Even I know that's not the same thing. And you don't look sleepy to me. Not nearly sleepy enough to need a walk around the block."

"I'm not. As a matter of fact, I'm wired. That was a hell of a cup of tea."

"Iron Buddha tea," I told him. "Gave you the strength to get up and do what had to be done?"

"Uh-huh."

"And that was?"

"I just wanted a look around. Wasn't that why we went there?"

"Of course that was why we went there. Find anything?"

"Uh-huh."

"What?"

"Iron Fist Chang."

I stopped still. *"What?"*

"Come on. He's probably still there."

I closed my mouth and caught up again. "What do you *mean*, you found Iron Fist Chang?"

"I was—what did that guy say?—spying through windows. There's a crew unloading crates and boxes, and one packing stuff up again in other boxes."

"The shipment coming in and the one going out."

"I guess. Anyway, between the forklift, guys yelling at each other, and the radio going, I didn't hear that guy sneaking up on me."

"I'm not sure you can call it sneaking. You're the one who was trespassing."

"If you want to look at it that way. Anyhow, Iron Fist's on the unloading crew."

"You're positive it's him?"

"I tailed him for a hour. I may not be able to tell you the color of his eyes but I sure as hell know the way he moves."

"He's Chinese; his eyes are brown. What's he doing here?"

"Unloading crates. Maybe the stuntman business is slow right now."

"Let me rephrase that: What's he doing *here*?"

"Wouldn't you like to know?"

We had made our way to the other side of the block. The lighted windows above the loading dock in the mid-block building would have told me without the little sign— this one in Chinese only—that this was the rear entrance to Lion Rock Enterprises. Both steel truck doors were down, but light leaked around their edges onto the steel-canopied concrete platform.

We crossed the street to someone else's doorway, some-one who'd shut down and gone home at a decent hour, and in the small shelter of its recess settled in to wait. Bill leaned back against the door, hands in his pockets, perfectly still. His deliberate control, his restrained, tight-muscled calm, made me sure he was desperate for a cigarette, and only not lighting one so the glow wouldn't be spotted from across the street. Some other time, I would have poked fun at him about that, about his ability to control the jitters but not the addiction they came from; but some other time, I'd have been sure he'd see what was funny. Right now, I wasn't sure what he saw, so I just watched the rain fall steadily, illuminated by streetlights and the distant, pale windows of the housing project's towers.

"What makes you think he'll come out this way?" I finally asked.

"What's his other choice, the front door? Laborers don't use the front door. Anyway, the timeclock's back here. I saw it."

"How did you know that's what it was?"

"Certain things are the same all over the world."

True, I thought. And certain things are different. "And what makes you think he's still in there?"

"He's on the unloading crew. They're not finished."

"And what makes you think he'll be out before morning?"

His eyes moved to me, then back to Lion Rock. "They're *almost* finished."

"Oh," I said.

After another few minutes, during which the rain fell and I shifted my weight and Bill didn't move, I said, "This could explain how someone who wasn't in the family knew about the jade. Something as simple as Wei Ang-Ran mentioning his great-nephew's inheritance to his trusty employees."

"Did you get the feeling," Bill asked, "that he trusted that particular employee?"

I looked at him. I couldn't really see his face, shadowed against the dim streetlights, the far-off windows and the falling rain. "I did think there was something strange in how they spoke to each other," I said. "But that was in Chinese."

"If you can't understand the words, you look for other things."

It was half an hour before Iron Fist Chang came out the rear door, in the company of three other sturdy, tired-looking men. The rain had changed back to a drifting mist by then. Through it we watched them light cigarettes and amble down the stairs, one turning right at the sidewalk with a brief wave, the other three heading left.

"Look," I said, following the three-man group with my eyes. "That's your pal Tony, the one who wanted to beat you up."

"Right. And the one in the white tee shirt's Iron Fist Chang."

"Who's the huge one?"

"You're asking me?" he said, gratuitously irritable. I thought about how long it had been since he'd had a cigarette and tried not to get annoyed.

Bill and I gave the group a block's lead—there wasn't much chance of losing them on sidewalks this deserted— and followed along.

The three talked and smoked—I wondered if that drove Bill nuts—as they turned left, right, left again, then crossed a wide street where I imagined the traffic, now sparse, must be a nightmare during the day.

"Don't you suppose this is something Mark Quan would be interested in?" I asked Bill as we walked. "Iron Fist working for Lion Rock?" We were keeping close to the buildings a block behind, for the shadows.

"I bet."

"But we didn't call him."

"That's true."

"Because we figured he'd tell us not to do anything on our own," I said. "Cops being cops all over the world. And we figured if *he* took over he'd come on like gangbusters and scare them off. Cops being cops all over the world. But I wonder if we're right?"

Bill looked over at me, then returned his gaze to the men ahead. "Cops are cops," he said. His voice, it seemed to me, was quiet and calm, controlled in the same way his stillness in the doorway had been. "All over the world."

The three men up ahead suddenly stopped. The big one, the one whose name we didn't know, glanced at his watch. They held a quick sidewalk debate. Iron Fist took out a cell phone and made a call, stepping away from the others. Finished, he stuck the phone into his pocket. The group turned to double back in our direction.

They were over a block way, but Bill and I pressed against a steel gate at the mouth of an alley as they came down the sidewalk. My heart raced. If they passed us it was big trouble; we weren't hidden well enough for that, and we had nowhere to go. I tried on and threw out ideas, grabbed wildly for ways to talk ourselves out of a confrontation with three muscled men on an empty night street if it came to it. Where were those teeming Hong Kong masses when you needed them?

But at the corner they made a left, down a smaller street, into an area of lit shop windows and glowing signs.

We gave them some distance, following in time to see them turn into one of the storefronts in the middle of the block. Sheets of paper Scotch-taped to the windows of the fluorescent-lit establishment advertised various cheap soups and noodle dishes. Like a lot of shops in Hong Kong, this place kept its door propped open as though air-conditioning were free, presumably so the scent of ginger and the hiss of frying dough could reach out into the street and coil around passersby along with the cool air.

It worked on us, even though the closest we came was across the narrow street.

"Jesus," Bill muttered. "That smells good."

"Not to mention how not hot and not sticky it feels."

He looked at me. "You're really miserable, aren't you?"

"Miserable? It's a hundred degrees out and I'm just about soaked, only I can't tell if it's rain or sweat. You're not even uncomfortable?"

"As a matter of fact it's just occurred to me I'm uncomfortably hungry."

I sighed. Across the street, the three men were ensconced at a table in the back of the noodle shop, drinking beers and exchanging remarks with the tee-shirted chef. Well, we certainly couldn't eat there.

But this was Hong Kong. And night was falling. According to everything I'd heard and read, we might have another option.

I peered up and down the street, and sure enough, two blocks on, where this street ended at another one, I spotted what I'd hoped to see.

"Well," I said to Bill, "as usual, your needs come first." I headed up the block.

"Hey, wait a minute," Bill said, striding to catch up with me. "Whose bright idea was it to come to Hong Kong in July in the first place?"

"Grandfather Gao's."

"You notice he's not here."

"Yes," I said, turning to look at him. "I noticed that."

The street where Iron Fist's dining establishment sat ended at a curved and even narrower one, and if Bill thought Iron Fist's place smelled good, he must have been in heaven on Hong Ping Street.

During the day this area was probably a lot like the one around the Lion Rock warehouse. The buildings were the same squared-off red brick or sooty concrete, with big steel-and-glass windows where there was manufacturing, small windows or none at all where the space was used for warehouses. But now, at night, something entirely different had taken over.

The guidebooks, and my mother, had told me about this: the night markets of Hong Kong.

Where I grew up, in New York's Chinatown, they practically roll up the sidewalks at night. At least, they roll up the action on them. The restaurants stay open, but the fishmongers, the vegetable merchants, the jewelers and tee-shirt men and toy sellers all pack up their tables, their boxes, and their awnings. The ones prosperous enough to actually have storefronts pull down their steel shutters, and they all disappear into the night.

When I was a kid I used to wonder where they all went. Standing here on Hong Ping Street, I'd have believed it if you'd told me they all come here.

Red-and-blue-striped plastic fabric thrown up on aluminum poles made impromptu rain shelters crowding both sides of the street. Under them, hawkers shouted the virtues of wares mounded on folding tables. Strings of bulbs glowing with power stolen from utility poles brought out the garish colors of fake Calvin Klein tee shirts and knock-off Swatches. Women's bright flowered dresses swayed from cables overhead while windup toys spitting sparks from their eyes chased each other across tabletops, tripping over cheap eyeglasses, rubber sandals, and painted teapots. From above displays of portable CD players speakers blared dueling Canto-pop and American rap into the crowd.

That was the scene along Hong Ping Street. A bit more to the point, however, was what was happening right here at the intersection.

With the market stretching away in both directions, a series of temporary fabric roofs had staked their claims to small sections of asphalt, each holding half a dozen tables set around a huge bubbling wok. The crowd of shoppers was so thick, even on this soggy night, that it was difficult to make our way to seats at one of these improvised restaurants. Bill drew some stares as we sat down at a table, especially from the four men already there, but staring isn't rude in Chinese culture, and this was a good spot to eat in and watch the door to Iron Fist's restaurant from. When the men came out I expected they'd head back to the street we'd all been on when they'd suddenly detoured for dinner. Bill and I, if we hurried, would be able to make it back there after them in time to see them reach the corner and make their next decision.

The young woman at the wok, her hair plastered to her forehead and neck by sweat, called over to us for our order. Bill finally got to light a cigarette as I took a quick look at the bowls in front of her, each holding mounds of chopped vegetables, fish, or meat, and shouted back. She dumped this and that into the wok, stirred as the wok sizzled, then added rice and kept stirring. With a flat paddle she scooped the mixture into two big bowls, squirted some sauce on them, and left the wok just long enough to bring them over. I asked how much, she told me, and I paid her.

In the U.S. you couldn't have made a phone call for what this dinner cost.

"What are we eating?" Bill asked, squashing his cigarette out. The men at our table watched intently as he picked up his chopsticks. "Smells great."

It did. "Fried rice with scallions, tofu, cabbage, and peas." I tasted mine. The saltiness of soy sauce blended with a dark, mushroomy taste. "I don't know what's in the sauce."

I reached into the center of the table for the communal teapot, the same stainless-steel pot as on countless restaurant tables back home. I poured steaming tea into a cup, swirled it around, and dumped it onto the street; then I did the same for another cup, and poured tea for me and Bill. My mother still cleans cups this way, the traditional way, in Chinatown restaurants; legally mandated high-temperature automatic dishwashers mean nothing to her.

The men across from us dug their own chopsticks into their own fried rice, resuming their meal but not taking their eyes off Bill.

"Well, find out," Bill said, swallowing. "So you can cook this for me when we get home."

"Oh, right."

"Maybe your mother will," he mused. "This is Cantonese food, right? I'll just tell her how much I've always loved Cantonese cooking, and she'll invite me home and ply me with plates of this stuff. . . ."

"Of course she will." I patted his hand. "I didn't know jet lag made people delirious."

"No, it's a good strategy," he said. "I don't know why I never thought of this before. I'll convert. If I get to be

Chinese, she can't keep hating me, can she?"

"You underestimate her. If you got to be a Buddhist priest she'd stop going to the temple."

Bill's successful chopstick wielding did nothing to satisfy the men at our table, who kept watching him, waiting for the inevitable *gweilo* mistake. Seeming not to notice them, he ate expertly, lifting his bowl the Chinese way, managing the rice, the chopped scallions, the squishy tofu as though he'd been eating like this all his life.

It seemed to me his mood had improved. After such good fried rice, so had mine. I asked him, "When you lived in Asia when you were a kid, did you eat local food, or American food?"

He drank some tea, putting his cup carefully down. "We lived on Army bases. My father was never big on local cuisine, so mostly we ate some version of American food wherever we were. Asia, Europe, wherever. I used to sneak off base and eat local stuff with the local juvenile deliquents. It was always better."

"The local juvenile delinquents were your buddies?"

"Sure. They were better company than the other Army brats."

"Wherever you were?"

"Wherever."

I had a lot of other questions about Bill's childhood, and here, under the glow of bare lightbulbs in the Hong Kong mist, surrounded by a night world that, as solid and raucous as it was, would be gone by morning, seemed like a good place to ask them.

But they'd have to wait.

"Look," I said, nudging Bill. "Iron Fist and his friends."

The group from the warehouse was exiting the restaurant. They stood, cigarettes glowing in the steamy damp, and chatted in the street. Iron Fist turned to look at the market. He spoke to the others, who turned also. After some brief discussion, they headed in our direction, the big one looking at his watch again.

A nighttime shopping expedition.

Damn.

Surrounded by tables, chairs, and diners as we were, Bill and I had no place to go. Any attempt to get up and manuever out of here would surely get us seen right away. Our best hope was to sit right here, heads down, focusing on our chopsticks and fried rice, and hope they wouldn't notice us and would just keep walking.

Right, Lydia. And your mother will cook for Bill when you get home.

Only Tony had ever seen us before, of course. If his attention had been grabbed by a blinking-eyed remote control robot or a Taiwanese pop singers pinup calendar, he might have passed us right by. But it wasn't. What stopped him was the sight of a six foot two broad-shouldered American having dinner at a night market fried-rice stall.

And then the double take as he realized this was an American he knew.

Tony put out his arm to stop his pals. He spoke low to them. Iron Fist and the other one stared at us.

The other men at our table, seeing the fists begin to curl on this group of young toughs, shifted uneasily in their seats. One of them made his excuses and slipped away. Two women who had been about to sit at the table next to ours changed their minds and walked on, with one quick look back. The young woman at the wok glanced up sharply, her mouth a thin angry line as she took in the standing trio and their focus: us.

"So," Tony smiled, addressing Bill but speaking in Cantonese, "now you come to spy on the market."

"He doesn't speak Chinese," I said to Tony.

"No shit." Tony surprised me with an answer in accented but completely understandable English. I saw Bill's eyebrows rise. "Big man," Tony went on, still in English, to Bill, dismissing me. "Hides behind boss, behind girl. Business with you, not finish." He took a step closer.

"No," Bill said, not moving. "We're finished."

Tony shook his head. "Who sends you?"

"No one sent me," Bill said. "I was out for a walk."

"Bullshit."

Bill said nothing.

The other three men at our table abandoned their fried rice and scurried away.

"Spying," Tony said. "For who?"

"Maybe, for police," smiled the guy we didn't know. He was taller than the other two, almost as tall as Bill, and wider across the chest than I thought anyone could be without being actually fat. He spoke English, too.

"Who's your friend?" Bill asked.

"Shit," Tony said, slapping himself on the forehead. "Sorry, so rude. This Big John Chou. This, Iron Fist Chang. Myself, Tony Siu. Who the fuck you?"

Not a bad command of English idiom, I thought, for a Hong Kong longshoreman.

"I'm Bill," Bill said. "This is Lydia. Does Iron Fist speak English, too?"

"No. Never can learn. But Iron Fist don't need speak English. Speak kung fu."

Big John laughed at that and translated it for Iron Fist. Iron Fist smiled too, but he didn't look happy.

"Why would the police spy on Lion Rock?" I asked. All eyes turned to me.

"No reason," Tony said. "Never stops police. Just to be pain in the asses."

"We're not police," I said, resisting the impulse to point out that *asses* should be singular. "We're Americans."

Tony sneered. "So, American police."

"Wish we could help you guys," Bill said. "But we're just nosy American tourists trying to finish our dinner here."

"Nosy," Tony said. "Damn right, nosy. Big damn American nose. You have enough guts stop hide behind girlfriend, get up, we break big nose for you."

"It's been done," Bill said. "But last time it didn't need three guys."

Tony reddened. Big John stepped forward, put a hand

on Bill's shoulder. Bill snapped his arm to shake Big John off. He started to stand.

"Wait," I said.

The woman at the wok was staring angrily. Most of the other diners had fled.

"Come on," I said to Bill. "What's the matter with you? It's not worth it. Sit down." I turned to the other men. "You, too."

Slowly, Bill sat. Tony and his friends stayed on their feet.

"If you sit down so this lady can get back to making a living," I said, "I'll tell you why we're here. Otherwise, if you want to keep your jobs, get lost. Wei Ang-Ran won't be happy if he hears about this."

I wasn't sure Wei Ang-Ran's name would have much of an effect, but it was all I had. For a minute it didn't seem to be working. Then Tony signaled his pals, and they all sat down. Iron Fist asked Big John what I'd said and got an answer. They watched me, waiting.

"Order something," I said.

Tony frowned. "What?"

"You've driven this lady's business away. Now order something."

"Shit," said Tony, but it must not have seemed worth arguing over. "Beer!" he called in Chinese to the woman at the wok, pointing at his friends and himself.

I decided that was good enough.

I took a breath and looked at the three. "You're right. We were spying," I said.

Bill lit a cigarette. So did Tony.

"We were sent by an American company with an interest in buying Lion Rock Enterprises," I went on. "What seems good on paper isn't always good close up, so they wanted us to get a look at the place. Apparently it's not a good time for Wei Ang-Ran; he said you're very busy and he wouldn't let us see the warehouse. Of course, he doesn't know where we're really from. We told him we're friends of a friend of his. So we couldn't insist. That would have made him suspicious."

The beers arrived, clomped down on the table by the young woman who then angrily stood her ground, waiting to get paid. Tony stuck some bills in her hand and waved her impatiently away as she started to make change.

Big spender.

"Our employers wouldn't want us to go home without seeing the actual operations," I said. "It's why we came. So I was keeping Wei Ang-Ran occupied while Bill took a look around. Until you screwed things up for us. Thanks a lot, by the way." I gave Tony a disgusted look.

He took a pull at his beer bottle. "Why American company wants buy Lion Rock?"

"How do I know? American companies are investing all over Asia these days. That's not our business. We just do the legwork."

Iron Fist, who'd sat there looking confused for a while, pulled on Big John's sleeve for a translation. He got a summary of what was going on. Frowning, he drank his beer.

"So let me ask you this," Bill said, dropping his cigarette to the street and grinding it under his foot. "What about the operation back there is worth working so hard to keep me from seeing?"

Tony grinned. "Not so hard," he said. "Stop one big-nose spying in windows? Not so hard."

"Okay," Bill said. "But why bother?"

Tony slugged back some more beer. "Just, don't like. Don't like no ones spying. Wei Ang-Ran say you can see, you can see. Say can't see, no spying."

"Are you really that busy back there that it would disturb your operation if we looked around?" I asked.

"Wei Ang-Ran say so busy," Tony said, then stopped to finish his beer, "must be so busy. Got good idea. Want hear?"

"Sure," I said. "Tell me."

"You tell American company, Lion Rock no good. Tell American company, go buy something else. Then you, Big-nose too, you don't come Lion Rock again." He pushed back from the table and stood. Big John and Iron Fist did the same, Big John with his beer bottle still in hand. "Because I see you again, no good. Big trouble. Business—" he pointed at Bill "—still not finish."

Bill said nothing, just returned Tony's stare with a long look of his own.

"We'll tell them," I said. "But I don't know what they'll do."

"Tell them," Tony repeated. "Don't see you again."

He turned and walked away. Big John, drinking his beer, followed. Iron Fist stood looking at us a little longer. Then he turned too, and followed his friends into the night.

seven

"I'm sorry," Bill said.

The mist was turning to a drizzling rain again. We sat alone at the night market table listening to the percussion on the plastic draped overhead. The young woman had gone back to frying rice for new customers, but they were all at other tables. No one would come sit with us.

"Sorry about what?" I asked.

"Now they've made us, and now we've lost them. My fault. I'm sorry."

"If you hadn't gone spying we'd never have known Iron Fist worked for Lion Rock in the first place."

"If I were any good I'd have been able to find that out without getting caught." He leaned back in his chair and lit a cigarette. "That was quick thinking, that story you gave them."

"I was worried about your nose."

"You don't think it could stand improvement?"

"I don't think they were planning to improve it."

He smoked his cigarette and didn't answer. The stall's lightbulbs swayed as the wind picked up, gliding our shadows across the tabletop, though we stayed still.

"Bill?"

He met my eyes.

"You let those guys get to you. You were about to take them on, which would have been crazy. What's wrong?"

He shrugged. "I didn't like them."

"You don't fight everyone you don't like. There's more than that."

Once again he didn't answer. Well, maybe he knew he didn't need to.

"I think," I said quietly, "that we should call Mark Quan. But I think not from here."

Bill squashed his cigarette out and stood.

We left the market after a quick consultation with my map. It turned out that following Iron Fist and his pals had done for us what we probably couldn't have done for ourselves: brought us within four blocks of the bus depot. We dashed through those blocks in a worsening rain. By the time we reached it, the falling drops were big and splashy and the gutters were flowing with fast-moving streams.

And there were no cabs at the bus depot.

Bill, gazing at the deserted cab stand, asked me, "Want to head for the subway?"

I looked into the curtain of rain falling from the edge of the overhang we'd scooted under. "No. We'll drown before we get there. Let's take a bus."

"Which bus?"

A bus pulled in just past the cab stand. I read the big black characters over its windshield and said, "That bus."

We climbed on behind other soggy people, mostly night market customers, their newly purchased socks and alarm clocks, pajamas and CDs stuffed into plastic bags.

"How do you know we want this bus?" Bill asked while we waited for the lady in front of us to roll up her umbrella.

"The sign says it's going to Central," I explained. "That's where the ferry goes from."

"You know," he said, "you're kind of handy to have around."

The downstairs of the double-decker bus was air-conditioned. Soaked with rain, I felt like I was walking into a freezer. I led us up the curving stairs to the top deck. As I'd hoped, the air-conditioning didn't reach up here. We had to choose our seats judiciously, avoiding the ones already rained-on through open windows, but once we got settled, the steamy warmth was kind of cozy and we were almost alone.

"That's the first time I've ever seen you voluntarily give up air-conditioning," Bill said.

"It's this semitropical climate," I answered, "weather of my people." I took my phone from my bag. "I'm trying to connect with my ancestors."

"I don't think," Bill said, "that you can do that from a cell phone."

He was probably right; it took me two tries to find Mark Quan, and he wasn't even related to me. First, as a matter of form, I tried his number at the HKPD. He was gone for the day, they told me, but he'd be in in the morning. Could they take a message, or could someone else help me? Funny, I thought, how that cop tone of voice—guarded, prepared to hear anything, giving nothing away—was the same in the rising, falling, nasal sounds and cadences of Cantonese as it was in hard-edged American English.

I thanked them, hung up, and tried the cell phone number Mark Quan had given me. He answered it with, *"Wai!"* before the third ring.

"It's Lydia Chin," I said. I decided to speak to Mark Quan in English. It was arguably the native language for us both, although I had to admit the same argument could be made for Cantonese. But English gave Bill a chance to get in on what was going on, and it was less likely to be successfully eavesdropped on by the few people up here on the upper deck with us.

"I was going to call you," he said. "When I got home. I'm having dinner." Behind his words I could hear the clinking of dishes and the din of many people talking and shouting to each other in an echoing room.

"Is this a bad time?"

"No, no, I'm alone. I'm at my local noodle joint, and it's noisy, that's all. And I don't have much to tell you, anyway. You hear from the family?"

"No. I'd call them but I don't want to give them a heart attack when the phone rings. We spoke to the uncle about two hours ago, and he said there was no news then."

"The uncle? Wei Ang-Ran?"

"Right. I'll tell you about it, but first tell me: Did you come up with anything at all?"

"No. I turned over a few sources, but no one admits to knowing anything about the Wei kidnapping. And if Iron

Fist Chang's involved in anything, we don't know about it. No one ever heard of him."

"Did they ever hear of Tony Siu or Big John Chou?"

Mark Quan was silent for a moment. "Yeah," he said. "Yeah, I know Tony Siu. He's a comer. Rising triad talent. If Strength and Harmony were a legit business he'd be a management trainee. Did you run into him?"

"I'm afraid we did."

As the bus turned and twisted through the rain, up hills and down them again, picking up passengers and dropping others off, I watched through the window and told Mark Quan where we'd been and what we'd done.

"Why didn't you call me?" he said. "When you first spotted Iron Fist Chang? Never mind. I know."

"I'm sorry," I said, "We should have."

"Maybe not," he said.

I glanced at Bill, showing my surprise, but of course he had no idea why. He raised an eyebrow; I turned back to the window, the better to concentrate on the phone. "What do you mean?"

"If I'd put a tail on him and he'd made my man, that might have driven the kidnappers more underground. Maybe those guys didn't buy your story, but no matter what they said, they didn't really take you two for HKPD. First of all, who would? And if they had they wouldn't have gotten up in your faces like that. Now we know more than we did: that Siu might be involved. No, you probably did the right thing."

Now I knew I was in a foreign country. I said as much to Mark Quan.

He gave a laugh. "I told you, I'm not the most popular guy on the Department. What makes sense to everyone else doesn't always make sense to me. You have to remember, I'm a stranger here myself."

"But you've been living here for twenty years," I said.

"You've been living in New York all your life," he retorted. "Does everything there make sense to you?"

That made me grin. My grin made Bill throw me another

inquisitive look, and that, unexpectedly, made me blush. I didn't know what to do, so I looked out the window some more and went on talking to Mark. I gave him more details of our conversation, such as it was, with Iron Fist and his friends.

"I don't get it," he said when I was done. "If this is a Strength and Harmony job, there are enough rice-for-brains street punks who'd love me to owe them one that someone should have told me by now. But I'll go out and stir the soup some more."

"How do you suppose Iron Fist ended up working there?" I asked. "He's a movie stuntman, I thought."

"That's not uncommon. The film business is spotty, and those guys are used to hard work. A lot of them moonlight on the docks or in the markets for a few extra bucks."

"And he found out about the jade because Wei Ang-Ran couldn't keep his mouth shut? That's how this started?"

Through the phone, in Mark's silence, I heard dishes clatter, and someone shouted. I pictured him in a large, bright room, waiters rushing back and forth, steam rising from big bowls, families with young children eating, laughing, all talking at once. In my picture, Mark sat at a table on the side, alone.

With a start I realized he'd asked me a question, but I didn't know what it was. I also realized Bill was watching me with an odd look. Suddenly confused, I didn't meet Bill's eyes, and I told Mark I hadn't heard him: Some interference on my cell phone, I said, though the truth was Hong Kong had this cell phone business worked out much better than we did back home and there hadn't been a second's static since I'd bought the thing.

Mark patiently repeated his question. "Did he seem like that to you, the old man? Someone who can't keep his mouth shut?"

"No," I said. "No, he didn't. And he didn't seem all that fond of Tony Siu, either."

"Siu's a hard man to like, from what I hear."

"I wonder how much Iron Fist likes him?"

"What are you thinking? Some kind of double-cross going on?"

"Maybe. But don't ask me who's double-crossing whom."

"Well, it's a theory," Mark Quan agreed. " 'A sweet tongue, a sword in the belly.' " He sighed. "Crime isn't what it used to be. In the old days you could trust your triad brothers."

"Maybe you still can, but Iron Fist isn't one of them, so they can cheat each other and feel okay about it."

"Well," Mark Quan said, "I'll bet I could lock them all up and feel okay about it."

There were some other calls I wanted to make, but not from here. I folded up the phone and filled Bill in on the parts of my talk with Mark Quan that he'd missed. For a guy who'd only heard one side, he seemed to have gotten most of it pretty well.

"What happens now?" he asked.

"Mark doesn't have an address for Iron Fist, but he's going to go up to Thundering Mountain in the morning. Tomorrow's Sunday, but if they're filming they work seven days, and if not maybe he'll find someone who can tell him something. I want to call the Weis and I want to call Grandfather Gao, but from the hotel." I leaned back against the bus seat and closed my eyes. "I'm tired. What did you say before about a brick wall?"

"I said I'd never seen one as cute as you."

I opened one eye and fixed it on him. "You did not."

"Well, it's what I meant."

I closed my eye again. After a while I said, "Where are we?"

"I'm supposed to know?"

"Describe our surroundings."

"Skyscrapers. Lots of traffic. Neon."

"Gee, must be Hong Kong. Go on."

"Other buses. Big lit building. Water."

"Hey," I said, opening both eyes, "we're here."

Our bus had come around a corner and was waiting its turn to pull into one of the angled, numbered parking slots by the big lit building, which according to its sign in both English and Chinese was the Central bus depot. Other signs, also in both languages, pointed the way to the subway, various buildings people might be interested in, and a number of different ferries. The ferry we wanted was the Star Ferry to Kowloon, and it was the closest one.

The rain had come down to a drizzle again. We trotted across the expanse of wet asphalt that was the bus depot and through a short, moldy-smelling tunnel under the avenue. A ferry was loading when we got to the dock, so we hurried on it. I took the first seat I saw, beside the rail in the middle of the boat. Bill dropped into the seat next to mine.

The boat wasn't as empty as the upper deck of the bus had been, but it wasn't the jam-packed commuter container of morning. We sat in tired silence as the ferry cut through the pockets of fog and slid across the dark surface of the harbor. The smell of salt water came to me again, speaking of distances much farther than any I'd traveled, journeys measured in years instead of days, loneliness that could not be measured at all.

"Damn," I said softly, to myself.

Bill looked at me. "What's wrong?"

"That little boy. We didn't do him much good, did we? And we didn't do Steven Wei or his wife much good, and we didn't do Grandfather Gao much good, either."

"We did what we could," he said.

"It's not enough."

He didn't answer right away, just gazed over the water, watching the lights of the boats that passed ours, on their ways to places we'd never know.

"If the amah's with the boy," Bill said finally, "he may be all right for a while. There's a cop on the case now, and there wouldn't be if you hadn't told Grandfather Gao what happened. We know more than we did, and we'll start again in the morning. There's nothing else we can do now."

"If we hadn't come here at all this wouldn't have started."

"You mean, because of the jade? If we hadn't been the ones to bring it, someone else would have. It may be the jade but it's not us."

I looked at him. "And you don't even think it's the jade, do you?"

Still looking across the harbor, he shook his head. "No. The jade's part of it, but it's not the point. Even if that was the real call. I don't know what the point is, but it's not as simple as that."

Behind us the neon crowning the office towers blurred into softly glowing halos of color floating in the misty night sky. Ahead, the lights of Kowloon shone from streetlamps and windows much more earthbound than the soaring structures on the Hong Kong side.

When the ferry docked we walked slowly back to our hotel. The rain had stopped, the traffic was thinner, and the jackhammers were silent, but the sidewalks were still narrow and packed, the horns still honked, and the store windows were still brightly lit, waiting for the strolling crowds to stream in and buy. Young couples holding hands stood in front of shops displaying the latest European and American fashions, the newest CDs, the most digital electronic gear. The night may be made for romance, I thought wearily, but in Hong Kong I was getting the idea romance was made for shopping.

The hotel lobby was a cool relief. We checked the desk for messages, but there weren't any. Bill asked if I wanted anything, a drink, a cup of tea.

"A shower," I sighed. "What I want is a shower and dry clothes. I'm going to go do that and then call the Weis and Grandfather Gao. Then I'll call you. You'll be in your room?"

"Yes. Then what?"

"Then maybe I'll see if I can sleep. What are you going to do?"

"Pretty much the same, I think. That way we can get started early in the morning."

"When we get started," I asked, "what are we going to do?"

He shook his head as the elevator came. "I don't know. But I'm too tired to think. You'll have a great idea in the morning."

"I will?"

"Uh-huh," he said. "You always do."

The elevator doors closed and we stood in silence; then they opened on my floor, so I got out. I turned to look at Bill, feeling like I had something else to say, but the doors were closing and I didn't know what it was. I stood there for a minute while the elevator took him to his room three floors above. Then I wondered what I was doing there and headed down the hall.

My room was cool and quiet, lit by the bedside lamp the chambermaid had left on when she'd turned down the bed. The drapes were closed, but I opened them, and I stood looking out across the bright lights of Kowloon and the busy waters of Victoria Harbor to the multicolored, mist-draped Hong Kong waterfront in the distance. My room looked toward the harbor, toward the island where the first foreigners had come, toward the tumultuous, clamorous, frantic empire they had built, an empire that had outlasted Empire itself. Bill's room faced the other way, across Kowloon, to the hills, to China. Funny, I thought, that it should be that way.

I showered in the big marble bathroom and dried myself on the soft thick towels feeling more and more bone-tired every minute, and more and more guilty that Grandfather Gao's hard-earned cash should be putting me up in such style while I was accomplishing nothing. Slipping into my yellow silk robe—made in China, bought in Chinatown, no doubt imported through Hong Kong—I left the bathroom ready to face the phone calls I needed to make.

But the little red light on my phone told me someone had beaten me to it.

I picked up the phone and pressed the button for the voice-mail message. Maybe it was Bill. Or Grandfather Gao. Or the Weis, with news.

But no. According to the voice mail, it had been my mother.

Talk about guilt, Lydia, I thought. Your mother just spent about a million dollars calling overseas—your mother, who never met a pencil she couldn't sharpen down to an inch or a piece of Scotch tape she couldn't reuse— and you didn't answer because you were in the bathroom smoothing freesia-scented lotion on your legs.

Before I could talk myself out of it I called her back.

"It's Ling Wan-Ju," I said in Chinese when she answered the phone.

"Ling Wan-Ju! I called you only ten minutes ago! I had to speak to a machine!"

"I'm sorry, Ma. I was here, just in the bathroom. How are you?"

"I am well! How was your day in Hong Kong?"

"You don't have to yell, Ma. I can hear you fine." I knew that wouldn't stop her: She yells into any phone that's making a call farther than Queens. "My day was interesting, Ma."

"Interesting?" She sounded instantly suspicious. "Have you done successfully what Grandfather Gao sent you to do?"

Not hardly, I thought, but I answered, "We're working on it."

"Ling Wan-Ju! You will not disappoint Grandfather Gao in this?"

Was I that obvious? "We're doing what we can, Ma," I said, trying to sound reassuring. "The job turns out to be more complicated than we knew."

She sniffed. Modern technology, it's amazing, I thought: I can hear my mother sniffing with disdain from halfway around the world. "Perhaps, Ling Wan-Ju, you are distracted."

I knew she didn't mean by the bright lights. "No, Ma, it's not that. There's just more to this. I've talked to Grandfather Gao; he understands."

"Ling Wan-Ju," my mother said decisively, "you will succeed in your task. You must ignore distractions; you must act as though you are traveling alone."

Wishful thinking, Ma, but go right ahead. "I'll do what I can," I told her.

"You will succeed." She said it again, and, because it sounded less like a prediction than a command, I both thanked her and promised to try.

"Now you must hang up," she ordered. "This call, much too expensive. Ling Wan-Ju, do not call me again from Hong Kong."

Oh, sure, I thought. And hear about how I didn't for the rest of my life?

"Just don't *you* call *me*," I said. "Because you can't tell when you'll get me in."

As if that hadn't been why she'd called in the late evening, Hong Kong time, just to make sure I was safely tucked in my room.

So, two Chinese women across the globe from each other, each satisfied she'd understood the other though neither of us had actually said what she'd meant, my mother and I said good-bye.

Now, I thought, to the other calls. I rearranged the pillows behind my back and reached for the phone again, but before I picked it up my bag started to chirp.

The cell phone. Not a lot of people had this number, and all of them were connected to this case. I lurched off the bed, dug the phone out of the bag, and stuck it to my ear.

"Hello? *Wai?*"

"Lydia Chin!" It was Steven Wei, yelling in English, sounding livid. "How could you do this? Where is my father's jade?"

Taken aback, I frowned at the flowered bedspread as I sat back down. "I don't understand. What are you talking about?"

"My son's life may depend on this! How could you do this?" he demanded again. "Where is my father's jade?"

"The jade?" I tried to follow this. "I left it there. You don't have it anymore? It's missing?"

"Missing? No, the jade you left here is not missing. But it is not my father's."

"Not—what do you mean?"

"You know full well," he said, almost hissing in fury. "It is similar, so much so that no one saw at first what is obvious now. But Li-Ling has been keeping it, opening the box again and again, gazing at the jade as though—in any case, it was she who first noticed. The veins in the stone, slight differences in the Buddha's smile. This jade is not my father's! You have substituted a piece, no doubt of lower value, thinking to keep my father's jade for yourself. At a time when a child's life is in the balance—!"

"Wait," I said. "Just wait a minute. First of all, the jade I gave you is the jade Gao Mian-Liang gave me in New York. I didn't substitute anything, and it was never out of my possession from the minute I got it until I gave it to you. Second, just before I gave it to you, I had it appraised. It's worth twenty thousand American dollars, so even if it isn't your father's, it's not a cheap substitute. Third, you and your family have been under a lot of strain. Isn't it possible you're mistaken?"

"Mistaken! No, it is not possible we're mistaken! If not for all the confusion at the time you left it we should have seen this immediately." He paused, and I heard him taking a breath. When he spoke again it was in lower, calmer tones. "Natalie also thought perhaps we were mistaken. So we compared this jade to the insurance photographs we had taken some years ago of various family possessions. The photographs of my father's jade are large and very clear. This is not that piece."

He paused again. I was trying to get my tired brain to

think. He said warily, "You say you had this piece appraised? Why did you do that?"

"I was trying to understand why the kidnappers would take such a risk for what's actually not a very large reward. I thought maybe the jade was worth more than I'd been told. But it wasn't. At least," I said, "this jade isn't. Maybe the real jade, your father's jade, is."

"We had it appraised at the time of the insurance inventory," Steven Wei said. His tone was less furious, less sure. "One hundred and fifteen thousand dollars—that is, almost fifteen thousand, American," he said. "That was the appraisal."

"Well," I said, "even with inflation, that makes the substitute piece worth actually more than the real one."

Steven Wei paused, wordless.

"When you had it appraised," I said, "was there anything unusual about it? Was it a special piece in any way, something that maybe added to its value?"

"Special?" he said. "No. An antiquity, rare enough to be valuable, but not unique." His voice was fading back to the dull, hopeless sound it had had this morning. Poor Steven, I thought. What a relief it must have been to think you'd found something to fight.

There was another pause. I heard Steven Wei relating what we'd said to someone in the room.

The next voice I heard was Natalie Zhu's. "We must call Gao Mian-Liang in New York," she said. "If there has been a substitution not made by you"—And I could tell she was reserving judgment on that—"perhaps he can shed some light on it."

Hello to you too, I thought. But I agreed. "I'll call him right now."

"*We* will call him. A conference call."

Well, okay. "I'll have to call the desk to find out how to do that."

"There is no need. We can place the call from here. Steven has the number."

Gee, I thought, I get the feeling you don't trust me. "All

right," I said, "but first tell me: Has there been any further contact with the kidnappers?"

"There has not."

There wasn't really anything I could say to that.

"I will place the call immediately," Natalie Zhu said. "It will be five or ten minutes until the overseas conference operator calls you."

"All right." About to hang up, I added, "I would appreciate it if the call was in English. I want my partner to be part of it."

"Gao Mian-Liang speaks English?"

"Yes."

"Very well."

I hung up the cell phone and grabbed the hotel one. I dialed Bill's room number.

"Come down here right away," I said as soon as he answered.

"To your room?" He was incredulous. "You want me to come to your hotel room?"

"No, but you'd better. But only for a phone call."

"This is a phone call."

"Hurry up."

I hung up so he'd have to hurry. Then I got up and quickly got dressed. I was tucking a yellow striped tee shirt into my slacks when he knocked on the door.

"That was fast," I said as I let him in. He was wearing a tee shirt, too, a plain white one. I suddenly wondered if that was the tee shirt he slept in, if he'd been in bed when I'd called. Or maybe he hadn't been in bed. Or maybe he had but he didn't sleep in a tee shirt. Or maybe it was none of my business.

"You said to hurry," he reminded me. "Are you okay?"

"Oh, just fine. I hate this place and everything about it."

"What's wrong?"

I told him about the jade.

"Jesus," was his comment. He took the omnipresent pack of cigarettes from his back pocket, then looked around. "This is a no-smoking room, isn't it?"

"Sorry."

He pushed the pack back. "Maybe self-denial will make a man out of me. What the hell is going on around here?"

"Not only don't I know, I can't imagine."

He looked around my room. I suddenly wished I'd hung the yellow silk robe in the closet instead of leaving it draped over a chair.

"No offense," Bill said, bringing his eyes back to me, "but could Grandfather Gao have pulled that switch?"

I skipped the part about taking offense—under the circumstances, it seemed disingenuous—and said, "Probably. He had old Mr. Wei's jade for a week before Mr. Wei died, and according to the jeweler this afternoon, these pieces aren't all that rare. But even if he could have, why would he? Why substitute a piece worth more for one worth less?"

Bill didn't look like someone who had any light to shed on that matter. What he looked like was someone who wanted a cigarette. Well, after this phone call he could go back to his own room and smoke a whole pack if he wanted to.

The bedside phone rang. I answered it; it was the overseas operator, hooking us up. I gestured for Bill to pick up the desk phone, told the operator to go ahead as though Lydia Chin joined in on international conference calls every day of the week, and waited to hear how these things went.

This one went by the operator asking if New York was there, and when Grandfather Gao, in slow but clear English, replied that he was, she checked on me, which also meant Bill, and Steven Wei, which also meant Natalie Zhu. Then she told us to ring her when we were through and left us alone with each other.

Natalie Zhu, in a voice that brought to mind a small, swift fighter plane approaching from the distance, introduced herself as Steven's lawyer and then told Grandfather Gao the basic fact: "The jade we have here, the jade Lydia Chin has given us, is not Wei Yao-Shi's jade."

Grandfather Gao was silent, then asked calmly, "What is the difference between the two pieces?"

Typical, I thought, as I half-listened to Steven Wei explaining. Anyone else would have been startled by this news and would have demanded, "Are you sure?" But no one would make an overseas conference call in the middle of a kidnapping to say something like this unless they were sure, so Grandfather Gao had just moved to the next step.

"You understand why we have called you," Natalie Zhu picked up after Steven Wei was done. "Lydia Chin claims the jade she gave Steven is the same jade you gave her."

"If she says that," Grandfather Gao replied, "it is true. You have called, therefore, to ask whether the jade I gave Chin Ling Wan-Ju is the jade Wei Yao-Shi gave me. It is." Even speaking in English, Grandfather Gao used my Chinese name. That was how he had always known me.

"You are sure?" Natalie Zhu asked. "Could a substitution have been made without your knowledge, perhaps?" A whole unspoken sentence was contained in that *perhaps*. Or could you, perhaps, be lying to us and have made the switch yourself, or, perhaps, be protecting your protégée and Lydia Chin actually did it, which is what we think most likely?

Everyone knew all the words in that silent sentence, but no one responded to them. Grandfather Gao answered the question Natalie Zhu had actually asked. "No," he said. "I guarded Wei Yao-Shi's jade with the utmost care from the moment I received it until I handed it to Ling Wan-Ju."

"Pardon me, but how can you—?"

"I wore it."

That stopped that.

A moment's silence. I looked at Bill, in the easy chair across the room, his feet up on the desk. "Grandfather," I said, trying to shake off the disorienting strangeness of speaking to Grandfather Gao in English, "could the substitution have been made before Wei Yao-Shi entered the hospital? While he was ill, maybe too ill to notice?"

"I suppose that is possible."

"My father," Steven Wei suddenly came alive, "how long was he ill before he was hospitalized?"

"He called me in the morning," Grandfather Gao said, "requesting that I bring him a remedy for the symptoms he described. When I arrived, however, I found him more seriously ill than he had said. I called an ambulance."

"But he could have been ill for days before he called you?"

"A day, perhaps. More is not likely."

"Why not? He was alone in his hotel, wasn't he? Who would have known?"

"No, he was not alone. Although there was a period after he sold his home that Wei Yao-Shi stayed in hotels when in New York, that had not been his custom these last few years. As age increasingly overtook him, he found it more difficult to cope with hotel living."

"Then where did he stay?"

Wake up, Steven, I thought, just before Grandfather Gao actually said it: "He stayed with his other son. With Franklin, your brother."

After the overseas operator disconnected the lot of us, Bill and I just looked at each other across my hotel room. Steven had been so hot to call his brother that Natalie Zhu had had to restrain him from doing it from his cell phone while the rest of us were still conferenced together. I suggested making the call to Franklin another conference call, but that was vetoed fast. Steven promised to let us know what happened between them. I wasn't sure he would, but there was nothing to be done about it right now.

Bill swung his feet off the desk, got up and walked over to the minibar. He pulled out a beer and held up a bottle of orange juice. I nodded. He tossed me the juice, then plunked himself down in the easy chair again.

I drank some juice, cool and acidy in my dry throat.

"Franklin Wei," I said, "wanted his father's jade for sentimental reasons, but he knew his father was planning to leave it to Harry. He's a doctor; on Mr. Wei's last New York trip Franklin could see the old man wasn't well and might go at any time. He snuck into his room one night and lifted the real jade off his neck, replacing it with the phony one, while the old man kept on snoring. The phony one was worth more than the real one because after all this was for sentiment, not for cash, and Franklin didn't want to cheat little Harry. How does that sound?"

Bill popped the top on his beer. "Ridiculous."

I sighed. "In half a dozen places, right?"

"At least."

"The main one being that Franklin didn't know about Harry?"

"That's a big one."

"What if he did?"

"What?"

"What if he really knew about Harry all along? Harry and Li-Ling and especially Steven? Knew about them, or maybe found out recently?"

Bill drank and lowered the beer can. "Go on."

"Well, it doesn't explain any of this nonsense with the jades, but it's an interesting thought. He's got a fast-and-loose lifestyle to maintain. Maybe medicine just isn't doing enough for him right now. Old Mr. Wei is his way out: That will leave his half of a prosperous business—Lion Rock—which Franklin had probably been expecting to inherit, and which he would if it weren't for the other family."

"So after old Mr. Wei dies, Franklin comes to Hong Kong, kidnaps the kid, and demands twenty million Hong Kong dollars?"

"Don't you think?"

"Then who wants the jade?"

The orange juice was kicking my brain into gear. "The amah, who's in on it with Franklin and could be the only person who knows the jade is coming who doesn't really know what it's worth. She tries to double-cross Franklin and get the jade before the real demand is made. She probably thinks it's worth more than whatever share of the twenty million Franklin offered her, or maybe she doesn't trust him to come through with any of it. Franklin, knowing nothing about that, calls as planned and asks for the twenty million."

"And then calls again and offers to mortgage his apartment to raise half of it?"

"Why not? It throws suspicion off him and nets him a million American dollars, in the end."

"Hmmm," Bill said, rubbing his eyes. "If I open this window really wide can I smoke?"

"No."

"In the bathroom, with the exhaust fan on?"

"No."

"Come up to my room?"

"You have to be kidding."

"It was worth a try."

The phone rang, saving me the trouble of telling him it had not really been worth a try.

"Wai?" I said, "Hello?"

"He is not there," came Steven Wei's voice, again dull and lost.

It took me a second. "Franklin?"

"He is not at his hotel. I have left an urgent message for him to call me. If for any reason you hear from him you must—"

"I'll tell him. I don't know why he'd call me, but I'll tell him."

It didn't sound to me like Steven completely believed that, but there wasn't much he could do. I wondered briefly whether to share my suspicions about Franklin with Steven, but I wasn't sure whether, in the light of bright, non-jet-lagged day, anything in the scenario Bill and I had just woven would make any sense at all. There were things we could do, I decided, to check this theory out, and we ought to do them before we started going around making Steven Wei distrust a brother he had only just met.

"I'll tell him," I repeated. "And if you hear from him, you'll let me know?"

He said he would, he hung up, and Bill and I were alone once more.

"Now that we have the phone to ourselves, I'm calling Grandfather Gao again," I said, looking at Bill across the room.

"Why not?" He leaned back in his chair. "Maybe a nature metaphor or two will help."

"He didn't use a single one just now, did he?" I reached for my orange juice.

"Maybe he only does it in Chinese."

"You know," I said, dialing the endless series of numbers you need to get to the other side of the world, "I don't speak to him in English very often. He sounds exactly the same as he does in Chinese. He's the only person I know who does that."

"Most people sound different?"

"Definitely. Don't you think so? People's whole way of expressing themselves changes in different languages. They move their hands around differently and everything."

Bill drank his beer. I could see his hand itching to be holding a cigarette. I wondered if he were thinking about the cigarette in another language if his hand would look different.

"*Wai?*" came Grandfather Gao's voice in my ear, finally.

"Grandfather, it is Chin Ling Wan-Ju calling." I switched automatically back to Chinese, the way we were used to talking. "I wanted to speak to you privately."

"You are alone?" He sounded not at all surprised at hearing from me again.

"Bill Smith is here." Speaking in Chinese, I used Bill's full name, the Chinese way; but it didn't roll easily off my currently Cantonese-shaped tongue. Maybe, for these situations, Bill needed a Chinese name. Smith Soy Ngau, I thought. Water Buffalo Smith. That's good.

"Ah," said Grandfather Gao, meaning, in Chinese, that's fine with me. He went on in his usual calm manner, but his voice struck me as darker than I was used to. "Ling Wan-Ju, this matter of Wei Yao-Shi's jade is disturbing."

"Very," I agreed.

"Have you thoughts on this problem?"

"None that make sense to me."

"As you continue your work, do not fail to keep this matter in mind. I believe that when you understand this, you will understand all."

That would be nice. "Wei Di-Fen"—Steven—"thinks Wei Fu-Ran"—Franklin—"is responsible," I told him. "Actually, I think he thinks *I'm* responsible, but he can't understand what my motive would be. Grandfather," I chose my words carefully to avoid offending Grandfather Gao by insulting his friends, "*I* can't understand what Wei Fu-Ran's motive might be. Do you know him well?"

"I have known him since he was a child, Ling Wan-Ju, as I have known Quan Mai, as I have known you."

All right, I thought, you didn't bring up Mark Quan just to have more people in that sentence. Parallel construction: the next best thing to metaphor. "You told me Quan Mai could be trusted," I said. "Is this true also of Wei Fu-Ran?"

"Quan Mai is a police officer," Grandfather Gao answered. "It is his profession to uphold the law, his nature to be honorable. Wei Fu-Ran is a doctor. It is his profession to be of help, though there is much he cannot cure."

His profession, I thought. "What is his nature?"

"To make decisions quickly, with great confidence."

Well, that sounded like the Franklin I'd seen, the man who just popped up to his brother's apartment in a foreign country, carrying flowers and chocolate, because it seemed like a cool surprise.

"What about honor, Grandfather?"

"I have never known Wei Fu-Ran to be deliberately deceitful or ungenerous. I have, however, seen him surprised by the results of his actions."

I'd have to think about that. I filed it away and changed the subject. "We went to the Lion Rock warehouse tonight," I said. "We brought Wei Ang-Ran your greetings. The man we had seen watching Wei Di-Fen at the temple was there, working as a laborer, in the company of a member of Strength and Harmony."

From the other side of the world, a long silence. "Ling Wan-Ju, if this is true you must take great care."

"What does it mean, Grandfather? Is Wei Ang-Ran a member of the triad? Was his older brother, Wei Yao-Shi?"

"Tree branches can be swept away on the river's current," he answered. "Still they are not water."

"What did he say?" Bill asked after I hung the phone up and leaned back against the headboard.

"Maybe I should speak to him in English from now on. This Chinese business is exhausting." I detailed the conversation for Bill.

"Great," he said. "Franklin likes to help but he makes decisions fast and screws things up. Steven has a valuable piece of jade that was not his father's and someone, somewhere, has a piece less valuable, except that someone else somewhere else may be willing to trade a young boy for it. And the older Wei brothers may or may not be all wet. Is that accurate?"

"Yes," I said, "it's just perfect."

"I," he said, standing, "am going to bed. I'm hoping that what seems like *Alice in Wonderland* stuff now will make complete sense after a night's sleep."

"You think so?"

"No." Hands in his pockets, he looked over at me. I thought he was about to say something, but he just stood there, and then he left.

I sat on the bed sipping orange juice and looking at the door for a while after it closed behind Bill. Then I picked up the phone again and called Mark Quan.

"You never sleep?" was his response when I told him it was me. Behind him I heard music, American jazz played on saxophone and drums.

"I do, and I wish I were. But I thought you should know the latest."

"They've heard from the kidnappers?" His voice quickened. The music stopped abruptly; he must have turned it off.

"No. But Steven Wei just called me." I told Mark Quan

about the jade, about the call to Grandfather Gao, about my theory about Franklin.

"God*damn*," he said. "This is unbelievable."

I said, "I keep wondering whether it would make sense if I weren't jet-lagged, exhausted, and in a completely foreign country."

"It wouldn't," he said. "I'm none of those things, and it makes no sense to me."

"Did you understand this place?" I asked suddenly. "Hong Kong, when you first got here?"

"Understand it?" Mark Quan seemed surprised at the question. "I'm not sure I understand it yet. Everyone's always telling me Hong Kong is different from every place else. All I know is Birmingham, but it's true, it's real different from Birmingham. But do you mean you think this Wei case is so weird because of Hong Kong?"

"I . . ." I tried to think what it was I meant. "It fits," I said. "Hong Kong seems to know what it's doing, but I can't figure it out. All the confusion, the hurrying, the stopping and starting. The temple courtyard that people can watch from their apartment windows next to their laundry. The pipes down the outsides of the buildings. It's all on purpose, but I don't get the logic of it. Like this case. All this stuff must mean something, but I don't know what it is."

"Well," he said. "I don't either. But I'm just a cop. I'm like one of those windup Godzilla toys. Put me on a case and I just keep going until I get to the end of it or I fall over."

I had to stifle a giggle, because Mark Quan did sort of resemble one of those round Godzilla robots with the flashing eyes. I pictured the robot in a linen jacket, with a tiny gun under its arm, stomping across the night market tabletop.

"If you were wound up now," I asked, "where would you go?"

"This jade," he said. "This jade is the key. I know it is."

The same as Grandfather Gao, I thought.

"But I don't know what I can do about it right now. Meanwhile, I'm interested in your idea that Franklin Wei knew about Steven and his family. I don't much like Franklin for the kidnapper, but I can't seem to unearth anyone who can point a finger at Strength and Harmony, which is what I'd really like. At least this would be something to follow up." He was silent for a few moments. "I think I'll call the NYPD."

"The NYPD? Why?"

"For a printout of Franklin's phone calls. Maybe he's been calling someone here—if he's involved in this, he'd have to have set it up before he got here."

Of course. And if I were thinking, I'd have thought of that, too. "Will you call me when you get it?"

Mark Quan paused. "Now you have me in a tough position. You brought me into this case; I wouldn't know anything about it if it weren't for you, so I owe you. But I'm a cop and you're not and I live here and you don't. Anything happens to you, I'm an earthworm for the next dozen lifetimes, not to mention all the unpleasant things that would happen to me in this one."

"You're telling me to stay out of it now?" I bristled.

"No, that would be dumb. The Weis aren't about to call me; you're the only one who's keeping me informed. I need you to stay in it, at least until we figure out what *it* is. What I'm telling you is to stay out of trouble."

"The more I know, the more I can see trouble coming before it gets here."

"And then what?"

" 'Of the thirty-six stratagems, the best one is 'running away,' " I said, quoting a famous line from the Three Kingdoms period.

"Boy," Mark Quan said. "You sound like Grandfather Gao."

"I'm a little shocked myself," I admitted. "I'm not sure where I dug that up from."

"Chinese school?"

"Probably. Did you have Chinese school in Birmingham?"

"Every day after school-school, when I was a kid. There were only eight or nine of us, in old Mr. Ko's house. He tried to teach us the old songs, painting, calligraphy, all that. I liked the music, but my calligraphy was awful. Mr. Ko said pigeons made more legible characters scratching in the dirt than I did with a brush and ink."

"That's about how bad mine was. But what a mean thing to say."

"It didn't make me mad, only curious. I walked around for months after that trying to read what the pigeons were writing."

In the end, Mark Quan promised to call me if I promised to keep out of trouble. I negotiated to *try* to keep out of trouble—I didn't want to get to be an earthworm too, for not keeping a promise—and we hung up. I pulled off my clothes, slipped under the covers, and just managed to turn off the light before I was completely, totally asleep.

eight

When the phone woke me the next morning I had absolutely no idea where I was. I didn't actually even know it was morning, until the white streak glowing in the gap where the curtains didn't quite meet told me. I stuck my hand out from the sheets and groped for the thing making the odd double ring. That was a sound I'd only heard in movies up until yesterday.

"Hello?" I croaked into the receiver when I found it, and then, as a flash of insight finally hit me, added, *"Wai?"*

"Breakfast in twenty minutes," Bill announced.

"No way."

"Half an hour?"

"Maybe. What time is it?"

"Eight-thirty."

I pushed myself into a sitting position. "You sound suspiciously chipper. I thought I was the morning person around here."

"I've been up since six. I went out and walked around. I have an idea."

"You did? You do?"

"I did and do. Meet me in the coffee shop in half an hour and I'll tell you about it."

So I did, and he did.

"I want to go look for the amah," he said, buttering a piece of toast.

I sipped my tea—good strong black English tea, though the so-called coffee shop, actually an elegant oasis of potted plants and silver samovars, also offered various scented Chinese and green Japanese teas to suit every tourist palate—and considered this.

"Well, Natalie Zhu did hire us to do that," I said. "And if there's anything to my crackpot theory from last night, the amah would be key. But I'm not sure this actually qualifies as an idea."

"Why not?"

"For one thing, if the kidnapping's real, then she's being held wherever Harry is, and we won't be able to find her."

"But if we *can* find her, it'll mean it's not real. And we might begin to get a handle on what's going on."

I dipped a steamed pork dumpling into vinegary ginger soy sauce and bit into it. The pungent meat was wrapped in dough of the perfect thickness and doneness. I washed it down with tea and attacked the next one. "Our theory was that Natalie Zhu hired us to find the amah just to keep us out of the way," I reminded Bill. "Because it was something she thought we couldn't do."

"I know," he said. "I think she's wrong."

"What do you have in mind?"

He salted his scrambled eggs. "Last night you asked me about living in the Philippines. That started me thinking. One of the kids I knew there, he had four aunts working here. They would get together on their day off with other women from their neighborhood in Manila and write letters home. I remember that because he used to tell me the funny stories his aunts put in their letters. We thought Hong Kong must be the weirdest place in the world, if even half of those stories were true."

"Lucky for them they all had the same day off."

"That's the point. They all do."

"All do what?"

"All the Filipinas. They're heavy Catholics. They all had Sundays off. They'd go to Mass and then meet for lunch on the Hong Kong side, in the park by Statue Square. I asked around this morning. Seems that's still true."

"And you're thinking, today is Sunday?"

"Bingo."

"They may all have Sundays off," I said, "but they can't all go to the same park for lunch anymore. Aren't there like a hundred thousand of them?"

"Uh-huh," he said. "And they all still do."

I finished my dumplings before Bill polished off his eggs and bacon. While I waited for him, I called Franklin Wei's hotel on my cell phone. Neither Franklin nor Steven had called me yet, which didn't mean they hadn't spoken to each other, just that I wasn't on the top of either of their lists. The hotel connected me with Franklin's room.

"Hello?"

"It's Lydia Chin," I said, nibbling on a strip of bacon I'd liberated from Bill's plate.

"Oh," Franklin said. "I was going to call you but I wasn't sure you'd be up yet." He sounded a little less brash, more distant, than yesterday.

"Did you speak to Steven?"

"Late last night. He told me about Dad's jade."

"And asked if you were the one who made the switch?"

"Yes."

"And were you?"

"I—no, of course not."

"I wasn't either. Just for the record."

"He said you'd said that."

"But he doesn't believe me."

"I'm not sure he believes me either. He's in a bad position. Why should he believe anybody?"

Well, I thought, he could believe *me* because I really *didn't* have anything to do with it.

"He said Grandfather Gao said it wasn't him either," Franklin Wei went on. "He also told me the phony jade is worth more than the real one?"

"Seems that way. Do you have any idea what's going on?"

"God, no."

"Why didn't one of you call me last night, after you'd spoken to each other? Steven promised you would."

"It was two A.M. I couldn't sleep; I'd been out to a club. I got his message and called right away when I got back. We decided there was no point in waking you at that hour to tell you nothing. Have you spoken to him today?"

"No. That's why I'm calling you. I don't want to get

them all excited when the phone rings, and then it's only me."

"I know," he said. "I was dying to know what was going on last night but I didn't want to call for the same reason. That's why I finally went out."

"I understand you did call yesterday, though," I said. "To offer them money, for the ransom."

"Well, yeah."

"That was generous of you."

"Well, money," he said. "I mean, this is my brother's kid."

After breakfast Bill and I left the hotel, bracing ourselves for the moment the revolving door expelled us into the heat of the Hong Kong morning. Sunday in Hong Kong, I discovered, was not all that much different from Saturday, my only point of comparison. We headed for the ferry along the same streets we'd taken yesterday, and though fewer of the people charging along were dressed in business clothes, the traffic was as relentless and the jackhammers were once again in full rattling voice. I had showered and put on loose tan slacks and a crisp white cotton shirt, and I was walking around in sandals, but I could feel the film of sweat start on my forehead before we'd gone half a block.

"Hot here," I said to Bill.

"Great, huh?" was his answer.

We threaded through the crowds of people, mostly Chinese, all intent on being somewhere other than where they were and getting there fast. As I hurried with them I said something to Bill and got no answer; I turned back and saw that he'd stopped to light a cigarette and was a few yards behind. I waited, watching him as he shook out the match and made his way along the sidewalk. He was a head taller than almost everybody else, and muscular in a broad-shouldered sort of way instead of slight like most of the people around us. But that didn't keep them from pushing and shoving past him as though he were some kind of moving park statue left over from colonial days, some large

Western figure of no current importance whose name no
one remembered anymore.

"You okay?" I asked as he reached me.

"Sure," he said, raising an eyebrow. "Do I look not
okay?"

"You look tall," I said.

"Sorry. I've been meaning to work on that."

"No problem."

We dropped our coins in the turnstile and went up the
stairs and down the ramp to the ferry, old hands at this
now. We took seats at the front and watched the Hong
Kong Island skyline swell as it approached.

Yesterday's rain was just a memory. A few high wispy
clouds floated over Victoria Peak and I could see some
more far out to sea, but Kowloon, the harbor, and Hong
Kong Island glittered and sparkled in the hot, bright sun.
Later in the day, as car exhaust, cooking fumes, and smoke
from factories with Sunday shifts swirled and rose, the air
would probably thicken and blur, but for now the shadows
were sharp and the sky was about as blue as anything I'd
ever seen.

"I called Mark Quan last night," I said to Bill. "After
you left. I thought he should know about the jade."

"What did he say?"

"He's going to call the NYPD."

"About the jade?"

"About Franklin." I told him about Mark's idea that
Franklin would have to be working with someone in Hong
Kong to set up the kidnapping, if he'd really done that.

"Okay," Bill said. "That's probably a good idea, getting
the phone calls. But tell me this: If Franklin is behind this,
why did he come to Hong Kong? He wouldn't be on anybody's mind at all if he hadn't shown up here."

"Good question." The ferry passed a fishing boat with
nets mounded on its deck. "And why did he offer Steven
money for the ransom, if he's trying to make money off
the ransom?"

"So he could look like a good guy and still make a

million bucks. It's actually a pretty clever move."

"Okay. But it still doesn't explain the jade."

"As far as that goes, there is one dumb, mundane explanation I thought of last night."

"Yes?"

"Old Mr. Wei, at some point, gets into a bind. Sells his jade for some quick cash. He's embarassed so he doesn't tell anyone. His ship comes back in, he buys another piece as close to the original as he can find. Figures no one but him will ever know."

I looked at Bill as the ferry cut its engine and headed for its slip. "I hate that."

"Why? It knocks one of these problems right out of the box."

"The one that Grandfather Gao and Mark Quan think is the key to the whole thing."

"Maybe they're wrong."

"Maybe," I sighed. "Or maybe it would all become clear to me if I thought in Chinese."

"In that case," he said, "it will never be clear to me."

We walked the same way as yesterday, along the covered walkway, past the rickshaw men, through the wide tiled passage under the street. But this time when we came out we didn't hail a cab. We didn't need to; the underground passage came out just where we needed to be.

And Bill was right.

We stood on the edge of Statue Square. On the far side of the paved and fountained plaza, behind a colonial-era building with stone columns and a portico, a park stretched away to our left. Palm and pine trees waved in the breeze, walkways arched over roads, and skybridges threaded tall buildings together. On our right loomed the Mandarin Oriental, still imperturbable, as placid and unflustered on this bright morning as she had been yesterday when traffic zoomed around her through the misty afternoon. There was no traffic today: The avenue was closed. But the Mandarin Oriental seemed uninterested in the change. Stolid, regal, and focused on higher things, she took no notice whatsoever of the young women in their bright-colored clothes who sat on rattan mats or newspapers or the occasional folding chair tucked against her flanks, in the shade of her awnings and her pedestrian bridge, on the wide walls of the fountain pool in the square beside her, on the paving stones, benches, paths, and every other surface in the square and the park, on the sidewalks and the closed street itself as far as the eye could see.

There were thousands of them. Mostly they clustered in small groups, five, ten, a dozen; mostly they were animated, giggling, talking, handing photos around; mostly, they were young, energetic, smoothing their hair as the breeze mussed it up and laughing in the sun.

And mostly, they were eating. The aromas of roast meats and sauces pungent with unfamiliar spices made my mouth water, and as I watched plastic containers being popped open and paper plates being passed I wondered how many breakfasts I could really eat. Here and there a group was done with their meal, or maybe was not starting until they finished the business of prayer: Quiet circles of young women held each others' hands and stood, heads down, silently or speaking in whispered unison. And scattered through the massive crowd, reaching for the other extreme, CDs played while women laughed and waved and called to each other, taught each other new steps in dances to the music of home.

I stood on the edge of this sea of women, reluctant to wade in. "We'll be intruding," I said to Bill.

He looked in the same direction I was looking, out over the square and the park. "We usually do," he said. "That's pretty much our job."

That was something I couldn't argue with. "How are we planning to do this?" I asked.

"We stroll through the crowd asking if anyone knows Maria Elena Quezon from Cabagan."

"I'm beginning to get that needle-in-a-haystack feeling."

"I don't think it's that bad. I'm betting they get together in hometown groups, the way my friend's aunts did. Someone must know where the women from Cabagan hang out."

"Okay," I said, still dubious, "but what makes you think that even if we find someone who knows her, they won't think we're some sort of immigration officials or something and they won't talk to us?"

"Because like Mark Quan said, both the good news and the bad news is no one would ever take us for locals. I'll say I knew her family when I lived in the Philippines."

"You think that'll work?"

"If I say it in Tagalog."

I looked at him. "You remember enough Tagalog to do that?"

"You can't hang around with the local delinquents if you don't speak their language."

So we stepped into the ocean of laughing young women and Bill spoke to them, group by group, in a language I couldn't understand. Their eyes widened in amazement, they smiled and answered and we moved on. Sometimes a woman responded not in Tagalog, whose very sounds and cadences were strange to me, but in Spanish, which, though I didn't speak it, was familiar from the streets of New York. Bill switched into easy Spanish then, and the women beamed with delight. Not part of these conversations, I watched the young women, their surprise and amusement at the tall Westerner who spoke both their languages; and I watched Bill, watched the small changes in his face, his hands and shoulders, as he shifted from one foreign way of speaking and thinking to another.

"Did you learn the language every place you lived?" I asked him after a time. We had stopped at a vendor's cart for bottled water. The sun was standing almost directly overhead now and the crowd, almost unbelievably, had grown, as church services let out or late sleepers sheepishly arrived.

Bill wiped his forehead with the back of his hand and said, "I tried. I didn't want to be an Army brat; I didn't want to be an American. Language isn't that hard when you're a kid."

"Do you still speak them all this well?"

"I don't speak Tagalog well. They're talking to me like you would to a six-year-old, and they think it's a riot." He took a long drink of water. "I never spoke much Thai, and I didn't like German, but I bet I could still speak Dutch if I had to."

"Dutch?"

"Sure. *Hei, meisje, wil je even een sluipende tulp kopen?*"

"What does that mean?"

He winked. " 'Hey, cutie, wanna buy a hot tulip?' "

I smacked him on the arm pro forma, and we went on. Bill's mood had lightened; but it seemed to me the darkness was still there, lurking behind the sleep-, caffeine-, and in his case cigarette-fueled activity that kept us moving, gave us something to do. I hoped, mostly for Harry Wei, but partly also for Bill, that fishing in this ocean of young Filipinas would turn out to be more than just a way to idle away a sunny morning.

About a half an hour later, we had a catch.

We had left the sun-heated stones of Statue Square for the greener precincts of Chater Garden, where the young women, fastidiously avoiding the planted areas, were seated on every path, plaza, fountain, and footbridge. Their lunches and their CD players surrounded them, and the shopping bags they'd brought these things in hung from the garden fences. The shopping bags had come from home, their employers' homes, and the Chater Garden fences were decorated with shopping bags carrying the names of the most upscale shops in the world: Bijan, Hermes, Armani, Tiffany bags had come here carrying spicy rice and Spanish music.

We had been walking through the crowd for almost two hours, and I was about ready to give it up and think of something else to do—something that involved air-conditioning—when we hit one group of young women where Bill's question brought more than shrugs and apologetic smiles. A small, pretty woman, short-haired and

quick, lit up at his question, asked him one in return, and
laughed at his answer. They spoke some more, both smiling, and then he thanked her and we turned to leave. We
didn't stop at the next group, though, but headed up the
path toward a pedestrian bridge.

"Where are we going?" I asked.

"There's a group of women from the area around Cabagan who get together where this bridge hits the one going
across there." He pointed ahead. "The woman who told me
that has a cousin from Cabagan. She has lunch with them
sometimes. She couldn't believe a Westerner had ever
heard of the place."

We worked our way to and up the sloped bridge, picking
a path between groups of women marveling over photographs and others singing along with crooning CDs.

At the top of the slope, where the intersection of two
bridges formed a sort of skyway plaza, eight or nine women
sat on mats, their shopping bags propped against the bridge
railings. They ate chunks of beef and tomatoey rice from
paper plates, offering each other cans of sweet juice drinks
and plastic containers full of pickled vegetables. They paid
no attention to our approach until we stopped in front of
them and Bill, smiling, said something I by now recognized
as hello in Tagalog.

Most of the young women smiled back, some looking
curious, and one or two of them answered, also in Tagalog.
Bill said something which included "Cabagan," and the response involved smiles and nods, a few giggles, and a question or two. Bill answered the questions and then said
something else, and I recognized Maria Quezon's name
among the unfamiliar sounds. Heads turned to one quiet
young woman sitting cross-legged against the railing. The
others waited, apparently, for her to respond.

She had said nothing when Bill first started asking questions and she said nothing now. She did not smile, but fixed
Bill, and then looked me over, with large dark eyes.

She spoke, Bill spoke, she spoke again. Bill shook his
head. She said something else, something that seemed to

be a question. Bill gave a short answer. She glanced around
at her friends, whose faces had lost their cheerful smiles
and looked now concerned and confused. She stood, said
something to them, and drew Bill off to a place a few feet
away. I stayed behind. They spoke briefly. He took out his
passport, and then some things from his wallet, and showed
them to her. He nodded in my direction. They exchanged
a few more sentences, she shaking her head, he speaking
low, seeming to repeat himself. When they parted he left
her with a card from his wallet on which he'd scribbled
something. She came back to join her friends; he gestured
me over to him. I nodded to the women, who watched me
warily. I went on to where Bill stood, and walked with him
over the bridge.

"So?" I said after about two steps. Coming to another
intersection, we turned. We didn't head back down onto the
streets, but took yet another walkway that, ahead, plunged
into the side of a glass-walled building.

"That," said Bill, reaching the door in the building, pulling it open for me, "was Maria Quezon's sister."

A blast of cool air rolled out and nearly knocked me
over. "What?" I demanded. I went though the door into a
short carpeted corridor. My skin tingled in the twenty-
degree temperature drop. I turned to Bill as soon as I was
inside. "And? So? *What?*"

Trying to get through the door also, he bumped into me.
Then two Japanese tourists coming in behind him bumped
into both of us. We all apologized with smiles and bows,
and Bill and I moved over, out of the traffic lane.

I opened my mouth but before I could start again Bill
said, "She told me she didn't know where Maria was."

"What do you mean, her sister?"

"Remember Natalie Zhu said she thought Maria had a
sister working in Hong Kong, but she didn't have any idea
where to find her? Well, you find her where you find the
other women from her village. Right there"—he nodded in
the direction we'd come from—"at the corner of Bridge
and Bridge."

"Well," I said, "that's pretty bright of you, I have to admit. You get genius points. But she doesn't know where Maria is, so in the end it gets us nowhere."

"Wrong. She *said* she doesn't know where Maria is. I swore up and down that not only weren't we cops or officials of any kind, we weren't even citizens here, and we didn't want to get into trouble here any more than she did. But I said we knew about Harry, and I thought Maria was already in trouble, and if she was, we wanted to help."

"What did she say?"

"What she didn't say was that she didn't know what I was talking about, or what did I mean, 'knew about Harry'? She just told me again she didn't know where Maria was."

"Hmm. And you're thinking if she's really in the dark she'd ask more questions?"

"Wouldn't you?"

"Don't I anyway?" I stepped aside as a middle-aged couple opened the door to go out onto the bridge. A gust of hot humid air tried to sneak in, but the air-conditioning muscled it out again. "So what now?" I said.

"I told her again I wanted to help. I said I was worried about the little boy. I told her I knew about living someplace where you don't belong and feeling like you have no place to turn when you're in trouble. I suggested Maria could call me and we could talk."

Three Americans came in the door, flushed and wilted from the heat. I looked at Bill as they passed us. "You do, don't you?"

"I do what?"

"You know about living places you don't belong."

He shrugged. "We lived in a lot of places when I was a kid."

"It's not just that."

"Not just what?"

"Feeling like you belong. It's not just the place."

He didn't answer and he didn't look at me.

"And speaking of places," I said, changing the subject in my usual adroit manner, "where are we?"

"The Furama Hotel. I thought you might want a cup of tea."

"Ding-ding-ding-ding-ding-ding."

"What's that?"

"That's your bonus genius points being rung up."

Down the short corridor we turned left, which was the only possibility. The carpet, released from the narrow banks of the corridor, flooded out to become the floor of a grand upstairs lobby, high-ceilinged, dotted with easy chairs, sleek glass-topped tables, and newspaper racks in case you wanted to sit around in cool comfort and catch up on the world.

Or you could sit and look at the actual world through the glass wall on the far side of the lobby. We decided to do that, strolling across the endless carpet to choose a table right up against the glass, with a view of the Chater Garden and the ocean of Filipinas we had spent the morning among. No sooner had we sat down than a young woman in a discreet gray uniform appeared to ask us gravely if there was anything we wanted. I ordered hot tea and Bill ordered iced. Then we settled back in the easy chairs and looked at each other.

"This tropical-climate business," I said. "I don't know about it."

"You're gorgeous when you sweat. It makes you glow."

"Uh-huh. I bet I smell good, too."

"As always."

"Well," I said, "my personal hygiene aside, what do we do now?"

"We wait for our drinks before we try to do any more thinking?"

That sounded like a good plan. I leaned back in the chair, feeling my body temperature dropping one slow degree at a time. I was content not to think right now, just to watch the other Sunday tea-takers, the hotel guests checking in and out at the long lobby desk, the waiters and waitresses coming and going. The traffic and the palm trees and the amahs beyond the glass were a sunlit, silent spectacle, and all the sounds I could hear were hushed ones: soft footsteps, quiet conversations, the mild chirp of a cell phone.

A cell phone. Chirp, chirp. From my bag. I yanked the snap open and grabbed the thing out, stuck it to my ear, and shouted, *"Wai!"*

"Lydia?" came a tentative voice in my ear.

I dropped my voice to normal speaking tones. "Yes, it's me. Mark?"

"You sounded so Hong Kong," Mark Quan said. "I thought I might have the wrong number."

"I'm adapting. Do you have news?"

"As a matter of fact I do. Not about the boy—that's your department."

"No, nothing. I was thinking of calling them but if they're waiting for a call . . ."

"I know," he said. Then, "I don't suppose you're anywhere near me?"

"I wouldn't know. Not only don't I have any idea where you are, I'm not exactly sure where I am. We seem to be at the Furama Hotel."

He laughed. "Right down the street. Give me a few minutes. Where do I find you?"

"The lobby on the second floor. Having tea."

Our tea came exactly as I said that. I folded up the phone and, when the waitress was through laying out the milk, sugar, lemons, and spoons, I told Bill we were expecting a visit from Mark Quan, with something to say.

"He didn't say what?"

"Not even a hint."

"Then I don't suppose there's anything we can do except drink and wait."

"You could speak Dutch to me some more."

"Is that sexy and attractive?"

"No. It's pretty silly, as a matter of fact. Are you sure your accent's right?"

"I'm almost sure it's not."

"Well, then."

I used the lemon and Bill used the sugar, and I wondered if that meant anything about our approaches to life. He didn't try any more Dutch, or Tagalog, or really do anything at all. He just settled into his chair, sipping his iced tea and watching people as they moved around the leisurely lobby; but the shadow in his eyes, the tightness in his shoulders, though still there, were faded. Maria Quezon's sister, who knew enough about something to be troubled, to be silent and watchful as she sat with her friends; but was not panicked, not so frightened she had not joined them; who had not asked what it was Bill knew about Harry, and had slipped the card with his cell phone number into the pocket of her cotton skirt: Maria Quezon's sister had lifted a weight from him, and I found myself silently thanking her.

As we sat quietly in the cool lobby drinking our tea I decided this must be how my cell phone felt when, after carrying it around all day, I plugged it in to recharge its batteries at night. By the time Mark Quan came striding across the carpet, wearing a gray linen jacket and darker gray slacks, moving with that surprising grace, I was ready to pay him some serious attention.

"Hi," he said, pulling a chair from another table over to ours. The chairs were all on casters, the better to glide without a hitch through the peace of the lobby of the Furama Hotel. "Hotel lobbies R us, huh?"

"Bill found this one," I said. "We had a hot morning."

The waitress appeared again. Mark Quan ordered a lemon squash.

"What's that?" I asked.

"A drink only the British could have invented," he said. "Too sour *and* too sweet. Tastes terrible, but it works." He sat forward, forearms on knees. "I got Franklin Wei's phone records for the last six months."

"And?" I demanded. "Are there calls to Hong Kong?"

He nodded. "Two numbers."

"Could you trace them?"

"Could and did. One's the number at Lion Rock Enterprises."

"Oh," I said. "Well, he'd have that, wouldn't he? To find out when his father was coming in, or tell him he'd left his socks behind on his last trip. That doesn't really mean anything."

"No. But the other's better. It's to an antiquities dealer up on Hollywood Road."

"Antiquities?" I glanced at Bill. "I don't suppose this antiquities dealer sells jade? Little laughing Buddhas, maybe?"

"No jewelry, as far as I know. Bronzes, ceramics, that kind of thing. All genuine, on the up-and-up, but that's no surprise. I don't know much about that stuff, but I do know something about him."

"The dealer?"

"L. L. Lee." Mark looked from me to Bill. "A long-term high-up member of Strength and Harmony."

Bill drew a cigarette from his pocket, then glanced around the lobby.

"It's a Japanese hotel," Mark Quan said. "You can smoke wherever you want."

Bill lit a match, got the cigarette going. The waitress returned with a grayish-yellow drink in a tall frosted glass, placed it on a coaster in front of Mark.

"Well," I said, "that's not good news, but I can't say I'm surprised."

"I don't know the guy," Mark said. "Franklin, I mean. So I don't have an opinion one way or the other. But it puts Strength and Harmony right in the middle of this, whatever this is. If I had a reported crime here I could round up a bunch of them and start pounding."

"Maybe I should call the Weis," I said. "If they haven't had a ransom call since yesterday afternoon they might be desperate enough to bring the police in."

"Wait," Bill said, reaching for the ashtray. "Let's think about that. If Steven reports the kidnapping, Franklin will hear about it—Steven will tell him next time they talk.

Either that or we have to tell Steven not to, which will tell
Steven what we think of Franklin. From what I've seen,
Steven's not the type to grit his teeth and wait. He'll go
charging off to face down Franklin and things could get
worse."

Mark sipped his drink. "There's something to that. If
this really is Franklin's game, then he's put himself in a
position to know everything the other side does, or at least,
if he gets shut out, to know he's been shut out, so there
must be something going on."

"So what are you thinking?" I asked Bill.

"We have the police"—he gestured at Mark—"involved
already. Rounding up triad members might give us something, but it might not. We may get results we don't want,
and they may not bring us any closer to Harry."

Mark shrugged. "It's okay with me. I'd sort of like to
have the Department behind me, except," he grinned,
"every time they get behind me I find a knife in my back
anyhow. Okay, so let's think. I may not be able to pick
these guys up but I can dig a little deeper than I did last
night, now that I know where to look. And I can go up and
see L. L. Lee."

"What did you mean," I asked, "when you said his business was completely legit and that's no surprise?"

"Any triad high-up needs someplace to operate from,
some legit business that he keeps straight so we don't have
any reason to go poking around. Lee's known as a cultured
man, a guy with a passion for the ancient arts. An antiquities business makes sense for him. He may be laundering
money through it, but him being L. L. Lee, I'm sure people
have looked into that before and not been able to make
anything stick. Probably the business is squeaky clean. But
I'll look again. Okay, what else?"

"We did something interesting this morning," I said,
glancing at Bill. Bill nodded; I went on, telling Mark what
we'd set up. "She may not call," I ended. "Her sister may
really not know where to find her. But Bill got the feeling
that she did."

"Tagalog, huh?" Mark said to Bill. "That's pretty good. You ought to be a cop."

Bill shook his head. "Couldn't take the coffee."

"Can I find the sister again if I want her?" Mark asked.

"She wouldn't give me her address and I didn't want to push it. But her name's Alicia Carolina Quezon-Aguilera, and she works for a family on the Kowloon side, in one of the new towns."

"That ought to do it," Mark said. I started to say something and he stopped me. "No, I'll stay out of it for now. But if she calls—"

"Yes," I said.

"Right." He raised his glass in a toast. "Tagalog, huh?"

Bill raised his iced tea in response, and they drank more or less to each other.

Humph, I thought. But the Furama had no potted plants for me to talk to, so I said to Mark, "Did you check on Natalie Zhu?"

"Yes. If what everyone says is true, there's someone who won't have to come back in her next life. Not a hint of a shadow of anything bad. Reputation for complete devotion to her clients, especially the Weis."

"Well, that's comforting. And you checked on the Weis' finances?"

"As far as I could. I think it's true, they don't have fifteen million dollars—Hong Kong dollars; two million, American. They don't seem to have anything close."

"Could they raise it?"

"I suppose they could borrow against Steven's share of the business. They'd need the uncle's permission, but he'd give it. But I talked to a banker I know, gave it to her as a hypothetical situation. She said it would be hard to borrow until the will's probated. Steven doesn't really own anything yet. Anyone who was looking for that kind of money would have done better to wait."

"It's strange," I sighed, sitting back in my chair. "The timing on everything involved in this is just wrong."

"Probably not," said Bill. "It's probably right; we just don't know what it's right for."

We drank our drinks, finishing them in silence.

"There's something I want to do now," I finally said. "Just a little thing, but as long as we're here."

So, after a brief squabble over the bill which Mark won, we all set off.

I was, as I'd told Mark, adapting. And one thing I knew by now was that there'd be an elegant, small, expensive jewelry store somewhere in the corridors of any grand hotel.

We found it with no trouble, a tiny storefront sandwiched between a shop selling Italian leather wallets and keycases and one selling extravagantly wrapped boxes of chocolates and marzipan fruits. The jewelry store's windows featured pearls, on long strands where each pearl was identical to the others in color and size, in earrings where rubies surrounded them, in brooches where pearl-bodied fish blew diamond bubbles as they swam between strands of twenty-four-karat seaweed. They all shone with that sharp, brighter-than-sunlight glow that Bill had attributed to high-intensity lighting, but I was sure had at least something to do with the nature of jewels themselves.

A bell rang as we entered the shop, and a young man in gold-rimmed glasses and a quietly expensive suit put away his calculator and came forward to greet us. His eyes swept our little party, and then, coming to a decision, he addressed us in British-accented English. He took care to include us all, because it wan't obvious at first glance which of these gentlemen might be planning to buy me some little pearl fish.

"Good afternoon," he said. "May I help you? Have you had tea?"

"Yes, thank you," I answered. "We've just finished." I didn't want to start with the whole tea business; we weren't planning to buy anything, and we had other things to do. "I'd like to ask you something, if I may."

"Of course." He smiled at the others and turned his at-

tention politely to me, slightly surprised at the lack of sub-
tlety involved in my dealing directly with him, but wanting
to make sure we understood his willingness to work within
the current world order, whatever it was. I was a little disappointed to see that his glasses glittered with the same
bright glint as the jewels in the window. Bill might be on
to something, after all.

"My grandfather," I said, "has always worn a jade pendant, a carved Buddha. Something like the one you have
here." I pointed to a velvet-covered tray in the glass display
case. "It's about three hundred years old and valued at one
hundred thousand dollars, Hong Kong dollars. He bought
it in Hong Kong twenty-five years ago. Since I arrived in
Hong Kong I've seen others, like yours—" He slid open
the back of the case and withdrew the velvet tray, placing
it on the counter, in case what I'd come to do was buy
another one. "—but they're all new." As he lifted the pale
green Buddha by its golden chain and placed it in my hand
it seemed the least I could do to add, "Some of them are
beautiful, of course."

The young man smiled, and looked from Bill to Mark,
to make sure they both noticed how much I liked this piece.

"What I was wondering was how rare a piece like my
grandfather's is," I said. "I mean, something that old. If I
wanted to buy one like it in Hong Kong now, could I?"

The young man pursed his lips as he considered my
question, and some way to answer it that would end with
me walking out of here wearing the laughing Buddha I right
now held in my hand.

"Yes, it would be possible," he answered me. "Pieces of
that age are rare but not unknown. Hong Kong has a number of shops that deal in those items. Here, of course, we
only carry unique pieces, designed and made for us. A customer purchasing a piece here can be assured that he—or
she," he interjected with a smile, "—is the first to own it."

Good move, I thought, bringing up that first-owner
thing. There's a risk involved in buying old things, if you
don't know whose they were. They might come with some

karma you don't need, left over from the previous owner.

Smiling to acknowledge his consideration for the spiritual life of his customers, I asked, "Where do those pieces come from? The old ones, I mean? Hong Kong people who don't want them anymore?"

"Most will come from local collectors, or old families," he said, almost visibly disappointed that I hadn't risen to the new-and-unique-piece bait. "Others, despite the laws, are imported from China. Many antiquities were destroyed during the Cultural Revolution, but many were hidden and preserved. Now all China wants to be like Hong Kong, so China's treasures are being sold abroad. The government disapproves and tries to stop the trade, but who was it who said 'To be rich is glorious'?"

The answer to that was Deng Xiao-Ping, but it wasn't a real question, so I moved on.

"So if I wanted a piece like my grandfather's," I asked, "I could find it in Hong Kong?"

"Yes," he acknowledged. "You could."

I smiled again as we thanked him and left, because he clearly wasn't about to tell me where.

We stood, Mark and Bill and I, in the carpeted corridor of the Furama, surrounded by expensive shops and hushed sounds. "Well, guys," I said, "what now?"

Mark said, "I want to drop in on L. L. Lee."

"His shop will be open on Sunday?"

Mark nodded. "In the afternoon. If he's not there, I'll go up to his place. I always wanted to see it anyway."

"His place is famous?"

"He lives along Harlech Road, on the Peak. They say he has some of his most valuable antiquities up there, in the house and the gardens. A lot of the houses on the Peak have gates, but Lee's gates have two Ming lions just inside them, to keep the riffraff out." Mark grinned. "No cop's ever gotten past the lions."

I was about to ask him if Bill and I could come along, when a cell phone rang.

Bill's hand went to his jacket pocket, Mark's to his belt,

mine to my bag. When all the phones were out and opened, Mark won.

"Wai!" Then a brief silence, during which Bill and I put our phones away. In his American-accented Cantonese, Mark asked a few questions, listened to the response, and in a voice of resignation told them he'd be right there. He folded his phone up and said, "Damn."

"What is it?" I asked.

"I'm not on duty," he said, "but I'm on call. We rotate as backup in case the guys on duty are out taking care of something when something else comes in. Usually it doesn't, but it just did. A floater in the harbor." He shook his head ruefully. "Some poor fisherman gets drunk and falls out of his sampan, call Quan. The 14K and the Wo Shing Wo hold a shoot-out on Queen's Road, make sure Quan's got some fisherman who fell out of his sampan to keep him busy."

"Does this mean there's about to be a shoot-out on Queen's Road?"

"No. But it means I've got to go deal with this. I'll call you as soon as I can."

So Mark Quan left us in the middle of the lobby of the Furama Hotel, heading back out along the same bridge Bill and I had come in from. I watched him walk away, with his loose, easy stride; then I turned to Bill.

"Tang dynasty horses," I said, "are beautiful clay sculptures. I saw some at the Met once, in a show from the museum in Taiwan. Did you go to that show?"

"Yes."

"Then you know what I mean. And don't you feel a need to see those horses again?"

He looked at me. "I do," he said. "And soon."

"Well, if you really feel that way, I understand there's a dealer up on Hollywood Road who handles them."

"I think I've heard about him. L. L. Lee?"

"That's who I had in mind."

"Good," Bill said. "Let's go."

nine

I unfolded my map of the Hong Kong Island side and perused it. "If we go that way," I said, pointing out the hotel window, "and walk along that road, we'll get to the escalator." I headed to the staircase down to the ground floor.

"We'll get to what escalator?" Bill asked, following along.

"The one that runs up the hill."

"Oh, *that* escalator."

I glanced over at him. "You're clueless, aren't you?"

"Only a little."

"You should have read the guidebooks to find out all the stuff that happened here in the last twenty years. They have an outdoor escalator that runs up the whole side of the mountain. To solve the traffic problem, all those people living up there and working downtown. It runs downhill in the morning and uphill in the afternoon and at night."

Bill raised his eyebrows in acknowledgement of my superior erudition. Taking a breath, I plowed out from the air-conditioned hotel into the damp hot day and led the way superiorly along the avenue, wading through the ocean of young Filipina women. By the time we'd gone a few blocks, their numbers had thinned, reduced to small groups here and there in the shade, tide pools and rivulets the sea had left behind.

I turned us left off the avenue up a shortcut alley too narrow for the sun to penetrate, though I didn't notice it being any cooler in the shade. Bill stopped and bought us plastic cups of fresh-squeezed watermelon juice from a storefront juiceman, and from the shadows of doorways children and adults watched us drink it. We glugged it down and turned right at the end of the alley, walked another block, and there was the escalator.

Superior knowledge notwithstanding, the first sight of

the thing was breathtaking. It had an aluminum canopy for a roof, but it had no sides, and mostly it wasn't really an escalator, it was a series of moving walkways like at the airport, except inclined. And it went on up the hill for a mile, carried at second-story height above the streets on steel columns, very close to the buildings on one side, with staircases down from it every couple of blocks so you could get on or get off.

"Very clever," Bill said, "these Chinese."

We climbed the stairs and joined everyone else, part of the slow-moving stream of people floating past the windows of upstairs dentists' offices, dingy small factories, used bookstores, apartments. I could have leaned over and grabbed a teapot from a kitchen windowsill, or a potted plant from a balcony. Some of the places we drifted by had rice-papered their windows, and one or two offices in newer buildings used clouded glass; but mostly, the goings-on within the walls at ten, fifteen, twenty feet above the sidewalk were as open to our view as the things that happened at street-level would be anywhere else.

I stared as we rode by, trying to take in the lives of all these people: the dentist picking up his drill while from the chair the patient watched his every move; the frowning lathe operator oiling a recalcitrant gear; the student turning pages in her textbook. Little old ladies made tea, middle-aged men read the newspaper, children crawled on the floor in tiny kitchens and bedrooms, all on top of each other, and me and Bill and thousands of other moving people practically in their laps. Because of the traffic below and the escalator machinery and the Sunday jackhammer shift filling the air, you couldn't hear anything from inside these places, but you could see. I wondered if some of the moving people peered into some of the same apartments and businesses day after day, if it became like a soap opera you watched for half a minute in the morning and again in the evening, and you had to figure out what had happened in between for yourself.

"We can't go in together," I said to Bill as we came to

the end of the last walkway we needed, about halfway up. We stepped from it to the platform at the top of the stairs.

"To Lee's?" he asked.

"In case Franklin's told him about us. About Grandfather Gao's emissaries. Two individual Americans out shopping, no problem. But as a pair we're a little unmistakable."

"Granted. So how do you want it?"

"Me first. Give me a few minutes, then come on in."

"What are we looking for?"

"I have no idea."

"Oh," he said. "Well, I'm good at that."

We headed down to the sidewalk.

Hollywood Road ran perpendicular to the escalator, a curving, one-way, hilly street lined on both sides with shops famous for antiquities, carpets, old furniture, and quality reproductions. In most of central Hong Kong, the shop signs were in both English and Chinese. It was like that here on Hollywood Road, and because this merchandise was high-end, the English words were the big and flashy ones.

Getting from one side of Hollywood Road to the other, I realized, was going to be a major challenge, given the speed and density of the traffic, even on Sunday. We had to do it, though, because the address of L. L. Lee Oriental Antiques put it a few hundred yards west of us, on the other side of the street.

"I needed that," I said to Bill as I leapt onto the opposite curb, ignoring the blasting of horns and the curses of drivers. I straightened my shirt and smoothed my hair. Bill had arrived a few seconds before me, having taken advantage of a lumbering truck to stride across the street while I was staring into the window of a carpet store.

"Needed what?"

"That adrenaline rush. Fights jet lag, you know."

"I'll remember that."

"No, you won't."

"I would if I weren't jet-lagged. Okay, you have ten minutes."

I wiped the sweat from my forehead and headed down
the street to L. L. Lee Oriental Antiques. When I reached
the storefront I stood for a moment, just to look.

L. L. Lee's shop was narrower than some of the others
I'd passed. Like them it had a glass door and a glass show
window; but here the painted screen just inside the door
and the two large red lacquered armoires standing in the
show window blocked the shop's interior from the street.
The only way to find out what made up L. L. Lee's world
was to step inside it.

So I did.

The heavy glass door, as it shut behind me, totally silenced the horns and the tires and the jackhammers, refused
entrance to the dust and the glaring sun and the hot sticky
air: a miracle of modern building technology, transparent
to the eye, opaque to the ear. I'd have to ask Bill later, I
thought, how they did that.

I stepped around the screen with its peonies and pines,
and I stopped. The shop was unnaturally quiet, not only for
Hong Kong, but for any place I'd been, anywhere with cars
outside and radios in the next room and people talking on
the sidewalk. In old China, homes faced inward, solid walls
to the street and your neighbors, windows and doors and
columned walkways opening onto your own shady courtyard. The rooms in those houses might have been like this:
cool and quiet and rich, perfumed with the mingled smells
of sandalwood and camphorwood, incense and leather. In
those houses the generations lived together, and the ghosts
of the dead never left.

I started forward, trying to shake the feeling of being
uninvited, an intruder in someone's courtyard home. I
looked around me, at the past. Red bridal cabinets painted
with idyllic scenes of arched bridges and willow trees stood
next to teakwood trunks, below shelves crowned with
scrollwork. Square chairs lacquered red like the cabinets sat
patiently under elaborately carved tables, waiting for someone to come and contemplate the clay and bronze sculptures
resting on every surface. Painted scrolls of misty moun-

tains, spotted with the red chops of owners through the centuries announcing to later generations each one's approval of the work, hung on a dark red wall. On a shelf I spotted my Tang dynasty horses, four of them, little fat ponies with simple saddles, their heads turned slightly left as though they'd just noticed you and hoped you wanted to go for a ride.

In pools of lamplight and in the shadows between them, each piece of dark wood furniture, each clay or bronze figure that crowded the narrow shop seemed to be dwelling still in the age that produced it.

Gazing at this and that, wondering about the ages of paper and bronze and clay, the lives they had led, I had worked my way deep into the shop. I was inspecting a bronze temple bell, cool and heavy to the touch, when my eye caught a movement in the shadows. I turned. High on the back wall, near a latticework cabinet lined with ginger jars and cricket cages, smudges of smoke floated from incense sticks at a small altar. Beneath was a low opening surrounded by a deep and heavily carved wood frame, probably originally a temple entrance, of an age I could only imagine. In the opening's dimness I could just make out a slender shape, a man, unmoving, draped in loose cloth. It might have been an ancient monk, come to learn who was approaching the temple precincts. Motionless, he regarded me as I stood in this room, all of bright hot noisy Hong Kong beyond the door behind me, the shadowy, unfamiliar past enveloping me from walls, shelves, floor and tables, crowding me close.

Unexpectedly, I shivered; it must be that Hong Kong too-cold air-conditioning, though it didn't seem very cold in here.

The figure in the doorway didn't move. Neither did I. The scent of the incense drifting around me was sweet and familiar: It was the type Grandfather Gao used, in his orderly, quiet shop on the other side of the world. A memory of a time many years ago in that shop came to me, an image seen as through a vanishing of smoke: myself, lifting the lid of a porcelain jar as big as I was, standing on tiptoe to see its contents. My mother, embarrassed, scolding, uselessly ordering me to be still. And Grandfather Gao calmly reassuring my exasperated mother that my endless activity and inability to sit still were not a worry: "A person moving fast enough will come to be everywhere at once. Finally, being everywhere, she will find no need to move at all." As a child I'd known that wasn't true and I'd giggled at how silly this dignified old man could be. Now, looking at this indistinct, unmoving figure in a dim Hong Kong shop, I wondered whether, as usual, Grandfather Gao had meant much more than he'd said.

For once motionless myself, I returned the gaze of the cloth-draped form. A few more silent moments passed; then he took a step through the doorway. My heart skipped. He moved forward, stopping in front of me in a circle of yellow lamplight. He revealed himself to be a thin elderly man, his gray hair cut very short, his monk's robes resolving into a dark silk tunic and pants of the old style. Really, Lydia, I thought, ordering my heart back to normal. An ancient monk. Please.

The old man didn't smile and his eyes didn't leave me as he said formally, "Welcome to my shop." He spoke in Cantonese. I smiled with more ease than I felt and answered him.

"Thank you," I said. "Are you Mr. Lee?"

He folded one hand over the other and held them out to me, bowing in the Chinese manner.

"I'm afraid my Cantonese is poor," I went on, trying to put a lot of New York into my words. "Do you speak English?"

That, of course, was for Bill's benefit, for when he got here.

"If you prefer," Mr. Lee answered, unruffled, in clear, precise English. Gazing directly at me, he asked, "Is there something in particular which you wished to see?"

I had the disconcerting feeling that that was not the question to which he wanted an answer. Determined to act as

S. J. ROZAN

though this were a normal shopping expedition, I smiled
again and said, "I'm in Hong Kong visiting my brother,
and I wanted to get him a gift." I spoke apologetically. "I
know he likes antiques, but I don't know anything about
them. All these different things." Mr. Lee's face was impassive. I turned to a shelf. "But these horses, for example.
How could anyone not love them? They're so charming.
And those figures—tell me about them." I pointed to two
flat-fronted little bronze men at a bronze table, tiny wine
cups and game pieces on the gameboard between them.

L. L. Lee held my eyes another moment; then, ignoring
the Tang ponies as though we both knew I already knew
all about them, he reached over, lifted the tray the men and
their table were set on and slowly turned it so I could see
them from all sides. "Good friends sharing the pleasures of
the day," he said quietly. "From the Zhou period. They will
bring harmony to any household."

"And those ink washes?" I asked. "The waterfall, and
the pool, over there."

"They are Yuan," he said. "A single stream, in motion
and at rest. It is not usual," his black eyes returned to me
once more, "to encounter an American of such discernment.
Your countrymen usually prefer court embroidery, or the
furniture of Tibet: large things, brightly colored. Have you
had tea?"

"I'm parched," I said. "Thank you."

"Please give me a moment." He vanished into the back.
I could hear the delicate clink of cups on a tray, the soft
whoosh of water flowing from kettle to pot. He returned
with tray, cups, pot, before I could do more than glance at
the paperwork on his desk in an attempt to do I don't know
what.

L. L. Lee, with hands long, pale, and clean, pointed me
into a black-lacquered chair in front of his scholar's desk.
Latticework railings sharply guarded the desk's corners so
ink pots and brushes wouldn't fall off, but there were no
rails at the back or sides so the scrolls as they were worked
on, whether horizontal or vertical, would not run the risk

of being crumpled. On L. L. Lee's desk sat a set of traditional scholar's tools: brush holder with brushes, some soft and round, some thin and sharp-looking, one with no more than three fine badger's-hair bristles at its tip; inkstone and grinding stone; water dish; brush rest. Everything was carved and worked: The brush holder was a mountainside, the water dish a gourd. Even the inkstone itself, waiting to be ground into powder, mixed with water, and applied to that most transient of artists' materials, paper, bore the molded character for longevity.

L. L. Lee poured tea into small white cups with blue flowers on them. "So you have come to Hong Kong from America to visit your brother?" he asked as he handed a cup to me. "A long journey."

I took up my cup, marveling at its smoothness of glaze, its perfection of shape, its translucency even in the cool dimness. How many reclusive scholars, gregarious court officials, rich merchants' wives over how many centuries had sipped tea from the cup I held in my hands right now?

"Not so long," I said. "If it's to see your family."

Mr. Lee nodded. "Again, an unusual sentiment from an American. Americans," he went on, though I had been about to speak, "largely look forward, into the future. They seem to rarely care about the past. They come to Hong Kong not to understand, only to buy: to buy cloth, to buy antiquities, to buy pearls and jade. And Hong Kong is only too eager to accommodate them. Even," he said, sipping his tea, "when they come to buy entire commercial firms."

Commercial firms. "Is that so?" I murmured, lifting my own tea to my lips.

"In most cases." L. L. Lee replied. He sipped unhurriedly from his cup. "On occasion, though rarely in Hong Kong, other values prevail. To take one case, an import-export firm with which I have some dealings has recently learned an American concern wishes to acquire them."

"Really," I responded politely. "Does the firm wish to be . . . acquired?"

"The Hong Kong firm is a family business; I do not

believe they will sell. And it would be a bad business proposition for the Americans. Owning a Hong Kong firm can
involve serious risk. Nor do I know," he went on, not interested in any answer I might make, "what value such a
small specialized firm could be to anyone. But it is hard to
dissuade Americans, once they have made up their minds.
Yourself, for example."

"Me?" I spoke calmly and returned his gaze, but it
wasn't easy.

He paused before answering, taking another sip of tea.
"You wish to purchase a gift for your brother," he said.
"Yet you do not know his taste, what he would prefer.
Perhaps it would have been better to spend time with your
brother, learning about him, about what things he considers
important. Possibly you would find a gift unnecessary, time
together being the greatest gift of all."

That was not, it seemed to me, a great way for a merchant to make a sale. I was at a loss as to what to say next;
I wasn't even sure what game we were playing. It was
obviously my turn, though, and I was about to take a stab
at it when to my immense relief the door at the front of the
shop opened, letting in a tidal wave of car horns and jackhammers and, just behind, a flood of swampy air.

I had never realized before just how fond I was of heat
and noise.

L. L. Lee looked up, then back at me. He rose from his
chair and spoke to the figure who had stepped around the
painted screen at the front of the store. "Welcome to my
shop. Will you have tea?"

The figure moved toward us, to where I didn't have to
twist around to see him, though I'd known from his sil-
houette, from the way he walked, that it was Bill. I felt a
wash of gratitude just to see his modern-day polo shirt,
never mind his face. As he stepped closer, the incense still
swirled, the lamplight still glowed, and silence was restored
with the click of the latch. Only now it was less the stillness
of the air of old China, more the quiet of a softly lit shop
with a thick front door.

"Perdoname?" Bill said to Mr. Lee. With a start I realized he was speaking Spanish. Well, that would make it
less likely that Lee would identify us with each other. Except I had a feeling it was too late to put one over on L. L.
Lee.

"Please join us for tea," Mr. Lee said again, his long
fingers indicating the tea service on the tray.

Bill said, "Ah." His glance and his smile took in the
scholar's desk, the cups and pot, Mr. Lee and me. "Gracias,
no. Please do not let me disturb you." He had switched to
Spanish-accented English, not heavy, just enough to convince. His smile was soft, and even the set of his shoulders
was a Latin slouch, radiating a connoisseur's appreciation
of life's finer things and a refusal to rush. He leaned over
a three-story pagoda-roofed pottery building with little
chickens and goats in its courtyard.

"Very well. If there is anything you wish in particular
to see, please let me know," Mr. Lee offered formally.

Bill, smiling gallantly, looked directly at me. "Bueno,"
he said. "If the lady will not object, perhaps just
briefly—?"

"Go right ahead," I said, putting on my most gracious
self. I sipped at my tea to hide my mixture of gratitude and
annoyance. The gratitude came from Bill engaging Mr. Lee,
giving me a few moments to recover from whatever it was
that had made me founder, feel so lost, in this dim shop.
The annoyance was because I knew that was why he was
doing it, the same as he had touched my hand at the Weis'
when I had felt like I was floating up there in the sky.

Mr. Lee, with a nod to me, approached his new customer.

Bill removed the building's roof to peer inside. "Exquisite," he murmured as Mr. Lee reached his side. I smiled
to myself; it was rare to hear Bill murmur. "Burial art, yes?"

"Han dynasty," Mr. Lee responded. "Almost complete."
Bill lifted the top story off the house, then set it carefully
down again. I hadn't known the things came apart.

"Almost complete?" he inquired.

"In the courtyard," Mr. Lee pointed a slender finger, "a pond, but no ducks. Surely there were once ducks. If such things concern you, I have another, complete, but not as finely crafted." He reached another, smaller building off a shelf, though his tone had clearly said that if such things *did* concern Bill then he wasn't half the customer Mr. Lee had thought him to be.

Bill admired the second house, then turned his attention back to the first, which, I thought, must please Mr. Lee, if anything ever pleased Mr. Lee. They had a brief conversation. Some of it I caught ("Old Hong Kong families, or Taiwanese; this, two brothers, Persian traders," as Mr. Lee picked up the little bronze game-players I had liked); most of it I ignored in favor of trying once again to read, upside down and in Cantonese, the papers on Mr. Lee's desk.

That attempt got me about as nowhere as it had the first time, and after another exchange or two with Bill, Mr. Lee returned to the desk, sat again, and poured me more tea. Bill continued to study my little bronze game-players, picking them up and examining them closely. Bill knows a lot more about art than I do, so I felt quite clever for having noticed them first.

"About my gift for my brother," I began to Mr. Lee, feeling able to hold a normal conversation once again. "Hong Kong has produced so many beautiful things. Will you help me choose?"

"Hong Kong has produced none of these things," L. L. Lee said coldly. "All of these beautiful things, which you admire so greatly but know nothing about, were made in China, in the past. Hong Kong, like America, cares nothing about the past except how to sell it."

If L. L. Lee spoke to all his customers this way, I thought, no wonder his shop was so crowded. He probably hadn't sold an antiquity since, well, since the past.

I sipped my tea, searching for something to say. I was saved by, literally, the bell. From the cell phone in my bag came an attention-demanding chirp.

"Oh!" I said, trying to hide my relief. "Excuse me." I took out the phone, opened it up. "Hello?"

"It's Mark," said the voice in my ear. "Where are you?"

"Up on Hollywood Road," I said, with an apologetic smile at Mr. Lee. I felt Bill move closer to me, still leaning over, looking at bronzes. "I'm shopping."

"Oh, my God," Mark said. "You went to L. L. Lee's, didn't you?"

"Of course. I'll be meeting you later, I hope?"

"We'd better. I wanted to tell you about the floater in the harbor. It's not some drunk fisherman. It's Iron Fist Chang."

"Oh," I said, while Mr. Lee sipped tea and looked into a distance I couldn't see. "Oh, my. Well, that is a surprise. What's he been up to?"

"No way to know. But he was beaten, his hands were tied behind him, and he drowned. They've got him down at the morgue now for the autopsy, but I don't think *how* he died is the big question here."

"Well, I don't want to be rude"—Mr. Lee, across the desk, flicked his eyes back to me and made a small gesture with his elegant hand, denying that I was being rude at all—"so let me call you later."

"Are you talking to Lee? Does he have any idea why you're there?"

"Of course not, silly."

I could hear him blow out a breath; I wasn't sure if it was in relief or exasperation. "I want you here, now."

Suddenly Mark Quan sounded like a cop. I looked at my watch. "Well . . ."

"Now."

Uh-huh. "I guess I could do that," I said. "Sounds like fun. You're at your office?"

"Yes. You know where it is? The Main HQ Building, in Wan Chai."

"Sure. Okay, I'll be right over. See you soon. Bye." I folded the phone and smiled at L. L. Lee again. "I'm so sorry. My brother. He ran into an old friend of ours down by the harbor and couldn't wait to tell me about it. He took him up to show him his office and he wants me to go meet them for a late lunch." I stood, and Mr. Lee did, too. "I hadn't even gotten started shopping, either. I'll have to come back. Thank you so much for the tea."

L. L. Lee stood and bowed. I excused myself as I brushed by Bill. He moved chivalrously aside for me, then recommenced his study of yet another clay building with dogs and children in the yard. As I pulled open the heavy glass door to rejoin the dust and noise and palpable sunshine of Hong Kong, I felt L. L. Lee's eyes on my back. I scolded myself for even thinking they pressed like the weight of the past.

I watched Hollywood Road for a good ten minutes, sweating at my vantage point at the top of the escalator stairs, before Bill came ambling along. Because of the bend in the road you couldn't see this place from L. L. Lee's door, so I felt safe trotting down the steps and meeting Bill on the sidewalk.

"This is east," he pointed out as he reached me.

Bill and I have this thing we do when we're separated while we're working. Whoever can leave heads north a block or two from the last place we were together and waits in some likely spot until the other one comes along. On Hong Kong's twisty streets, though, there was a problem. "I wasn't sure which way was north," I said, maybe a little defensively. "But this worked."

"Because your mind is transparent to me."

I sighed. "Or just plain transparent. He's on to us."

Bill stopped in the middle of lighting a cigarette. "Lee? Is that why you left? The phone call wasn't real?"

"No, I was just getting warmed up. If he's on to us and he didn't throw me out, I figured he must have something to say. I was waiting to hear it, even though he's about as confusing as Grandfather Gao. But that was Mark who called."

"That's what I thought." By way of explanation he

added, "You didn't sound surprised enough for it to have been anybody else."

"Actually I was surprised, but not because it was him." I told Bill what Mark had told me.

Bill drew deeply on his cigarette, breathed smoke out into the hazy Hong Kong air. "Shit," he said. A heavy truck lumbering around the corner scattered a group of pedestrians about to cross the street. Everyone briefly yelled at everyone in Cantonese, and then the truck driver drew his head back into the cab and everyone moved on.

Bill and I moved on too. The sidewalk took a drop steep enough to turn it into steps. People passed us in both directions, young women laughing together, a middle-aged couple arm-in-arm, an elderly woman laboring uphill with a tiny baby on her back. "Shit," Bill said again.

He doesn't usually use those words around me. I thought about the weight I'd seen lifting from him while we were drinking tea at the Furama Hotel. This time I touched his hand, just briefly. For a short time as we walked neither of us spoke and there was nothing to hear but cars shifting gears as they strained up the hill, footsteps, conversations, children laughing, a baby crying.

Bill finished his cigarette and tossed it away. "How do you know Lee knows who we are?" he asked.

"He told me some Americans are interested in buying out a family-run import-export firm he does business with, and what a bad idea it is," I said. "He said it could be risky."

"It was a threat?"

"Oh, I think so."

Stepping aside for a woman using a flowered umbrella as a parasol against the unrelenting sun, Bill said, "So Lee does business with Lion Rock."

"He's got to get that furniture from somewhere."

"Umm. That may be how Franklin connected with him in the first place, to set this up with. If it's Franklin who set it up."

"Why else would he have called Lee from New York?"

Bill shook his head. I looked at him, but his eyes were fixed on the glitter of the harbor, below.

I said, "And I guess Lee heard about us from Tony and Big John, last night."

"Probably. They're Strength and Harmony, he's Strength and Harmony. But," Bill said, still watching the water, "that was just your cover story, about buying Lion Rock. It might not be so bad to have him believing that. Do you suppose he knows anything else?"

"You mean, who we really are? If he and Franklin are working together, Franklin would have told him about Grandfather Gao's emissaries. If he did, it has to be obvious to Lee that we're the same people. Or at least," I amended, "that I'm the same person. He probably thinks you're the Duke of Plaza-Toro."

"Uh-huh. In other words, waste of effort, that cover."

"Well," I said, "it was nice, anyway."

"Thanks." He was silent for a few moments. "But he may not know we're investigators," he said. "Just that we came from Grandfather Gao. Because Franklin may not know that."

"That's true. In which case let him keep believing we represent someone who wants to buy Lion Rock. Keep him distracted."

"Well, but here's another question: Why do you think he cares?"

"About someone buying Lion Rock?" I considered the question. "He doesn't like Americans?"

"Americans have been all over Hong Kong for a hundred and fifty years, doing all kinds of business. Including buying up firms. Including buying up the antiques Lee sells. It's a hell of a rear-guard action to try and stop the sale of one little import-export operation, if it's just that he doesn't like Americans."

"Well, maybe he's afraid that new owners would change his relationship with Lion Rock. Raise the prices, or start importing lower-grade stuff."

"I'd like to know just what his relationship with Lion

Rock is. Why he's got at least one guy working there."

"You mean Tony."

He nodded. "And for all we know, three—Big John and Iron Fist could be Strength and Harmony, too."

"I get the feeling," I said, "that we're about to find out more about Iron Fist than we wanted to know."

A little farther down the hill we came to a main street. We hailed a cab and I told it where to take us.

"We should we call the Weis, don't you think?" I asked as the cab lurched into traffic. "Not to tell them about any of this, but to see if they've heard anything."

So I took out my cell phone and did that. Although we both had the feeling that if anything good had happened, the Weis would have called us.

Nothing had happened.

After Steven Wei's predictably loud and anxious, *"Wai!"* I identified myself, told him I was calling just to see if things had changed.

"No," he said, and I imagined his heartbeat slowly returning to normal as he sank dispiritedly into a chair. "No one has contacted us. I don't know what to think."

I offered my sympathy, which he seemed sadly grateful to have. Then, because I thought she'd get suspicious if I just hung up, I asked to speak to Natalie Zhu.

"Natalie is not here," Steven told me.

That was a bit of a surprise. "She's gone out?"

"Early this morning. And since then she has called to say she would be detained, and to expect her later this afternoon."

"Where did she go?"

"She had business with another client that could not be put off."

On a Sunday? When there's a kidnapped kid whose parents you've put yourself in charge of?

"There was nothing she could do here in any case," Steven Wei added. I thought maybe I heard in his voice relief that he was, for just a while, alone with his wife. Or maybe I was projecting.

"Nothing," I told Bill when I hung up. "Except Natalie
Zhu went out. To take care of some business, another client
who couldn't wait."

"Really?"

"Fact or opinion?"

"Fact."

"That's what Steven said."

"Opinion."

"Not likely."

"You think whatever she's doing has something to do
with this case?"

"I think wild horses couldn't have pulled her out of that
apartment if it didn't."

The main headquarters building of the Hong Kong Police
Department, back down the hill and not far from the water,
looked like any other Hong Kong skyscraper. An expanse
of gray-blue glass, midday sun glinting off it, faced an avenue of roaring traffic. Our cab screeched to a halt at the
curb and bounced forward and back while I peeled off bills
for the fare. Inside the building, the usual too-cool air-
conditioning greeted us like an old friend. Not so the stone-
faced police officer at the front desk, who inquired after
our business in a way that implied that whatever we said
was probably a ruse his vigilance would get to the bottom
of. I explained our names and our mission in Cantonese to
see if it would soften him up. It didn't, but a curt phone
call upstairs got us visitor badges and a grudging explanation of where to find the elevator and what floor to get
off on.

Mark Quan was waiting for us when the elevator
opened. He wore a gold badge on his belt and an automatic
in a shoulder holster. He said nothing except, "Come this
way," so we followed him through a blue-carpeted warren
of office partitions. At scattered desks uniformed and plainclothes cops, mostly Chinese, a few Westerners, mostly
men, a few women, typed on computer keyboards, drank
from mugs, and insulted each other with the same offhand

ease you'd see at the Fifth Precinct on Elizabeth Street, back home. They looked up when we passed, saw we had a cop with us, and went back to what they'd been doing. We were another cop's case, another cop's problem.

We stopped at a glass-walled conference room on the window side of a corridor. Mark Quan pushed the door open and held it. I hoped he would give us a map to find our way back to the elevator when we were through. I moved past him into the room, noticing the scent of his aftershave: green and citrusy, not a bit perfumed, but fresh as morning. I wasn't really surprised that I noticed. I'm a detective; noticing details is my job. I was a little surprised, though, that Mark Quan had so clearly just shaved, in the early afternoon.

I crossed to the window. Below us, water sparkled and ferries plowed and sampans bobbed and yatchs both under sail and under power skimmed across the harbor to the outlying islands for a Sunday picnic. A regatta was going on far off on the horizon, small boats with bright-striped sails all swooping together this way and that like a flock of birds. Beyond the harbor, Kowloon's gray buildings shimmered in the heat and its round hills blurred into the blue of the distant sky.

Mark pointed Bill and me to chairs and we sat in them, with him across the table. Our backs were to the window and Mark faced it, the brightness of the Hong Kong afternoon lighting his face. That was a good sign, I thought: If he were really mad and wanted to show us who was boss, the first thing he'd do is put us facing the window, so we'd be the ones who had to squint.

Mark looked from me to Bill, then asked, "You want some tea?"

"I just had some," I said, and in the spirit of full disclosure added, "with L. L. Lee."

"Great," Mark said. He turned to Bill. "You?"

"You have coffee?"

"No, but the tea's so old you might not be able to tell the difference."

"No, thanks."

I said, "This is where you tell us we're trouble, right? Or, *in* trouble?"

Mark shook his head. "Pointless. And not true." He picked up a pencil, one of six set carefully around the table next to six ruled pads. The HKPD, ready for anything. "I'm the one in trouble."

"You are? Why?"

"Well, not yet. I probably have twenty-four hours. After that people will start asking why I haven't cleared the Chang case yet."

"Iron Fist? You work that fast here?"

"We don't do wholesale homicide in Hong Kong. Murder is a retail business here. They expect us to be efficient with it." He bounced the pencil on the polished table. "I'm supposed to be out pounding the streets already. You don't get a lot of chances like this on this Department. Every other cop in the joint is jealous. I mean, I wasn't even on duty, just on call." He couldn't suppress a quick grin, the look of a man whose lemons had turned to lemonade all by themselves. "But," he said, "I stumble, they take it away from me." He lifted his eyes to the window. From where he sat he could see the gray buildings, the hills, China. He looked once more at us. "I don't want to lose this chance."

He threw the pencil down and leaned back in his chair. "But," he said again, "I go out and look around, I guarantee I won't be more than ten minutes on the street before someone tells me Chang worked at Lion Rock. I run across Tony Siu there, I have to pick him up because he's known. Between Siu and old man Wei, someone's going to tell me something I can't ignore. And then we have what we didn't want: the Wei kidnapping public and the Department involved."

I looked at him, the Alabama-born cop with the American accent, a man surrounded by people who didn't want him to do, didn't think he could do well, the job he loved.

I said hopefully, "Maybe Iron Fist's murder has nothing to do with the kidnapping."

Mark and Bill both gave me looks, the looks I'd have given either one of them if they had suggested such a thing. Iron Fist had, after all, been at the temple. "Well," I forged on, "maybe Tony Siu doesn't know about the kidnapping, anyway. And maybe Wei Ang-Ran won't say anything, and you won't officially know."

Mark shook his head. "It'll still be obvious cops are poking around Lion Rock. That might scare the kidnappers, or piss them off because they'll think the family called us in. You heard from the Weis lately?"

"We just talked to them. They haven't heard anything from anyone."

"That's not good."

"No."

"Or," said Bill, "maybe it is."

Mark and I turned to him. "How?" I asked. "It sounds to me like nobody's calling because . . . something's gone wrong. Because nobody has anything to trade."

"Meaning Harry's dead," Bill said bluntly. "But maybe not. Maybe nobody ever had anything to trade."

"What are you saying?"

"Look at it," he said. "It's been screwy from the beginning. Us getting buzzed up. That park in the middle of the morning. Two demands, equally irrational. And no one willing to produce proof. What if neither of those people has the kid?"

"Then what's this about?" I said. "And where's Harry?"

"I don't know."

"You have a theory?" Mark asked.

"No. But if I had one, Maria Quezon would be at the middle of it."

I gave him a long look. "Even if she is," I said, "that doesn't mean everything's okay."

He returned my look. "Obviously," he said slowly, "everything's not okay. I'm just saying that maybe Harry is."

Maybe, I thought, maybe. I didn't want to say that, though. I wasn't sure what I did want to say, so I let my eyes have a chance, saying something to his. Mark waited.

Briefly, there was only silence and the sparkling of the harbor.

Then Bill moved his eyes from mine. In a straightforward, businesslike tone, he said, "But I do have a theory about something else."

He drew a cigarette from his pocket and looked at Mark. Mark shrugged and pointed behind Bill to an ashtray sitting guiltily on the windowsill. Bill leaned back and reached for it.

"Did you know L. L. Lee does business with Lion Rock?" Bill asked Mark, shaking his match out.

"He told you that?"

I didn't know where Bill was heading, but I gave Mark a brief outline of my conversation with L. L. Lee, finishing with Lee's advice about Lion Rock: "He pretty much warned me to stay away from the place."

A female cop in a uniform skirt hurried down the corridor, giving Mark a smile and a wave as she passed. He smiled back. Skirts were not flattering on cops, I decided. Mark said, "Well, I didn't know, but I'm not surprised. Lion Rock imports from China, Lee deals in Chinese antiquities."

"And Strength and Harmony has guys working at Lion Rock. Tony Siu and his buddy. And maybe Iron Fist," I said.

Mark shook his head. "Not Iron Fist. I did some checking with the Triad Task Force. Word is he wasn't bright enough, or he was too nice a guy, depending on if you're talking to his enemies or his friends. But Tony Siu definitely, and that other guy, Big John Chou. Chou's not management material like Siu, but he's an all-purpose thug. I wonder if Strength and Harmony runs a protection racket on Lion Rock?" he said thoughtfully. "Lee puts his bums inside, then gets some nice discount on his goods for keeping them in check? Maybe he was guarding his own turf when he warned you off."

Bill said, "I think he was guarding something else."

"What else?"

Bill shifted in his chair, recrossing his legs. "I had a good look at his shop," he said. "I don't know all that much about Chinese antiquities, but I've seen some of those things before. Particularly those clay buildings. They had some at a couple of museum shows over the last few years—that show from Taiwan," he said to me. I nodded; I'd seen them, though I didn't remember much about them. They were a little crude, a little somber, I thought: not nearly as appealing as my Tang horses. "And I know a gallery that shows them sometimes," Bill went on. "It took me awhile to dredge up what I know about them, but I have. They're what a friend of mine calls tomb trash."

This was a phrase I didn't know, and, I thought, an unattractive one. Mark was regarding Bill quizzically. Clearly the idea that Bill knew anything at all about Chinese antiquities had not crossed his mind. With me it was different. Though I've known him a long time now, there are still things about Bill that surprise me; but they're not the same things that surprise other people.

"Tomb trash?" Mark asked, and I chided myself for being secretly glad I wasn't the only ignorant person in the room.

"Otherwise called burial art, but not made as art," Bill said. "They're for graves. They go back about a thousand years. You buried them with people so they could have a home—and chickens and ducks and servants—in the next world."

Mark and I looked at each other. "We do that in paper now," I said. "Not bury things, burn them. Money, and houses. And," remembering my father's funeral, "clothes. And kitchen things." My father had been a chef, so my mother had bought and burned paper knives and a wok for him to use in the next world. And because he had never had a car but always wanted one, my oldest brother, Ted, had bought a red paper Ferrari, and burned that.

"So," I asked, "you're saying Mr. Lee's buildings were dug up out of graves?"

"They must have been. And some of the other things in his shop—those little game-players, say."

I thought of the happy little men at the table. "They sent friends along with you?"

"Everybody needs a friend," Bill said. "But the point is, if the things in Lee's shop are genuine, they're a thousand years old. And it's not legal to export them from China. Remember what the jeweler told us—this is a trade the government tries to stop?"

Mark and I were both silent a moment. Mark said slowly, "That's true. During the Cultural Revolution they couldn't smash things fast enough, the older the better. Now they've rediscovered them, and rediscovered that tourists will come to see them. The jeweler was right, you can't export antiquities now."

"But Lee's selling them in the open in his shop," I said. "How can it be legal to sell them here if it's illegal to export them from China?"

"It's legal to sell anything here," Mark answered. "Except drugs, and even that was legal once. If you can get it in, you can sell it or ship it out."

"But this is China, now. Don't the same restrictions apply?"

Mark shook his head. "Special Administrative Region."

"What does that mean?"

From Bill: "That means: whatever the capitalist running dog market will bear."

Mark agreed. "It's meant that for a hundred and fifty years, and they're making too much money to change the rules now. Customs here is supposed to stop goods that are illegal to export from the country of origin, but if they miss them, tough luck. Pro forma, Lee would have to have papers for his stuff, but it can't be very hard to forge those."

"What kind of papers?"

Bill, again: "Something that says the things he's selling have been floating around outside China for long enough that the government can't demand them back."

"Old family papers," said Mark. "Customs stamps from

eighty years ago. Bills of sale proving something was bought in Rangoon in 1953."

Bill said, "And I'm sure he does. I asked him where he got these things—who would give up such treasures, I wanted to know. Old Hong Kong families, he told me. Or Persian traders. Persian traders." He shook his head and Mark rolled his eyes. I gave a disbelieving snort, but no one noticed me.

"So," Mark said, "what you're saying is, L. L. Lee's goodies are newly coming out of China and someone's bringing them out for him."

"And who better to do that than an established import-export firm?"

"Lion Rock. In the furniture crates."

"In the furniture," Bill amended. "The buildings come apart." I thought of him in L. L. Lee's shop, lifting the roof off, removing the top story of the courtyard house. "All the pieces are relatively small," he said. "Tape them up in dark corners, slip them into drawers. Bribe an official now and then not to look too closely. If people are raiding graves, they're shipping out stuff there's no record of, so no one's going to be looking for it."

"Then when it gets here," Mark said, getting into the spirit of the thing, "Lion Rock bribes the customs people on this side to release the shipment quickly, without examining it much. This is Hong Kong, time is money, the respectable Wei brothers have customers waiting."

"And your customs people are probably preoccupied with drugs like everyone else," Bill said.

"They are. And if Lion Rock were bringing in drugs the Wei brothers would be a lot richer, and the bribes would be bigger. Any customs officer could see that."

"So," said Bill, "they move Lion Rock's stuff to the front of the line. They take a few extra bucks home and they don't have to start crowbarring crates."

"And they can get back to looking for the big drug bust that'll make their name."

It was time for me to elbow my way back into this con-

versation. "That would explain why Wei Ang-Ran shut the
warehouse door. And why Tony Siu was so unhappy with
Bill looking in the windows. Because they were unloading
the shipment from China."

Bill and Mark, as though they'd just remembered I was
in the room, looked at me and nodded. Okay, you guys are
so smart, I thought. "And?" I said. They both looked at me.
"So what does it mean?" I asked. "What about Harry?"

Smart guys. Neither of them had an answer to that.

"But," Mark said, "one thing it means is that I need to
talk to Wei Ang-Ran. I can't avoid it."

"You're going to Lion Rock?"

He thought. "No. I'll call him and ask him to come here.
'To assist with our inquiries.' A neat phrase we learned
from the Brits. That's what you guys are doing now, by
the way. And I want to ask you guys to do something else,
too."

"What's that?" I asked, although I had a feeling I knew.

"Except for staying in contact with the Weis, could you
back off? I have a homicide, maybe smuggling, possible
Triad involvement, an unreported kidnapping. What I don't
have is any way to explain it if you either screw things up
or get hurt."

"We won't—"

"But you might get hurt."

He grinned. I met his eyes and to my surprise felt my
cheeks warm up. Well, I thought, I've never been thrown
off a case so elegantly before.

I didn't want to agree. I didn't see how we could do
anything else. I didn't know exactly what to do.

Then, in the Hong Kong Police Department fifteenth
floor conference room above the blue and sparkling harbor,
Bill's cell phone rang.

ten

The phone's ring electrified the air. Just about everyone we knew in Hong Kong with Bill's number also had mine, and most of them were more likely to call me than him. Except one. Bill fumbled the phone from his pocket, flipped it open and barked, "Hello!"

Silence. Then Bill, leaning forward, took a breath and answered what had been said to him, calmly, softly, and in Tagalog.

I grabbed one of the HKPD's pencils and scribbled *Maria Quezon* on one of the yellow pads, showed it to Mark. I added, *Or her sister*. He nodded.

The next few minutes were hallucinatory: silence, alternating with Bill, someone I knew well, speaking a language I couldn't understand at all, in a glass-walled room with ships floating by in the harbor on one side and Chinese cops strolling through the corridor on the other. I didn't know what Bill was saying or hearing, whether this call was good or bad, whether everything would be all right now or just get worse.

I stayed still, close to Bill, in case he had a question or needed something. Mark pushed back his chair and went silently to the door, to keep out any stray cops with an urge to say hi. One thing about a cell phone: You don't know where you're calling. The last thing Maria Quezon or her sister needed to know was that Bill was in the cop house.

Occasionally, as the time went on, I caught a few English words, usually after Bill made a halting attempt to put something together in Tagalog, something he couldn't manage. His voice, even as he switched languages back and forth, remained calm and steady throughout: the tone you would use to talk a jumper down off a bridge. Unless you saw him, you wouldn't have known about the lines concentration was carving onto his face, the tension in his shoulders as he leaned forward in his chair, elbows on knees, eyes focused on the carpet.

The conversation lasted a few minutes if you asked my watch; if you asked me, it lasted years. An ocean liner crawled across the water, inching its way from the confines of the harbor out to the South China Sea.

Finally, after saying something that sounded no different in tone or meaning from anything else he'd said before, Bill listened for a few moments, then lowered the phone, thumbed the OFF button, and ran a hand over his face.

"Jesus," he breathed. He looked up at me. "That was Maria Quezon," he said, about as redundantly as I'd ever heard anyone say anything.

"What did she say?" I whispered. Mark, though he hadn't moved, seemed full of action, like a parked dynamite truck.

"She says Harry's all right."

Please, I thought, let it be true. "What happened? What's it about?"

"She wouldn't tell me."

"That whole time? What was she saying?"

"Some of that was me checking her out—I asked things about the Wei apartment, I asked what she knew about why we were here—and then when I was convinced it was really her, I had to convince her I was okay. She's scared, almost hysterical. That's why I kept speaking Tagalog—I figured she'd be most likely to trust me in it." He gave a rueful grin. "She speaks English."

"She does?"

"The Filipinas all do," Mark said, finally crossing the room. "Where is she?"

"I don't know," Bill answered. "But she wants to meet with me."

"Out of the question," said Mark.

Slowly, Bill brought his eyes to Mark. "It's not a question."

"She's the link to the kid," Mark said. "And a homicide

I have to assume is connected until someone proves otherwise. I can't let a civilian—"

"She said me, no one else. It was hard enough—"

"You can't—"

"You don't—"

"Wait!" I snapped at the two of them. "Before you start.
What did she *say*?"

Bill stood, partly to stretch, and partly, I'd have bet,
because Mark was standing already. What happened, I
wondered, to the buddy-movie, no-girls-allowed spirit of
ten minutes ago?

"She said Harry's all right," he repeated.

"He's with her?"

"She wouldn't tell me. She says he's still in danger.
She's claiming she didn't kidnap him, she rescued him, but
she's not bringing him back or telling anyone where he is
until she's sure it's safe." He looked out the window at the
ocean liner, barely visible now on the hazy horizon. "She
asked me to tell his parents he's okay."

"We'll do that," I said. "In a minute. Do you have the
feeling she's telling the truth?"

Mark shot me a look and seemed about to speak. This
was, after all, his turf; it wasn't my job to say what we
would do, or when. My eyes still on Bill, I waved my hand
to silence Mark. It would be absolutely unproductive if the
testosterone really started flying.

Bill looked at me. "That Harry's all right, yes. About
what happened and how much she had to do with it, I don't
know." He turned back to the window. "She wants to meet
me on a place called Cheung Chau, but I don't know if
that's where she is now. It's one of the outlying islands?"
He phrased that as a question and turned to Mark to ask it.
Maybe it was a peace offering, I thought, so I waited for
Mark's answer.

Mark hesitated. Then, "About an hour by ferry," he said.
The cop temporarily took over from the male beast chal-
lenged in his lair, and Mark pointed out the window to the
left. "Ferries every hour from here, twice a day from Lan-

tau. Or if you have a boat, or hire one, you can get there from anywhere: Kowloon, any of the other islands. She could be anywhere."

"She told me the three o'clock ferry." Bill looked at his watch.

"I can't let you do it."

"Look," Bill said, facing Mark squarely, "I could have not told you any of this. I could have said she was just making contact, then walked out of here and gotten that ferry. Christ, I could have said it wasn't her. I'm giving you everything I have but she's the only link to the kid and I'm going to meet her."

"Everything she said could be a lie," Mark said. "For all we know she's working for Strength and Harmony and they've decided you're a bigger catch than the kid. Or you're trouble and it's time to get you out of the way."

"Then why not me, too?" I asked.

"He's big and Western and he's a man, and he was the one questioning the Filipinas. That could have set off someone's alarm bells. You're just another Chinese woman. You could be his local guide, for all they know. I'm sure they hardly noticed you. Sorry, but this is Hong Kong. That's how it works."

"What about last night?" I wouldn't give up. "Strength and Harmony would know that I was the one dealing with Tony and Big John."

"Because you speak Cantonese. So you're his translator, big deal. Or maybe Maria Quezon has something going on the side and Strength and Harmony's not involved. I don't know. I agree we need to find out and I agree someone's got to keep this date." To Bill he said, "She's never met you. I'll send a cop."

"Her sister will have described me. You have a Western cop my size who speaks Tagalog you can brief and mobilize in twenty minutes? Forget it. I'm out of here."

"Wait," I said.

"No." Bill knew what I wanted. "She said alone."

"Not alone."

"Her sister would have described you, too. It's too risky."

"No," said Mark.

"Crap," said Bill.

"I can't let you."

"You can't stop me."

"Yes, I can."

"Then arrest me."

"Oh, knock it off, you two," I ordered. "How do men ever get anything done?" I turned to Mark. "He's right and you know it. He has to go. But not alone. Send a cop to watch his back." Before Bill could speak I added, "From a distance. So she doesn't get spooked." Then to Bill: "I don't suppose she's actually meeting the ferry?"

He seemed about to say something else, then gave it up and answered my question. "No. She said she'd call me once the ferry docked."

"So she may send you somewhere else from Cheung Chau. She may even be on this side, waiting to see if you do get on the ferry, alone. So your man stays way back," I said to Mark. "And you," I said to Bill, "you don't let her get you into any situations where your back can't be covered."

Our eyes met. Mine told him what I was asking; his told me what he was going to do.

Bill turned to Mark. "I don't want to see your man at all. I don't want to know he's there."

Mark didn't answer. His jaw was set, and the scar on his lip that usually became more obvious when he smiled was white and sharp now, though he was about as far from a smile as a man could get.

"You'll call the Weis?" Bill asked me. I nodded. He kissed me on the cheek. He looked at Mark. Then he moved between us to the door, and strode fast down the corridor without looking back.

Suddenly I found myself worried that Bill wouldn't be able to find his way back to the elevator, or to the Cheung

Chau ferry. I wanted to go after him, to be with him, to help.

I mentally shook myself. Bill's ability to find his way around was not the problem.

But I still wanted to go with him.

I turned and said as much to Mark, but he might not have heard me: He pushed past and went striding through the door himself. I hurried after him, prepared to stop him from stopping Bill, but that wasn't what was on his mind. He twisted through the partitions, past desks and Xerox machines, until he pulled up at a cul-de-sac where three plainclothes cops sat shooting the breeze in Cantonese.

They greeted Mark with grinning advice to each other: "Look out, it's Quan." There were inquisitive nods for me, but Mark had no time for that. He addressed himself in Cantonese to the youngest and most cheerful-looking of the cops. "You busy, Shen An-Se?"

"Just finishing my reports, Sergeant," the young cop said, half curious, half defensive.

"Forget it. You see that tall European who just left here?"

All the cops nodded. Anywhere else a man walking through an office might not be noticed at all, but these were cops. They could tell you the color of Bill's shirt and the design on his belt buckle.

"He's making the three o'clock Cheung Chau ferry," Mark said. "Follow him, but stay way back. He'll be watched; don't let them see you, don't let him see you. He may go somewhere else from Cheung Chau. Stick with him. Ko Pan," he turned to a tall, thin cop dangling his feet off Shen's desk, "go along. If he meets someone—probably a woman—you take her if they split again. Invisible, guys. The point is invisible."

The two cops stood immediately. Shen grabbed his jacket and shrugged into it. "What's up, Sergeant?"

"I don't know. We're looking for a seven-year-old boy, maybe with the woman, but if you see him, don't move in, call me. Call me anyway when it's safe. I want to know what's happening."

"This guy," Shen said. "He could hire a boat, to Lamma or someplace."

"Then get an urge to fish," Mark suggested. "Or grab a local girl for a romantic boat ride. Be creative, Shen, but stay with him."

They were off. The third cop, slipping Mark a disappointed look, left also, to find someone else's desk to sit on.

"You can't go," Mark said to me, his gaze following Ko and Shen. He'd switched back into English to answer what I'd said in the conference room doorway, what I'd thought he hadn't heard.

"I know," I said.

He watched his cops; I watched him. He let his shoulders relax. The male beast, I thought, reasserted as ruler of his lair, with other members of the pack out doing what they were supposed to do. I wondered what Grandfather Gao would say about that.

"Those guys," I said. "You said you were unpopular around here, but they don't seem to have a problem with you."

"Unpopular with the bosses," he said. "The young guys like to work with me. Something exciting could always happen, and if there's a screwup, Quan was giving the orders and they were just being good cops, and everyone knows about Quan."

Mark led me through the office warren to a partitioned corner far from the windows. "Is he always like that?" he said as he gestured to a chair in front of the desk and dropped himself into one behind it.

"Bill?" I said. "Yes."

"Must make him hard to work with."

"No. It makes him easy."

Mark gave me a long look. "Those guys are good," he finally said. "Ko and Shen. You don't have to worry."

"Do I look worried?"

He didn't answer that. "What are you going to do now?" he asked.

"Sit here and worry. What about you?"

He picked up a pencil and bounced it on the desk the way he had on the conference room table. "Before all that, I was going to call Wei Ang-Ran and invite him to help with our inquiries. I think I'll do that. That ferry won't get to Cheung Chau for over an hour anyway."

Something suddenly hit me. "I'm starving," I said.

Mark grinned. He left his chair, went around the partition, and came back with a steaming teapot and two paper containers that, for all that they were covered with Chinese characters and the smiling faces of Chinese children, looked suspiciously like Cup-o-Noodles to me. He tossed me a container and poured the hot water in after I'd torn the top off. Sitting again, he opened his desk drawer and handed me a pair of chopsticks. I stirred the stuff around.

"Smells awful."

"Tastes worse."

I sighed. "I thought all the food in Hong Kong was supposed to be good."

"You thought this trip was going to be a cinch," he pointed out. "A nice, relaxing vacation."

"No," I said, "I don't think I really did."

"Because of Grandfather Gao?"

I nodded and filled my mouth with noodles. Even hungry as I was, I couldn't persuade myself this meal was any better than lousy.

"When this is all over," Mark said, "I'll take you to this seafood place near Happy Valley where your fish is swimming until they cook it for you. And you have to buy bottled water if you want it, but beer is free."

"Bill will like that part," I said. "If he's invited?"

Mark shrugged. "Table for three, could get a little crowded."

I thought maybe I wouldn't answer that. I scooped in more noodles and said, "What kind of a place is Cheung Chau?"

Mark picked up noodles in his chopsticks and let me get away with the change of subject. "It's got a big fishing fleet. It used to be just an island with a fishing village, but now people retire there, villas and everything. There are a couple of schools and academies because land's available. A Buddhist college, a music school. About half a dozen martial arts schools, the old kind where academics fills as little of the day as they can get away with and the kids practice kung fu the rest of the time."

"Is that the kind of place you went to?"

"Me?" He seemed surprised at the question. "I learned kung fu in Birmingham."

"Oh." I went back to my mediocre noodles.

"People go to Cheung Chau for the day, to go to the beach or to hike," he went on. Lifting another noodle mass, he added, "It's got a huge graveyard."

So much for the picture I'd just begun to paint of an idyllic resort. "Graveyard?"

"Great *feng shui*—covers the whole hilltop down to the sea, good ocean breezes, water wherever you look. You can't get buried on Hong Kong anymore, land's too valuable. There's the big mausoleum at Sha Tin on the Kowloon side, but on Cheung Chau you get a real grave if you want one, not just a file drawer."

"Don't be disrespectful. That's where old Mr. Wei's getting buried, Sha Tin. As soon as this is over." The idea of this being over brought me back to something, and thinking about graveyards wasn't something I wanted to do right now, anyway. "I told Bill I'd call the Weis. To tell them Harry's okay."

Mark asked, "What if it isn't true?"

"Bill thought it was. I think it's only fair that they hear about it. And," I added, "if I call them I can find out if they've heard anything."

Mark chewed thoughtfully. "Assuming Maria Quezon is telling the truth," he said, "then look at this: She won't tell anyone where the kid is until she's sure it's safe. Not even the parents. So she doesn't really trust them. But she wants them to know he's okay. So she doesn't think they're part of it. What does that mean?"

"Maybe she thinks if they get him back they won't be able to protect him from something like this happening again."

"Like if Steven Wei's brother's involved."

"Or Strength and Harmony."

"Or both."

"And she can?"

"Obviously she doesn't think she can, or she wouldn't be taking the risk of meeting Smith."

Maybe it was something in my face when he said *risk*; this time he was the one who changed the subject. "What are you going to say if you call them?"

"Not very much."

So I called the Weis from Mark's desk phone, trying to preserve my cell phone's charge so Bill, if he needed to, could call it. And I didn't tell them very much.

"I wanted you to know," I said carefully, after Steven Wei's excited *"Wai!"* and the dispirited greeting when he found out it was only me, "that we've been in contact with Maria Quezon. She says Harry's okay."

"Maria?" he shouted into the phone. I pictured him shooting to his feet, mashing the phone to his ear, trying to get closer to this news.

"Where is she? Where is Hao-Han?"

In his excitement Steven Wei reverted Harry's name to Cantonese, I noticed, though we were speaking English. "I don't know," I told him. "We're supposed to hear more later." That was hedging, but I wasn't sure how to explain to him that Bill, the big foreigner, was on his way to meet the amah, who claimed to have his son; and that he, Steven, wasn't going because the amah, who loved his son like her own, wouldn't allow it.

"What do you mean *later*?" Steven demanded. "What happened? How did you find them? Who took them?"

"I'm sorry, I don't know that. We were only able to contact Maria because we were able to find someone who knows her, and passed the word along that we wanted to speak to her." I offered him that almost unrecognizable description of our morning in the Filipina sea. "We haven't actually found her, and we don't know where she is; she called us, on the cell phone."

Steven Wei took a moment to digest this. "Passed the word to someone who knows her? But that would seem . . . but it sounds as if . . . as if she's not being held."

"As if she took Hao-Han and ran away," I finished for him.

"No," he said firmly. "That cannot be true."

"Steven—" I began gently.

"No. Maria loves Hao-Han. She is a part of this family. She would not put my son in danger any more than we would."

Well, that's what Natalie Zhu said you'd say. "She told us," I said, "that she was saving him from danger."

"Saving him? From what danger?"

"That's something else she didn't say. Do you have any idea?"

"I . . . no," he said. "This is all difficult for me to understand. I just want my son to come home. Can you—?"

"I'll do whatever I can," I said. "How is Li-Ling?"

"Resting. With her condition, this has been very hard for her."

"I'm sure. Go tell her what I said. I'll call you as soon as I hear anything else." Casually I asked, "Has Natalie Zhu come back, or called?"

"No. I expect her soon. Why do you have to wait until you hear from Maria? Why can't you go to her, or to these people who know her? Who are these people? And why hasn't she contacted us?"

"We can't go to her," I lied, although at that very moment, we were. "And I don't know why she hasn't called you." Except that in one sense or another, she doesn't trust you. "But tell me something else: Have you heard from anyone? Either party making ransom demands?"

"No. No one at all. We were beginning . . ." He trailed

off, clearly reluctant to tell me what they'd been beginning to do, or more likely, to think. "How did you find these people, the ones who know Maria? You're new to Hong Kong. How could you do something we could not do?"

Well, for one thing, you didn't try.

"We were lucky," I said. I decided it was time I got out of this conversation before the asides I was making to Steven in my head started coming out of my mouth. "Let me get off the phone, in case she calls again," I said, feeling a little bad because that wasn't about to happen, not on this phone, but I knew it would work. "I'll call you as soon as I hear anything else, I promise. I just wanted to let you know."

"Wait," Steven said, but when I did, he didn't have anything for me to wait for.

"The phone," I said gently.

"Yes," he finally said. "But you will call immediately when you hear something? Anything at all?"

"Yes," I promised again. "Yes, I will."

I hung up. Mark and I met each other's eyes over the remains of reconstituted noodles.

"He sounded relieved," I said. "Surprised. And confused."

"That all makes sense."

"So what's not to trust?" I asked. "A family man of strong loyalties, a father worried sick. What's on Maria's mind?"

"Let's hope your partner finds out."

I was about to correct Mark, to say that Bill and I weren't partners, we just worked together sometimes, but I stopped myself as I remembered that wasn't true. It had been, for a long time; but a little while ago, things had changed. Boy, Lydia, I thought, the next thing you'll forget is your own name. Well, it's the damn harbor, I thought back. The windows and the glittering water and the charging, smelly traffic; the crowds and the incense and the small hushed shops; the kidnapped seven-year-old and the roast pigs at the temple; the street signs and store signs and bus signs all in Chinese.

"Are you okay?" Mark asked.

I was startled to hear his voice in all the swirling confusion. I realized I had closed my eyes. I opened them and there was no confusion, nothing swirling, just Mark's solid desk and the office partitions and the quiet comings and goings of cops.

"Jet lag," I said.

"It never stops," he said, in a gentler voice than I'd heard him use before.

"Jet lag?"

"No. Hong Kong. You think if it just *stopped* for a minute, or even slowed down, you could get a handle on it, see what was going on around you. But it never does."

I rubbed my forehead, surprised to discover the beginnings of a headache. "I feel like it keeps me from thinking," I said. "Everything racing around. I feel like *I* can't stop, either."

"You can use it," Mark said. "You can let it pull you along, instead of doing all the work yourself. Or you can keep still and let it flow right around you. But you have to keep your eyes on where you're going, or you'll drown here."

If you knew where you were going, I thought wearily, that might work. Mark, watching me, said, "Maybe you should go back to the hotel and get some sleep."

With Bill on some boat on the way to some cemetery island? I thought, you have to be kidding. Bill doesn't even like boats, from when he was in the Navy. "No," I said. "I can't do that. But the hotel, that reminds me." Without asking, I picked up the phone on his desk again. "I want to see if Grandfather Gao called me at the hotel."

Mark made no move to stop me, probably because it was Grandfather Gao, so I dialed the Hong Kong Hotel. According to the desk clerk, I did have a message. He put me through to the voice mail in my room and I waited, prepared—maybe even a little hoping—to hear Grandfather Gao's familiar calm voice.

But that's not who it was.

At first, in fact, I had no idea who it was, although the scratchy Cantonese voice identified herself at once. "Mo Ruo is speaking. Come to Number Eleven, Po Kong Lane. I can tell you many things." Then the hang-up click. It wasn't a voice I recognized. Frowning, I pressed the button to replay the message, trying to pry the name Mo Ruo from the recesses of my brain. On the third replay I got it, and it sent a sizzle up my spine that thoroughly woke me up.

I hadn't recognized her voice because I'd never spoken to her before, though I very much wanted to. Mo Ruo, the old lady prayer-seller from the temple at Wong Tai Sin.

As I hung up the phone Mark asked, "Who was it?"

Oh, I thought. No. Sorry. If I tell you, you'll tell me not to go. This is the woman who may be able to tell us who sent Steven Wei to the temple, and you'll tell me not to go.

"The front desk," I said, lying out loud, apologizing silently. "Something about my room charges, but I can't figure out exactly what they're telling me. And you know what? I don't care. I'll worry about it later."

I stuck my chopsticks back into my noodles, now cold and congealed. I poked them around a little, then stood. "I'm going out. I need to move. Maybe I will go back to the hotel. I'll try to stay out of trouble," I said, seeing Mark about to speak. "Let's make a deal: I'll call you as soon as Bill calls me, if you call me as soon as your cops call you."

Mark stood also, and eyed me. "You sure you're okay?"

"I'm fine. Just antsy. What are you going to do now, bring Wei Ang-Ran in?" Maybe discussion of his next move would deflect any curiosity he might have about mine.

He nodded. "I'm going to call him right now. Do you think you can find your way out?"

"No problem," I said, with more confidence than I felt. "Talk to you soon. Thanks for the so-called lunch." I waved as I rounded the partition, and, with not so very many false moves and dead ends, worked my way out of the maze.

It would be best to get out of the building, I thought, before consulting my map. Not that I felt paranoid in any way, but it might also be good to walk a block or two, to where I couldn't be seen from any of those big HKPD windows.

The dusty hot walk along Gloucester Road was like a stroll on a narrow, afterthought sidewalk next to any major expressway anywhere in the world. The cars roared and whished, honked and swerved, and I felt like a mutant life-form that had emerged unexpectedly and for which, therefore, no provision had been made.

Eventually, in the semishelter of a building's recessed entrance, I pulled out the Kowloonside map. Po Kong Lane was no place I'd ever heard of, but my guess was that it was close to Wong Tai Sin temple. I studied that corner of the map, and eventually, in an area of twisting narrow streets dividing tiny uneven blocks one from another, I found it.

I took the ferry across the harbor and the subway up to the Wong Tai Sin stop, calculating that, as in New York, the subway would be faster than a cab, even on Sunday. Impatient with what felt like the ferry's unhurried, aimless drifting, I was right up in the front of the crowd at the ramp when we docked, and I hustled through the plaza where only yesterday morning I'd stood openmouthed by the water, bowled over by the vast Hong Kong skyline. Today I didn't give it a look. I had someplace to go, and like everyone else in Hong Kong, getting where I was going was more important than being where I was.

The subway took forever to come (though my watch claimed it was only four minutes) and forever to get to Wong Tai Sin (though again, my watch, thinking it could fool me, said fifteen). And exactly what's your hurry, Lydia, I asked myself. The old lady will be there or she won't, and she'll tell you something useful or she won't, and what are you going to do about it if she does? Call

Mark Quan at the police station, when you wouldn't even tell him where you were going? Or call Bill on his cemetery island, when God only knows what he'd be in the middle of that you'd scare off with the ringing of a phone?

I checked my watch again as I climbed the subway stairs, making that now-familiar Hong Kong transition from too cold to much too hot. Bill wouldn't even reach Cheung Chau for another twenty minutes, so there was no point in any of the worrying I was telling myself I wasn't doing. At the top of the subway steps I stopped for a moment to look around. The temple was still there, its golden roofs glittering in the sun above the courtyard wall; and above the roofs loomed the high-rises with their laundry flying proudly in the breeze. I scurried up the temple steps and stuck my nose into the fortune-teller's area to make sure Mo Ruo wasn't there, chasing after Wong Tai Sin's faithful with her paper prayers. Of course she wasn't: If she'd been planning to come to work today, she would have told me to meet her there, and not in Po Kong Lane, which I expected was her home.

Sunday was a day of rest for much of Hong Kong's workforce. The crowds in here were thicker than yesterday, and paper prayers seemed very much in demand. An odd day, I thought, for a prayer-seller to choose to take off.

I trotted back down the steps and headed east, past the temple forecourt, the incense stands and the clothing stalls where I'd bought my blouse, now hanging safely in the closet of the Hong Kong Hotel where it could embarass nobody. Beyond the stalls the view opened up to show, on the other side of six lanes of roaring traffic, a huge housing development of high-rise apartment buildings, and lower ones with restaurants and shopping malls on multilevels, and parks and playgrounds, movie theaters and an auditorium; and ahead, on both sides of the road, more of the same. Slim high-rises stood in clusters with shorter buildings at their feet, like tall reeds among heavier, more tangled aquatic plants, all growing through the surface of an asphalt lake. A few miles down the road, garish against the soft green hills, a stand of pencil-slim white-tiled buildings with side walls striped in bright red or blue or yellow had the smug look of cultivated plants in a formal garden overlooking the chaos at the edge of the wood.

Between them and the stand of high-rises closer to me, I could see an area the concrete gardeners seemed to have forgotten. Unruly stretches of corrugated metal roofs undulated above two- and three-story steel-sided huts patched together with tar paper and plywood. Bursting exuberantly through the rudimentary, twisting pathways between them, palms and broad-leafed rubber trees sent cheerfully chaotic nods to their more organized brethren in the carefully spaced rows of the housing development parks. Television antennas stuck out at inexplicable angles from the roofs, and balconies and walkways clung so precariously to the tilted walls that I wondered how anyone dared walk along them, much less operate or patronize the upstairs barbershops, tailor's shops, shoemakers or dentists or TV-repair shops I could see from the raised sidewalk I stood on. I also wondered if this sprawling, untended patch had street signs at all, or if I was going to have to ask directions of this person or that as I wandered through it, searching for Po Kong Lane.

I descended from the sidewalk down the one steel stair that provided entry to this place over the moat of jungle shrubbery. Everyone else on my raised sidewalk hurried right by, taking the direct route from Modern Hong Kong to Modern Hong Kong. I was the only person going somewhere else.

I wasn't the only person there when I got there, though. Like any jungle, this one was teeming with life.

Hidden by the palm trees and roofs from the sight of the raised sidewalk, but close enough that I was almost knocked over by the intensity of aroma the minute my feet hit solid ground and I left the belching traffic exhaust behind me, was this jungle's Restaurant Row.

I could smell delicious things stir-frying in woks, deep-frying in oil, dry-frying on flat steel plates. Spices and soy sauce and sesame oil all called to me, reminding me what a poor excuse for lunch Mark Quan had provided. Ahead, facing a path crowded with customers, a row of tin huts without so much as shop signs or tables was doing robust business.

Me, too, I decided, making a beeline for a hut where skewers of root vegetables and squid sizzled in pots of hot oil. I ordered two skewers and got them in a flash. The proprietor slipped them into a paper bag for me, jutting his scraggly-bearded chin at the bottles and dishes of sauces, seeds and spices at the end of the counter. I paid him, thanked him, sprinkled sauce into the paper bag, and asked him for Po Kong Lane.

He gave me a good-natured, curious glance as he stirred and fried. "You want to see someone in Po Kong Lane?"

"Mo Ruo," I told him.

"Ah? Do you know Mo Ruo?"

"No. Can you tell me how to find her?"

He smiled and shook his head. "Better if I don't tell you how to find Mo Ruo. You'll come back, complain, tell everyone my fish is no good."

"I'll tell everyone your fish is sensational." I pulled a chunk of squid from a skewer with my teeth. It was salty, chewy, rich and spicy. "Whether I find her or not."

"You say that now, because you haven't found her."

"Is she that bad?"

"Oh!" he said innocently. "She's a venerable old woman. She's someone's mother."

"But not yours."

"No," he grinned. "Not mine." He pointed along the line of food stalls with his iron paddle. "Do you see the knife sharpener's stall? Turn just beyond it. Walk to the wet market, go between the stalls to Po Kong Lane. Mo Ruo lives beyond the egg-seller's." He picked up another skewer, slid vegetables and squid down its length. "Maybe she'll be there, maybe not. Don't blame me if you don't find her." He dropped the skewer into the oil, where it hissed and spun. I could have sworn he winked at me, but winking is not particularly Chinese. "Don't blame me if you do."

The knife-sharpener's, the wet market, the egg-seller's. With each step I left behind the Hong Kong I was just coming to know and moved more deeply into the Hong Kong that used to be.

The knife-sharpener shooting sparks off the blade grinding on his wheel didn't give me a glance as I passed his stall and turned right, through a lane so narrow I would have thought it led only to his backyard. I stepped carefully over the ditch flowing down the lane's center. Brown water carried soggy leaves and stems, scraps of paper, bits of plastic wrapping, and other things I didn't look closely at. The heavy, moldy smell of damp concrete and soggy earth was everywhere. A black chicken scurried out from a doorway and ran ahead of me down the path.

I could see the sky only in fragments: Above my head, walkways draped from building to building like steel jungle vines, and rooms hung across the alley as though gigantic birds had built swollen nests on the sides of the buildings, supporting them back to the walls here and there by clusters of random bamboo poles.

On my right and my left as I walked along, open doorways, some with doors and some without, led into dim passages, or sometimes directly into rooms. I could see tiled floors and slanted stairs, or wobbly-walled alleys with daylight at their ends, where they connected to other lanes or opened into washing-hung, junk-piled courtyards. Some rooms were homes, dark little one-room dwellings or relatively grander downstairs kitchens with stairways to upstairs bedrooms. Toddlers crawled on floors; TV sets lit dark interiors with an eerie blue light. From one of the kitchens an old woman snapping the tops off green beans gave me a silent stare as I passed. A few doors down three undershirted men sat around a table and a fourth stood over them with a kettle in his hand in what I realized must be a tea shop; they stared also, cigarettes dangling from their lips or held between thin fingers. I didn't return any of these stares; their stares weren't rude, according to Chinese custom, but it would have been a direct challenge if I, a young female stranger, had stared in return, and I had no reason to get into a fight with any of these people.

Quite the contrary. If the wet market didn't turn up soon, I'd have to give up on what the squid-seller told me and start asking the people around me for Po Kong Lane.

But I wasn't quite ready to do that yet. I had been right to worry about the lack of street signs: Occasional characters painted on peeling walls were the only hint of where I was, but since none of the lanes or alleys they called out were on my map, they weren't much help. But the squid man had said just keep going, so I kept going. And with a breathtaking abruptness that reminded me of how a meandering stream, minding its own business in the forest, can unexpectedly plunge over a waterfall, my dark little alley ended and shoved me out into the wet-market clearing.

A wet market is a place where vegetables and fruit are sold. It doesn't have to be big, which this one was not, although the clearing was wide enough that a ragged-edged circle of blue sky, hemmed in by tilted walkways and leaning rooms, actually showed overhead. It doesn't have to be clean, either, which this one was also not: Sodden leaves, squashed oranges, and broken melon husks littered the muddy ground around the warped plywood sheets set on oil drums that served as vendors' tables. Mothers with babies on their backs picked through limp greens wilting in the late-day heat. Sharp-prickled fruits were mounded in wicker baskets on the ground, watched over by a walnut-skinned woman who had no teeth. Furtive flies lifted off a pile of tangerines one wing-flap ahead of a young child with a flyswatter. The place, busy with shoppers buying and haggling, had the thick, overripe aroma of a garbage dump. I wondered if, back here in these lanes, hidden from neon-filled, bustling Hong Kong as much by the straight-ahead glances of the rushing people on the sidewalk as by the steel roofs and overgrowth, anyone ever collected the trash.

I stood in the heat in the center of the clearing, surveying the shoppers, the sellers, the cabbages, the flies. Between the stalls to the egg-seller's, the squid man had said. Okay; but which way was that? From where I stood I could see at least four ways out of this marketplace. I was about to ask a chubby bald man behind a table of parsnips and carrots, when the black chicken I'd seen on the path darted out of the alley I'd come from and into another one. Well, all right, I thought. You're a chicken; I'll bet you know where the eggs are.

And so she did. I walked over to the mouth of the chicken's alley. Faded red paint on a rough concrete wall told me this was Po Kong Lane. I blinked, trying to adjust my eyes back to the dimness as I followed the chicken inside. Maybe twenty feet in I found, on my left, another opening, this one leading to a dizzy-angled slot between two buildings. A middle-aged man with a thick head of hair and scratched, dusty glasses squatted there next to three baskets, each holding a pile of eggs.

He looked up from the newspaper he was reading as I said, "Excuse me," and waited to be presented with my egg box, so that he could pack up my purchase for me.

"I'm sorry," I said. "I'm not buying eggs. I'm looking for Mo Ruo."

For a moment he didn't respond, just blinked at me from behind his heavy, smudged glasses. I thought of the jeweler in the Furama Hotel. He'd had sparkling glasses and a golden bird's nest brooch with tiny pearl eggs in it, and I hadn't bought anything from him, either.

Silently, not rising from his squat, the egg-seller pointed his newspaper over his shoulder. I thanked him, but he'd gone back to his reading by the time I stepped gingerly over the baskets and was on my way.

It wasn't a long way. At the other end of this narrow lane was a dirt-floored courtyard about the size of my hotel room but much more crowded, strewn with junk and motion. My friend the black chicken was there, scratching on the ground along with a dozen or so colleagues. Black smoke rose from an old oil drum, someone's cooking fire;

I didn't know what they were burning, but it had an acrid, chemical stink. Between that and the stench of the chickens I was dubious about the fate of the laundry flapping overhead. Three or four tinny radios tuned to different stations, a couple of TVs, and at least one screaming baby provided a steady background to the erratic hammering and sawing coming from somewhere off to the left. I had thought it was hot when I'd come out of the subway, hotter in the lanes; but no breeze could reach into this hidden, stagnant world. Even Bill would hate it here, I thought, wiping my brow. Bill. I looked at my watch. Bill's ferry would have docked on Cheung Chau ten minutes ago. My phone hadn't rung. I guessed that was good. Unless it was bad.

Never mind, Lydia. You're busy. You have a job of your own; do it.

Three or four doors scattered around the periphery of this choked courtyard suggested ways out, or deeper in. At a loss for any brighter idea, I was about to start trying them when a small flurry of action caught my eye. Opposite the alley mouth I was standing in, a crooked, tin-sided shack clung to the wall of a concrete building like a child afraid to let go of its mother. A couple of chickens had wandered into the shack's open door; an angry voice was screeching at them to get out. They ran—one even flapped its wings— as a round figure dashed, arms waving, into the light, screaming that such scrawny, ill-tempered chickens weren't good for anything but soup anyway and the only reason they weren't soup yet is that they weren't much good for that, either.

"*Taitai!*" I called. "Mo Ruo *Taitai!*" *Taitai* strictly speaking means wife; the way I was using it now, it meant what ma'am would have meant back home: a word of respect to open a conversation with an older woman you don't actually know.

The figure in the doorway stopped with her flabby arms in midwave and looked at me. I hurried across the courtyard, scattering chickens as I went. "*Taitai!* I am Chin Ling Wan-Ju! You called me at my hotel."

Her eyes had widened in surprise when she first heard me yell. Now as I said my name they narrowed, and I was hit with the uncomfortable feeling she was deciding just what I was good for, like the chickens. "You called me," I repeated, stopping before her. "I gave one of the other ladies my number and asked you to call. I gave her ten dollars." I added that to remind Mo Ruo that just knowing me could be profitable. I was speaking to her in Cantonese; even if she knew English, I calculated I had a better chance of her trusting me in her language than in mine.

Mo Ruo, with a black-toothed grin, grunted, turned, and gestured for me to follow her into the shack.

It was dim, darker than the alley, and it smelled bad, worse than the courtyard. The one window was grimy; the dirt floor was damp in spots. I just about made out a cot with a metal box under it, a shelf with a few battered bowls, a rickety card table with a chair on one side and a low stool on the other. A torn jacket hanging from a peg for when the weather got colder, and an incongrously new-looking, well-made umbrella: that was what Mo Ruo had. I found myself wondering who had put the umbrella down for an unguarded moment in what public place.

"So. You have come to Mo Ruo." The old lady eyed me from the shaky chair, waiting for me to sit on the stool. Her greasy gray hair came to an uneven line about the level of her chin, as though she had hacked it off herself with a dull scissors. The pattern on her sleeveless blouse was so faded I couldn't tell what it had once been.

The stool wobbled in the dirt and I turned it, resetting its legs so I wouldn't fall over. "Yes," I said. "I have some questions I would like to ask you."

Mo Ruo's narrowed eyes took me in another few moments; then she leaned over and pulled the metal box out from under the bed. She opened its top, pawed through it, and lifted out a battered book, some charts, and a clutch of other papers so old, torn, and grease-stained I would have had trouble reading them. She held out her dirt-streaked hand and waited.

I took out ten dollars. Her eyebrows lifted. She laughed derisively, stuffed the bill into her blouse, and held out her hand again. More? I thought. So fast? Then I looked again at the papers and charts and I caught on.

She was waiting for me to show her my palm.

"I don't want my fortune told," I said.

She frowned. "You have come to Mo Ruo. Mo Ruo will tell your fortune. Not like the cheats at the temple, oh, no." She spat in the dirt, repeated, "Mo Ruo will tell your fortune." She stuck out her hand again.

"No," I said. "I have a different question."

"A question. What question?"

"Yesterday, at the temple," I said, "you approached a young man. You gave him a paper to read, but it wasn't a prayer."

At first she didn't answer me. Then, carefully, as though tasting a dish to see what it needed, she said, "No."

"Yes. A young man. He looked at your paper, then made two phone calls. Then he left in a taxi. Who gave you the paper to give to him?"

"No."

"One hundred dollars."

Mo Ruo showed her black teeth again. "So much money."

"If you tell me."

She kept her chicken-appraising eyes on me for a few moments. "If telling you is worth one hundred dollars," she finally said, "it is worth two hundred."

Well, Lydia, that's what you get. I took two one-hundred-dollar bills from my wallet and placed them both on the table. "Who?"

With surprising speed Mo Ruo reached over and tried to lift the bills, but my hand was on them. Leaving her hand covering them also, she smiled. "The old man."

I let go of one of the bills. "His name?"

"I don't know."

"That's not worth two hundred dollars. Describe him. Tell me what happened."

Without removing her hand from the remaining bill, without losing the mocking smile, she said, "He came to the temple. I saw him, watching the prayer-sellers. He picked Mo Ruo. He could tell Mo Ruo was the best, that Mo Ruo would find his young man, that Mo Ruo would not fail the way those other fools would."

"What did he want you to do?"

"He gave me a paper. It looked like a prayer but it was not a prayer."

"What did it say?"

"I did not read it."

Oh, sure, I thought, but since I already knew what the paper said, I let it go.

"What did he tell you to do?"

"Give the man the paper."

"That's all?"

"No more."

"How did you know what the man would look like?"

"He showed me a picture."

"All right. What did he look like himself, this old man?"

She gave me the chin jut. "An old man. Thin, with white hair. Old men, pah. All the same to Mo Ruo."

My money had been on L. L. Lee anyway; now I was sure of it. "If you saw a picture of this old man, would you recognize him?"

"Mo Ruo does not forget."

Can't tell old men apart, but does not forget. Still, it was worth a try. "I want you to come with me. I want you to look at a picture." Mark Quan, I was sure, could dig up a photo of L. L. Lee.

Mo Ruo tugged at the hundred-dollar bill still on the table. I released it and it disappeared into the faded blouse.

"No," she said.

Sighing, I said, "Another hundred dollars."

I was not a bit surprised when, with a reappearance of the black-toothed grin, Mo Ruo said, "Another two."

Our trip out of the lanes was quicker than my trip in. Mo Ruo led the way, trotting along with an energetic quickness I would not have suspected, slipping in this door and through that courtyard, never once looking back to see if I was with her. We emerged at the knife-sharpener's and turned down the row of cooking huts. I waved at the squid man, who let out a cackle of delight when he saw the company I was keeping. Mo Ruo threw a scowl in his direction and told me, "Pah. Disrespectful turtle's egg. His fish is no good."

We climbed the stairs out of the jungle and reentered high-rise, high-traffic Hong Kong. I had to stop and clear my head, readjust, but Mo Ruo hoofed it toward the temple, plowing through crowds of her fellow pedestrians as though she expected them to flap their wings and hop out of her way. She seemed to have no trouble with the transition from the twisting, hidden pattern of the lanes to the bright broad grid of boulevards. Maybe it was because she did it every day, I thought as I hurried to keep pace with her. Or maybe the two were not actually as different as I thought them.

Just before we reached the temple I managed to flag down a taxi. Mo Ruo climbed in with obvious satisfaction. I gave the driver the address as a street number instead of the building's name, in case Mo Ruo had an aversion to police headquarters. She settled back in the taxi seat, clearly gratified that her own importance had been acknowledged in the form of transport I'd chosen. Her joy didn't keep her from screeching at the driver to watch how he turned, or at pedestrians who dared cross a street we were barreling down. The driver made it his business to hurry; he was probably noticing, as I was, that the rank smell of Mo Ruo's little tin hut had not come entirely from the hut. When we arrived, I broke Hong Kong protocol and tipped him, to cover the cost of the time he was going to have to take out of his busy day to air out his cab.

Mo Ruo, nodding in pleasure at having been brought to the Hong Kong side in a taxi, followed me along the sidewalk almost into the building before she caught on. Eyes popping, she slammed to a halt.

"Aiyeee!" she howled. "Where do you bring me? Oh, no, Mo Ruo is not coming here!" She spun on her heel and hurried away down the sidewalk. Why, I thought, oh, why couldn't I have gotten one of the other old ladies, one who didn't know how to read?

"Taitai!" I called. I raced after her. "Mo Ruo *Taitai*! There is nothing to fear! Just to look at a picture. That's all you need to do here, just look at a picture!"

Scurrying, she waved me away. I caught up with her at the corner. Luckily the whizzing traffic made it impossible for anyone to cross. *"Taitai—"*

"Police!" she spat. "Not Mo Ruo, talk to police! Go away, police!"

"I'm not a cop," I said. "I just need your help. They won't even know who you are. I won't tell them your name." Desperately I offered, "Another hundred dollars."

That stayed her headlong plunge into traffic. "You are not police?"

"No. It's just, this is where the old man's picture is."

I expected her to continue balking, on the logical basis that if the picture was at police HQ the man pictured was probably a criminal, and therefore someone to avoid fingering, as that might make him mad. But that didn't seem to bother Mo Ruo. Maybe she thought of herself as a match for any lowlife, and maybe she was right. Two things happened. She demanded the expected: "Two hundred dollars." And, with the shrewd, mocking smile of the person with the upper hand, she said, "They can bring the picture out."

I agreed to the two hundred, glad that Hong Kong dollars were worth only eight to the American: Still, they were mounting up. About the other, I said, "Maybe. Maybe they can. I'll find out. But if they can't, you have to agree to come inside."

"Maybe," she echoed me, and I knew what that meant: If she did, it would cost me another two hundred dollars.

We backed off from the street corner, although Mo Ruo would not come all the way to the front door. The sun was low now, glowing from behind the Peak, and Gloucester

Road was in shadow. Heat still rose from the baked concrete sidewalks, but the glare was gone from the chrome of rushing cars and the glass of lofty towers. Accepting Mo Ruo's compromise sidewalk position, I dialed Mark Quan from my cell phone.

"Wai!"

"It's Lydia," I said, but I said it in Cantonese, so Mo Ruo wouldn't think I was trying to put one over on her and dash off again.

"Lydia? What is it?" Mark demanded, responding also in Cantonese, his quick and wary. "Did you hear from your partner?"

"No," I said. "Did you hear from your cops?"

"No. I'd have called you if I had. Why aren't you speaking English?"

Hearing him say he'd have called me, I knew it was true, and I also knew something else: I could trust Mark Quan to do what he said he'd do. And I knew he wasn't sure he could trust me to do the same.

And I wasn't either.

And I wished I were.

But that wasn't the point here. Come on, Lydia, I thought, you have a skittish old lady on the sidewalk ready to bolt, and a simple request. Worry about whatever it is you're worrying about later.

"I'll explain, but not right now. Do you have a photo of L. L. Lee?"

"Do I—sure, I guess so. Why?"

"I think I have a witness who can identify him as the man who sent Steven Wei to the temple."

"A witness? What kind of witness?"

"The prayer-seller."

"From the temple?"

"I'll tell you all about it, but she's kind of nervous. I think we should show her the picture soon, before she changes her mind."

I had the feeling that *we* had not passed him by, but all he said was, "So bring her here. Where are you?"

"On the sidewalk outside. Can you bring the picture down?"

"Can I do what?"

"I told you, she's kind of nervous. She doesn't want to come in."

Mo Ruo stood near me, picking her teeth and darting glances in all directions. "It'll only take a minute," I said. "Please?"

"Outside police headquarters?"

"Yes."

A moment of silence. Then: "We don't have a lot of PIs in Hong Kong," Mark said. "I never really understood before why American cops think they're such a pain."

"Please?"

"Oh, why not? I'm just about finished with what I was doing anyway. HKPD, here to serve the public. Sure, I'll be right down."

"Thanks," I said, but he'd already hung up.

I spent the impatient waiting moments trying to hold Mo Ruo's attention so she wouldn't scram. The first thing I did was take two more one-hundred-dollar bills from my wallet and slip them into my pocket. The gesture was not lost on her.

"Someone's coming down with the picture," I said. "But first I'd like to ask you something else."

She eyed my pocket hungrily.

"I just wondered," I said. "Why didn't you go to the temple today?"

No answer.

"Did the old man tell you not to? He paid you enough to stay away for a while? He paid you a lot of money?"

I thought that would get her, and it did. "A lot of money! Pah, a cheap old man! He would not give Mo Ruo nearly as much as he should have. He was very anxious that this job be done, but was he willing to pay for it? Scarcely!"

"But he did pay you to leave the temple as soon as you gave the young man the prayer? To stay away for the next few days?"

"He paid me," she grudgingly confirmed. "He said to me, stay away from the temple for three days, or I would find trouble. As if Mo Ruo were afraid of trouble!"

She said the word as though trouble were something that should be afraid of Mo Ruo.

But she wasn't finished on the subject of the old man. "Three days!" she complained. "Mo Ruo makes a great deal of money in three days, I told him. To stop work for three days!"

"So he paid you for those three days?"

"Not enough," she repeated.

This explained why I hadn't been able to find her when I went back to the fortune-teller's area yesterday, after Steven Wei raced off in his taxi. It also implied that L. L. Lee expected this whole thing to be over in three days. It also made me briefly wonder how much money Mo Ruo actually made. Maybe prayer-selling was as lucrative as she said it was. Maybe she was one of those nutty folks who turn out to have millions of dollars stuffed in the mattress when they die.

"He said, don't tell anyone," she added scornfully. She spat on the sidewalk. "Stupid old man. Mo Ruo will tell whoever she wants to."

Or whoever pays her to, I thought. Though, thinking back on L. L. Lee's hard, ancient eyes and the icy contempt in his voice when he made it clear he knew how little I knew about the treasures of my own past, I gave Mo Ruo credit for more courage, or avarice, than I might have been able to come up with, if L. L. Lee had told me to keep *my* mouth shut.

So there I was, standing on a sidewalk next to a smelly but possibly wealthy chicken lady in the shadowed heat of late Sunday afternoon Hong Kong, waiting for the validation of a theory that, if true, would lead me, I had to admit, to pretty much where I was right now. If L. L. Lee had sent Steven Wei to Wong Tai Sin, what of it? That would prove Strength and Harmony was involved in the kidnapping of Harry. This would not be news. And it would not be anything we—me, as a foreign PI without gun or local license, Mark as an HKPD cop with all the resources of the Department available to him—could do anything about. Except sit and wait. Or, as I was doing right now, stand and wait.

Through the glass of the HKPD HQ doors I glimpsed Mark Quan, book of mug shots under his arm, strolling past the reception desk with a wave to the cop behind it. Someone was with him; with a little start, I realized it was Wei Ang-Ran, Steven's uncle. Well, of course. Mark had been going to ask Wei Ang-Ran to come to the police station to aid in the inquiries; that must be the business he had just finished when I called. The two men were in conversation, Mark inclining his head to catch Wei's words. Still talking, they pushed through the glass front door.

Mark saw me and, annoyance notwithstanding, smiled.

Wei Ang-Ran saw me and Mo Ruo and, eyes wide, slammed to a halt.

And Mo Ruo saw Wei Ang-Ran, screamed, "The old man! You tricked me! You cheated me!" and with a baleful glance at me that made me wonder what it felt like to be cooked for soup, sped away, arms waving, scattering pedestrians like chickens as she raced down the sidewalk and across the street.

eleven

I charged after Mo Ruo, shouting, yelling, making promises, offering cash. Nothing stopped her. Behind me I heard Mark also shouting, then some scurrying activity, then thudding footsteps as Mark came chasing after us. Mo Ruo had zipped across the street, creating a blast of horn-honking chaos. We stirred it up again when Mark caught up to me, waving his gold shield as though it could protect us from the cars we dashed in front of. Everyone on the street was mad at us, and the people on the sidewalk didn't think much of us either as we ran past and around them, forcing them to jump aside or be knocked out of the way just as they were recovering from the typhoon of Mo Ruo's passage.

Mo Ruo turned left and blasted up a side street. Mark pulled away from me, gaining on her faster than I did. I was hampered by my bag, bouncing along over my shoulder. At home I rarely carry one, because it gets in your way in situations like this. In Hong Kong I hadn't expected any situations like this, I thought as I sped along; still, you'd think Lydia Chin could at least keep up with, if not outrun, an old lady and a chubby cop.

But Lydia Chin couldn't. Mo Ruo made another turn, this time to the right; by the time I reached the corner, she was gone. Somewhere among the doorways, alleys, open-fronted stalls, and shadowed shops of this narrow street a few blocks from Hong Kong Police Headquarters, she had vanished.

Mark stood in the middle of the sidewalk, looking around, cursing. Locksmiths and sandal-sellers studiously avoided his eye. As I reached him he was demanding of a fruit-juice man whether he'd seen Mo Ruo; he settled for a cup of juice, melon and tangerine, the best the house had to offer, no charge for our gallant police officers, a small thing to apologize for the juice man's poor powers of observation and deeply regretted inability to help. When I got there Mark pointed at me without a word and I got in on the deal, too.

"She's gone," Mark said, his voice disgusted.

I worked at bringing my breathing under control and sipped my juice. We had run maybe five blocks total, in ninety-degree heat and ninety-nine point ninety-nine percent humidity. I was dripping with sweat. Mark was also, I noticed, but his breathing was absolutely normal.

"How could she do that?" I asked, and then on the next breath, "Run so fast? And disappear like that?" Glancing around at the cigarette-sellers and the dusty bookstore and the restaurant with roasted chickens hanging in the window, I added, "Where are we?"

"Wan chai," Mark said, his eyes still searching the street. "She could have run into anywhere and paid someone to hide her. We can turn the place upside down and maybe shake her out, but I'd have to know why." He finished his juice and turned to look at me. "Why were we doing this? What's going on?"

"You mean you chased after her and didn't know why? And how come you can run that far that fast in this weather and not even be breathing hard?"

He shrugged that off: "Kung Fu. And I'm used to this weather. It's not that different from Alabama."

Kung Fu indeed, I thought. I practice Tae Kwon Do, and I'm panting like a dog. The thought crossed my mind that anyone who could run like this might, when it came to Kung Fu, be very, very good.

"And I chased her," he said, "because you were chasing her."

Oh. I finished my juice. It was sweet and blessedly cool, and I could have used another, but I wasn't sure what the protocol was about demanding a second bribe.

"And it could be," he went on, "that that old lady might have some practice in running away."

I thought about the speed with which Mo Ruo had led

us from the lanes, eager to earn her next two hundred dollars, and I thought about the expensive new umbrella on her dirt floor, and I had to admit he might be right.

"So," he repeated, "what's going on? You said she could identify L. L. Lee as the guy who sent Steven Wei to the temple. You said she'd look at a picture if I brought it down. So I brought it down, and she took off. Why?"

Why? Why? Because Lydia Chin is a blind and birdbrained idiot, that's why.

"Did it take her that long to figure out where she was?" he asked.

"You mean, police headquarters? No, she knew that. I don't think it was that, and I don't think it was you." Before I could say anything else Mark took my arm and moved us a few yards down the sidewalk, away from the juice man who had become elaborately interested in the inner workings of his tangerine press and was ignoring us much too completely.

At our new position in front of a restaurant specializing in poultry, I told Mark what a mistake I'd made: "She said 'the old man' had paid her to give Steven the paper. She kept talking about 'the old man.' I thought she meant L. L. Lee. I just *assumed*." As I said that, I could just hear what Bill would have had to say about assuming. I pushed that aside and went on. "And then just now, when you guys came out, she looked at Wei Ang-Ran as though she'd seen a ghost. Just before she ran away she screamed, 'The old man!' "

Mark frowned. "Wei Ang-Ran? You're saying he's the one who sent Steven to the temple?"

"Not me, Mo Ruo. And you were behind him—you didn't see his face when *he* saw *her*. He was as shocked as she was." Two men stepped out of the restaurant, trailing behind them a puff of cold air scented with soy and roast duck. "And now she's gone. And so's he," I added glumly, picturing Wei Ang-Ran taking advantage of our Keystone Kops routine to slip away to God knows where.

"I don't think so," Mark said.

"You don't think what?"

He just said, "Come on." I'd made enough of a mess, so I shut up and followed him. We crossed a street, this time waiting docilely for the light, and took some twists and turns. We were heading back; even I could figure that out.

The sidewalk in front of police headquarters was empty. That didn't seem like a good sign. But Mark held the door open for me, just as he had for Wei Ang-Ran, and I went inside, and there was Wei Ang-Ran.

He slumped, dejected and defeated, on a bench by the window, his back to the Gloucester Road traffic, under the watchful eye of a uniformed cop.

"I didn't know what the hell was going on," Mark said. "I didn't hear what she said. But something spooked her, and just in case it wasn't me, I thought I'd ask someone to make sure he stuck around. That's why it took me so long to catch up to you," he added.

And then to pass me, I thought. And to not even be breathing hard.

"You," I said, "must be the smartest cop in Hong Kong."

"Do me a favor?" he asked, as we came to stand in front of Wei Ang-Ran, who didn't look up. "Tell my boss."

Wei Ang-Ran accompanied Mark Quan and me back upstairs without a word. Mark brought us back to the glass-walled conference room he and Bill and I had used just a few hours ago. The brief heart-thudding excitement Mo Ruo had provided had taken my mind off Bill and his island; now, back in this room, I found myself craning my neck to see if I could see the Cheung Chau ferry, and absently accepting Mark's offer of a cup of tea while discreetly pulling out my cell phone to see if it had lost its charge.

Of course, if it had, and Bill had needed something, he could have called Mark. And Mark's cops would have called if anything had happened, meaning, gone wrong. So probably there was no action at all on Cheung Chau. I drank Mark's tea, hoping it would help relax the knot that had formed in the pit of my stomach when I watched Bill leave this building and had not, for all my ignoring it, gone away.

Wei Ang-Ran drank some tea, too. He didn't meet Mark's eyes, or mine. The glass conference room was full of the dancing golden sparkle of the late-day sun on water, and silence.

"I believe you have something you'd like to say?" Mark finally asked, addressing Wei Ang-Ran in deferential Chinese. Though he spoke gently, I noticed that this time he had seated himself against the window, pointing me to the head of the table, and leaving Wei Ang-Ran to squint against the glass.

Wei Ang-Ran responded only with a small sigh, so I demanded, "Did you kidnap your great-nephew, Hao-Han?"

To which Wei Ang-Ran, looking into his teacup, replied, "I wish I had."

"The prayer-seller," I said, my voice sharp. "She identified you. You paid her to give Di-Fen"—Steven—"the paper at the temple."

"Yes," he said morosely, "that's true."

I banged my cup down, about to demand that he stop mooning around and talk, but Mark threw me a look that stopped me. My show, the look said. Well, so it was. Get on with it then, my look said back. I picked up my cup as Mark turned to Wei Ang-Ran and said respectfully, "Wei Ang-Ran *Sinsaang.*" *Sinsaang* meant about the same thing in this context as *Taitai* had when I'd used it on Mo Ruo. "*Sinsaang*, you had some part in this. It's important now that you tell us what happened. For your great-nephew's sake."

Wei Ang-Ran sighed again, and I clenched my teeth to keep from grabbing his shirt collar and shaking him. Maybe I should count the number of sparkling waves in the harbor, see how many I got up to before he opened his mouth.

Mark reached over and, far from grabbing the old man's

collar, poured Wei Ang-Ran more tea. The old man sipped at it, then spoke.

"I'm just a practical man," he said sadly. "I don't have ideas. I don't make plans. For our business, my older brother always made the plans. I did as he said. The business always prospered."

Mark waited, so I waited, too, my toes curling in my sandals.

"For other things, other people have always had ideas. But now, I needed an idea," Wei Ang-Ran said. "I did my best. This is the sorry result."

"Why did you need an idea?" Mark asked.

"My nephew, Di-Fen,"—Steven—"is taking over my brother's responsibilities at Lion Rock Enterprises."

"That's not good?"

"It's very good. My nephew can make plans. It will be very good for Lion Rock, for the future of the business. But just at this time—at this time, it was not good."

"Why?"

Wei Ang-Ran didn't answer. He looked again into his teacup as though he wanted to crawl into it and swim away. I gave him as long as I could stand. Then, "I know," I said.

Both men looked at me, Wei Ang-Ran with a sad nod, Mark with irritation. Well, what was I supposed to do, wait until we *all* got old?

"The smuggled artifacts," I said. "Last night you were unloading a shipment from China, including smuggled artifacts. You and your brother have been smuggling for years, working for L. L. Lee, but your nephew doesn't know."

Realizing I didn't know L. L. Lee's Chinese name, I had to use its English version. But Wei Ang-Ran didn't seem to have any trouble figuring out who I meant.

He was anxious to correct me on one point, however. "Not my brother. He knew nothing about it. He would not have allowed it. That was the reason I had to hide my crime from my nephew."

"What was?" Mark asked.

Wei Ang-Ran sighed again. "I was tempted to admit everything to Di-Fen. I considered that. It would have been simple. There would then have been no need for plans. Then none of this . . ." He faltered, then went on, "But I feared he would not believe his father was not involved. I could not bear to tarnish my brother's memory in the eyes of his son. Or . . ."

"Or—?"

"Or his opinion of me," Wei Ang-Ran admitted. "To my brother, I was always a younger brother, to be taught, guided; but to my brother's son I am a wise old uncle." This brought forth from Wei Ang-Ran a wistful smile.

Then: "To be practical," he said, and looked up at us, as though practicality might be something we would admire under the circumstances, "I also feared his response, for himself. My nephew has many virtues, but he is not a patient man. The man you name is not someone I would wish my nephew to become involved with."

"The man we name," Mark said, clarifying. "Lee Lao-Li?"

Well, there was L. L. Lee in Cantonese, in case I ever needed it.

"So . . ." Wei Ang-Ran started.

"So—?" Mark prompted, after a long interval of silence and glittering water, during which I heroically kept my mouth shut.

"I planned a distraction." Wei Ang-Ran said this with hushed voice and downcast eyes.

"A distraction? The kidnapping of your great-nephew was a distraction?" Mark spoke with the calmness of a cop who'd heard worse, many times; and he probably had, though I doubted he'd heard stranger. His matter-of-fact approach, or maybe more important, the lack of accusation in his voice, seemed to both surprise Wei Ang-Ran and give him strength.

"That was my plan," the old man said. "You see how badly it has worked out."

"What do you mean?" Mark asked. "Badly."

Wei Ang-Ran looked at Mark, and then at me, as though he were telling us something he was sure we already knew. "Very, very badly," he said. "I have lost him."

The story, which Mark pried out of Wei Ang-Ran while I jiggled my foot and sipped my tea and tried mightily to squelch my urge to pace, was this: He had conceived the kidnapping of Harry as a way to keep Steven occupied while he, Ang-Ran, had the last shipment of smuggled artifacts from China unloaded at the Lion Rock warehouse.

"Nothing less than a threat to his family would have kept my nephew from discharging his new responsibilities in the business," Wei Ang-Ran explained. "From the day of my brother's death I worried about this, that my nephew would discover the treasures within the expected furniture shipment. He is determined to acquaint himself with all aspects of the business, to not fail in his new responsibilities. Even yesterday evening, not long before you arrived"—turning to me—"he offered to come to the warehouse to help, as I told you. I told him his place was at home with his wife."

But by that time, Wei Ang-Ran said, things were already disastrous.

Earlier he had enlisted Maria Quezon in his plan. At first she had been surprised and suspicious, he said, but later had given in and agreed. He had not told her anything about his reasons, only that he wanted her to take Harry to Ocean Park for a day or two. Ocean Park, Mark threw in for me, was a huge amusement complex around the other side of Hong Kong Island. There, Maria and Harry would stay in a hotel, swim at the beach, go on rides, and generally enjoy themselves, all courtesy of Wei Ang-Ran. The only catch was that Maria must not mention any of this to the Weis, and when they came back, must claim to have been kidnapped along with Harry by kidnappers who for some unknown reason gave up and ran away. The large sum of cash Wei Ang-Ran had promised Maria when the whole thing was over, along with a barely whispered but clear understanding about the flimsy nature of Filipina work visas, was expected to overcome any queasiness on her part about the plan.

"At first," said Wei Ang-Ran, "everything seemed to go smoothly. The shipment came in, the unloading was going well. Because you were coming," with a nod to me, "I had the idea to ask for my brother's jade as ransom. That way it would not be necessary for my nephew to involve his bank, which might have raised questions." He smiled sadly. "I was pleased to have thought of that."

"Why send your nephew to the temple?" Mark asked.

"Only to keep him busy. Di-Fen must take action; he is a man of plans. I was not sure where that would lead, but to be practical, also to keep his mind from Lion Rock, I supplied steps for him to take. I had . . . other things planned. Had things not gone so wrong, my nephew would have received further instructions to be carried out.

"But in any case, by tomorrow morning all was to be complete. The shipment of treasures will have been removed from the warehouse. Di-Fen will be welcome there once more. Maria was to have brought the child home, clearly unharmed, even happy from his days at Ocean Park. His tales of rides, bathing beaches, sweets, Maria would explain as their captors' method of keeping the child happy, easily controllable. Many kidnappings happen in Hong Kong; most end well once the ransom is paid. The kidnapping of Hao-Han was intended to end better even than others, because in the end there would have been no ransom paid. My nephew would have thought no more about it. Everything would be well."

Except for a glance over his shoulder every time he goes out of the house, a clutch in his stomach every time Harry, and soon the new baby, are out of his sight. A tingle he'll never lose, even if he forgets the reason for it, every time the phone rings for the rest of his life. Except for those, I thought, everything would be well.

"But," Mark said, "something went wrong?"

Wei Ang-Ran nodded again. "My nephew called to tell me there had been a second ransom call, demanding a great deal of money. I called Maria Quezon on her cell phone; she did not answer. They are not at Ocean Park in the room I had reserved for them, under the name we agreed on." He looked up at us, me and Mark. "You can see what happened. Maria Quezon is taking this opportunity to extort from my nephew a great deal of money for herself."

If she were, I asked him silently, could you blame her? If Steven got wind of her involvement in your loony scheme, she'd be tossed out of Hong Kong before you could say *amah,* and that would be if he didn't just have her arrested. The least she could do would be to go ahead and get herself a nest egg.

Only I didn't think she had. And as crazy as this old man's desperate scheme might be, the deep furrows in his brow and the trembling of his hands as he lifted his teacup made his fear and regret so excrutiatingly obvious that it was all I could do to watch the shadows of the mountain spine of Hong Kong Island creep across the harbor water, covering the sparkling wavelets inch by inch, and not blurt out to Wei Ang-Ran what we knew that he didn't.

Which was, of course, that Maria Quezon, appalled by Wei Ang-Ran's scheme, had taken Harry and run to safety on Cheung Chau Island, where Bill was with her right now.

I looked at Mark and spoke in English. "I don't think so," I said.

He returned my look, then stood, courteously asking Wei Ang-Ran to excuse us. Equally politely, as though he had a choice in the matter, the old man did. Mark held the glass door for me and we stepped into the hall.

"She's not behind that second demand," I said as soon as the door shut. "If she were, she would never have called Bill and asked to meet with him. She would have stayed lying low until the money was paid."

Mark nodded. "I was thinking the same. What he's saying fits in with what she said: that the boy isn't safe, and won't be if he's returned to his parents. She doesn't know what this is about. She must think it's the real thing, that the old man's desperate enough for money to kidnap his own nephew's kid. So she can't let Harry go back to where he could get a second shot at him. She must figure if she told Steven he'd never believe her. He might even toss her out for defaming the old man, and then who'd protect Harry?"

"Supposedly Steven thinks of her like family."

"Yeah, but Wei Ang-Ran *is* family. In a pinch, whose story do you think would win out, his dead father's brother's, or the Filipina amah's?"

"Poor Maria," I said. So the amah did love the boy like her own son.

I was, at least, glad to hear that.

I glanced back into the conference room, watched the shadows of the mountains on the water, the shadows of unhappiness on the old man's face. "This explains why neither ransom caller could produce evidence that they were holding Harry," I said.

"Because neither is."

"Right."

"So the second caller is some opportunist who found out Harry was gone and decided he'd work the situation?"

"I think so."

"Who?"

I said slowly, "Franklin."

"Franklin Wei?"

"Sure. So he didn't do the kidnapping like I thought. But the rest still fits. He gets here and Harry's gone. He's an impulsive guy, we know that. He calls in a two-million-American-dollar ransom demand, offers to lend Steven a million which totally diverts suspicion from him, and figures to end up with his own million back plus another one before the real kidnappers return the kid."

"And if the kid's returned first?"

"Then everybody can see the second demand's bogus, but what's Franklin lost? It was worth a shot."

A cop on an errand hurried past us. He and Mark exchanged quick Cantonese greetings, and then everything was still again.

The thought struck me that this was exactly the kind of conversation I was used to having with Bill, when we were working out the possibilities of a case. But Bill was out on Cheung Chau with the amah, and I was here in police head-quarters, talking things over, working out the possibilities, in a quiet hallway with Mark.

Mark's eyes met mine. I wasn't sure what I was feeling, and I don't know what he felt, either, but what he said was, "I want to ask the guy a few more questions," and he held the conference room door for me once again.

I went in and sat down, telling myself that working on a case was just working on a case, no matter who you worked with. Mark lifted the teakettle and poured us all more tea.

Saying nothing to Wei Ang-Ran about our discussion in the hall, Mark switched back to Cantonese and asked, "Your nephew's flat had been searched before Chin Ling Wan-Ju—" that was me "—got there. Why?" He still spoke in that mild, inquiring tone, as though none of this were very important, but he did need to fill in all the blanks, just part of the job, you understand.

"I don't know." Wei Ang-Ran blinked. "Maria Quezon must have arranged that."

That didn't make any sense to me, and it must not have to Mark either, but he didn't follow it up. Instead he asked, "I suppose you didn't make the ransom call yourself?"

"Of course not. Anyone in that household would have recognized my voice immediately."

"Who did?"

This time the silence lasted almost longer than I could stand it. I fixed my eyes on the harbor again, where the dusk-softened colors made following the movements of the chugging, sailing, streaming boats harder. I got the feeling, though, that, seen or not, the harbor traffic never stopped. Far off on the horizon, to the east where the night had long since come, a large military ship had set its lights twinkling. Mark sat patiently waiting for the answer to his question, and I sat, trying to be patient, too.

And when it came, it was worth the wait.

"Iron Fist Chang," the old man said.

Kung Fu is an interesting martial discipline. If practiced assiduously from a young age it can develop the lung capacity and muscular strength that will permit a stocky cop in his thirties to outrun a fit, athletic private eye still in her twenties. It also can convey a level of mental control that makes it possible for a practitioner to respond with nothing but slightly raised eyebrows to news that can make a student of Tae Kwon Do choke on her tea.

Kung Fu Man shot me another look—as though, trying to swallow and not make a mess, I needed it—and said patiently, "Wei Ang-Ran *Sinsaang*, an hour ago we sat here discussing the death of Iron Fist Chang. You assured me you knew nothing about his death, nothing about the man himself beyond the fact that when he wasn't working for you he worked in films as a stuntman."

"What I said was true," Wei Ang-Ran maintained, though he didn't even try for a tone of aggrieved innocence. "I know nothing about him. My brother hired him, on a recommendation, as I told you earlier. I know nothing, either, about his death."

"But you had a relationship with him that may have had something to do with his death. Surely you must have thought of that when I questioned you."

"I did. But you must see that anything I might have said would have revealed my part in this terrible situation?"

Mark let a tiny, exasperated sigh escape. It was my chance; I sneaked a question in. "*Sinsaang*? Who recommended Iron Fist Chang to your brother?"

Wei Ang-Ran turned to me as though I had a perfect right to be asking questions here, and Mark, though he frowned, didn't contradict that. "I don't know. It would not have occurred to me to ask. If my brother trusted the recommendation, I needed to know nothing more."

"And why did you choose him to make the phone call?"

Once again Mark, looking wary, stayed silent.

"I needed someone trustworthy. There was no possibility

of involving any of the other young men. Two of them, as
I suppose you know, are members of Strength and Harmony. They are there to look after the shipments."

Mark and I both nodded.

"Some of the others may also be members, or they may
not. But Iron Fist Chang came through my brother, recommended by someone my brother trusted."

A good reason to involve the poor guy in kidnapping
and extortion, I thought: Still, I knew what he meant.

Again casually, as though he were only trying to clear
up some personal confusion, Mark asked, "But *Sinsaang*,
if Lee Lao-Li was involved in your plan, your diversion—
after all, the smuggled treasures are his—why not use a
member of Strength and Harmony?"

Wei Ang-Ran stared in horror. "Lee involved? No, no!
I would never have done that. It would have been far too
dangerous. Oh, no, Lee knows nothing about this!"

Which was exactly what Mark had wanted to know.

"But Iron Fist Chang knew about your plan all along?"
he asked.

"No, of course not. Yesterday morning, I explained the
call I wanted him to make. I offered him a good deal of
money. I assured him the child was in no real danger. I
said . . . I said I felt my nephew was too lax in his attention
to his family, that he took them too much for granted. Before the new child came, I told Chang, I wanted to make
sure my nephew understood what treasures he had." He
slowly shook his head. "My nephew. Nothing could have
been further from the truth."

"And then you sent Chang to the temple, to make sure
Steven did as he was told?" I asked.

The old man's sad nod was more eloquent than speech.

It didn't answer all my questions, though. I had a lot
more, and it seemed as though Mark was going to give me
a chance to ask them. What Franklin's role was, and Natalie
Zhu's; what Wei Ang-Ran made of the fact that the jade
we'd delivered wasn't his brother's. I wish, still, that I'd

gotten to them, although I don't know that anything would have changed if I had.

But I didn't. As I was framing the next one, my cell phone proved that its battery charge was still intact, by ringing.

A small part of my brain noticed that my phone's shrill chirp got as much of a reaction from Mark as from me, and was gratified. The rest of me was occupied by the plunge into my bag to retrieve the thing and the slapping of it onto my ear.

"*Wai!* I mean, hello!" I shouted. I felt a flood of hopeful relief. This must be Bill. He must be all right: What could have happened, since the danger to Harry had all been made up? The rest of this, everything else we didn't understand, could be sorted out at leisure now that the really important part—restoring Harry to his family—was about to be taken care of.

But it wasn't Bill.

It was a woman's soft voice, speaking in English accented with something that wasn't Chinese. She asked for me.

"This is Lydia Chin," I said.

Before I could say anything else, she went on in a hurried whisper: "Your friend. I think your friend is in trouble."

"Who is this? What do you mean, trouble?" I mashed the phone harder against my ear, as though that would help me understand.

"I am Maria Quezon. He tell me to call you. He say you know where he go and why."

"I do."

Mark had leaned across the table when he'd heard me say *trouble*. His hand stuck out, as though to grab my phone and plaster it to his own ear. I shot him a warning look and said, "What happened?"

"Your friend, we talk. He . . . advise me. Then he see two men. Tony, he say to tell you, and the big one. They watch us drink coffee but do not come to talk. Your friend tell me, go out the back, go away. He go talk to them. He say, if he don't come meet me, I call you. He do not come."

"Where are you?"

Carefully, she said, "At the harbor, along Praya Street on Cheung Chau Island, is where he see the men."

"You didn't see where they went?"

"No. I run away, like he say to do."

"Where are you now?"

A pause. Then, "I cannot say."

"Is Harry with you?"

Desperately: "You must see. Your friend, he seem like a good man, but I do not know him. I do not know you. My Harry—"

"Maria," I said urgently. "I know what happened. I know about Harry's great-uncle, and that you took Harry away to keep him safe. But that's all over now; the danger is past. You can come back."

She paused. Then, "Your friend," she said, "he tell me to run away. These men, they frighten me. I think they frighten him, too, but he go to them, he do not run away with me. They are danger. Maybe he is danger too. I do not know you. I do not tell you where I am." Her voice, soft as it was, was firm. I suddenly thought of my mother, turning down with calm finality the pleas of all her five children to be allowed to go play in the park if we promised to finish our homework *after* dinner.

And I couldn't argue with Maria Quezon. Tony Siu and Big John Chou seemed like dangerous men to me, too. I stared across the water at the yellow lights stringing the Kowloon waterfront.

Mark reached out for the phone again, and I realized the room had gone silent. I spun away from him and said, "Maria? Maria, give me your cell phone number."

"Your friend tell me don't use the cell phone. He tell me, don't use no phone more than once."

Now it was my voice that sounded desperate. Part of me listened to it, the higher pitch, the rapid words. "Maria, I have to be able to keep in touch with you. It's important."

"Yes," she finally said. "Yes. I call again."

The phone went silent in my ear.

I slowly lowered it as Mark demanded, "Lydia? What the hell's going on?"

"That was Maria." I spoke in English, as he had. "Tony Siu and Big John Chou showed up on Cheung Chau. Bill kept them busy while she escaped. They were supposed to meet up, but she hasn't seen him since."

I heard my voice, composed, reporting, and marveled at it; I saw myself, as if from across the room, fold the phone and clip it to my belt. It was closer, there, than in my bag, for next time I needed it. I noticed Wei Ang-Ran's puzzled look, and thought, he must be waiting for someone to explain this to him; he doesn't speak English.

"Lydia? Lydia!" Mark's hand hit the table. The slap rang, the table shook. "What else? Where did they go? Where's the boy?"

Startled, I stared at him. The Kowloon lights glowed brighter and I could hear the faint hiss of the air-conditioning as it washed cool air over us from the ceiling. I shook my head hard, to clear it. Don't go losing it, Lydia, I demanded. Not now. Not now.

I swallowed and spoke. "Harry's with her but she won't tell me where," I said. "She doesn't know where Bill and those guys are."

"How did they know to go to Cheung Chau?"

"I don't know."

Mark's eyes met and held mine. He reached out and very briefly covered my hand with his, and for that moment his large warmth made me feel brave and hopeful. He withdrew his hand and turned to Wei Ang-Ran.

"*Sinsaang*," he said, in sharp and commanding Chinese, "the two members of Strength and Harmony who work for you, the ones who call themselves Tony Siu, Big John Chou"—those names he gave in English—"are on Cheung Chau Island, where Maria Quezon took your great-nephew. How did they know to go there?"

But the old man had another question. Eyes wide, he asked, "Is that where Maria Quezon is? With Hao-Han? The boy is all right?"

"We don't know that," Mark said. I thought that was a little cruel, but right now I didn't care. If that's what it took to shake Wei Ang-Ran up and get him to talk, it was fine with me. "How did these triad members know where to go?" Mark repeated.

The old man shook his head, a slow movement. "I know nothing about them. They come to Lion Rock when the shipments come in. They take what is theirs, they leave again. I try to keep away from them. They frighten me."

Great, I thought, a consensus.

Wei Ang-Ran's eyes, which would not look at Mark or at me, glistened. He turned them to the window, to the gray harbor, the ships you couldn't see. "When I started smuggling," he said to the water, "it was the time of the Cultural Revolution. I knew what was happening in China. Everyone knew. Ancient treasures smashed in the streets, fed into bonfires while gangsters howled. Lee Lao-Li came to me. I knew him only as a dealer in fine antiquities; at that time I knew nothing about Strength and Harmony. He begged me to help save the treasures of China."

In the harbor a headlamp on a ferry caught a sampan crossing the ferry's prow. The sampan was for a moment visible, then, outside the lamp's reach, vanished again.

"I knew I could not tell my brother; he would never have agreed. He was an upright, virtuous man. But he loved the ancient ways. I watched him grieve over each new report from the mainland. I thought by joining with Lee, I was doing right." In a low voice echoing with the sadness and regret of a lifetime, he said, "This was the only important decision I ever took without my brother's counsel. I knew, all through the years, that something bad would come of it. I am not a man of plans."

Mark seemed about to speak, but Wei Ang-Ran went on. "At first, the smuggled treasures were few. They were small. I felt proud to have rescued them. In one shipment were three jade Buddhas, pendants to wear. They made me think of my brother. Of his jade. I could not believe I was doing wrong.

"But they grew more numerous, came more often. I began to worry. I stopped wanting to know what was in the shipments, to see them. I wished Lion Rock were not involved in this business.

"After China changed," he went on, still speaking to the harbor, "I tried to end Lion Rock's involvement. Three times I went to Lee, saying the danger is over, I would like to sever our ties. He would not permit it. Now, of course, now that my brother has died, now that my nephew is entering the business here in Hong Kong, not in New York far away—now at least he understands continuing is impossible."

To the east along the shoreline the colored neon crowns of the buildings were starting to shine. Enough, I suddenly decided. I don't care. Damn the smuggling. I stood because I couldn't keep still anymore.

"Mark—"

"I know," Mark said. He turned to speak to Wei Ang-Ran, but as he did the conference room door opened and a uniformed cop stuck his head in.

"Sergeant, call for you. Your desk phone."

Mark's eyes met mine as he rose swiftly. Heading around the table and out the door, he pointed at Wei Ang-Ran. "Stay with him," he ordered the uniform. "He doesn't leave."

"Yes, sir."

I was right on Mark's heels through the maze to his desk. He leaned across the desk to grab up his phone, barked, *"Wai! Wai!"*

Beyond the partitions, in the maze, the sounds of cops coming and going. In here, silence. Mark, holding the phone to his ear, walked around the desk and sat in the chair behind it. Listening, listening—finally, in Cantonese, he asked, "What about the woman? Does Ko have her?"

More silence while he listened to the answer.

"No," Mark said. "Yes, okay."

I squeezed my hands into tight fists of frustration while I followed Mark's half of this conversation. It was like listening to a radio broadcast constantly interrupted by static.

"Shit," Mark said. "Damn. No, it's not your fault, Shen." Glancing at his watch: "Well, that depends—you're off duty by now, you want to stay with it? . . . They're triad, Strength and Harmony. The European's an American cop. . . . No, unofficial. . . . Because you didn't need to know until now, Shen." Longer pause. "No." Pause. "All right, good." Another silence, ending with, "We will. Good work, Shen."

He hung up, looked up at me, switched to English. "Shen stayed on Smith while he talked to Siu and Chou and followed them when they went off together. Ko tried to stay with Maria Quezon but he lost her. I can see that; the town there is worse than Wan Chai, where we lost the prayer-seller."

"And?"

"Smith, Siu, and Chou got on a boat, a small launch, and headed around the south side of Cheung Chau. Shen says it looked like Smith went under his own steam, that he wasn't coerced. Shen and Ko rented a sampan, all they could get. The launch was too fast for them. They lost it. They're still on the water, but it's getting dark."

Boats. Bill doesn't like boats. "You told Shen Bill was a cop," I said. "He's not a cop."

"But Shen is. He's likely to take a personal interest in what happens to another cop. He and Ko are going to stay out there, see what they can find."

I met Mark's eyes. They were dark and unguarded, and they looked like mine. Bill's eyes were deep-set, shadowed. "Thank you," I said.

He nodded. "I think—"

But I wasn't about to hear what Mark thought. Cutting off his words, a cell phone rang. Mine, cheeping from my belt. I hate you, I thought as I yanked at it and flipped it open. You stupid thing, I hate you.

And then was immediately sorry, because the voice was Bill's.

"Lydia, it's me." His words, I thought, sounded wrong: tight and strained. A chill touched my spine.

"Are you all right?" I said. "Where are you?"

"A boat, off Cheung Chau." No more answer than that.

"Are you all right?" I asked again.

"Been better," he said. "Not as tough as I thought. Should have trained longer. Maybe as a stuntman." A laugh, without humor.

He's hurt, I thought, hurt badly enough that he's not thinking straight. "Bill—"

Then a voice that wasn't his.

"He's definitely been better," Tony Siu said in Cantonese. "But he could definitely be worse. How're you doing?" As though we were making casual conversation.

"What the hell's going on?" I demanded.

"I want the kid," Tony Siu said, in the same easygoing manner. "What I really want is to throw your friend here into the ocean so I can watch him kick for a while before he sinks. But I can wait. I can probably wait until morning. If I don't have the kid by morning, splash."

Careful, Lydia, I told myself. Take a deep breath and play this carefully. "I don't have him," I said. "Harry. I don't know where he is."

"That's what your friend says. It's what he says now, at least. An hour or so ago on the Praya he said for the right price he'd take us straight to him." I looked up at Mark. His jaw was tight with the same frustration that had clenched mine a few minutes back.

"We worked out a deal," Tony Siu went on. He was much more articulate in Chinese than in English, but it didn't make him more likable. "He'd been sitting there with the kid's amah looking into each other's eyes like they just got out of bed, so I figured he knew. Actually, I still think he knows, but he wants to be a fucking American hero.

Anyway, he says he knows, so we rent this stinking boat.
Sail around to the ass end of this stinking island. Now he
tells me he doesn't have any fucking idea where the kid is,
he was just buying the amah time to run." In English he
suddenly exploded, "Cocksucker!"

I heard a thud, and a groan. "No!" I shouted into the
phone.

"Oh, yes," Tony Siu's voice came back. "I don't like
this guy at all."

"What do you want?"

"I told you, I want the kid."

"Why?"

"Fuck you, sweetie. All you need to know is that I'm
offering an exchange of merchandise. What I have here is
damaged, maybe, but still usable. I thought of you because
last night you seemed to care. It's too late for that nose, by
the way, but it wasn't so great anyway."

"Tony, I can't—"

"By morning, sweetie. What I want isn't even yours, so
what's your problem? Unless," he said, as if something had
just occurred to him, "unless you don't care. Unless you,
or whoever the hell it is you work for, don't really give a
shit what happens to this motherfucker. Tell me, because if
that's true I'll just go on, have a little fun out here, not
bother you anymore."

"No," I said. "No. I'll see what I can do. Leave him
alone."

"Well, no, that's not part of the deal. In fact, this merchandise is losing its value as we speak. I'd recommend
you get moving."

"Tony, if he's hurt—"

"What?" A mocking laugh. "What? You'll do what?"

Another thud, another groan.

Another laugh.

"Get moving, sweetie," Tony said.

My stomach churned; I squeezed the phone so hard I
thought I'd break it. "How do I contact you?"

"I'll take care of that. You have enough problems." One more laugh, then silence.

I lowered the phone and folded it.

"Lydia?" Mark came around the desk. I felt his hands warm on my arms. "Sit down. You're shivering. What happened? Yang!" he called over the partition to another cop, his voice taking on the cadences of Cantonese. "Bring me some tea in here." Back to English: "Lydia, what happened?"

I looked up at him. "They're on a boat. They want Harry in exchange for Bill."

A uniformed cop came around the partition with a steaming cup of tea. Mark nodded at me. I wrapped my hands around the teacup. So damn cold in here, I thought: Why do they keep every place so damn cold?

"Better?" Mark asked.

I realized it was the second time he'd asked that. I nodded, sipping.

"That was Tony Siu?"

Another nod.

"Is Smith all right?" Mark asked quietly.

I shook my head, all I could do.

"But he's alive? You spoke to him?"

"Yes."

"All right." Mark crouched in front of the chair I sat in. "All right. We'll do everything we can. Tell me what they said."

I gave him what I could, Tony Siu's words so glaringly bright in my mind that I couldn't clearly see them.

Mark didn't move until I was done. Then, perching on the edge of his desk, he picked up a pad and made some notes. "Who's your cell phone carrier?"

I told him.

"Smith's too?"

"Yes."

"Okay. I can put a trace on those, maybe triangulate. It's a long shot but worth trying. Shen knows what the launch looks like, and Smith says they're still off Cheung Chau. I can call Marine District; they have boats, and Cheung Chau's theirs. They can be looking for the amah, too." He breathed deeply. "Siu said, until morning."

"Mark, what are we going to do? Even if we find Harry, we can't turn him over to them!"

"Of course we can't. But if we find him we can talk to them as people with something to trade. Draw them out, bring them to us."

Something to trade, I thought. Damaged merchandise.

"But," Mark asked, "why the hell do they want him?"

"I don't know," I said. "If the whole thing was a phony kidnapping set up by Wei Ang-Ran, why are they suddenly trying to make it a real one now?"

"Maybe," Mark said, tapping his pencil on the pad, "they heard about the second ransom demand, the one you're trying to tell me Franklin was behind, and they realize there's two million U.S. to be made by whoever has the boy."

"Trying to tell you. You don't think so?"

"You told me Grandfather Gao said Franklin's impulsive but not malicious."

"Maybe he had an impulse to make two million dollars."

He shook his head. "It doesn't fit. And we have him calling L. L. Lee from New York. If you told me he was part of the smuggling operation, I'd think about it. But not this."

Franklin working with his father's brother to smuggle artifacts out of China? Maybe. Maybe not. I didn't give a damn about that now. Something else had just broken through my thoughts, something very dark lit up by Tony Siu's glaring words.

"Beaten up and thrown into the water with his hands tied, to drown." I stared at Mark. "Isn't that how Iron Fist Chang died?"

Mark nodded but he didn't look at me, and I realized he'd already thought of that but hadn't told me.

"Work something else out with me," he said. I didn't know if he really wanted something else worked out, or if he just wanted to change the subject. I sipped my tea; it was bitter and overbrewed, but it was warming me up. My mind began to work again; I felt as if a wave had crashed over me, making it hard to see or hear. It was receding now, and I could think again, though everything looked different, strange, rearranged by the tide.

"If Siu and Chou heard about the second demand, whoever the hell made it, and Franklin's offer," Mark said, "how?"

"Maybe they didn't," I said slowly, exploring the landscape around me, the new shapes of things turned up by the waves. "Maybe they didn't hear about the demand. Maybe *they* made it."

Mark gave me a long skeptical look, then shook his head. "They knew the boy was gone and they decided to get in on the take?"

"Why not?"

"Because the question's the same. How did they know?"

Odd the number of things you can see, things that were hidden but always there, once the tide goes out.

"The Weis apartment was a wreck when we got there," I said, still speaking slowly. "Mark, it hadn't been searched. It had been bugged."

"Then why—?"

"To hide their traces. Maybe they broke something, spilled something, I don't know. They couldn't hide the fact they'd been there, so they made it look like something else."

"Siu and Chou? They were in on it from the beginning? Wei Ang-Ran's lying?"

"I don't think so. Maybe they found out from Iron Fist."

"Wei Ang-Ran says he only involved him after, to make the phone call."

"All right, I don't know how they found out, but suppose they did. They bugged the apartment, so they knew everything that was going on. They made the second demand themselves." And, I thought to myself? And so what, Lydia? Does this help find Harry? Does it help Bill? "What's the difference?" I heard my voice rising, getting a little wild. Breathe, I thought, control, breathe. "Mark, we need to find Harry. We need to find Bill."

Mark looked at me, saw in my eyes my need to be up and moving.

"All right," he said, looking down at the pad in his hand. "I'm going to get these things started. Then we'll go up and see the Weis. Then we'll go to Cheung Chau."

"The Weis won't talk to you."

"I have another case now. Two: Smith, and Iron Fist Chang. These guys want Harry in exchange for Smith, now I can go see the Weis. They can deny anything's wrong if they want. But at least I can tell them I think their place is bugged. If they let me I can send someone up to sweep."

I nodded. "Mark?"

"What?"

"Thank you. And thank you for not telling me, 'Don't worry, everything's going to be all right.' "

"It will," he said, "if I can make it." He ripped the sheet off his pad. "Hold on," he said. "This will take a few minutes." He gave my hand a quick squeeze, the way he had back in the conference room. I didn't feel quite as hopeful now, but it still helped. Then he left.

I sat without moving in Mark's cubicle, listening to the sounds of cops coming and going. Police stations never stop, I thought. You have to keep doing this, do it forever, over and over, because the bad guys, men like Tony Siu, never stop either. Maybe this isn't really the world. Maybe it's the afterlife, some kind of purgatory where the punishment for being evil in your last life is to be endlessly, futilely, hopelessly battling evil in this one.

I tried to remember whether any of the stories I'd heard as a child, any of the ancient tales my father had told, had said anything about that. It was true that the tales said you went on in death according, one way and another, to how you'd been in life. That's why my mother had sent chef's knives to my father, why those pottery houses in L. L. Lee's shop had ducks and chickens and servants. Although

I'd rather have the little game players sent into the afterlife with me; I'd rather have friends.

A thought shot straight through me, almost throwing me out of the chair. L. L. Lee. Oh, my God, Lydia. Bill would do better with those little bronze game players for friends than he's doing with you.

But one good thing about this thought being so late in coming: Mark wasn't here when I had it.

I grabbed the pad Mark had left behind and scribbled him a note. *I'm sorry*, it said. *I thought of something and I have to do it alone. I'll call you.*

I propped the pad against his lamp and hurried out of the cubicle, finding my way to the elevator by memory and prayer.

twelve

I was afraid Mark, or another cop, or someone, would see me and stop me, but no one did. I walked past the security desk and found myself outside, pushing through the soft blanket of evening heat. I hailed a cab and in Cantonese told the driver, "The home of Lee Lao-Li, on Harlech Road." Maybe L. L. Lee's place was as famous as Mark had said and the driver would know right where to go. If not, we could cruise the Peak, looking for Ming lions inside gates on Harlech Road.

But the driver did know, although the look he gave me in the mirror expressed his doubts about whether, once we found those gates, I'd be allowed through them. I got his point. I'd never in my life felt so wrung out, damp, rumpled, and used-up, and I knew I looked it. It felt like a million years since I'd put on crisp linen and set out with Bill for the Filipina sea.

I set my phone to vibrate instead of ring, settled back against the seat, and tried to think of nothing as the cab climbed from the glittering neon and whipping traffic of Central through the high-rise residential neighborhood on the hillside above and from there into the leafy darkness of the Peak.

Here, the road snaked beside rough stone walls, under banyan trees as wide as I was tall, under stands of rubber and maple and shaggy-barked pine with the lights of houses glowing between them. Here, money bought distance from your neighbors, from the smells of their dinners and the noises of their children playing and crying. It bought gardens that were more than pots on windowsills, gardens with paths and palm trees, ponds and benches, where you could stroll and think. It bought rooms where you could read, or study a bronze figure, without having to fold up a daybed or move the breakfast dishes from the table. What money bought here was the privilege of slowing down.

The cab made a couple of turns on roads that, as far as I could see, did not have road signs. My phone jiggled on my hip twice as we drove. Both times I snatched it up, hoping, but both times the number on the readout was Mark's, at the station. I let the voice-mail message tell him I'd call him back as soon as I could.

Finally, as though he did it every day, the driver pulled to a stop at a pair of iron gates. Just inside them two huge curly-maned stone lions, the female on the left with her paw on her cub, the male on the right with his paw on the globe of the world, watched us with glaring eyes and snarling mouths.

The driver took my money and looked me over once again. "Do I wait?" he asked.

I thought. "Yes." Just because I wanted to see L. L. Lee didn't mean he was home. And if he was, and I saw him, I still wanted to be able to get down from here fast, and go with Mark to Cheung Chau.

I gave the driver fifty Hong Kong dollars for his waiting time, wondering as I got out whether he'd disappear with it and leave me alone in the dark. Well, if that happened, I'd worry about it later. I pressed the bell. After a foot-tapping wait, during which I was slightly surprised to find that the cab did not drive away, but even turned its radio on and its engine off, a voice issued forth from the speaker set into the gatepost. It asked me in Chinese who I was and what business I had.

"I am Chin Ling Wan-Ju," I told it. "I wish to speak to Lee Lao-Li about a gift for my brother. Also about Lion Rock Enterprises."

That should identify me for L. L. Lee. I tapped my foot some more in the quiet dark, listening to leaves rustling against each other and cicadas whirring. What had been the haze of early evening below was drifting mist up here on the Peak. It floated across the road and paused lazily in the treetops, as though it had nothing urgent to do, no worries, no fears. The speaker didn't say anything more, but finally, just as I was about to jab the button again, a soft electronic click preceded the silent, slow opening of the gates.

I hurried up the path. Probably, a corner of my mind said, this was a lovely place, especially now, as twilight changed to night. Gravel crunched peacefully underfoot; more statues hid, pale among the greenery; here and there a lantern shone softly, to show the way, and pine and palm trees shadowed a fragrant flower border. Yes, lovely. I charged through it as fast as any Hong Kong citizen on a crowded sidewalk at high noon.

The house loomed before me as I came around a curve in the path. A square white house, I was surprised to see, stucco with a dark tile roof, big windows with wooden shutters: nothing Chinese about it at all. But then, the mansions on the Peak had been built by Europeans, not Chinese, and they, like anyone, had built the houses of home.

Columns flanked the front door, sheltering a porch and lifting a balcony over the treetops. The view from there must be spectacular, Hong Kong Island falling away below you, the sea to the south, the out-islands. Maybe from that balcony you could even see Cheung Chau. But not on a night like this, with a blanket of mist hiding from view everything below. And most nights on the Peak, from what I'd read, were like this.

I tried to guess the age of the house, but I'm not good at that. The 1920s, maybe, or a little earlier. That was the kind of question I always asked Bill; these were the things he always knew.

I climbed the three steps; as I reached the door, it opened. Apparently, once you were inside the gate, there was no need to ring any more bells; the hospitality of L. L. Lee was yours.

Of course, that also meant someone was at all times keeping careful track, on that lovely path, of exactly where you were.

A young man in a navy tunic and pants, black hair brushed straight back from his solemn face, held the door as I walked through it, then closed it quietly behind me.

Bowing, not once speaking, he turned and walked across the wide marble foyer to another heavy wooden door, which he opened also, and held.

My sandals slapped against the marble as his silent footsteps had not. The sound abruptly stopped when I crossed through the door and onto a cream-colored carpet where huntsmen rode the forest, sending arrows after elephants and deer. A prince and his courtiers galloped from the left, bows taut, banners flying. They were matched exactly, arrows and horses, men and dogs, by another prince and more men-at-arms coming from the right. The luster of the carpet in the soft lamplight made me understand it was not wool, but silk.

"Do you like the hunt?" asked a voice, speaking in English, not loud but hard as stone. Across the room, L. L. Lee sat in a carved chair in a pool of light. The three walls surrounding him were open wide to the night, their shuttered doors thrown back. Sweet scents and soft sounds floated in from the garden to drift around the lacquered furniture and brush against porcelain jars holding slender yellow blooms. The age of the house my own ignorance kept me from knowing, but this room was different. It might be newly built, finished even yesterday: no matter. It was ancient, the scholar's study unchanging through two thousand years of the Chinese past.

I crossed the carpet and stood before L. L. Lee. "No," I answered him, in Cantonese. "Shedding blood for pleasure has never appealed to me."

"The hunters hunt from necessity; the people must be fed. That it also gives them pleasure is a fortunate thing."

"It's all the same to the prey."

"Speak to me in English. As you told me earlier, your Cantonese is poor."

"My Cantonese," I said, switching into English, "is the language I was raised in. But as you say."

He nodded. "Sit."

I did, on a mahogany bench scattered with cushions. The young man returned, opening the solid European door in the solid European wall to enter this Chinese garden pavilion. He carried tea things on a tray. He set the tray on an ebony table, bowed, and left.

When the young man was gone, L. L. Lee lifted the pot, swirled it in the traditional gesture of welcoming a guest, and poured golden, sweet-smelling tea into tiny cups. The pot was small and white, painted with plum blossoms in the snow. Plum blossoms also circled the cups, both inside and out.

He waited for me to taste the tea. It was as sweet as it smelled, tropical, mild, for evening. He lifted his cup after I drank from mine, sipped his own tea, then spoke.

"Why have you come to see me?"

The formal grace of ritual hospitality did nothing to soften the stone in his voice.

"Two men who work for you—they call themselves Tony Siu and Big John Chou—are holding my partner," I said, in a measured, hard voice myself. "He's injured and they're threatening to kill him. They're demanding that I give them the great-nephew of Wei Ang-Ran, the man who smuggles antiquities from China for you, in exchange. I don't know where the boy is and if I did I wouldn't turn him over to men like that. I want them to release my partner and I want to know why you want the boy."

I didn't have to identify Wei Ang-Ran for L. L. Lee; he knew perfectly well who he was. I did that to cut out any dancing around we might otherwise have to do, about what I knew, about who he was.

"Your partner." He nodded. "The Spaniard."

"That was a ruse. He's as American as I am. We came here to bring a gift to the boy from his grandfather, who recently died in New York."

In the slight lift of his eyebrows and the nod L. L. Lee gave me, I read a connoisseur's cold appreciation of skill in an art he doesn't care for. "A ruse. Well done, then."

"I'm sure he'll thank you if he gets the chance."

"What do you want?"

"I told you: I want them to let him go. I want to know why you want the boy."

"What are you offering?"

I'd been expecting that. "I don't know." I took a breath. "Whatever reason you have for wanting the boy, maybe I can help you achieve your goal another way."

L. L. Lee's eyes rested on me then, and we sat in silence for a time, in this room both indoors and out, open and enclosed, solid and here and ancient and legendary.

"No," he said. "Your value is limited. This is the way you will be most useful."

My cheeks blazed. No, Lydia! I ordered myself: Think why you're here. Forcing myself calm, I spoke. "There must be another."

"This is the way I choose."

"Why? To accomplish what?"

"That is not your concern. You must find the boy."

"My partner—"

"Will live, if you find the boy."

"I think," I said, trying to keep my voice hard, "that Tony Siu will kill him before morning."

Another long look. Then: "No. That will not happen."

"You can promise that?"

"Yes."

"And that he won't hurt him further?"

A pause, and then a nod. "Yes."

"And if I can't find the boy?"

"Then I can promise nothing."

L. L. Lee put his teacup down. A tendril of mist from the branches of the pines outside crept into the room, wandering past a scroll painting of pine trees and mist.

"This is about the smuggling," I said. "You intend to use the boy to pressure his father into continuing smuggling for you."

"A father," he said, as if instructing me on a law of nature, "will look for a way to express gratitude at the rescue of his son."

Rescue. But I let it pass. "How did you know the boy was missing?"

"I was told."

"By Tony Siu?"

"By someone who knew."

"How do you know the father will do as you want?"

"Indebtedness is a powerful motivation."

"So is fear."

"For many people."

"How did Tony Siu know to go to Cheung Chau?"

His stony gaze rested on me. "Shall we sit here until morning, discussing the past?"

"No." I stood. "But I have until morning. And I have your promise."

L. L. Lee spoke not another word, nor took his eyes from me, as I crossed the hunter's carpet. The door to the room I opened myself. The silent young man pulled wide the front door as I crossed the marble hall, and shut it without a sound behind me, leaving me standing alone on the porch facing the path through the trees.

I raced down the path as quickly as I'd come up it. Outside the iron gates, which swung wide as I reached them and closed when I was through them, my cab was still sitting, engine off, radio on. Whatever the fare for the ride down the mountain, I decided, this cabbie was getting double, protocol be damned. I told him where I wanted to go and pulled out my cell phone. Twice more during my talk with Lee it had shaken discreetly on my hip. I'd glanced down, but both times it was Mark. I hadn't answered.

Now, without listening to the messages, I called him back.

"Wai!"

"Mark?" I said, closing my eyes against the blast to come. "It's Lydia."

It came. "Where the hell are you?" Mark roared.

It was obvious nothing I said would be okay, but I gave

him the truth anyway. "Up on the Peak. I went to see L. L. Lee."

"You went to—Jesus Christ, Lydia! You sit there handing me this shit, Siu and Chou, Franklin Wei—you just couldn't wait until I was out of the room, could you?"

"It wasn't like that. I didn't think of this until after you left. But Mark—"

"Where are you now?"

"In a cab on the way back."

"To where?"

"Police headquarters."

"Good. I'll arrest you when you get here."

"Mark—"

"Goddamnit, Lydia! What the *hell* were you thinking?"

"I was thinking Lee could stop Tony Siu from killing Bill!"

Momentarily, Mark was silent.

"And I was also thinking," I admitted quietly, "that if I told you I wanted to come up here and talk to him you wouldn't let me."

More silence. My cab took a sharp turn and the harbor opened below us, sparkling lights on black water.

"Goddamn right," said Mark, but in a calmer voice, his three-alarm fury subsiding into a controlled burn. "Goddamn right I wouldn't have let you."

"If I were the cop I wouldn't have let me either," I said. "But I had to come."

"Yeah," he said. "Yeah, okay. We'll go into that later. I guess you survived. Did you get anything?"

"He's intending this to be the 'rescue' of Harry. He expects Steven, in his gratitude, to continue the smuggling operation for him."

"I thought of that. I may be just a dumb cop—"

"I never said that."

"—but it did dawn on me that Siu and Chou work for L. L. Lee. Except I was thinking more along the lines of extortion than gratitude."

"What you see depends on where you stand."

"I was going to suggest it to you when I got back to my desk."

"I'm sorry, Mark. I really am."

"You should be. Don't go back to headquarters."

"No?"

"No. Meet me at the HKPD Marine Piers." He gave me the address. "I was about to take off for Cheung Chau."

I let out a long breath. "Thank you," I said, and meant it.

"Oh, no problem. Anything for our American cousins."

"Does that make you your own cousin?"

"Just get here. You'll want to hear what I've been doing, too."

"You haven't been sitting around obsessing over where I went?"

"Don't push it."

"Sorry."

I closed up the phone, gave the driver our new destination, and for the rest of the ride tried, by breathing in and breathing out, to bring a rhythm of calm to the pounding of my heart.

At the foot of the mountain, across the rushing highway, the HKPD Pier was ringed with a chain-link fence. My cab dropped me at the gate, where the driver seemed on the verge of expressing his outrage at the insult my large tip implied. Then, probably contemplating how hard it would have been for me, after all, to find another way down the Peak, and contemplating also the upcoming race day at Happy Valley, he grudgingly stuffed my money in his pocket and U-turned away.

I crossed the asphalt to the guard booth. Before I reached it, its door swung open and Mark jumped out. He waved to the guard, took my elbow and, wordless, hurried me along down a concrete pier to a sleek launch rocking impatiently on the harbor waves. It had an HKPD ID number painted on the sides and cabin roof and the cabin lights were lit. Growling, its engine exhaled diesel fuel into the sea air. It tugged on the thick rope tethering it as though anxious to get going. Or maybe that was me.

A uniformed cop on the dock pulled the boat close enough for us to leap onto. He slipped the single rope that had been holding it to the concrete, glass and asphalt of downtown Hong Kong, and we were at sea.

I watched the skyscrapers and neon recede fast, signs and logos blurring into a ragged rainbow in the mist. Rushing wind blew my hair into my eyes. I brushed it back. The snarl of the engine was louder now that it was released to run, and the wind covered me in a fine salt spray and tore my words away. I had to yell twice to Mark to make myself heard. "How long will it take us to get there?"

"Half an hour," he answered. "Come below."

In the cabin I could feel the engine pound but its noise was less. The trim room, in fact, seemed like a miraculous place of peace after the spray and the growl and the wind. Forward of us, in a glassed-in cockpit, the launch's captain, his HKPD uniform including discreet nautical insignia on the shoulders, held the wheel. Another Marine District cop on deck did whatever else you have to do to get a boat from here to there.

Mark closed the cabin door. Now it was quiet enough to talk in this room, and we were alone.

Before us, a small table was folded out of the wall between two benches that were also bunks and storage bins, depending on what you needed. On the table, a battered kettle released a thin trail of steam from its spout. The steam coiled through the air like the ghost of the electric cord snaking along the table to an outlet behind it. Next to the kettle sat two Styrofoam boxes. The smell of diesel fuel was no match for the aromas of fish paste and soy sauce filling the cabin.

Silently Mark handed me a pair of chopsticks.

"You're feeding me?" I was amazed. "I thought you were going to kill me, and instead you're feeding me?"

"Maybe I poisoned it."

"Maybe I don't care."

We dropped onto opposite benches and attacked the boxes. Slippery wide *chow fun* noodles shared space and sauce with bitter greens, carrots, and shrimp.

"It's to make up for the noodles before," Mark said.

"Forgiven."

A squat, slow ferry drifted up beside us. Mark said, "That was crazy, what you did, Lydia."

I lifted a shrimp off its noodles. "No," I said. I looked at the shrimp, not at Mark, as I went on. "I'm not dangerous to L. L. Lee. In fact he needs me. I'm the only person who cares enough about Bill for this to work. Without me he'd have to find Harry himself."

The launch bucked, slapping the water, as we crossed the ferry's wake. Lifting my eyes to Mark I added, "Lee promised me they wouldn't hurt him anymore. That Tony Siu wouldn't kill him before morning."

"And after that?" Mark asked softly.

I looked away again and shook my head.

For a brief time there was only silence in the cabin, and the aroma of food I seemed to have lost my appetite for. Then Mark went back to something else I'd said.

"About L. L. Lee finding Harry himself: Siu and Chou came close."

"Yes," I said, grateful for something to focus on, "and I wish I knew how."

"I do."

"What?" I braced myself against the table as the launch veered. "Tell me!"

"I don't know," said Mark. "It'll probably just give you another bright idea and you'll go charging off someplace."

"Mark—"

"You're not going to do it again, Lydia, okay?"

"Just that once. I had to."

"Twice, actually. I don't remember you telling me you were going to look for the prayer-seller."

I nodded guiltily. The launch resumed a steady course. "That's true. But—"

"—but you had to. And you knew I wouldn't let you."

"Am I wrong?"

"No, you're right. I wouldn't have. I'm trying to keep you from getting killed."

"I don't need—"

"Oh yes you do! Maybe you can run around New York like that, but this is Hong Kong. It's different here."

"It's not different! People want the same things and go after them in the same ways. Money, love, respect." God, Lydia, I thought, this is what Bill said to you in Kwong Hon Terrace Garden, a million years ago, yesterday. "The balance may be different but it doesn't really matter. You, for example," I told Mark. "Right now you're acting like every other cop I've ever met."

"Proving you must be as far out of line back home as you've been here."

I slumped back against the cabin wall. "Okay," I said. "Okay, you're probably right. Can we table this? I'm trying to save Bill's life. I'm trying to bring a little boy home. I'm doing the best I can."

Mark put down his chopsticks, too, and looked at me. I met his eyes, and I didn't look away, but the cabin began to feel small and confined, and I wished I were on deck, alone, with only the wind and the spray, moving very fast across the huge ocean.

"Okay," Mark said. "Okay, now listen. I'm out on a limb here. I've requisitioned a boat and two Marine District cops. I have Shen and Ko out there doing overtime, and Wei Ang-Ran, a respected businessman, not quite under arrest back at Headquarters. I have you, a civilian—worse, an *American* civilian—heading with me out to Cheung Chau, which is against every regulation we have. My excuse, when someone finally asks—and they will—will be that you had knowledge essential to the case, that you were the only person who could have led me where we needed to go when we got to Cheung Chau. Of course, that's complete bullshit. You don't know anything I don't know already, and that's not why I'm letting you come."

He picked up a chopstick and bounced it on the Styrofoam box. "All this probably kills any chance I had left of ever making lieutenant but I can live with that. What I can*not* live with is if you, or Smith, or Harry, or *anybody*, winds up worse off because you're here than they would have been if I'd left you standing on the quay."

He reached for the teakettle and poured hot water into a chipped white pot. He swirled the pot around, then put it down to settle and steep. "Now eat your dinner, because you'll need it. And listen to what I've been doing, because by now *I* know a lot of things *you* don't, and the more blanks we can fill in before we get to Cheung Chau, the better off we'll be."

Eyes on Mark, I picked up my chopsticks, too, but I didn't use them right away. " 'Casting a brick to attract a piece of jade,' " I said.

Mark frowned. "What?"

"Those two Tang Dynasty poets, I don't remember their names. You must have learned about them in Chinese school. One of them wrote two lines of poetry on a monastery wall because he knew the other one, who was a much better poet, couldn't resist finishing an unfinished poem. Then the world would have two more lines of great poetry."

"And?"

"I feel like the brick here."

He stared at me, shook his head, and went back to his noodles. But I saw the corners of his mouth tug upward, and that was enough.

"Okay," I said, a few *chow fun* later. "What have you been doing?"

Mark poked around in his noodles, hunting shrimp. "After I got back to my desk and found you gone," he said pointedly, "and after I'd reamed out a few innocent cops who had no idea they weren't supposed to let you leave, I went to see the Weis. I didn't know when the hell you'd ever show up again, and talking to the Weis was as good an idea without you as it had been with you."

Ignoring the accusatory tone, which I deserved, I asked, "What did you find?"

"One: The flat *was* bugged."

"No kidding! You found the bug?"

"I found one. I sent a sweeper. He should be there by now; he'll find any more. I did this whole stupid mime-show thing, flashed my badge and made the elevator guy take me up without announcing me, made the Weis come out into the hall before I opened my mouth. Franklin was there, by the way."

"Franklin? Did you—?"

"I ran it through in my head and decided whatever he's up to, let him think we're on to it but not on to him. Maybe he'll tip his hand. So I told them about Iron Fist Chang, about Smith, about the trade for Harry. I asked them how long he'd been missing, just to hear what they'd say."

"What did they say?"

"One little hesitation from Steven, then it all came out. I don't think the lawyer wanted him to tell me, but once he started, he didn't stop."

"Natalie Zhu? She was there?"

"Is that surprising? I thought you said she was always there."

"She seems to be, except she wasn't there earlier today, and Steven was vague about where she'd gone. To see another client, he said. That *was* surprising."

"Well, she's back. Anyway, I told them I had reason to believe Harry was on Cheung Chau. I said we had no intention of making the trade, but I was going to try to find him whether or not they admitted he was gone, because now there were some pretty nasty customers also wanting him. That seemed to be what decided Steven to talk."

"Did he tell you anything new?"

"No, pretty much exactly what you'd said. I fudged a little on how I got into the thing, by the way—they think it was through the Iron Fist Chang case—so they wouldn't think you went to the police when you were told not to."

"Thank you."

"I didn't do it to do you a favor. I wasn't in much of a mood to do you favors right then. But I thought it might be useful if they still trusted you, if we ever need them for anything."

Like, I thought, letting us use poor little Harry as bait to lure Tony Siu and Big John Chou to us. But that was probably against any remaining HKPD regulations Mark wasn't breaking right now, so I didn't mention it.

"They did say you'd also told them Harry was on Cheung Chau," Mark went on. "That the amah had taken him there."

"How did Steven react when you told them Wei Ang-Ran was responsible for the whole thing, and what it was about?"

"I didn't."

"You—why?" A noodle slithered off my chopsticks and fell back in the box.

"What would have been the point? I didn't have time for the whole drama, denials, family loyalty, all that. I was there to find out if they knew anything that could help, and to see if the place was bugged. I let them think I had no idea what the connection between Smith and Harry was, or why Siu wanted Harry except maybe to extort a fortune from Steven because no one would pay that kind of money for Smith, who he already had."

No one? I thought, but didn't say it.

"I didn't mention L. L. Lee, but I did mention that Siu and Chou were triad members, in case Steven needed persuading to talk to me."

"Sounds reasonable." And since it would just about break Steven's heart to hear the truth about his uncle, the longer he waited, the better. "Tell me about the bug," I said to Mark, lifting the noodle again.

"In a lamp on the desk. Probably good for the whole room. I ripped it out. The sweeper will find anything else. I told them not to say anything in the flat they wouldn't want to read in the newspapers until he's come and gone."

I chewed and swallowed a mouthful of bitter greens. "If I say, *good work,* will it sound patronizing?"

"No." He grinned, the scar on his lip paling. "But it would be premature."

"What do you mean?"

"There's more and it's better. I found the connection."

"Between what and what?"

"Harry Wei's kidnapping and Iron Fist Chang."

"Besides Wei Ang-Ran getting him to make the phone call?"

"Uh-huh. I think I can explain why the Wei's place was bugged and who bugged it."

"You can?"

"Why are PIs always surprised when cops do something smart?" he mused, scratching his head theatrically.

"Hey, how do you know? You said you don't even have PIs in Hong Kong!"

"We have some, just not many," he said, mock defensive. "And anyway, I've seen enough American movies to know this is how it works."

"Mark!"

"All right," he said. "Remember Natalie Zhu told you Maria Quezon had a boyfriend?"

"Yes, and?"

"And, Iron Fist Chang had a Filipina girlfriend."

"What?" I stared in disbelief. "You're kidding."

"Nope. That's how Iron Fist ended up at Lion Rock. See, stick with me instead of running all over town alone, you could learn things."

I considered throwing my noodles at him, but managed to restrain myself.

Mark went on: "Wei Ang-Ran told us he was recommended to his older brother, and that was good enough for him, but he didn't know who by. Well, it seems he was recommended by Harry's amah. The Weis all know him. Knew him," he amended. "That's how they got into the flat. The doormen had standing instructions to let Iron Fist up anytime. Steven said he was a polite, respectful guy, not overendowed in the brains department but always anxious to be helpful."

"Helpful." I tried to think, absorbing these new facts. "So maybe he was helping."

"That's what I'm thinking."

"Maria tells him what Wei Ang-Ran wants her to do. She's stuck—she doesn't trust Ang-Ran that it's all as innocent as he says, but if she refuses, she's afraid he'll just get her fired and even booted out of the country. That wouldn't do either her or Harry any good."

"And Iron Fist goes to his buddies, Siu and Chou, because they're smart." Mark picked it up. "He tells them the problem, and they get a brilliant idea: They'll bug the Wei flat and find out what's really going on."

"That's not such a brilliant idea. The Weis don't know what's really going on."

"But if you're Iron Fist Chang and Tony Siu tells you it's a brilliant idea, maybe you fall for it. And if you're Tony Siu, what you're looking for is not a way to help out your buddy Iron Fist and his girlfriend, because you're Tony Siu and you don't give a damn about them. What you're looking for is an angle of your own. So you go up and bug the flat, and you knock something over so you set about making the place look trashed, and in the middle of that the intercom buzzes and Iron Fist, not the sharpest knife in the drawer, answers it."

"Iron Fist—oh, God. He's the one who let me and Bill in?"

"Looks that way. What could he say to the doorman after he'd answered, except to tell him to send you up as though everything was normal? Then he and Siu probably beat it down the stairs."

"They were there," I breathed. "They were right there, just before we were. Oh, damn. Damn. Damn."

Mark nodded. "Okay. So: You're Tony Siu, looking for your angle. You head to wherever your listening post is and—"

"—and you find one," I finished for him. "Freelance extortion. You're working it—the second demand—when the boss calls and says go find me this kidnapped kid, I want to use him for something." I drank some tea, trying to straighten all this out in my head. "I wonder how L. L. Lee would feel if he found out Siu was freelancing?"

"He might not care, as long as when he snapped his fingers Siu dropped his own project and jumped."

I had to admit that could be true. But I decided it was okay to harbor a revenge fantasy anyway.

"All right," I said, "okay, I'll buy every word of it. But where does it get us? It still doesn't tell us, for example, how Siu and Chou knew to come to Cheung Chau."

"No, but something else does. The Weis' phone wasn't the only one that was bugged. There was a tap on Maria Quezon's cell phone, too."

I just stared. "Damn," I breathed. "Oh, damn."

Mark nodded. "The conversation between Smith and Maria. He had to get someone to translate the Tagalog, or maybe he speaks it, but he was right on top of things. I thought of that—that someone might have tapped that phone—when I was setting up the taps on yours and Smith's. I called her carrier. They were surprised I didn't know: A guy answering Siu's description came to them a few days ago with HKPD ID, a court order, everything. I have someone on his way down there, but you know that stuff was forged." He added, "I was going to tell you that when I got back to my desk, too."

"Bill thought of that," I said quietly. "He told Maria not to use the cell phone."

Briefly, there was no sound in the cabin but the growl of the engine.

"There would have been another way, too, if Siu had thought of it," Mark said. "Steven Wei told me."

"Another way to do what?" I lifted my teacup. It felt heavy and took effort. I realized suddenly how bone-tired, how drained I was. Maybe this was how a teapot felt when there was nothing left inside but old used-up leaves. I couldn't think what Mark meant. "To do what?" I asked again.

"To figure out Cheung Chau might be a good bet. It's where Iron Fist Chang's from."

"Iron Fist? From Cheung Chau?"

"Don't look so surprised. Everybody's from someplace, and a lot of people are from the out-islands. But that might explain why Maria picked this one."

"Or she and Iron Fist did together. He knew a good place there to hide."

"He knew one, but he wouldn't tell his buddies. They tried to get it out of him, and then they killed him."

I thought of Iron Fist, struggling and sinking in the harbor water, and I thought of Bill, on a boat with Tony Siu and Big John Chou.

"And now," Mark said, maybe as much to break the silence as to actually say anything, "they're expecting us to find it for them. This hiding place."

I thought: In the dark. At night on an island in the middle of the ocean on the other side of the world from anywhere I know. An island I've never been to, with a huge graveyard and a town with narrow winding streets and homes on the hillsides and schools and academies because there's room.

I looked up at Mark, my eyes wide. I felt as though buckets of icy water had just washed over me out of the sky.

"I know," I said.

"You know what?"

"I know where they are."

Mark stared as though he could see the buckets of water, too, and had no idea what to make of them. "What are you talking about?"

"I don't know. Maybe I'm crazy." My flash of inspiration was already beginning to seem dubious. I tried shoring it up with logic. "Where's the best place in the world to hide a little boy?"

"If knew that I'd have looked there already."

"With lots of other little boys. If Iron Fist's from Cheung Chau that's where he must have learned his kung fu. There are academies out there, you said so. You have to start young and study for years to get as good as Iron Fist was. Bill was even wondering where the kung fu schools were, when he found out who Iron Fist was. He—oh, my God!"

"What?"

At first I couldn't answer, hearing in my head what I'd heard a few hours ago.

"What?" Mark pushed.

"Bill told us." That was a whisper; I made my voice stronger and went on. "He told us that's where Harry is. I thought he was just rambling, that he didn't know what he was saying, but he was telling us! He said, 'I should have trained harder. As a stuntman.' "

Mark frowned. "He said that on the phone?"

"I thought he was just rambling," I repeated. "Oh, God." I sank back against the bench again. "I must be the stupidest person alive."

"You think Maria told him?"

I nodded. "She told him. And he knows. And Iron Fist knew, and he didn't tell Tony Siu either. They—"

"Lydia!"

Mark yelled my name. I looked at him.

"Don't," he said. "Don't lose it now. I know you're exhausted. I know you're scared, and right now you're pissed off at yourself. But I need you to keep it together. A lot of people need you to keep it together right now."

Not true, I thought. No one needs me. Who needs an idiot like me? Running around like a headless chicken, never stopping to think—well, Lydia, your headless chickens are coming home to roost. That was pretty funny, and I laughed. Everyone always told you to slow down, Lydia, I lectured myself, and look, everyone was right. Well, not everyone. Bill never minded the running around, he even likes how you jump the gun, how fast you move. I'm sure he doesn't like being out on a boat with Tony Siu, getting beat up, but he likes how fast you move.

I closed my eyes, took a deep breath, another, another. All right. So I was stupid. I could still move.

When I opened my eyes again my breathing and my heart were under control. I didn't feel like laughing anymore, and I wasn't tired at all.

Mark, across the table, was watching me warily as he spoke into his cell phone. He raised his eyebrows in a question and I nodded in answer. His shoulders relaxed and he gave me a reassuring smile. I found my teacup and sipped my tea; I couldn't quite manage the smile.

The conversation Mark was having involved the kung fu schools on Cheung Chau—there were eight—and how to identify the one we wanted. He hung up from that call and made another. I listened as he spoke to someone at the HKPD station in the town at the center of Cheung Chau. They arranged things. Through the window behind Mark, lights floated by, not boats but buildings speckling a dark mass of hills. Our launch turned, heading left in a wide arc. I could see more lights now, and more hills. Straight ahead, a kaleidoscopic glow resolved itself, as we approached, into a waterfront strung with multicolored lanterns and lined with open-air restaurants and cafés, curving right and left from a large ferry pier.

Mark's phone rang as a change in the engine's growl told me we had slowed, approaching our dock.

"Wai?" He listened, nodded, thanked the person on the other end. Folding the phone and putting it away, he stood up. "I've got it."

"The school?"

"Tiger Gate Academy. In the northern hills. Iron Fist Chang still holds some records there, in each age and rank category."

"Poor guy."

"Yeah," Mark said. "Come on, let's go."

So much for sympathy. I wondered suddenly whether Maria Quezon knew about Iron Fist yet, that he was dead. I decided she must not: She'd have been too scared to talk to someone like Bill, whom she didn't know, if she knew people she cared about were getting killed. And who, I wondered, would tell her? And what would that be like?

The captain in the glassed-in booth cut the engine as the launch gently bumped a wooden dock, and the cop on deck threw the rope over a wooden post. Mark jumped out of the launch onto the dock and then reached a hand back to help me. I took it, even though I didn't think I needed it: I can jump too.

We walked quickly up the dock, toward a man hurrying to meet us. He and Mark saluted each other, then shook hands, introducing themselves. The other man was slight, younger than Mark, his straight-shouldered presence matching his crisp uniform. The two of them spoke quietly, privately, while I tried not to look as though I were eavesdropping. Then the other man was introduced to me, too, in Cantonese. "Lieutenant Zhang Yun, Marine District. Lieutenant Zhang," Mark addressed the other man respectfully, "this is Chin Ling Wan-Ju. She's assisting in our inquiries."

Zhang looked me over, and I wondered if this was the moment Mark had said was coming, when someone asked just what I was doing there. I also wondered how it felt for Mark to say *Lieutenant,* to hear himself say it, addressing someone so young. But Zhang just gave me a brief nod and shook my hand. This was Mark's case; Zhang was just providing requested assistance, Marine Region helping out Wan Chai. If Mark's civilian screwed things up, that would be Mark's problem.

We followed Zhang along the dock. The night was warm but wide, without the palpable weight of Hong Kong's city heat. Stars glittered overhead. The air smelled of distances and the sea. In the harbor's circling embrace the fishing fleet of Cheung Chau rocked softly at anchor. Couples, hand-in-hand, strolled the waterfront under lanterns of red, yellow, blue, and green. Small groups, largely Chinese but some Westerners, largely men but some women, sat at café tables, drinking bottled beer, talking or playing chess but mostly just watching the couples and the harbor and the night. Large dogs were everywhere. They wandered, sat, scratched themselves. None of them seemed to be any particular breed, none of them were leashed and none of them seemed to have an argument with any of the others. Like the people, they were meandering, amiably visiting, going no place in particular because where they were was just fine.

And there were no cars. Where the dock we were on met the waterfront street, a van idled, the Chinese characters for Emergency Plumbing Repair painted on its sides. It was the only vehicle in sight.

"What *is* this place?" I asked Mark, marvel in my voice. "It's like a negative. It's the total opposite of Hong Kong."

He shook his head. "It's the rest of Hong Kong. We try not to let the tourists know about places like this."

"Selfish of you."

"Can you blame us?"

I couldn't. The softness of the night and the slow quiet rhythm of the strolling couples and sleeping dogs were even working on me, making me think the world could be an okay place and the things I was worried about might turn out okay, too.

Lieutenant Zhang reached the idling plumbing-repair van and, sliding open the side door, stood aside politely, waiting for Mark and me to climb in.

Mark did, so I did too. Zhang shut the door and went around to the passenger side. He got in the front seat and gave an instruction to the driver, who, unlike Zhang, was not in uniform. This undercover plumbing van was probably his regular gig. He shifted smoothly into gear and we began to roll down the waterfront street.

Mark said to me, "They don't have cars here, except the Marine District patrol cars, two fire trucks, and an ambulance. And service vans. Siu and Chou are probably still at sea on the south side of the island, but I thought it was a good idea if we didn't go roaring up to Tiger Gate Academy in a patrol car."

The van didn't roar, but it traveled at a good clip. In less than two minutes we'd manuevered along the waterfront and entered what Cheung Chau probably thought of as its downtown: narrow lanes of two- and three-story stucco-sided, balcony-hung buildings, their ground-floor storefronts largely shuttered now, their upper-floor living quarters glowing with the soft yellow light of domestic tranquillity or, occasionally, the cooler blue light of television.

Within another two minutes we'd emerged from town and begun to climb into the hills. At first the houses along the curving road sat in companionable closeness, though often behind fences. But gradually they grew apart as their gardens got bigger, tiled courtyards with well-tended potted plants giving way to jungly undergrowth. Leafy trees and pale flowers glowed faintly under the moon, which had risen when I wasn't looking. I was glad to see the moon: it was almost full, and I knew from the few times I'd been on a boat myself that the moon gives a lot of light at sea. It might help Mark's cops, Shen and Ko, spot the boat where Tony Siu was holding Bill. And whatever was going on on that boat, seeing the moon and the light it gave might help Bill too.

"Does the school know we're coming?" I asked Mark, speaking in Cantonese so Lieutenant Zhang wouldn't think I was trying to cut him out of the discussion.

"Yes," Mark said. "Lieutenant Zhang spoke to the school's master. He thought it would be worthwhile to find out if they'd taken on any new pupils in the last day or so."

"Have they?"

"Four. Saturday's a popular day for kids to start. Two of the new ones are seven-year-old boys. Neither is called Wei Hao-Han or Wei anything else, but the school doesn't ask for much proof of ID. It's probably not a big problem, kids' faked identities at kung fu schools."

I agreed it probably wasn't.

"One of these two boys was brought here by his folks," Mark went on, "who went back to Kowloon. The other came with his Filipina amah. She took a room in a guest house nearby. Lieutenant Zhang asked the master to call the amah, get her to the school without saying why."

"Good," I said. "That's very good."

Lieutenant Zhang, who had heard every word of this from the front seat, shook his head to acknowledge, by denying it, the compliment.

The van kept climbing, bouncing along over roads more and more deserted. Houses, gardens and trees grew fewer and farther apart. As we reached the crest of the hill they disappeared completely. It was treeless at the top, flat and rocky and bald. Cheung Chau's northern slopes fell away below, surrounded by endless black ocean. White surf frothed in the glow of the moonpath and the sea was dotted with the lights of ships as the sky was with stars. I could see the horizon curving, bending, reaching for the farthest distances, to connect them to here.

Then we headed down again, and the trees grew more numerous and the houses reappeared. "Where's the graveyard?" I asked Mark as we drove under an arch of palms. "You said Cheung Chau had an enormous graveyard."

"Around the other side of the island," he told me. "The south side."

We bounced along in silence for a while after that, until the road forked off to the right under a painted wooden gateway in the old style. The characters for Tiger Gate Kung Fu Academy were emblazoned overhead. We drove under the gate, curved around a little more, and pulled up in front of a white villa, a three-story affair on a rise overlooking the sea. French doors opened onto a tile porch running all the way around it and stars winked through the pine trees towering above it.

"Built by an Irish seaman in the 1870s, they say," Mark told me as the van stopped in front of the door. "Jumped ship, married a local girl. Her father gave them a fishing boat for her dowry, figuring a gift that expensive would give him big face and at the same time make sure the *gweilo* fell on his ass. The guy kept the boat tied up in port for six months while he crewed for nothing for one of her brothers. When he'd figured out how they fish here he took his boat out. Ended up owning his own fleet and making a fortune. He and the girl had nine little freckle-faced Chinese children. Built this house and brought his in-laws here to live with them. Built an ancestor altar and everything, very respectful." He added, "The locals love that story."

"Is it true?"

"Who knows? Every time a kid with freckles is born here you hear it, though."

The driver stayed in the van while the rest of us piled out into the scent of flowers and the sea.

The front door was flanked by male and female lion figures, smaller than L. L. Lee's but probably just as capable of guarding the door. Lieutenant Zhang pounded the brass knocker. Before the echoes had died away the door was opened. A young man bowed to us and showed us in.

Down a short hallway on the left a teak door stood open. The room it led to faced the rear of the house. There were French doors on that side, too, and through them, as we stepped into the room, I saw a wide, lighted courtyard where children and teenagers, both boys and girls, threw punches, snapped kicks, and practiced the fierce faces and fiercer concentration serious martial arts required.

I was last into the room, last to bow to a handsome, muscled man of perhaps forty, in polo shirt and khakis, whose formal manner and calm, controlled movements reminded me of the sensei at my own Tae Kwon Do dojo back home. I was last also, therefore, to see the pretty Filipina woman perched on the edge of a chair, her arm protectively around the shoulders of the little boy standing next to her. The woman's face was flushed; she sat in thin-lipped anger, based in fear and edged with defiance, at the sight of Lieutenant Zhang's uniform and the gold badge on Mark's hip. The boy, though obviously confused, did not seem to share her anger or her fear. His face was wide-eyed with interest in the three strangers who'd come to see him, and his face, as in the photos in the Robinson Road apartment, was a cheerful, seven-year-old version of his father's face, and his grandfather's—and, I now realized, his half-uncle's and his great-uncle's, too.

I knew him right away, and to me it was redundant when Mark, crouching in front of him, said, in Cantonese, "Hello, Wei Hao-Han. I'm Quan Mai," and Harry Wei politely answered, "Hi."

thirteen

The rest wasn't easy but it was predictable. The master of Tiger Gate Kung Fu Academy, used to the heavy responsibility of acting in loco parentis for his pupils, took the calm but unmovable position that whoever Harry was, he was here under the master's care and was going nowhere until someone could prove both a legal and a moral right to make decisions on his behalf. The amah who had brought him here had given false names both for him and for herself, and the authorities in the person of Mark and Lieutenant Zhang were now accusing her of something very close to abduction, although a quiet agreement Mark and Zhang had made as we left the van was keeping the actual term from being used so as not to back anyone into a corner. The amah had, therefore, forfeited that right.

However, the master explained courteously over tea and sweets brought in by two young pupils, this did not mean that Mark or Lieutenant Zhang by virtue of their badges had acquired it.

I, a foreign stranger, was completely out of the running.

Mark and Zhang could have insisted, of course. What the master was doing was technically abduction also: a private citizen holding another citizen against his will, or, in this case, against his parents' will, Harry himself seeming to have no problem with the idea of a long stay at Tiger Gate. They could have threatened with arrest—or, the master being the quietly unintimidatable man he seemed to be, actually arrested—everybody in sight, and carted them all, including Harry, off to the main Cheung Chau police station.

But the master wasn't really the problem. Even if he had been willing to hand Harry over to us, we couldn't have just waltzed out with him into a situation as chancy as the one Mark had in mind. The plan was for me to let L. L.

Lee know I had found Harry and to set up the trade for Bill, which would turn into an ambush of Siu and Chou arranged by Lieutenant Zhang. The danger to Harry would be minimal, but you couldn't involve a child in that sort of thing without the permission of his parents.

Which, not surprisingly, they would not give.

As we sat in the master's study drinking his clear green tea and watching his pupils finish their evening practice session in the garden, Mark called the Weis in their high-rise apartment on Robinson Road.

Steven Wei's joy and relief could be felt flooding out from Hong Kong Island to wash in waves over Cheung Chau. I imagined his half of the conversation while I listened to Mark's half: first, his identification of himself and an instruction to Steven to take his cell phone out into the hall. Second, the question, "Has the sweeper been there? Were there other bugs?" Third, whatever the answer to that, the statement, "I've found your son. He's fine," followed by, "Yes—I—You—" Then Mark, smiling, gave up and handed his cell phone to Harry.

The seven-year-old put the cell phone to his ear in an offhand, practiced way. Speaking in Cantonese, he quickly dispensed with a respectful greeting to his father and launched into an excited description of Tiger Gate Academy. He seemed surprised when twice he was interrupted with a question to which his answer was, "Yes, Baba, I'm fine." At the next interruption, his face fell.

"But I don't want to come home," he objected, in response to what he'd heard. "I want to stay here."

Forget it, Harry, I thought. That's a losing proposition.

Harry seemed to figure that out, because he spoke a few more sentences which included phrases like, "Yes, Baba," then gave Mark back his phone. Maria Quezon put her arm around him again, giving him a comforting squeeze.

Mark, back on the phone with Steven Wei, explained the situation at Tiger Gate: the master's position, which Mark referred to in such terms as *responsible* and *correct,* and our need for action.

Steven Wei seemed to agree that the Tiger Gate master was doing precisely the right thing. He agreed to hire a boat if possible, or at any rate take the next Cheung Chau ferry, and present himself at Tiger Gate Academy with documents to prove to the master's satisfaction both Harry's identity and his own.

What he did not agree to was Harry's being involved in any way with any scheme that was dangerous on any level.

Mark had a long discussion with Steven, most of which he carried on standing off by himself at the French doors to the garden. There, the last of the pupils were rolling up the mats and taking down the hanging bags. I couldn't hear what Mark was saying but I watched him, patient, formal, asking, stating, responding, reassuring.

This is a good cop, I thought. This is a cop who should be promoted, maybe even given his own command, not be fracturing regulations on some out-island, politely requesting assistance from the young Lieutenant Zhang and waiting for the ax to fall.

Finally, Mark took the cell phone from his ear, still looking out at the now-empty practice area. He folded the phone and slipped it into his pocket. Turning, he returned to where the rest of us sat. He requested that Harry leave the room for a few moments. The master summoned an older girl who escorted Harry away.

Mark spoke to the master. "The boy's father will be here as soon as he can, with identification papers for both of them. He has agreed to stay here in hiding with the child until our operation is concluded. We may also need your assistance in other ways. Will you permit this?"

Providing none of these ways endangered Harry or any of his other pupils, the master agreed.

To Lieutenant Zhang Mark said, "I'd be obliged if you would station a man here also."

Zhang made a call, to get someone up here who could stay.

To Maria Quezon Mark said, "Wei Di-Fen"—Steven— "has been told only that you brought the boy here to take him out of danger. Since the situation isn't resolved, I'd appreciate it if you don't say anything more right now. You can say that you don't know who set up the original plan to kidnap Hao-Han, that you ran away with the boy because you panicked."

Maria Quezon, in no position to argue, agreed.

To me Mark said, "We have to talk."

Mark and I, with the master's permission, went out into the garden. Lieutenant Zhang, his phone call concluded, joined us. The garden smelled of the sea. We stood at the edge of the moonlit courtyard practice area under the breeze-stirred leaves of a palm tree.

"We can do this," Mark said. "We just have to plan it out carefully."

"What are you thinking?" I asked.

"He won't let us take Hao-Han anywhere"—speaking in Cantonese for Lieutenant Zhang's benefit, Mark used Harry's Chinese name—"but he'll let us put him on the phone with Siu. I want you to call them now. Tell them you found him. Say you're ready to set up the trade. Let them talk to him."

"What's the setup?"

"We'll try to make them come to you. If we're good, we can have Hao-Han on the phone from here, no matter where you are, to keep them convinced he's with you until it's too late."

"They'll want to see him before they make the exchange."

"I just want them on land. They still don't know you've got us involved. Lieutenant Zhang can set up whatever he needs to as soon as we know where the meeting place is."

Lieutenant Zhang, clearly already weighing strategies, nodded.

"What if they won't land? What if they want me to hire a boat and go find them?"

Mark considered. "They might. Try to talk them out of it. If they insist, we'll send you on a police boat. We'll put as many of Lieutenant Zhang's men in it as it can hold."

"All right," I said slowly. "All right. It's not great, but it's not like I have anything else more brilliant. But I can't call Tony Siu. I don't know his number. The only one I can call is L. L. Lee."

So I called L. L. Lee.

Before I did, Mark and Zhang and I talked a little longer, although not much of it was me: Mostly, it was two cops considering places I could suggest for the exchange, places on Cheung Chau that would sound remote and isolated to Tony Siu, but would actually offer Zhang's men good cover and possibilities for an ambush.

Then Mark, Lieutenant Zhang, and I went back into the master's study. Harry had returned and was sitting on his amah's lap. Tiger Gate's other pupils had gone to bed, and Harry, only seven, seemed to be flagging.

Mark crouched down before him. "Hao-Han," he said, "we're going to make a phone call. The man we're calling will want to talk to you. I'd like you to say hello, tell him your name if he asks, but don't tell him where you are. It's supposed to be a big secret." He grinned at Harry. "Okay?"

Harry smiled back and nodded.

I flipped open my phone and dialed L. L. Lee's number on Hong Kong Island, on the Peak.

After a few rings the call was answered by the solemn young man who'd let me in and brought tea: houseboy, bodyguard, whatever he was. He put me through, immediately, to Lee.

"I've found what you wanted," I said without any of the niceties respectful courtesy would require.

L. L. Lee paused before he spoke. "You've done that fast, for one who did not know where to look."

"I was lucky." I curtly dismissed that. "I'm ready to make the trade. What should I do?"

"I cannot make arrangements."

No, of course not. In my mind I saw, resting on his scholar's desk, his clean, thin-fingered hands. "Then tell Tony Siu to call me. He has my number."

I hung up. It was a lot easier to be rude to L. L. Lee, I

reflected, when he was miles away over the sea.

It wasn't five minutes, all of us sitting in tense silence in the master's study, before my phone rang again.

"Hey, sweetie. I hear we have business to do."

I gritted my teeth; I felt like Tony Siu's voice was grating against my bones. I stood because I couldn't sit, and answered him. "I'm ready to meet."

"Prove it."

I took the phone to where Harry was sitting, his head resting now on Maria's shoulder. He put it to his ear, and I leaned close and listened in.

"Wai?" Harry said.

"Hi," said Tony Siu. "My name's Tony. Who are you?"

"Wei Hao-Han," Harry responded promptly.

"Who's there with you?"

I pointed at myself. Harry's brow creased. "A lady," he said. "I can't remember her name." I smiled at him and put my finger to my lips, hoping he'd understand not to say any more. His look became confused, but luckily Tony Siu wasn't a patient man and moved on.

"Where are you, Wei Hao-Han?"

"I can't tell you." Harry grinned. "It's a secret."

I took the phone back. I saw Mark smiling at Harry and whispering, "Thank you." Harry smiled back and snuggled up closer to his amah.

"All right," I said to Tony Siu, "that's enough." I walked over to the French doors, as Mark had, to be beyond Harry's range.

"Better be the right kid," Tony Siu said to me.

"You won't know until we make this trade, will you? Let's set it up."

"Get yourself a boat. We'll do it on the water."

"Are you crazy? It's the middle of the night. I don't know anything about boats."

He laughed. "They have two hundred sampans in the harbor. Wake a fisherman."

"I don't like that," I said. "A witness. The ocean. There must be beaches around here you could land on where no one would see you. I thought smugglers used to land here all the time."

"A witness to what? You're bringing out my nephew, I'm sending back a dumb *gweilo* who got himself banged up in a boating accident. You pay the fisherman enough, he'll swear that's what he saw. Hell, give him enough whiskey, he'll *think* that's what he saw."

"I don't want to do this on the water."

"I know," Tony Siu said in mock sympathy. "You're worried about boating accidents. Because they can be pretty bad, after all. People get killed in boating accidents all the time."

"Let me talk to Bill."

"Well . . ."

"Your boss wants this trade, Tony." I stared through the glass to the palms and the moonlight. "He wants it a lot. I want it, too, but only if there's something to trade for."

Briefly, no more words came through my phone, but I could hear sounds, nothing I could make out but enough to convince me Tony hadn't hung up.

Then Bill's voice, scratchy and weaker than I was used to. "Lydia?"

"It's me," I said. "Are you okay?"

"Hanging in."

"Good," I said. "Good. It won't be much longer."

Whether he answered or not I didn't know, because Tony's grating voice was back. "Out here, sweetie. On the water."

I clenched my teeth and agreed. "How do I know where you are?"

"Around the south side of the island. Get your fisherman to pass the smuggler's cave, the Tin Hua temple, all that shit. Tell him to head east along the south coast. Tell him to hang, I don't know, three lamps on the port side, one starboard. I'll spot you. When I do I'll call again."

"This will take time," I warned. "I'm not in town. I have to get to the harbor, find someone to take us, come around the island."

"Then you'd better get moving."

"Give me your number. I don't like the ocean. I want to be able to call you."

A laugh. "No."

After that we had nothing more to say to each other, so Tony Siu and I hung up.

Lieutenant Zhang had a talk with the master, involving phones and numbers, then made another call back to the station and after that one to Hong Kong Telecom. When he was through, we had an open conference line between the master's cell phone and mine. Any call coming to my phone would ring here too, so that the fiction that Harry was with me could be maintained.

At the same time Mark used his cell phone to call Ko and Shen again. He told them we were headed to a rendezvous with Siu's boat around the south side of Cheung Chau, somewhere east of the Tin Hua temple. He described to them what our sampan would look like, three lights hanging on one side and one on the other. They were in those waters now, they said; they hadn't spotted Tony Siu's boat but they'd keep looking, and they'd try to pick us up coming around.

I knew all this was necessary and I tried to stay calm while it was going on. I paced and breathed, working on controlling the adrenaline rushing through my blood, trying to save some for later when I'd need it. I wasn't doing all that well: My skin felt prickly and I was just about ready to explode when Mark finally said, "Let's go."

The plumbing van drove us back through the night, rising briefly once more to the bald and windy hilltop. I wondered as I gazed over the lights of the boats sprinkled on the sea which one Bill was on, and why it didn't look different from any of the others. Then we were under the trees once more, then among the houses, then in the town.

The colored lanterns still outlined the waterfront street, but most of the cafés and restaurants were closed now, most of the strolling couples gone. We pulled up to the harbor where the fishing fleet lay at anchor. A thin mist had gath-

ered on the surface of the sea. The sampans and trawlers
floating next to the dock appeared solid and substantial,
their cabins dark and no sound to be heard but the creaking
of wood and the lapping of water. Beyond the first boats
an endless number more seemed to spread out over the
water, growing less and less real, more faint and ghostly as
the distance to them grew.

Waiting at the end of the pier where the police launch
had docked—it was gone now—was a sampan, weathered
green paint on its sides and cracked glass in its cabin windows. Mark spoke briefly to Lieutenant Zhang, then saluted
him before climbing aboard. He reached out an automatic
hand to help me, and I took it, not quite as sure of my
ability to get onto this boat as I'd been about getting out
of the last one.

The sampan's engine gave a soft growl, coming to life
without anything near the aggressive roar of the police
launch. We turned in the water, *putt-putt*ing as we picked
our way carefully among the other boats. They appeared
and disappeared again as we approached and then passed
them in the mist. Then their ghostly, silent presences became fewer, and we were once again at sea.

Besides the sweatshirted, unshaven, chain-smoking
helmsman who guided the boat from a rudder near the engine, and besides Mark, there were three other cops aboard,
sitting in the cramped cabin. This sampan was one of Marine District's undercover boats, used to patrol the waters
around the out-islands for smuggling and other illicit sea-
borne activities. According to Mark, the *putt-putt*ing little
engine had all the power of the launch, but now was not
the time to give the game away by using it.

Mark and I went below and introduced ourselves. We
shared a pot of tea with the men in the cabin while Mark
went over with them what we expected and what we intended. I half listened as they exchanged Cantonese cop
talk; Mark was the highest rank aboard, but these men were
experienced in seagoing matters, and there was the inevitable—though veiled and always polite—jockeying. Then,

because I couldn't sit still, Mark and I came out on deck again. We stood leaning on the rail as the mist thickened and thinned. It smelled salty and damp, floating by in soft gray patches and glowing white where it was most dense, especially on our port side, where it reflected the three hanging lights.

"Will they find us?" I asked Mark, my voice startlingly loud over the *putting* of the engine and the soft *whoosh* of water parting for us. I spoke more quietly: "In this fog?"

"We'll keep close to the shoreline. So will they. They'll find us."

We did keep close. The lights of Cheung Chau's coast broke through the mist on our port side, and sometimes the lights of other boats, on both sides. Every time another boat drifted out of the fog I tensed, even though Mark told me the cave and the temple were half an hour away, and the island's south coast stretched east for an hour beyond that. I couldn't help it. I had told Tony Siu I didn't like boats, which was not true when I said it but was growing truer by the second. Maybe if the air were clearer, maybe if I could see to the distance the way I had from the hilltop, I wouldn't mind so much. Or if there were a path, a road you had to stick to, like on land. But right now the water seemed very strange to me: a surface from which going up was impossible and going down deadly, above which floated a mist too insubstantial to touch but solid enough to block all sight, on which you could wander anywhere without any more reason to do one thing than another because everything in all directions was the same.

Mark took off his jacket and slipped it around my shoulders. I looked at him in surprise.

"You were shivering," he said.

"Is it cold?"

"I guess. If you're not used to it."

Which meant no. But I was glad for his jacket, because I had been shivering.

The mist thinned as we came around the southern headland, and we could see the shore. The helmsman pointed out the smuggler's cave, which looked like just a mass of rocks to me. After a while, outlined against the sky, rose the curving eaves of the temple for the worship of Tin Hua, protector of sailors and those lost at sea. Tin Hua was not a goddess I knew well; my mother never had much reason to take us to pray for sailors when I was a child. But all goddesses liked oranges and incense, and I found myself silently promising Tin Hua the best of both, and whatever else her special joy was, if only this worked out.

But it seemed like she didn't hear me. We *putt*ed up the coast, and my phone didn't ring. We reached a spit of land jutting into the sea. There the coast turned south again, and we went around a point where the light of a lonely lighthouse blinked slowly on and off. We drifted east some more, and then turned around, heading back along the south shore the way we'd come. My phone didn't ring. Mark, from his cell phone, called Lieutenant Zhang. Everything on land was as it had been. Steven Wei had not yet arrived at Tiger Gate Academy, nor had anything else of note happened there. We briefly considered my calling L. L. Lee, but decided against it for now.

"They may have spotted us already," Mark said, and the helmsman, through his cigarette smoke, nodded. "They may be just making sure."

Mark made another call. Ko and Shen had found us, and were paralleling our trail, staying as far from us as they could while keeping us in sight. The helmsman smoked and steered. Mark sat on the deck, against the wall in the shadow of the cabin's overhanging roof, where he wouldn't be seen. I had never been on a sampan before, never realized how small they were, how many ropes and buckets and things crowded the deck, so you couldn't pace. The boat had a fishy smell. I asked the helmsman if actually fishing was part of their undercover work. He laughed and said the HKPD boats, when not in use, were available to cops on a sign-out basis, for day fishing trips. He offered to take Mark to fish for shark on their next mutual day off.

We reached the Tin Hua temple, made another leisurely

turn, and headed up the coast once more. A breeze had come up and blown the mist away. Ahead of us, in the east, I could see a thin white line on the surface of the sea.

"The sun's coming up," I said to Mark. "It's morning. Where are they?"

Mark looked at his watch. "The sun rises early on the water, in the summer. It's only four-thirty. It's only been a few hours."

The coast of Cheung Chau, I saw now, was steep here, all rocky hills and grassy headlands black against the starry sky. The thin line on the horizon grew, a rose blush starting to color it. No one spoke. Boats at anchor rocked as we slipped by them, some of them starting to show lights in their cabins as fishermen woke to prepare the day.

The stars began to fade. The line on the horizon was striped with crimson and the sky was turning from black to gray when I took my phone from my pocket. "Something's wrong," I said. "I'm calling Lee."

I should have taken the thing out sooner. As Mark was nodding his agreement, it started to ring.

I flipped it open. *"Wai!"* I yelled into it. *"Wai!"*

"Hi, sweetie. How's the boat ride?"

"Where are you?" I barked. "What's going on?"

"Just calling to tell you your merchandise has been delivered."

"What are you talking about?"

"We just dropped it off. You can pick it up any time."

"I don't understand."

"Change in plans."

"What change in plans?"

"No trade."

"What?"

"We don't need what you're bringing."

Mark was on his feet now, jarred there by the confusion in my face and voice.

"What do you mean, you don't need it?"

"Like I said: change of plans."

"Your boss wanted a trade."

"My boss says he got what he wanted. He doesn't need the kid anymore."

"Got what he wanted? What does that mean?"

"It means I can get off this stinking boat. Look, sweetie, you want your merchandise or not? Me, I wanted to dump it in the ocean, but my orders were to give it back."

I swallowed. "Yes. Yes, of course I do."

"Thought so." I could hear his mocking smile; I wanted to jam it down his throat. "There's a place where the cemetery comes almost down to the sea. Your fisherman will know."

"What—?"

"See you, sweetie." And Tony Siu hung up.

I looked at Mark. "They don't want the trade."

"What?"

"L. L. Lee says he got what he wanted; he doesn't need Harry. Tony Siu said they just left Bill on land."

"Where?"

"Where the graveyard comes down to the sea." I looked at the helmsman. From behind his cigarette he nodded, turned the boat, and, after a few words with Mark, gunned the engine to full HKPD life.

Mark flipped open his own cell phone as one of the cops, feeling the change in the engine, stuck his head from the cabin to ask what was happening. The helmsman told him. Mark was by then on the phone with Lieutenant Zhang.

Their conversation was brief, Mark having to shout over the roar of the engine. When it was over Mark shut the phone and filled me in.

"I don't know," was the first thing he said, standing close to me, almost yelling. "I don't get it. Harry's still at Tiger Gate. Steven Wei came an hour or so ago, with all the ID you could ask for. I told them to keep him there in case it's not really him, but he's made no move to leave, so if he's up to something I have no idea what it is. Zhang's sending men to the cemetery, and he's calling Shen and Ko in." He nodded to the sea, to the sharp lines of masts and the diagonal rigging I could see now cutting across the stripes of the dawn. He added, "We'll get there first."

The wind whipped my hair around. I pushed it from my eyes. "Could it be a setup? At the cemetery?"

"Why? Siu had all the cards, doing the trade on the water. The cemetery's not a great place for it, if you're thinking about an ambush—where would he hide?"

"What if he knew there were cops involved?"

He shook his head. "The water's still the best place."

I didn't like my next idea but I spoke it out loud anyway. "Maybe he's lying. Maybe there's nothing at the cemetery at all. He knows you're involved and he's trying to distract us, while he grabs Harry from Tiger Gate."

"I thought of that. I asked Zhang to double the guard there, just in case, but if that's it, why call at all? We were enough out of the way just sailing up and down the coast."

The helmsman swung the boat around and pointed it straight toward shore. Against the sky, now a pale, gentle gray, what looked like a craggy headland swept down to a low cliff above a thin stretch of beach. We drew closer. With a suddenness you could almost hear, the sun burst above the horizon, hitting the headland like a golden searchlight, and I saw that the crags were not rocks. They were graves.

A Chinese graveyard isn't like a Western one. Traditionally Chinese people buried bodies in temporary graves for seven years, until the bones were bare. The final, permanent grave, the real one, held only the bones, cleaned and placed lovingly in an urn. Now almost everyone's cremated, and it's the ashes that go in the urn, but the result is the same. A Chinese grave isn't six feet long. The stone slab on the ground that covers the urn is shorter than the headstone is tall, and it has two little side pieces that make the whole thing a private altar, where relatives come to light incense and bring offerings—real ones like wine, and paper ones to burn. So Chinese graveyards, like Chinese cities, are much more densely packed than Western ones. And there's another difference, an innovation of the last hundred years. From ancient times the name of the dead has been inscribed on the headstone. Now along with the name, there's often a picture, a photograph silkscreened onto a tile and set into the stone.

And this photograph thing, I wasn't sure I liked it, I thought to myself, as the helmsman stopped the sampan in the shallow water off the beach and the faces of a thousand of Cheung Chau's dead, glowing in the first bright rays of the morning sun, watched Mark and me jump from the deck into the surf.

The water was cold, shocking. Waist high, the small waves first pushed me and then tugged me as I slipped over the stones below them. Two of the cops from the cabin leaped in with us, holding their guns well above the water and ready to fire, as Mark had his. The third cop stayed on the boat, to cover us.

Cover wasn't necessary. Nothing moved on the beach but the surf, and then each of us struggling out of it. Seabirds wheeled and screamed in the sky. In the graveyard, nothing moved at all.

A path from the narrow beach twisted through a mound of weathered boulders, pitted from their years standing guard for the dead. Mark was first onto the beach, but despite his shout for me to hold back and let a cop go first, I raced by him and scrambled up the path. I heard him curse. Small stones, dislodged by our intrusion, clicked down the path, some splashing into the sea as Mark and the others charged up behind me.

Just around the boulders the path flattened. The first graves stood ten yards away, where the slope began. Between them and the cliff edge spread an uneven plain, all sand and stones and short spiky grass. The faces of the dead, someone's ancestors, stared from the headstones in silent disapproval at the human form that sprawled there, spoiling their view of the sea.

I ran over and dropped to the ground next to him: Bill, face down, shirtless, unmoving as the stones. I stared at, but didn't register, the swollen ridges crisscrossing his back, purple and blue, some spotted with dark blood. I heard a bird call to another and someone come up behind me as I pressed my hand to the artery in Bill's neck. For a moment, nothing, and I was a stone at the bottom of a cold black sea. Then I found it, a strong and steady pulse, and I saw the morning sun blazing and heard the screech of the birds and thought this graveyard must be the most beautiful place on earth.

Mark called for an ambulance. It was a while in coming and when it did, it had to stop at the top of the hill, its two medics trotting down the path to where we were. By that time three more of Lieutenant Zhang's cops had arrived, cops he'd sent when Mark told him where we were heading, but there was no point, because in this graveyard at this hour there were no living people but us.

Waiting for the ambulance, I took off Mark's jacket, which I'd been wearing for hours, folded it, and slipped it under Bill's head, thinking it would make a better pillow than the spiky grass. He stirred when I did that, saying something I didn't get. He had a lump on his jaw and a gash on his forehead, but the major feature of his face was the twin pair of black circles rimming his eyes from the blow that had broken his nose.

"Shh," I said, taking his hand. His wrists were raw with rope burns. "Tell me later. Everything's okay now."

He spoke again, one word, and this time I heard it: "Harry?"

"He's fine. He's safe. It's okay."

Slurring words, he asked, "What happened?"

"I don't know."

Broken nose, black-rimmed eyes, purple back and all, I swear he grinned at that.

The medics came. One of Zhang's cops went back to the sampan with the helmsman, who'd run up the path to join us, gun drawn, as soon as he'd beached the boat. They headed back around the island. Mark's cops from headquarters, Shen and Ko, had a quiet conversation with Mark before they went back to their rented sampan and did the same. I couldn't hear what they said, but from the way Shen and Ko stood—elaborately casual, hands in their pockets, smiling small smiles and watching the seabirds—I could tell that neither cop macho nor Chinese reticence could quite surpress their pride at the compliments and thanks they were getting from Mark.

Zhang's other two cops hitched a ride to town with the three cops who'd just come. Mark and I rode in the ambulance, he up front with the driver, me in the back with Bill. The driver negotiated as quickly as he could, which was slowly, through the vast cemetery, along paths barely wide enough, paths that separated large areas of close-crowded graves one from another. The paths were overhung with the green branches of trees, but the graves sat splendidly in the sun, falling away down the hillsides, looking out in all directions to the sea. Through the ambulance's rear window I could see that many held oranges and the powdery remains of incense, evidence of the visits of conscientious relations. As we twisted along a leafy path we came to an area where the headstones stopped having photographs on them, and were no longer rectangular. Upright half-moons set among a tangle of greenery, they bore only the names of the departed, painted on them in red characters. This was the oldest section of the graveyard, all these people dead more than a century; and yet there were oranges and incense here, too, people honoring ancestors they had never known.

We descended into the town and came soon to the hospital, a two-story building at the end of the waterfront street. It was small, peaceful-looking: not the place of crisis and disaster I'm used to a hospital being. "Mostly for births, too much sun, and broken legs," Mark told me. "Anyone who's seriously injured they send to Hong Kong by helicopter."

As it turned out, that wasn't Bill. Bruised and battered as he was—he'd been beaten, said the doctor who worked on him, with something both hard and flexible, most likely a bamboo pole—X–rays and tests showed no serious internal injuries, nothing broken with the exception of his nose.

I sat in a sunny waiting room while Mark, outside on a terrace overlooking the sea, made one call after another on his cell phone. The doctor set Bill's nose, did some other things, gave him a shot of morphine for the pain, and told me I could go in to see him.

He was lying on his side facing an open window beyond which white boats danced on sparkling blue water. A bandage seemed to cover half his face, making a startling contrast to the black rims around his eyes. His wrists were bandaged too, but his back was still bare. His eyes were closed, so I whispered, "Hey," prepared to leave if the morphine had begun to work and he was asleep.

"Hey." Soft but clear, and he opened his eyes. "Harry," he said, in a voice not strong but determined. "Did you tell me Harry's okay, or did I dream that?"

"No, he's okay. Steven's with him. I think it's over."

"What was it about? What was the point? Maria said it was the uncle, but how can that be true?"

"It was," I said. "It's complicated. I'll tell you the whole story later. Harry was where you said," I added. "At Iron Fist's kung fu school."

"You got that?"

"Late, but I got it."

"Hot damn." He gave me that grin.

I leaned over and kissed his cheek. "Tony got your nose," I said.

"First thing he did. Only thing he actually did. The rest he farmed out to Big John."

"I don't suppose Big John minded."

"He loved it. They did Iron Fist, you know."

"I thought they probably did. They told you?"

"Said they were going to do me the same way. Tony wanted to peel the tattoo off my arm first, sew it to the back of his jacket. They had plans for you too."

"I'll bet they did."

"Iron Fist pissed them off, though. This beating the crap out of people, with them it's just openers. He wouldn't tell them where Harry was, so they brought out the blowtorch. He jumped into the harbor."

"He jumped?"

"Hands tied behind him, beat to shit. Had to know it was the end. Tony's sure he jumped because he knew they could make him talk. Me they strung up to the goddamn mast in case I had the same idea. I was waiting for the blowtorch, but they never brought it out."

"I said they couldn't."

His eyebrows rose above his black-circled eyes. "They listened to you?"

"They listened to their boss. L. L. Lee. I went to see him and made a deal. He gave me until morning."

"Oh." His voice was getting slower, sleepier. "That explains it. About half an hour after they called you Tony got a call. In Chinese, so I don't know what the hell went on. But Big John cut me down, dumped me in the cabin. Even threw me a beer. I was ready to nominate him for sainthood."

"You can thank me for that," I said.

"Thank you."

"Any time."

"Lydia?" He was struggling to keep his eyes open now. "Why did they want Harry? Why didn't they make the trade? What's going on?"

"I'm not sure. L. L. Lee was going to use Harry to make Steven agree to keep up the smuggling operation, but now he says he got what he wanted and he doesn't need Harry."

"Got what he wanted? Steven agreed?"

"Doesn't sound likely, does it? But I don't know what else to think." A soft salt breeze drifted in the open window. "Getting on a boat with them," I said. "Tony and Big John. That wasn't a very good idea."

"Didn't mean to. Just trying to give Maria time. Big John pulled a gun on me at the end of the dock. Thought of hitting the water, but too many people around, in case he started shooting. Besides," he winced as he shifted position, "I never said to love me because I was smart."

"You never said to love you at all," I clarified for him. "Just to marry you."

"Is that right?" He appeared to be thinking about this new information. "Are you planning on it?"

"No."

"Oh. Then go away and let me sleep."

His eyes closed. The soft breeze came back. I kissed his cheek once more, walked to the door, turned again to look. The tattooed blue snake lay as peacefully on his arm as he did on the fresh white sheets. He was still, probably asleep already. It was a good thing that the question he'd asked me was whether I was going to marry him. That was the one I had an answer to.

I joined Mark on the terrace, where he was leaning on the railing looking at the sea. He turned as he heard me walk up. The stubble on his chin and the shadows under his eyes would have told me, if I hadn't known already, that it had been a long time since he'd slept.

"How is he?" Mark asked.

"Lucky. He'll be fine."

"Good." He leaned on the rail again, turned his eyes back to the sea. "They're gone. Siu and Chou. Zhang has Marine District men out, and I have people all over Hong Kong and Kowloon, but word is they're gone."

"This fast? Gone where?"

"Right now, deep underground. In a few days, probably Taiwan. There's a strong international trade in gangsters both ways."

"Can you follow them? Will Taiwan cooperate?"

He shook his head. "Not big enough fish. Now that we're PRC, they won't deal with us unless there's something really big in it for them." A sleek speedboat skidded over the water, motor roaring. "But I know cops there. I gave them a heads-up. If Siu and Chou show up they'll be watched. If they get out of line, maybe they can at least be taken out of circulation."

He looked over the ocean, and I looked at him. "But you won't get them," I said. "You won't be able to bring them in for killing Iron Fist. You won't be able to clear that case."

He shook his head.

"I'm sorry."

He shrugged, not the Chinese chin-jut but the good old American shoulder shrug. "It might not matter. I can't clear the case, but I identified the perps and everyone will know that. You could say I chased them out of Hong Kong. And I cleared two abductions, one reported, one unreported."

"Still."

He didn't look at me, just at the boats and the birds and the water. I leaned on the rail and helped him look.

"I'm sorry about your jacket," I said after a while. Seawater, sand, and Bill's blood had made Mark's linen jacket just about unsalvageable. I surveyed Mark and started to giggle. "And about your pants." His pants, like mine, were still damp, sticky, and smelling of the surf we'd waded through. Trying to restrain my giggles, I said, "And your shirt's had a hard day, too. And your shoes don't look happy."

He turned to face me. After a moment he shook his head, and a smile lit his tired face. "Private investigators, what a pain in the ass. Come on, I'll buy you breakfast."

"There's a place that will take us, looking like this?"

All he said was, "Yes." He offered me, formally, his arm. I took it. We strolled off the terrace, back through the waiting room, and, sticky smelly clothes and all, we headed out onto the wide, carless, waterfront street of Cheung Chau.

fourteen

Breakfast was delicious, though it wasn't breakfast by either American or Chinese standards. Mark Quan and I sat at a picnic table under a canvas roof in the breezy sunshine of the waterfront street. The tables ran in an unbroken length for what would have been two New York City blocks; the changing colors of the roofs marked the different restaurants. Red, blue, yellow, orange, solid, striped, and dotted, with the sun glowing through them all: Ours was green, which I thought might have an unfortunate effect on the food, but Mark assured me otherwise. "You'll feel like you're eating in a tropical forest, fish you just pulled out of the water yourself. Or," he suggested, "you could close your eyes."

I couldn't, though. I'd have missed the aquamarine of the ocean and the round whiteness of the clouds, the cheerful gray bulk of the Cheung Chau ferry pulling into its slip, the happy surprise as it disgorged an entire summer-school's worth of fourth graders, a hundred excited black-haired children in identical yellow shirts and shorts come to spend a day at the beach.

I'd have also missed our whole steamed grouper, covered in chopped red peppers and a spicy bronze-colored sauce. It sat on the table between us next to a bowl of pork fried rice and a plate of steamed greens. We drank an entire pot of tea while we waited for the fish and rice and greens, and another while we ate them. We had green plastic plates to eat on and white plastic chopsticks to eat with and I had never had such a good meal in all my life.

For a while there was nothing but the click of chopsticks, the lapping of the sea, and the whispered words of other diners who ate their steamed buns and breakfast dumplings and gave each other slyly knowing looks as they discussed the question of what Mark and I had been doing all night that we looked and ate the way we did.

As the fish was beginning to look a little picked-over and the greens were almost gone, Mark said, "I have a favor to ask you."

His back was to the ocean; I was facing it. I looked away from the drifting sailboats and bobbing sampans and met Mark's eyes. "I owe you," I said. "Whatever you want, I owe you more."

"You don't owe me. This is my job."

"You broke every regulation they have. You broke regulations they haven't written yet. That's not your job."

He grinned. "They'll write them now." The grin faded. "Listen: A kid was missing. I wanted to get him home. That's my job."

"Okay," I said. "If that's your story, you stick to it. What do you need?"

He poured us each more tea. "They didn't make the trade because L. L. Lee said he'd gotten what he wanted. What he wanted was for Steven Wei to keep Lion Rock smuggling for him."

"It's hard to believe Steven agreed to that, but he must have."

"That's part of what I want. Lee will talk to you. I want you to call him and ask him what happened."

"He *may* talk to me. He may not. In case you missed it, he doesn't actually like me. And he certainly won't give me any details."

"I just want to hear him say what Tony Siu says he said."

"All right, I'll try it. What's the other part?"

"Assuming that's what happened, I want you to pretend you don't know. To Steven, I mean. And especially to make him think that *I* don't know. That I know nothing at all about the smuggling. He has no reason to think I do. I want him to believe he's in the clear. Later on, I can use this to bring down L. L. Lee."

Teacup in both hands, I looked at him. "Oh, Mark."

"I know. I don't like it either. But Lee's a bad man and I can't pass this up."

"You'll destroy the firm. Steven, Wei Ang-Ran . . . Mark, there'll be nothing left. Wei Ang-Ran could even go to jail."

"Not if he cooperates."

"But . . ."

"Lydia, look what Lee's guys did to Smith. On his orders."

"They also delivered him alive, on Lee's orders. He'll recover."

"Iron Fist Chang won't."

I was suddenly very tired. I put my chin on my hand.

"Iron Fist's not the only one, over the years, Lydia. I'm a cop. This is my job."

"But poor Steven . . . If he did agreed to this it was only to save his son. What else could he do?"

"Nothing. There was nothing else he could do. It's not his fault he was in this bind, it's his uncle's. He'll be paying the family debt. *Zhong xiao dao yi*. But that's sometimes how it works."

I knew that was how it worked. Someone in your family causes trouble or brings dishonor, it's your obligation to sacrifice whatever you have to, to make it right. Wei Ang-Ran had been breaking the law for years, working hand in hand with a triad chief. Someone would have to pay. Steven, for all his high-rise modern-day Hong Kong trappings, was a very traditional Chinese family man. He'd be the first to understand.

"It's not fair," I said.

"No. But it's how it works."

I lifted my eyes from the fish on the platter, its head and tail still complete but all its bones exposed, and looked again at the sea. "I have to think," I said. "And I can't think now. I'm exhausted."

Mark didn't speak.

"I won't say anything to anyone for right now," I promised. "And I'll call Lee for you. And I know you're right, Mark. But it's so unfair."

Mark paid for our breakfast and we walked out onto the waterfront street, away from the restaurants and the town. The morning was no longer new and the day had grown hot. We stopped along the railing at a place where no one else was stopped and I dialed L. L. Lee at his shop on Hollywood Road.

"I wanted to thank you," I said, after he knew it was me. I spoke in English. "Tony Siu said he'd have killed my partner, but his orders were not to."

"It was unnecessary." L. L. Lee's voice was rock-hard, as before. I found myself thinking of the rows of polished headstones crowded together on Cheung Chau's southern slopes, with their pictures of the dead.

"I can deliver the boy," I offered. "Tell me where."

"That is also unnecessary."

"I don't understand," I said, as if hearing this for the first time. "Tony Siu said you'd gotten what you wanted. I thought that meant you knew I'd found the boy."

"It did not mean that. Neither you nor the child are of any value to me now."

"How will you pressure the father then?" I said, in my most gee-whiz voice. I'm just a girl, Lee, just a dumb American-born Chinese, of limited value and limited threat; go ahead, tell me anything.

"Again," he said contemptuously, "unnecessary."

"Wait." I tried to sound as if the light was dawning. "He's already agreed? Without—?"

"Last night. An American, hollow bamboo, cannot be expected to understand. But the boy's father is a true Chinese and has a subtle mind. He saw ahead and made things easier for all concerned. I advise you now," he said, "along with your partner, to leave Hong Kong."

"Bill can't travel yet. They didn't kill him, but they made sure he'd remember them."

"Do not delay your departure."

"We'll go as soon as we can. Did you—?"

"No more questions. All you seek is information. You have no use for knowledge."

What I did have was the start of a headache and no use for L. L. Lee's insults. "I called to express my gratitude," I said. "I've done that. Now let me also tell you this." I thought of Bill's bandaged face, his back, his night on that boat. "If I ever see Siu or Chou again, I'll kill them."

Mark's eyebrows went up. In my ear there was silence. Then L. L. Lee's stone voice said, "Good-bye, Miss Chin. I don't expect to see you again."

The connection went dead in my ear.

"I'm not sure I'd have done that," Mark said, as I folded the phone and put it away.

I shrugged. "He can't take something like that seriously, coming from me. He'd squash me like a bug if he thought I was worth the effort, but he doesn't. But he's been warned."

Mark was smart enough not to say anything. We turned and headed back along the waterfront, walking side by side but without a word. Just before the ferry pier we reached the police station. Mark spoke briefly with the man in charge; Lieutenant Zhang had long since made his report and gone home for some well-deserved rest. I felt like I deserved some, too, but there was more to do. We climbed into the police car that had been arranged, and the uniformed cop in the front saluted Mark and drove us north on Cheung Chau to Tiger Gate Academy.

It was a beautiful drive, through the narrow streets of the town, up through the houses and the hills, over the bald hilltop with its wide and windy view of the sea. The pines in front of the Irish seaman's house rustled their branches in greeting as we drove up and parked. The young pupil on door duty brought us through the house to the practice area in the garden.

Students in black cotton uniforms stretched, punched, kicked, and practiced the slow, graceful movements that to my mind make kung fu the most beautiful of the martial arts. My own art, Tae Kwon Do, isn't nearly as ancient, and is much more straightforward, more focused on power and practicality. I looked at Mark, who was following the students' movements with an appreciative, critical eye. This was his art. Ancient, meditative, graceful. Mastered through years of serious study, the first of them, in his case, in Birmingham, Alabama.

The Tiger Gate master was in the garden too, observing his pupils, calling out commands first to this small girl, then to that boy, then to a pair of teenagers sparring with poles. He nodded when he saw us, crossed the garden to where we stood.

"I've come to thank you for your help," Mark said to him, bowing. I bowed also. "I'd like to see Wei Di-Fen. He can take his son home now."

The master summoned a young girl who led us to another part of the garden. Here, half a dozen young children were being drilled by a teenager of high rank. Harry Wei was there, his little brow furrowed in concentration, snapping kicks and defensive blocks against an imaginary opponent. Steven sat on a low wall watching, his round face soft and smiling in the sunlight, the relaxed and happy face of the photographs I'd picked up from the floor of the apartment on Robinson Road. This was the first time, I realized, that I'd seen him look like this.

He stood when he saw us, and, smiling, bowed first to Mark and then to me, one hand fisted, the other covering it in the traditional gesture of gratitude.

"Thank you," he said. "You have given me back the greatest treasure a man can have: his family. I will be in your debt forever."

To which Mark protested, "No, no, I only did my job," and I answered something similar about being glad Bill and I could be of some small help. It would have been rude of us to say anything else. To accept his thanks would have been to acknowledge that we'd played as major a part as Steven Wei said we had, which would have been boorish, as well as dangerous: The jealous gods eavesdrop on conversations like this, waiting for a display of pride that will make it worth their supernatural while to bring your world crashing down around you.

But we all knew where the kernel of truth lay. Steven Wei *was* in our debt. And when Mark called that debt in, in a year, maybe two years from now, Steven would have no choice but to respond.

No matter what world came crashing down.

A small dark figure walked around the house and entered the garden. It was Maria Quezon, looking tired but, like Steven, relaxed. She gave Harry a quick look filled with fierce pride. When she spotted the rest of us her face changed; she brought out an unsure smile. Steven returned her smile, a little unsurely himself at first, but in a few seconds they were beaming at each other like thousand-watt searchlights.

"Maria told me what happened," Steven said to us, switching into English for Maria's sake. "She acted very courageously to protect my son."

"Can you fill us in?" Mark asked. "Remember, I came into this late."

Maria looked at the ground, color rising in her cheeks. Steven waited, but then spoke.

"During the kidnapping attempt Maria heard one of the men say that our flat was—what is the English, bugged? She managed to slip away with Harry from the kidnappers; she hid but she was afraid to call us. She called her young man, the unfortunate Chang"—Maria, still looking down, shook her head slowly—"and he arranged for her to come here. He was supposed to come to us, to tell us what had happened, avoiding the listening device. She waited but he never called her. Poor Maria panicked, at a loss. When Mr. Smith came she was willing to let him decide what to do, but he disappeared, too, telling her to run away. So she did."

Maria added, in a soft, clear voice, "I believe I must have been in shock. I did not think at all clearly. I am so sorry," she added, to Steven.

Hmm, I thought. Sounds awfully thin to me. But I didn't

for a minute believe that Steven believed it. If he'd gone
to L. L. Lee, he knew at least part of the truth. This story
was for us.

Though, to be fair, Steven Wei did not actually look like
a man who had just found out that his uncle had been be-
traying the family for decades by being involved in criminal
activity with a ranking triad member. Or one who knew
that this uncle and the woman standing in front of him had
put him through hell by arranging and then losing control
of the disappearance of his son.

The six little kids finished their drill and lined up in three
rows, bowed to their instructor, and then, temporarily dismissed, ran screaming with laughter to splash each other
with water from a fountain at the end of the garden. I
watched Steven and Maria watching them and thought,
maybe what Steven had just told us was what he really
believed happened. Maybe his bedrock dedication to family
loyalty would not let him think evil of either his uncle or
his son's amah, and maybe this was the story Maria had
told him and he bought it.

No, Lydia, I thought, as the master called a break, and
the rest of the kids flopped on the grass, ran to the fountain,
laughed and teased and poked each other. You're exhausted, you're hot, you're running on empty, and this is
not a good time for you to try to think, I lectured myself.
Obviously, if Steven Wei knew enough to go to L. L. Lee,
he knows most, if not all, of what's been going on here.

Except, myself said back, answer me this: No matter
how much he knew, how *did* he know to go to L. L. Lee?
Maria didn't know about Lee. Mark didn't tell him. The
only one who knew about Lee was Wei Ang-Ran, and he'd
been not-quite-arrested in HKPD headquarters all night.

All right, I said to myself, all right, we'll make a deal.
The deal is: Shut up. This is a question you want the answer
to because there's no such thing as a question you *don't*
want the answer to, but it's not an urgent question. Nothing
is urgent now because this business is over. Probably when
you get some sleep, and talk this over with Bill, or with

Mark, the answer will be so obvious you'll feel dumb for not having thought of it right now. So worry about this later, how about that?

Myself seemed too tired to argue, so the deal was struck.

I waited while Mark checked over the ID Steven had brought with him: passports, birth certificates, fingerprints from a time he'd done an audit for a government agency, school photos of Harry. All this had been gone over by the Marine District cops already, of course, and it all checked out; Mark just wanted to be sure, for himself. In the end, he was, and so was I: This man was Steven Wei, and Steven Wei was this man.

Mark told Steven, the Tiger Gate master, and the Marine District cop still stationed up there that Steven, Maria, and Harry could leave. We shook hands and bowed all around; then he and I climbed into our patrol car and headed back to town.

At first no one spoke as the car tooled along past peaceful houses with terraced gardens snoozing in the sun. Then: "I have to go back to Hong Kong," Mark said. "I have reports to make, all that sort of thing." He leaned back against the seat and breathed a tired sigh. His day, which had started yesterday morning, wasn't over, and he seemed like he was suddenly feeling it.

I touched his hand. "You look exhausted."

He turned to me with a small smile; then he folded his fingers over mine. "I don't know about American PIs," he said, "but this isn't really the everyday life of a Hong Kong cop."

"Us either."

He looked a while longer. "Us?"

I shrugged.

He nodded. We didn't say anything more on the ride to town. But he didn't let go of my hand.

Mark took the next ferry back. Now that the case was wrapped up, a sleek, fast-running police launch would have been a luxury difficult to explain.

"It's okay," he said. "In fact it's better. The slower the ride, the more sleep I'll get."

I waited for the boat with him; then, just before he boarded, I gave him a quick kiss good-bye. At least, I meant it to be quick. He had other plans for it, and when it ended he was grinning. "Sorry," he said. "That wasn't fair."

"Yeah, you look sorry. I might have to report you for abusing your authority."

The scar on his lip stood out the way it always did when he grinned, white now in his tired face. What is it with you and men's grins, Lydia? I asked myself sternly, but myself had been ordered earlier to shut up and had nothing to say.

After the ferry left I turned and walked back along the waterfront street. It was only a few hours since breakfast, but I was starved, so I sat at a small round table outside a Taiwanese teahouse and had one of the thick neon-colored fruit drinks the Taiwanese like so much, and a couple of lemon cookies. I called the hospital, where they told me Bill was asleep but could be discharged later in the day. I watched the boats in the harbor and the strolling couples and the sleeping dogs until my drink was finished, and then I walked up one of the narrow streets into the town.

I went from shop to shop, buying first a sundress, a white cotton sleeveless affair with red piping and a sash that tied in the back. The proprietor let me change in the room behind the shop, which as it turned out was her kitchen. A shower would have been nice, too, but on the other hand the day was promising to be so hot that there was probably no point. I bought a bright blue backpack at the next store and stuffed in it the shirt and pants that had been so crisp and fresh yesterday morning, before the running around and the chasing people and the surf. I bought a bag of oranges and a bottle of wine, and though I was tempted, at the funeral-supplies store, by the paper boats and cars, the TV sets and cell phones, I didn't know the people I was going to see. So in the end I just bought incense and tiny wine cups, and I set out.

The walk to the cemetery from the center of town was hot and hilly, though most of it was in the shade of wide-leafed palm trees. My steps fell into a rhythm, an easy, relaxed one, and I emptied my mind and just watched the houses and gardens go by me on each side, the tiles and the flowerpots and the trees. I reached the graveyard and passed through the oldest section first, the one with the half-moon graves and no photographs. Eventually I came to the newer areas, and with the aid of posted maps, I found the section that swept down to the sea.

At the bottom of the slope, on the spiky grass plain, twelve graves stood in the front row. The faces of the dead watched me now as they had watched us all at dawn, Bill and Mark and the cops and me. Seabirds called and the sun leaned hotly on my back as I poured a cup of wine at each of the front-row graves, lit some incense, and left an orange. The photos showed old men and old women, mostly, but two were young men and one was a child. Two were named Chin, and I knew I was as much American as I was Chinese when I wasn't sure if that warmed or chilled me.

After I was done I climbed back up the hill and, again consulting the map, headed for the temple of Tin Hua. The walk there took another hour, some of it in shade, some in the full glory of the morning sun. The path climbed up and down, twisted and turned, taking every opportunity it could find to burst from leafy splendor into a clearing with a breathtaking view of the sea. After the fifth or sixth of these exuberant events, I paused to wipe the film of sweat from my face, to watch the white surf break on the golden boulders along Cheung Chau's shore, to see the sun sparkle on the deep blue water and listen to the wheeling seabirds' cries. If I were a path with views like this, I conceded, I'd probably be a little overdramatic and flamboyant, too. I wondered briefly what stone made golden boulders instead of regular gray ones, but I didn't give it too much thought, because that was the kind of thing that Bill always knew. Although this was Hong Kong, a place so foreign and strange that maybe he wouldn't have the answer. But if he didn't, I could ask Mark.

The Tin Hua temple was a smallish affair carved into solid rock, its pagoda roof and half-closed shuttered front making the interior dim and cool. Every inside inch was painted crimson or turquoise or gold, every surface covered with embroidered cloth, statues of Tin Hua and her fellow deities, candles and incense burners and plates of offerings. The air was thick with smoke. Candlelight glanced off gilding and brass offering plates like lights winking on and off in the smoky distance. There was no sound but the surf crashing on the rocks below, but I imagined Tin Hua liked that.

I lit my incense and left my oranges, and then on an inspiration I bought an incense spiral from the monk who seemed to be the temple's sole attendant. With a slender bamboo pole, he found a spot to hang the spiral on the crowded ceiling, and I lit that too. It was very long and thick; it would burn for a week. After I'd left Hong Kong, I thought, watching my smoke curl and blend with the smoke from other peoples' offerings, after I was home, back in Chinatown, New York, America, this incense in the Tin Hua temple on Cheung Chau Island would still be burning.

It took me another hour to walk back to town, half of that along a flat path by the waterfront. I took a long, long drink from a water fountain on the path, and then stuck my whole head under the cool stream, rinsing my face, soaking my hair, letting water run down the back of my new sundress. By the time I reached the row of colored-roofed restaurants Mark and I had had breakfast in I was totally dry again. I went beyond that row to a shady plaza dotted with large dogs who seemed to think this cool, stone-floored spot was a great place to spend a day this hot. I agreed, so I chose a table at one of the cafés that fronted it. I ordered lunch— fish soup with carrots and noodles, and a pot of tea—and drank another gallon or two of water while I took out my cell phone and called my client.

It was 2 A.M. in New York, but Grandfather Gao's *"Wai!"* sounded both calm and alert.

"It's Chin Ling Wan-Ju," I told him. "Everything's fine."

Grandfather Gao is not the type to sigh with relief, but the barely discernible relaxation in his tone when he spoke was the next best thing. "I am pleased to hear that, Ling Wan-Ju. Can you tell me what has happened?"

I laid it all out for him: Iron Fist, the prayer-seller, Tony and Big John; Wei Ang-Ran, Steven, and Harry; Mark, Maria Quezon, and L. L. Lee. My lunch came and started to cool on my table and I was still talking.

"I am sorry for what your partner has suffered," was the first thing Grandfather Gao said when my story was done. I took advantage of his continuing, "Please convey to him my sympathy. I am deeply in his debt," to slurp down some noodles.

"Thank you, Grandfather. He will be pleased to know he's served you well." I sneaked a quick piece of fish and, hoping the connection wasn't quite good enough that he could hear me chewing all the way in New York, asked, "Grandfather, one thing has been troubling me. From what you know about Wei Di-Fen,"—Steven—"does he seem like the kind of man who would make a deal with Lee?"

"A man may do many unexpected things for the sake of his family," was his reply.

"That's true, of course. But even assuming he made the deal, I'm not sure how he found out Lee Lao-Li was involved in this at all." He didn't answer. I sighed, sipped from my teacup. "Maybe it doesn't matter. The little boy is safe. Bill's safe. But Grandfather . . ."

"Yes?"

"What should I do about what Quan Mai asked of me? Can I really just let him shut a trap on Wei Di-Fen to bring down Lee Lao-Li?"

For longer than I expected there was silence from New

York. I covered the speaker part of my cell phone with my hand so I could eat more fish and some crunchy strips of carrot. Probably, Grandfather Gao was thinking up some polite way to point out the path that would have been obvious to anyone more clear-thinking than Chin Ling Wan-Ju. My problem was, I couldn't anticipate him. Either he was about to tell me that it wasn't my concern, that Steven Wei was going to have to, as Mark had said, pay his family's debt, and I should butt out; or he was going to say of course I couldn't let that happen, that my long-standing relationship with himself, Grandfather Gao, created a debt I owed to the son of his oldest friend—a man my own grandfather had known—and that it was therefore my obvious obligation to warn Steven. Both approaches were very Chinese, totally believable. I waited to see which it was.

It was neither. "Perhaps, Ling Wan-Ju," Grandfather Gao said as I lifted some noodles out of my soup bowl, "when you find the answers to the questions still troubling you, you will find that they solve this problem also."

I was a little surprised at the implication here. "Find the answers?" I said.

"You will not walk away from an unanswered question." All the way from New York I could hear Grandfather Gao smiling. "I have known you too long to think otherwise. Now, Chin Ling Wan-Ju, enjoy the rest of your lunch."

And Grandfather Gao rang off, leaving me alone in the shade with my soup and the sleepy dogs.

After lunch, still thinking over what Grandfather Gao had said, I walked along the waterfront street past the ferry terminal to the hospital. I was beyond exhausted now, beyond adrenaline-fueled, beyond determined. I was hot and pleasantly sleepy, maybe even a little stupid, but I didn't care. Grandfather Gao might be right, but there wasn't an unanswered question on earth I was capable of doing anything about right now. I'd collect Bill from the hospital, we'd go back to our hotel on Kowloon, I'd sleep, and then

I'd start worrying about rounding up any stray answers I needed.

Some of it worked out that way. But the thing about answers is, if you don't find them, they have a way of finding you.

Bill was perched on the edge of a chair by the window drinking tea when I got to his room. He wore a hopital gown open at the back and a pair of boxer shorts.

"Nice legs," I said, entering the room.

"The same to you," he replied politely.

"Aren't they ever going to let you get dressed?"

"They wanted me to, but I said you were coming so why do something that would just have to be undone again?"

"Quick, I'll call the doctor, you're delirious."

"Nah," he said, "I'm fine. You do look great, though."

"You like it?" I turned around to model my dress for him. "It's what all Cheung Chau's best-dressed twelve-year-olds are wearing. You want to stay or leave?"

"Is that a question?"

"Okay." I unslung my backpack. "Here, you'll need this. And don't think it was easy getting something that size on a Chinese island." I handed him the shirt I'd bought him, a soft, loosely woven tan cotton short-sleeved XXL. "Seriously," I said, "do you think you can wear a shirt?"

"If it's the price of leaving. The good thing about this hospital is I can't understand a word anybody says, so I don't know how bad off I am. Still, you can't smoke in here, you can't get a cup of coffee, and with the exception of you all the pretty girls seem to be out there."

"What about the nurses?"

"Well, with the exception of them, too."

I stepped out into the hall while he changed. When he came out he was moving slowly and stiffly, but he seemed steady enough on his feet. We did the hospital paperwork and headed toward the ferry. People stared as we made our way, gawking at the little Chinese woman in the white dress in the company of the big, black-eyed, bandaged Westerner.

I began to feel like Dr. Frankensteinette out for a stroll with her newest monster.

"I can hire us a boat," I said to Bill. "If you want to get there faster."

"Another small boat? As they say back home: fugge-dabadit. The only things I'd consider instead of the ferry would be a helicopter or the Queen Mary."

"Can't do it."

"Well, then."

The next ferry was in less than twenty minutes, anyway, so we waited across the waterfront street at the Taiwanese teahouse. Bill ordered iced coffee, and though it came whipped up with frothy milk and crushed ice and sugar, he pronounced it delicious. I had some gorgeously sunset-colored thing that had to do with mango and tamarind, and while we drank I filled him in on all the things he didn't know, all the things Mark and I had worked out or found out or theorized after he'd left for Cheung Chau.

"Wei Ang-Ran," Bill said when I'd gotten through that part, shaking his head with wonder. "What is he, nuts?"

"Desperate," I said. "And as he told us, not a man of plans."

When the ferry came we bought first-class tickets, which gave us the option of the air-conditioned forward cabin or the breezy upper deck. Bill preferred the deck, saying it was actually easier for him to stand than sit, and besides, outside he could smoke. So he leaned on the rail and I sat in a plastic deck chair with my feet up on the same rail, companionably near his elbow. He dragged on a Chinese cigarette, which he claimed bore about the same resemblance to an American one as the Taiwanese iced coffee had to the coffee he was used to: revolting, unless you're desperate and you're on a Chinese island where it's all they have, in which case it's totally terrific.

It was late afternoon by now, and the rounded green mounds of the out-islands drifted past us, softened by a thin heat haze. Other boats scudded along the water and birds flew overhead and the wind pushed my hair around.

"Listen," I said after a while. "Are you smart enough to think right now?"

"I thought we decided smart wasn't my strong suit."

"Just answer the question."

He took his cigarette from his mouth. "I guess I'm no dumber than usual. What's up?"

"I can't figure out how Steven Wei knew to go to L. L. Lee, to make the deal."

He watched the islands float by. "I have another one."

"What's that?"

"How did Lee know Harry was missing in the first place?"

I frowned. "That doesn't seem so hard. Tony told him. Tony and Big John knew what was going on almost from the beginning, because Iron Fist went to them for help after Maria went to *him* for help."

"Not bad, but not true. According to Tony they were freelancing. Tony was surprised when Lee called and said he wanted Harry. I think he was pissed off, too, because he'd been looking for a big score. But Lee's their boss, and on the plus side, they figured they'd impress the hell out of him by how fast they could get this done."

"When did they tell you that?"

"When we were still friends, before the boat."

"So who told Lee about Harry? And who told Steven about Lee?"

Bill shuffled in to where the concession stand was and came back with tea, coffee, and coconut cookies, but none of that made either of us any smarter. I sat in my deck chair and sipped my tea and watched the islands slip by, and I thought I was thinking about L. L. Lee, but something must have happened, because the next thing I knew a hand was gently stroking my hair and Bill's voice was saying, "Wake up."

"Huh?" I said incisively.

"We're here."

I looked around. My feet were still up on the rail, my

half-finished tea sat on the deck under my chair, and a row of skyscrapers stared me right in the face.

"Oh."

"It's those trenchant comments," Bill said, reaching for my backpack, "that way you have of cutting to the core of the issue—"

"Oh, quiet. And give me that." I grabbed the pack before he could pick it up. "Monsters can't carry the supplies, only doctors."

"What?"

"Nothing."

The walk from the Cheung Chau ferry to the Star Ferry was short, and the wait for the ferry was short, and the ride across the harbor to Kowloon was short. The walk from the ferry to the Hong Kong Hotel was also short, but as frantic with cars and jackhammers and surging tides of people as an end-of-the-day Monday in Hong Kong might suggest. We stepped aside and gave way and generally were so slow-moving and unaggressive that three different people actually snapped at us.

At the hotel we checked for messages, but the only one was from Grandfather Gao, from yesterday, asking to be kept informed. Okay, I thought, you're informed. And I'm off duty until I shower, eat, and sleep.

"Here's the plan," I told Bill. "I'm going to take a shower, put on some clean clothes, and make myself feel human again. Then I'll come up to your room and we'll order the best meal room service has. Then I'll go back to my room and sleep until morning, or afternoon, or whenever I want. Unless," it occurred to me, remembering I'd just retrieved him out of a hospital, "you just want to go to bed and you don't want company."

The grin started to spread across his bandaged face.

"No!" I said. "Don't even bother. You know exactly what I meant."

He sighed in acknowledgment. "But you'll come to my room?"

"Only for dinner."

"It's a start."

"No, it's dinner."

We parted in the elevator. When I reached my room I spent a little time staring out the window as the neon crowning the buildings of Hong Kong Island began to glow through the purple dusk. Then I spent a lot of time in the shower, first under hot water to scrub off the salt and sand and sweat, then cold water to bring my brain back to life. I dried my hair and put on a thin white cotton sweater and a pair of khakis. I took my cell phone with me, because you never know, and headed to Bill's room.

He had showered too, and shaved, and changed. In his room as in mine the air-conditioning was on, but here the windows were also open, to empty out as much cigarette smoke as possible. This might be a losing battle, considering he was adding to it as he opened the door to let me in, but it was Be Nice To Bill Day so I didn't point that out.

He had the TV on. A crisp young Chinese woman was delivering the news in English; Hong Kongers must be the same as Americans, watching the news with their dinner, making sure they hadn't missed anything while racing through another day of getting and spending. The young woman summed up what looked like a very slow and soggy Legislative Council meeting; then she moved right on to the prospects for two fillies new to Hong Kong in Wednesday's big-purse race at Happy Valley.

"You can turn it off," Bill said, handing me the leather folder from the desk with the room service menu in it. "I just thought it would be useful to see if anything about the Weis or Cheung Chau or anything had hit the news, and if it did, what spin they're using."

"As usual, a step ahead. Let's leave it on for a while. It's really kind of interesting."

Actually it was fascinating, a collection of information useful to the English-speaking Hong Kong community—meaning, expatriot and probably upper class—or at least, what a TV station thought would be useful to them. The

kinds of local-interest stories that fill American newscasts—
fires, political squabbles, hero pets—were completely absent, replaced with stories about a new even higher-speed
train connection to the airport, or rumors reported as news
about a land development deal on the border with Guang-
dong. Absent also were any crime stories. Not a mugging,
jewelry-store robbery, or talking-head defense lawyer to be
seen.

"I don't think we're going to make it onto this news," I
said, handing the menu back to Bill. "There seems to be
no crime in Hong Kong, probably bad for business. I'm
having Hainan Island chicken."

"That sounds good. What is it?"

"How can it sound good if you don't know what it is?"

"Because I'm hungry enough to eat the menu." He took
a club soda out of the minibar for me, and a beer for himself. There was an empty bottle on the desk; he'd already
finished one in the time it took me to shower and get up
here. Well, he was entitled. He ran his eyes over the menu
while I explained the coconut and spicy dipping sauces that
were the glories of Hainan Island chicken. I was doing a
pretty good job, too, when suddenly my mouth froze open
and my head snapped around to the TV as though I were
a marionette.

"We take you now to the Peninsula Hotel," the crisp
young woman was saying, "where an American doctor, Dr.
Franklin Wei, has, in a very unusual move, called a press
conference. He promises information of great interest to the
authorities concerning triad activity."

"Oh, my God," I yelped. "What's going on?"

The TV anchor's face was replaced on the screen by the
grassy slope in front of the Peninsula. Franklin Wei, looking very somber and determined, stood at a set of microphones before a small knot of reporters. He wasn't
speaking, but seemed to be waiting for something. Maybe
more reporters. The dusk of evening had drained the green
from the slope, but I didn't think it was dusk that had
drained the color from Franklin's face.

Bill stared at the screen also. "Get down there," he said. "You move faster than I do. I'll come as fast as I can."

He was reaching for his shoes; I was gone before he picked them up.

The elevator didn't move nearly fast enough for me, but once I hit the street I moved fast enough for myself, zipping through the sidewalks full of people, once charging across a street against Hong Kong traffic. Yes, okay, I thought to the cursing, honking drivers, fine, everything you're saying is true. I ran faster. The Peninsula was only a few blocks from the Hong Kong Hotel; I felt like it was taking me forever to get there, but in truth, when I screeched to a halt at the grassy slope, it seemed that Franklin had only just started to talk.

". . . first came to Hong Kong only a few days ago," he was saying, in English. White TV lights cast sharp shadows on the grass and on his face. "However, I've been involved in an illegal smuggling operation in partnership with members of a Hong Kong–based triad for many years. My family owns an import-export firm, Lion Rock Enterprises. The firm was founded by my father, Wei Yao-Shi, and his brother, Wei Ang-Ran. My father died recently and my brother, Steven Wei, came into the business. None of these men had any knowledge of my illegal activities or were involved in any way."

He paused, looking around at the assembled reporters. He looked down, swallowed, then squared his shoulders and continued. "For years this triad has paid me to arrange for antiquities from the Chinese mainland to be smuggled into Hong Kong and through Hong Kong to the U.S., hidden in furniture Lion Rock was importing. I was able to do this because the strict honesty and uprightness of my father, uncle, and brother made it impossible for them to even see what was going on, much less, if they had seen, to suspect that I was involved. Recent events—the death of my father and the entry of my brother into the business—have made me decide to end my relationship with the triad. However," and here Franklin managed a small smile, "ending a relationship with a triad isn't easy. I thought the best way to do it would be like this, in public." One more pause; then, "That's all I have to say for now. I'll give details of the operation to the authorities in the morning, if they're interested. Thank you very much."

Franklin Wei turned from the microphones, ignoring the shouted questions of reporters, who began crowding after him. The doormen at the Peninsula, accustomed to famous guests, politely but unshakably refused entry to the reporters, who were left to yell requests for interviews at the revolving door as Franklin disappeared inside.

fifteen

As I stood there stunned I heard Bill's voice beside me.

"What happened?"

I looked up at him. His forehead was beaded with sweat; he was standing oddly. His back must be very stiff and sore, I thought. He belonged back at the hotel, in bed, not out here on the tip of the Kowloon Peninsula where lunatics prevailed.

"Franklin announced to the world that it was he and he alone who was responsible for the smuggling," I said. "As a partner with an unnamed triad. What the hell is he thinking? First, it's a lie; and second, it's suicide."

"Come on," Bill said.

We ambled slowly to the door of the Peninsula, trying to look as unlike reporters as we possibly could. Bill's bandaged face got narrow eyes from the doorman, but just because a guy's had a nose job didn't seem enough reason to be denied admission. We didn't rush through the columned, gilded lobby, either, just made our slow way to the elevators, stood placidly like any other tired tourists at the end of a long Hong Kong day, and entered the elevator when it came. I pressed Fanklin's floor, which luckily I remembered from having phoned him here. We nodded friendly greetings to our fellow Peninsula residents and faced front. It wasn't until the doors opened on the seventh floor's carpeted hallway that I broke and ran.

Bill followed as fast as he could, but by the time I reached Franklin's room I was half a hallway ahead of him. I knocked, or really I more like pounded. Bill pulled up next to me just as Franklin opened the door.

When he saw who we were a very strange expression crossed Franklin Wei's round face: disappointment and relief fought each other to a draw.

I pushed past him into his room. He opened his mouth

to protest, then shut it, as he shut the door after Bill, too, was inside.

"What's wrong with you?" I demanded, facing him squarely.

"Nothing," he said. "I think you should leave."

"Franklin, you're nuts. One, what you said out there, I know it isn't true, because your uncle confessed to the whole thing. Two," I overrode whatever he was about to say, "what can you possibly think Strength and Harmony is going to do now that you've done that in public? A news conference? What is *wrong* with you?"

He paused, as though surprised at something I'd said. "My uncle? He was lying."

"No, *you* were lying. There's no way you could have run an operation like this from New York. I'm willing to believe you were involved, but not alone. And this public announcement—!"

"I don't really care what you're willing to believe," he snapped. The soft lighting in this elegant room and the peach-colored stripes on the Peninsula's silk wallpaper were doing nothing to restore the color to Franklin's face. He looked at Bill. "What happened to you?"

"Strength and Harmony," Bill said.

Franklin kept his eyes on Bill's face for a few more brief moments. The sight of the broad white bandage—or maybe something in Bill's eyes—seemed to bring him to a decision.

"All right," he said. "You're right about some things, I have some questions for you, and there are a couple of other things I want you to know. I'm going to tell you about them and then you're going to leave."

He gestured us to silk-upholstered armchairs and brought the desk chair over for himself. Before he sat he opened the minibar. "Anyone want anything?"

Bill asked for a beer, and I asked for a club soda, and there we were, resuming our interrupted drinks in Franklin Wei's grand room in the Peninsula Hotel.

Franklin had taken out two tiny bottles of single-malt

Scotch for himself. As he poured them into a glass and sat
down before us I noticed the room's two telephones were
unplugged, their jack cords snaking emptily along the carpet.

"Ang-Ran," Franklin said. "What do you mean, he confessed?"

"He was helping the police with their inquiries," I said
dryly. "I was there, with Mark Quan, the detective who
went to Steven's apartment later."

Franklin frowned. "The police were questioning Ang-
Ran? Why?"

"It's a long story." I hesitated a moment; then I thought,
what the hell. If Steven knew enough to go to L. L. Lee,
nothing would be secret from any of these people for long.
"Harry's kidnapping was his idea."

"Uncle Ang-Ran?" Disbelief was written all over Franklin's face.

"Because of the shipment coming in from China. He
didn't want Steven to be at Lion Rock until the smuggled
goods were all removed, but apparently it's hard to keep
Steven from discharging his family obligations. The kidnapping was only supposed to be a distraction, no real danger to Harry, but things got out of hand. But because he
told us all about it, that's how we know what you said out
there is a lie."

It took Franklin a moment to be able to do anything but
stare at me. "My God," he said. "Ang-Ran didn't want
Steven—Is that what started all this?"

"No." That was Bill, quietly. "What started it was when
Wei Ang-Ran agreed to the original deal with Strength and
Harmony thirty years ago."

Franklin drank and then nodded. For a long time the
elegant room was filled with silence, the silence of thick
carpets and heavy drapes and other people's work insulat-
ing you from the world. It's a comforting silence, but un-
real, and Franklin finally broke it.

"You're right." He drained half his drink, closed his
eyes, opened them again. Color was returning to his face.

"The operation was obviously Ang-Ran's. I was a kid when it started, the late sixties, the Cultural Revolution. He didn't bring me in until seven years ago."

"Why bring you in at all?" I asked.

"I didn't realize it until a few weeks ago, after Dad died and the will was read," Franklin said, "but that's when Harry was born. I didn't know that, of course, because I didn't know about Steven, but I do remember around then Dad changed, started talking and thinking more long-term. I thought it was because he was sick. His heart was starting to go. Uncle Ang-Ran saw it too, and worried that Dad would start looking more deeply into the business, to make sure everything would be okay for Harry to inherit."

"How do you know that?"

"I had a long talk with Ang-Ran about all this two weeks ago. That's when I decided to come to Hong Kong, partly for Dad's funeral but mostly to meet the rest of the family. I always liked Ang-Ran—he sent birthday presents and wrote long funny letters when I was a kid, and boy I loved working with him on this smuggling stuff, but I'd never met him. My mom had no family, and with Dad gone . . . I mean, all I have is skiing buddies and three ex-wives who don't speak to me."

Franklin drank some more Scotch and fell silent again. His eyes fixed on the carpet, but I was sure that whatever he was seeing, it wasn't that.

"So Wei Ang-Ran brought you into his smuggling operation?" I asked. "And you liked it?"

Franklin looked up, a little startled, as though he'd forgotten we were there. He nodded. "He knew I needed money—the ex-wives," he said, with a sad smile. "And he was so afraid Dad would find out what was going on. He just wanted someone to oversee what was happening in New York, make it come out all right and keep Dad out of it. I didn't see a problem in that. Dad was sick by then, and to know Ang-Ran was messing with stuff like this could have killed him. And the way Ang-Ran put it to me, we were helping save, my God, the artistic heritage of

China from barbarians. All I was was a club-hopping Upper East Side doctor with three divorces and a specialty in squash-court injuries."

"What did you do?"

"In the operation? Like I said, not much. Some of the stuff came to New York. There was a guy at the New York warehouse whose job was to unload and distribute, but Ang-Ran didn't trust him. My job was to visit the fences— fences, for Pete's sake—" Franklin grinned briefly, shaking his head. "—and make sure they got what they were expecting. That the guy wasn't skimming some little piece of jewelry or some bronze figure that he thought no one would notice."

"That explains the phone calls," I said to Bill. He nodded.

Franklin raised his eyebrows.

"Mark Quan got your phone records," I said. "From New York. You called L. L. Lee from time to time."

"My—why?"

"We thought you might be behind the kidnapping," I said matter-of-factly.

"*Me?* You can't—I'm just—" He seemed about to become righteously indignant, but he looked from me to Bill, relaxed and smiled instead. "Franklin Wei, criminal mastermind," he said. "What a career that could have been. Yes, I called Lee. Sometimes I had to double-check with him on something."

I asked, "Who were the fences?"

"About half a dozen guys in and around Chinatown. I can give you a list."

That might be a useful list to have, I thought, though I wasn't sure what I was going to do with it.

"I know what a mess this is now," Franklin said into his drink. "But I'm not sorry Ang-Ran asked me and I'm not sorry I did it. The whole thing made me feel like the Scarlet Pimpernel. I'd go down to Chinatown in shades and a leather jacket—God, it was a blast."

Well, I thought, but the Scarlet Pimpernel, brainless aristocrat by day, hero by night, was saving lives when *he* switched identities. Although if you actually believed you were preserving China's artistic heritage, plus protecting your sick father—plus making a few bucks and getting to walk on the wild side—I guessed I could see it.

Franklin downed some more Scotch. The drapes at his windows were open. The neon Hong Kong skyline shimmered in the ultramarine sky and again, upside down, in the black harbor water. In the sky and in the water a cloud drifted across the face of the moon. I looked at Franklin. The Scarlet Pimpernel. My skin began to tingle.

"You were there when Mark Quan told the family that some triad guys wanted to trade Bill for Harry," I said slowly. "You were there. And you were the only one there who knew any triad guys, or why they'd want this trade."

He met my eyes. "I wasn't sure," he nodded, "but I guessed. I knew Lee wasn't happy when Ang-Ran told him we wouldn't be smuggling anymore now that Steven was in the business. I figured Lee thought if Ang-Ran couldn't make Steven agree to keep going, maybe he could."

"My God," I said, the tingle sharper now. "Oh, my God. You went to Lee and told him you were Steven, didn't you?"

Franklin looked at me silently for a moment, then shrugged. "I'd spoken to him on the phone a lot, but he'd never met either of us, Steven or me. And we do sort of look alike."

Sort of. I thought of my own reaction when I'd first seen Franklin standing outside the door to the Robinson Road apartment.

"You told him you were Steven," I went on, still slowly, still half expecting Franklin to tell me I was crazy. "You said he didn't need to complete the trade for Harry. You said you agreed to the deal just knowing what he had in mind, and please, let there be no more trouble. He was gratified," I added. "L. L. Lee said you were a true Chinese, with a subtle mind."

To which Franklin threw up his hands and responded, "Great."

Bill, perched forward on his chair, pulled on his beer and asked, "But you weren't the one who told Lee about Harry's kidnapping in the first place."

Franklin shook his head. "God, no. That's not the kind of information I'd want a guy like Lee to have. No," he said, finishing his Scotch, "that was that lawyer. Natalie Zhu."

"Natalie Zhu? *Why?*" I said. "What was she thinking?"

"And how do you know that?" Bill added.

"I asked Lee and he told me. I think he was trying to impress me with how tied into my family's affairs— Steven's family's affairs—he was. And apparently she was thinking he could help."

"Help?" That was me again, my amazement growing at this entire extended mad family.

"Help find Harry." Franklin sighed, shook his head. Maybe he was amazed too. He got up, got himself two more Scotches from the minibar. "Natalie Zhu stumbled on to the smuggling a couple of years ago. Uncle Ang-Ran almost had a stroke when she told him she knew."

"What happened?"

"She was disgusted by the whole thing, but she agreed to keep quiet about it for my father's and Steven's sake. Ang-Ran kept promising her it would end but she totally dismissed that: You don't end a partnership with a triad unless *they* want it ended, she'd say. She thinks Ang-Ran's pretty pathetic."

"Did she know about you?"

"I didn't think so before I'd met her, but now I bet she did all along. Ang-Ran never told her, but I don't think you can slip much past her."

"Did she know Wei Ang-Ran was responsible for the kidnapping?" Bill asked.

"She didn't know that, according to Lee, but she did think the whole thing smelled funny. And she was sure of two things: One, you two messing around could only cause trouble. She was sure you couldn't find Harry, and any close look at the family might open the whole can of worms."

I nodded. "She sent us on what was supposed to be a wild goose chase, looking for the amah. She must have been unhappy when Mark Quan told you all that Bill had found her."

Franklin smiled. "Her face didn't exactly light up, like Steven's and Li-Ling's. I didn't know all this at that point—I just thought, well, they're Harry's parents, of course, they're more excited than the family lawyer."

"You said she thought two things," Bill said. "What was the other?"

Franklin looked at Bill. "That a long-term relationship with a ranking triad member had to be good for something. One of the reasons Lee was ready to believe I was Steven and I was making the deal was because that was what she'd promised him: that if he found Harry she'd guarantee Steven would keep up the smuggling."

"How was she going to deliver that?" he asked.

Franklin blinked. "Well, don't you think he would have? She'd made a promise on his behalf, for one thing. It would have been a matter of honor for him to keep it, even if he hadn't wanted it made. But also, if Lee had actually found Harry, Steven would have been grateful, and would have wanted to show that."

Very Chinese and logical: Grandfather Gao would have approved. I wondered if he knew it was possible to proceed according to Chinese logic and be insane at the same time.

"When you went to Lee," Bill said, seeming less amazed by these crazy people than I was, "Harry was still missing."

"Yes. I didn't know what had happened to him, but that detective—Quan?—said the cops were looking for him, because of the trade for you. If they were, I had to think he'd be better off if Lee wasn't. I wasn't sure I was doing you any favors," he added apologetically, to Bill, "but a kid . . . I mean . . . anyway, I hope I didn't make it any worse."

Bill shook his head and drank his beer.

"Okay," I said. "Okay. Every last one of you is nuts, it must be a Wei family thing. But listen: What were you planning to do once it was over and Lee expected Steven to keep smuggling and Steven had no idea what he was talking about? Because Steven really has no idea, does he?" I thought of Steven Wei's relaxed and smiling face in the garden at Tiger Gate Academy, a face that was the sunny, daytime mirror of the pale, shadowed one I sat across from right now. Steven really believed the story Maria Quezon had handed him. Steven really knew nothing about his uncle's involvement in his son's kidnapping. Steven really had no clue.

Franklin said nothing, but Bill did. "That's what the press conference was for. You've exposed the whole thing and laid it on yourself. Steven won't have to know about Ang-Ran—the kidnapping or even the smuggling—and Lion Rock is useless now to L. L. Lee. If he saw you on TV, he'll know he was had. Why didn't you mention him or Strength and Harmony by name?"

"Tomorrow," I said. "You said you'd give the authorities details tomorrow."

Franklin smiled and swirled his whisky. "American melodrama," he said. "I couldn't resist it."

"Franklin," I said, "you may not have thought about this, but what you just did isn't going to make L. L. Lee very happy."

"I have that under control."

"How?"

Franklin looked out the window at the clouded moon, and then back at me and Bill for a very long time. "Listen," he finally said, "I'm exhausted. You must be too. You especially," he said to Bill. "I really don't want to talk anymore right now. Come over in the morning, I'll give you the rest."

"You need a bodyguard," I said. "Bill and I are both trained and experienced at that. We—"

"No," Franklin said.

"Franklin—"

"It's the Peninsula," he said. "Nobody's going to come blasting down my door at the Peninsula."

"We're staying."

"I'll call security," Franklin said. "I'll have you thrown out." He stood, a little shakily, it seemed to me, from all that Scotch. He plugged one of the phones back in and started to punch buttons.

"Franklin—" I tried again.

He paused, then put the phone to his ear.

"No," I said. "No, you win." If security came to throw us out they'd also make sure we couldn't get within two blocks of the hotel in any direction. That wouldn't help at all.

I stood. "Franklin, you're crazy. This is Hong Kong. You can't do things like this here."

"Sorry," Franklin told the phone. "My mistake." He lowered the receiver and unplugged the phone again. "Hong Kong," he said. He stared for a moment out the window at the two moons, the two neon skylines. Then he turned to me. "Hong Kong. Didn't you just get here more or less the same day I did?"

"Yes, but—"

"I know what I'm doing."

"I don't think so."

"You're wrong. Now go."

He crossed the thick carpet, opened the door, stood waiting for us to leave. Without a choice, we left.

We didn't go far. My first thought was to stay in the hallway, planted like soldiers on either side of Franklin's door, but hotel security wouldn't have been happy with that either. What we did was to go back down to the lobby, where, on a maroon expanse of Oriental carpet among two-story columns with ornate tops, the Peninsula's famous tearoom became, at this hour, the Peninsula's famous lobby bar.

Not that a bar was what either Bill or I needed right then. I ordered tea and Bill ordered coffee and I called Mark Quan.

"Wai?" This was a hoarse and sleepy Mark, and I felt bad for waking him as I obviously had, but some things can't be helped.

"It's Lydia."

"Lydia? What the hell's wrong? I just got to sleep an hour ago. Are you—?"

"I'm sorry, Mark. But there's a big problem." I gave him a fast rundown of Franklin Wei's press conference.

"This isn't happening."

I knew how he felt. "Bill and I were just up in his room, but he threw us out. He thinks he's safe here. It's true the desk won't give out his room number and he's probably smart enough not to open his door, but I don't think that's enough if he's pissed off L. L. Lee."

"No," Mark said, completely awake now, his voice both urgent and unbelieving. "It's not. He's totally crazy. Everyone in that family is totally crazy. Okay. It'll take me twenty minutes to get down there. I'll call in a couple of cars to get the entrances watched. Maybe nothing will happen this fast. When I get there I'll arrest him."

"You'll arrest him?"

"He confessed to a crime, didn't he? At least he'll be safe with us."

"Can you get him kicked out of Hong Kong—shipped back to the U.S.?"

Mark sighed. "I doubt it. You and I know he's lying about being the brains behind this, but the government isn't going to think it's funny. A lot of people are going to want to talk to him. How long ago was this thing televised?"

"Maybe half an hour."

"Guaranteed there's screaming and yelling all over headquarters right now. Give them another half hour, I'd be surprised if the cops I send are the only ones who show up."

They weren't, though they were first. Within three minutes a glance out the stately front doors showed me a patrol car firmly ensconced in the Peninsula's curving driveway. The driver politely and completely refused the

doorman's, and then the night manager's, requests to re-
move to somewhere where he wouldn't make the guests
nervous.

Leaving Bill in the bar where he could watch the grand
staircase and the elevators, I strolled to the back and side
entrances. They were covered too. Well, all right: No one
was going to enter the Peninsula in the next half hour who
was either known to the police or was particularly concerned about becoming known. That should buy enough
time for Mark to get here, and then at least Franklin Wei
would be safely in police custody. At that point, from what
Mark said, Franklin's troubles would be just beginning, but
this was, after all, his own bright idea.

A pair of plainclothes detectives, badges on their hips,
strode into the lobby about twenty minutes later. A little
discussion with the desk clerks and then with the increasingly distressed-looking night manager, a little flashing of
the badges, and they got what they wanted, which was obviously Franklin's room number. They headed for the elevator in the reluctant company of the night manager. This
was good if they were real cops, not good if they were
Strength and Harmony ringers. Bill and I stood to follow
them, though what use we'd be if these were the bad guys
I wasn't sure. But we didn't have to find out. Before they
got to the elevator or we got to them, Mark himself pushed
through the Peninsula's revolving door.

He saw the detectives crossing the lobby and called to
them. They stopped and waited for him and the three of
them had a brief discussion, which the night manager listened to with growing dismay on his face. They started for
the elevator again. Bill and I joined them in time to hear
the taller of the two detectives say, "I guess we should have
known this one was yours, Quan. The guy's crazy."

Okay, so they were real cops. Mark gave him the Chinese chin-jut and introduced Bill and me to them. The elevator door opened and we all got in.

"Civilians?" the tall detective said significantly, but he
got no answer from Mark. I just smiled, faced front, and

watched the numbers light up. The cops were speaking Cantonese, so Bill had no idea what was going on, but on the other hand, they had no idea why his face looked the way it did, so I guessed they were even.

At the seventh floor we all followed the night manager down the hall to Franklin's room. Mark knocked, identified himself, knocked again, waited. Franklin didn't answer. One more knock; Mark told me and Bill to stay back. He and the other cops pulled out their guns. The night manager looked as though he wanted to run to the lifeboats. But this was his ship and he stayed on the bridge. He produced a key and unlocked Franklin's door.

The cops swept in. In the carpeted hall I waited: for a shout, a shot, a loud fight, a quiet arrest. But there was nothing, because Franklin wasn't there.

The three cops made a survey of every inch of the room and were out in half a minute. As we charged down the hall Mark yanked out his cell phone and started barking orders at the cops in the cars outside. No one even thought about the elevator except the night manager, who stopped there and then watched openmouthed as the rest of us swept by him to the stairs.

Bill couldn't run; he was being left behind. He yelled Mark's name. Mark turned. "Alone," Bill shouted down the carpeted corridor. "Somewhere deserted and alone."

I wasn't sure what that meant, and at first it seemed as though Mark, stopped still in the corridor, wasn't either. Then Mark's eyes widened. He nodded and took off.

When we hit the lobby the other detectives each headed to a side door. Mark took the front and I went with him.

The patrol car was gone from the front, sweeping the area as Mark had ordered. Mark stopped outside just briefly, then ran forward again. I chased after him.

We crossed the busy avenue in front of the Peninsula, Mark ordering me to go back inside and then, when that didn't work, grabbing my arm to at least keep me from dashing across the street against traffic. When we finally got to the other side Mark sped across the plaza, zigzagging his way among the Cultural Center buildings. I followed, under shadowy bridges and beside high blank walls, until we burst onto the harborfront promenade where I had stood wordless next to Bill at my first sight of the Hong Kong skyline.

Without stopping Mark headed left, along the promenade, away from the ferry. Away from everything, I realized as I ran after him. Strolling families and fried-dough vendors became fewer, the tiled promenade narrower and emptier. A few hand-holding couples here, a pair of night fishermen there. The air was hot and thick. My breath began to burn in my chest. My tired legs pumped, feet slamming the tiles, but I was well behind Mark when I spotted Franklin Wei, far up ahead.

Franklin leaned on the railing gazing across the harbor at the glittering neon skyline. On the black water fishing boats and sampans cut white lines across the city's shimmering reflection. Above the blazing neon, a thick dark cloud shrouded the Peak, cutting it off from the rest of Hong Kong.

"Franklin Wei!" Mark shouted as he ran.

Franklin didn't turn, didn't move. He just stood there, staring across the harbor. And when a figure stepped from the shadows much closer to him than Mark or I, raised his arm, and, in Tony Siu's voice, called Franklin's Chinese name—"Wei Fu-Ran!"—he didn't move then, either.

Mark shouted a warning. Siu spun toward us. The gun in his hand glinted. Mark hit the tiles and so did I.

A bullet screamed over our heads. Mark fired back; his shot flew useless into the night. Siu turned back to his business, to Franklin. He fired. Franklin jerked forward into the railing. Another shot. Now Franklin half turned. I couldn't see his eyes; I don't know what he saw, what was reflected in them. He slumped slowly to the ground and didn't move again.

Tony Siu, his work done, raced away along the waterfront. Mark jumped to his feet and sped after him. I heard another pair of shots, but neither figure stopped. Siu turned, charged down a walkway that would take him back to the crowded, frantic streets of Kowloon. He was far ahead, running as fast as Mark.

I stood and ran again too, hesitating when I reached the place where Franklin lay. But I couldn't help Mark: I had no gun, I didn't know the streets, didn't know the shortcuts or the hiding places, the merchants or the landlords. I didn't know anything, here, in Hong Kong.

I dropped to my knees next to Franklin Wei. Franklin's open eyes were blank and glittering. Automatically I felt his neck for a pulse. There was nothing. Blood was seeping from beneath him, flowing along cracks and joints, pooling on the tiles. Two fist-size stains on his chest spread as I watched them, merging into one, surrounding the amulet lying on his shirt like a sea of blood circling an island of jade. Feet pounded, sirens howled, voices called, but I sat unmoving, seeing only the neon skyline of Hong Kong reflected in Franklin Wei's blood.

Two days later, in the morning under a bright, hot sun, there was a double funeral at the mausoleum on the breezy hilltop in the New Territories town of Sha Tin.

We climbed a broad switchback staircase through lush mountain greenery in the company of chanting Buddhist monks. They rang gongs and tapped bells as the wind cleared the early clouds from the azure sky. At the top, among the gilt-touched crimson columns in front of the wall's wide sweep, Steven Wei, dressed in mourner's white, lit sweet, thick incense for his father and his brother. The rest of us did the same. We bowed, sometimes chanted, circling the open altar to stand our incense sticks in the sand of the burner and, at the iron cauldron beside it, to add our paper funeral gifts to the fire.

Li-Ling, heavy with the expected child, held Harry's hand as he dropped Hell Notes—paper money made to send to the dead—and paper rice bags into the flames. Wei Ang-Ran was next, also sending money, and a paper feast of fish; Natalie Zhu sent books and an image of Tin Hua, which curled and darkened and sprang suddenly into the air before it fell to ashes. Maria Quezon had brought Hell Notes and a set of recipes, in her own hand, for Filipino dishes old Mr. Wei had enjoyed. Mark was there; like Bill, he had brought only money, feeling it presumptuous to offer anything else. I had one gift beyond money. At a funeral supplies store on the shrine-sellers' street in Mong Kok I had found a paper image of Sun Wu-Kong, the Monkey King: joyful trickster and thief, laughing fighter, courageous companion. I put that in the fire for Franklin Wei.

As the monks, chanting, placed the two urns of ashes in the mausoleum wall, I gazed over the emerald hillside to the white waves and dark boats on the water far below. Old Mr. Wei had asked to be brought from America to be buried in this sunny, breezy place next to his second wife, Steven's mother. Now his first son was buried here too, their photographs added to the numberless others on the curving wall, forever looking out over the green hills and the sea.

I turned back to watch Steven bowing, to listen to him saying the prescribed prayers. He had been shocked and sickened to hear of Franklin's crime, his betrayal of his father and family, his death on the Kowloon waterfront. But Franklin was his older brother and there was no question about his funeral. All the proper rites were performed, everything done correctly, as filial loyalty demanded.

Filial loyalty, of course, was what had brought on Franklin's death. It was *Zhong xiao dao yi*, and Bill had seen it before Mark or I had. Franklin had calmly left the hotel by a side door—the cops had been watching for suspicious people going in, not tourists going out; none of them had Franklin's description—and walked down to the waterfront, and waited. Announcing that he would provide names and details the next day insured that Strength and Harmony would have to do something about him immediately. Lion Rock, as Bill had said in Franklin's hotel room, was useless now to L. L. Lee, though Lee himself had not been identified and had nothing to deny. Self-protection had required

Franklin's removal and honor had required revenge. L. L. Lee had gotten both. And the death of Franklin settled his score with the Wei family.

Steven, performing his filial rites, knew nothing about any of this.

I watched him, and watched Wei Ang-Ran, next to him, bowing, placing incense in the burner as sweet-smelling smoke swirled around him. I was afraid Wei Ang-Ran, driven by guilt, would tell Steven the truth. What a shame that would be, what a waste.

And Wei Ang-Ran might have, but for one final, stunning fact.

When the last incense stick was lit and the last gong rung, the monks stayed to tend the fire and the family prepared to leave. The Weis were planning to gather for the traditional postfuneral meal. Mark and Bill and I had been courteously invited, but declined, as we thought right. As the others started back down the hill, Wei Ang-Ran hung behind.

"Please wait," he said to me in Cantonese. "I have something I must show you." He included Mark and Bill in his look.

So we waited, letting Wei Ang-Ran draw us to a secluded bend in the curving wall. Once the rest of the family, descending the staircase, was out of sight, Wei Ang-Ran reached his hand under his shirt collar and pulled out a pendant on a slim gold chain.

"What's that?" I asked.

And he answered, "My brother's jade."

The sun beat down and the soft breeze blew and I stood with my mouth open, as speechless and staring as the high wall's rows of photographs of those who would never be confused again.

Finally coming back to life I said, "You've had it all this time?"

"In one sense," he said. "In another, no." His voice was barely above a whisper and his eyes were sad.

"What does that mean?"

"The envelope you brought me that I would not open. My brother's final advice, I thought, his final words to help me. It was my guilt, as you now can understand, as much as my fear for Hao-Han, that kept me from reading it. My brother was kind, a good man; I could not bear the thought that, dying, he had considered me. After what I had done, what I had been doing for so long! After the way I had deceived him!" Wei Ang-Ran gazed out over the hills and the ocean. He turned to us and spoke again. "This morning I opened it. The envelope, as you recall, was thick. We spoke about that: So much advice, so many worthy words, I thought.

"But that was not the case. Protected in many layers of fine rice paper was my brother's jade. With it, the business card of a Chinatown jeweler. Also, a single proverb, in my brother's hand." He smiled a smile full of a lifetime's regret and quoted the proverb to me: " 'A man's love for another must extend to the crows on his roof.' "

I knew this one. When I was a child my father had quoted it to me at those times—fairly common—when I had been brought to tears by the scoldings of my aunt, my mother's older sister who lived with us. He had been telling me that I must love my aunt despite her faults; and he was also, I knew, telling me that my aunt loved me that way too.

And Old Mr. Wei had been telling his brother the same thing.

"Do you see?" Wei Ang-Ran asked me. "Do you see? He knew."

"Knew?" I managed. "About the smuggling?"

"Yes." He carefully replaced the jade Buddha under his shirt, out of sight. "I told you," he said, "I had once, for Strength and Harmony, smuggled three jades similar to my brother's out of China. They went to New York, to a Chinatown jeweler."

"The jeweler whose card—?"

"Exactly. My brother must have known when they came in. I can only think now he knew when all the shipments came in. Clearly he knew also where they went. He visited the jeweler himself, where he bought one of the three. So many years ago . . ." He shook off the memory, the amazement. "That was the jade he sent to Hao-Han. His jade he sent to me. To tell me he knew. To tell me he forgave me."

I looked at the old man's wrinkled brown face. The breeze had stopped; the hilltop was hot and still and silent.

"Will you tell your nephew?" I asked.

"No." Wei Ang-Ran's answer was soft but sure. "My punishment in this life will be to bear this burden alone for my remaining days. What my punishment will be in the next life I do not know."

He bowed to me, and to Mark, and to Bill. He turned to follow his family down the hill.

Mark and Bill and I had an early lunch at a floating restaurant Mark knew: not one of the huge, garish ones the tourists go to but a place that was nothing more than a dozen picnic tables under bright canvas umbrellas on a barge. The kitchen consisted of a few huge woks and steamers also in the open air, and on this barge they turned out the best shrimp *har gow* and the best steamed crabs in Hong Kong. That was according to Mark. I would have to have done a lot of eating to test this claim, and though I was willing to try, time did not allow it: Bill and I were leaving in the morning.

"That's what Grandfather Gao meant," I said, cracking a crab claw as the barge rocked gently. "When he said when I found the answers to my unanswered questions I'd know what to do. But I couldn't even remember what my unanswered questions were."

"One was the two jades?" Bill asked.

I nodded, pulling a lump of crab out of the shell. "And the other was what Franklin had really been up to. If I'd thought to ask that—"

"Nothing would be different," Mark said.

"I don't know. Maybe we could have stopped him.

Grandfather Gao said Franklin was a guy who acted before he thought."

"Not this time," Mark said. "He knew when he called that press conference how it would end."

"And he just stood there. Waiting."

There was quiet on the barge for a while. I didn't know what Bill and Mark were thinking. I was wondering whether I would have had the courage to stand there, waiting.

"Now I want to ask you something," Mark said. "When you found the answers, you'd know what to do about what?"

"Me? About not warning Steven you were planning to pounce on Lion Rock to bring down L. L. Lee."

"You told Grandfather Gao I asked you to do that?"

"Of course. What's so funny?"

"So did I."

"You did? Why?"

"For one thing, in case he didn't like it, I wanted him to know it was my idea, not yours. For another," he shrugged, "getting Lee that way—I just wanted to be sure it was right."

"What did he say?"

"About getting Lee, if I could live with it, that was up to me. About what I asked you, he said, 'A fast-moving stream will find its own course.' "

"He didn't."

"He did." Mark grinned, and the scar on his lip practically blazed in the sun. "Of course, by now I knew that about you anyway."

I looked at Bill, beside me; he was grinning too.

"Oh, for Pete's sake," I said. I went back to my crab. "Well, I'm sorry you didn't get Lee, but I'm not sorry Steven and everyone else can go happily on with their lives now. And Lee did lose his smuggling operation."

A small cloud, carelessly drifting, meandered across the sun. The day went briefly dim. In my mind rose a picture of the scholar's study on the Peak, its pools of lamplight and its hunter's carpet. And L. L. Lee motionless in the carved dark chair, his face hard, his voice stony.

Then the cloud, probably shocked to see where it was, scuttled away, and sunlight flooded down again.

I poured myself some tea, steaming and strong. The hell with L. L. Lee. I was sitting in the sunshine on a barge in a crowded harbor, eating a really great lunch with two of my favorite people. I was not going to worry about L. L. Lee.

In the picture in my mind, Lee smiled like ice. The past, I suddenly knew, was a very long time; but the future was even longer.

A waiter brought over another steamer of crabs. Well, then, Lydia, I thought, eat now, because the present is short. I lifted the lid and divided the spoils.

"I didn't get Lee," Mark said, pulling on a new cold beer the waiter had also provided. "I didn't get Tony Siu for Franklin, or Siu or Big John Chou for Iron Fist Chang. But," he said, "I didn't get killed by Siu when I chased him, and I didn't get fired, either. So I guess I came out ahead."

"And I got a new nose," said Bill. "So I know I did."

We had been ferried out to the barge by sampan, and though we ate mightily and lingered over tangerines and tea at the end of the meal, there came a time when the tea was gone, the tangerines nothing but pits and peels, and the sampan had returned.

We didn't speak much as we crossed the water back to Sha Tin. The day had grown very hot but stayed wonderfully clear. As the sampan rocked gently over larger boats' wakes I could see the mausoleum far above us on the hilltop. Now we were one of the small dark boats on the water. I wondered if anyone was looking down to the sea from a funeral, and if the sight of other peoples' daily lives going on made the funeral easier or harder.

At Sha Tin we parted; Mark was going back to work, and Bill and I had decided to spend our last day in Hong Kong out here in a park in the country, walking on the hiking trails above the sea. Mark and Bill shook hands, and, because they were men, had little they could say to each other beyond Bill's "Thank you," and Mark's "Try to stay out of trouble." They gave each other nods and smiles. Then Bill ambled away down the street, as though he had developed a sudden interest in shop windows.

That left me alone, facing Mark. His eyes briefly followed Bill; then he turned back to me.

"It's too bad," he said.

"No, it's not," I answered. "Still, I know what you mean."

"Will it sound stupid if I say 'keep in touch'?"

"I don't know. Try it."

"Keep in touch."

"Sounds good to me."

Then he kissed me and I kissed him, a kiss a lot like the one at the ferry pier on Cheung Chau.

Mark hailed a cab and headed back to town. I watched the cab weave through the crowded streets until I couldn't see it anymore. Then I strolled down the block to join Bill, to see if he really had found something interesting in a shop window.

The rest of the quiet, hot day Bill and I spent walking under thick jungle greenery. We watched flocks of quacking ducks floating over mirror-surfaced ponds. Slowly, we climbed a long dusty trail to a rock outcropping from which we could see for miles over the hazy ocean. We paused at every water fountain to drink gallons of water and then sweated it out; we bought something to nibble on, steamed buns or pork satay or syrupy rice cakes, from every kiosk and vendor. We didn't talk much, just sometimes a few words to point out things to each other, something one of us thought the other might have missed, might like.

As the afternoon went on we came down the hill again and found a puppet show in progress in a children's area of the park. We sat on low benches and watched. The paper puppets, like puppets everywhere, were having a marvelous

BLOOD RITES347

time bashing each other over the head with paper clubs.
The audience, who seemed to know the story, booed and
cheered and called out warnings and advice. The puppets
ignored them, doing what they always did, and the audience
loved it. When the show was over we put money in the
puppets' red bowl.

"What did your mother say?" Bill asked as we walked
away.

"My mother?"

"Didn't you say you were going to call her this morning?"

"Why did you think of that just now?"

"The little puppet," he said. "The one who kept smacking all the others with the parasol."

"That was the Dowager Empress."

"I rest my case."

I stopped at a water fountain. Wiping my mouth when
I was done, I said, "She said she was glad you were all
right."

"Not possible."

"Well, okay, it wasn't that exactly. What she said was
that you're lucky your ignorance of Chinese ways didn't
get you killed."

"My ignorance of Chinese ways, though admittedly extensive, had nothing to do with it," he asserted.

"I tried to tell her you got hurt protecting a little Chinese
boy, but her position was, a Chinese person doing that job
wouldn't have gotten hurt. So I pulled my trump card,
which was that I couldn't have accomplished what Grandfather Gao sent me here to do without you."

"And was she impressed, won over, ready to ask my
forgiveness for the way she's treated me?"

"She got mad at me. She said that modesty was only
becoming when it reflected the truth, not when it was an
attempt to soften up one's mother. She said the reason
Grandfather Gao sent you here in the first place must have
been that in his wisdom he was trying to show me how
extensive your ignorance of Chinese ways really is. And

that the distraction of traveling with someone as ignorant as you was what kept me from being quickly able to accomplish my task. And that—"

"I give up."

"Very wise. I gave up long ago."

The shadows grew long, though the afternoon light was still bright, not golden as I was used to at the end of the day. Bill said that was because we were surrounded by water. I didn't understand that but I didn't care. We headed to the train, sat and watched the New Territories fly by our window. I remembered why I love air-conditioning. Bill felt better enough that he could lean back against the seat, and I was glad for him. We took the train to the subway and the subway to the streets of Kowloon, where the cars and the jackhammers and the people were familiar now, almost comforting, as everyone crowded, rushed, charged, yelled into cell phones, and hurried as fast as they could to the next place.

Bill and I went back to our hotel, showered and changed and met an hour later in the purple dusk to walk along the promenade to a restaurant with a glass wall facing the Hong Kong Island skyline. We ate vegetable dumplings and Mongolian beef, stewed black mushrooms and aromatic rice. The neon across the water blurred slowly as a tattered fog began drifting in.

"Can I ask you something?" I said, pouring headily fragrant jasmine tea. "You're a man."

"Is that the question?"

"If it were I'm sure you'd have a smart-guy answer. But no. What I want to know is, do you understand old Mr. Wei? Do you understand this two-family thing?"

Bill gazed out the window. He was drinking red wine. Tiny pinpoints of light from a boat in the water sparkled on his glass as he put it down.

"Maybe I do."

"Can you tell me?"

"I don't know."

"Is it about doing it because you can? Having it all?"

He was quiet a minute. Then he said, "I don't think so. I think it's about living where you don't belong." He looked into the night again. "Your grandfather never left China."

"My father said he couldn't leave the place where his family had always lived. If he left there'd be no one to tend his ancestor's graves."

"And Grandfather Gao left, but he seems to have taken China with him."

I thought about that. "Well, he had uncles and great uncles who'd gone to the U.S. before him. He went right to work in the shop when he got there." I thought about the shop that was now Grandfather Gao's, the carved screens, the lion-footed table, the sweet incense. "And he's—" I searched for the words, found none better than the ones Bill had used. "You're right. He took China with him."

Bill sipped his wine. "But old Mr. Wei seems to have been different. He went to New York and got married but he didn't live in Chinatown. He moved his family to Westchester and laughed at the old ways. His family was going to be American, charge headfirst into the modern world, leave the old ways behind. And so was he."

"But he didn't really meant it?"

"I think he did, while he was there. But he came back here over and over, for the business. And, wild and modern as this place is, it's still China."

"So here he was Chinese? And had a Chinese family, and lived the old ways?"

"I think so. I think that's what was going on."

A clearing in the fog beyond the window showed us the harbor water. Hong Kong had come about because of this harbor, deep and slow-moving water where huge ships could anchor, exchange cargo, move on. On the water's calm surface the crowded chaos of the buildings on the opposite shoreline glittered and shone. The moon hung above them, bright and unquenchable.

"Swiftly running water," I said. " 'Swiftly running water does not reflect the sky.' "

To the question in Bill's eyes I said, "That was my fortune at the temple."

He poured himself more wine, and me more tea, and said nothing else.

After dinner we went out to the promenade. The scents of salt water and diesel fuel reached through the fog as we walked. A boat plowed past us, its engine growling. It was near enough for us to see it clearly, its cabin lights and its numbers; all the other boats were blurred presences, lights and sounds without shape in the neon-crowned mist. I felt the fog, damp against my skin; the night was growing cool.

We leaned on the railing to look across the harbor. Bill lit a cigarette. Its smoke blended into the mist. There was no sound but the waves lapping the seawall and, occasionally, a deep horn from the distance: ships speaking, one to another. We looked out over the water for a long time.

I said to Bill, "Spend the night with me."

He turned and so did I. Our eyes held each other. Then he leaned down and I reached up and we met to kiss, and this was the kiss I wanted, warm and deep, slow and long, changeable and constant as water.

We separated.

Bill, without words, looked over the harbor again, and shook his head.

The lights of a boat passed by in the fog. I was wordless too, a little differently. Bill turned to me, saw that, grinned, shook his head again.

Flabbergasted, nonplussed, astounded, I said, "*You're* turning *me* down?"

He said, "It wouldn't be a good idea."

I heard the note of wonder in my own voice as I said, "I've been saying that for years. Now I stopped and you're picking it up?"

"For one thing," he said, turning back to the water, "I'm not in great shape. A guy with a broken nose and a screwed-up back—"

"We'd think of something."

He grinned again. "I'm sure we would." The grin faded. "That's not really the point."

"What is the point?"

He nodded at the harbor, the boats, the neon glowing through the fog. "All this," he said. "It'll be gone tomorrow."

"That's why," I said. "That's why tonight."

"If we spend tonight together, that'll be part of this."

"Would that be bad?"

"The next night we see will be on the other side of the world. This won't be real anymore. The only thing that's real is where you are." He turned from the harbor to me. "I want nights with you to be part of that, where it's real, not part of this. I want that ahead of us, not behind us."

I looked at him as long and steadily and silently as he looked at me. Then I turned to gaze out over the water. "I can't promise that."

"I know."

We stood that way a long time, leaning on the railing as boats appeared and disappeared in the fog, water rose and fell against the stone, and, on the opposite shore, the neon colors shimmered in the mist.

Finally we turned away and started back to our hotel. The fog was thicker; the night was chilly. We had to pack tonight; we had to get ready. Tomorrow, we were going home.

KEEP READING FOR AN EXCERPT FROM S. J. ROZAN'S
BLOOD TIES

When the phone rang I was asleep, and I was dreaming.

Alone in the shadowed corridors of an unfamiliar place,
I heard, ahead, boisterous shouts, cheering. In the light, in
the distance, figures moved with a fluid, purposeful grace.
Cold fear followed me, something from the dark. I tried to
call to the crowd ahead: my voice was weak, almost silent,
but they stopped at the sound of it. Then, because the language I was speaking wasn't theirs, they turned their backs,
took up their game again. The floor began to slant uphill,
and my legs were leaden. I struggled to reach the others,
called again, this time with no sound at all. A door swung
shut in front of me, and I was trapped, longing before, fear
behind, in the dark, alone.

The ringing tore through the dream; it went on awhile and
I grabbed up the phone before I was fully awake. "Smith,"
I said, and my heart pounded because my voice was weak
and I thought they couldn't hear me.

But there was an answer. "Bill Smith? Private investigator, Forty-seven Laight Street?"

I rubbed my eyes, looked at the clock. Nearly two-thirty.
I coughed, said, "Yeah. Who the hell are you?" I groped
by the bed for my cigarettes.

"Sorry about the hour. Detective Bert Hagstrom, Midtown South. You awake?"

I got a match to a cigarette, took in smoke, coughed
again. My head cleared. "Yeah. Yeah, okay. What's up?"

"I got a kid here. Fourteen, maybe fifteen. Says he
knows you."

"Who is he?"

"Won't say. No ID. Rolled a drunk on Thirty-third Street
just up the block from two uniformed officers in a patrol
car."

"Sounds pretty stupid."

"Green, I'd say. Young and big. I told him what happens to kids like him if we send them to Rikers."

"If he's fourteen, he's too young for Rikers."

"He doesn't know that. He's been stonewalling since they brought him in. Two hours I been shoveling it on about Rikers, finally he gives up your name. How about coming down here and giving us some help?"

Smoke twisted from the red tip of my cigarette, lost itself in the empty darkness. A November chill had invaded the room while I slept.

"Yeah," I said, throwing off the blanket. "Sure. Just put it in my file, I got out of bed at two in the morning as a favor to the NYPD."

"I've seen your file," Hagstrom said. "It won't help."

Fragments of stories I would never know appeared out of the night, receded again as the cab took me north. Two streetwalkers, one white, one black, both tall and thin, laughing uproariously together; a dented truck, no markings at all, rolling silently downtown; a basement door that opened and closed with no one going in or out. I sipped burnt coffee from a paper cup, watched fallen leaves and discarded scraps jump in the gutters as we drove by. The cab driver was African and his radio kept up a soft, unbroken stream of talk, words I couldn't understand. A few times he chuckled, so whatever was going on must have been funny. He let me out at the chipped stone steps of Midtown South. I overtipped him; I was thinking what it must be like to grow up in a sun-scorched African village and find yourself driving a cab through the night streets of New York.

Inside, the desk sergeant directed me through the glaring fluorescent lights and across the scuffed vinyl tile to the second floor, the detective squad room. Two men sat at steel desks, one on the phone, the other typing. A third man, at the room's far end, punched buttons on an unresponsive microwave.

"Ah, fuck this thing," the button-puncher said without rancor, trying another combination. "It's fucked."

"You break it again?" The typist, a bald-headed black man, spoke without looking up.

"Hagstrom?" I asked from the doorway.

The guy at the microwave turned, said, "Me. You're Smith?"

I nodded. He was a big, sloppy man in a pretty bad suit. He didn't have a lot of hair but what he had needed a trim. "You know how to work these things?" he asked me.

"Try fast forward."

The typist snorted.

"Screw it," Hagstrom said, abandoning the microwave, crossing the room with a long, loose-jointed stride. "Doctor says I should lay off the burritos anyway. Come with me."

I followed him into the corridor, around a corner, into a small, stale-smelling room. It was empty and dim. The only light came from the one-way mirror between this room and the next, where a big kid rested his head on his arms at a scarred and battered table. Two Coke cans, an empty Fritos bag, and a Ring Ding wrapper littered the tabletop.

Hagstrom flicked a switch, activated the speaker. "Sit up," he said.

The kid's head jerked up and he looked around, blinking. His dark hair was short; he wore jeans, sneakers, a maroon and white varsity jacket with lettering I couldn't make out on the back. They were all filthy. He rubbed a grubby hand down his face, squinted at the glass. That glass is carefully made: It will show you your own reflection, tell you what's behind you; it hides everything else.

Hagstrom switched the speaker off again. "Know him?"

"Yeah."

Hagstrom waited. "And?"

"Gary Russell," I said. "He's fifteen. Last I heard he lived in Sarasota, but that was a couple of years ago. What's he doing here?"

"You tell me."

"I don't know."

"What's he to you?"

I watched Gary shift uncomfortably in the folding chair they had him on. The knuckles on his left hand were skinned; his jacket had a rip in the sleeve. The dirt on his face didn't hide the bags under his eyes or the exhausted pallor of his skin. As he moved, his hand brushed the Fritos bag, knocked it to the floor. Conscientiously, automatically, he picked it up. I wondered how long it had been since he'd had real food.

"He's my sister's son," I said.

This small room was too close, too warm, nothing like the crisp fall night the cab had driven through. I unzipped my jacket, took out a cigarette. Hagstrom didn't stop me.

"Your sister's son, but you're not sure where he lives?" Hagstrom's eyes were on me. Mine were on Gary.

"We don't talk much."

Hagstrom held his stare a moment longer. "You want to talk to him?"

I nodded. He stepped into the corridor, pointed to a door a few feet away. He backed off, so that I was the only thing Gary saw when I opened the door.

Gary stood when I came in, so fast and clumsily his chair clattered over. "Hey," he greeted me, his fists clenching and opening, clenching and opening. "Uncle Bill. How's it going?"

He was almost as tall as I was. His eyes were blue, and under his skin you could still see a hint of softness, the child not yet giving way to the man. Otherwise we looked so much alike that all the mirrors I had seen that face in over the years rushed into my mind, all the houses I'd lived in, all the things I had seen in my own eyes; and I wanted to warn him, to tell him to start again, differently. But those were my troubles, not his. You could look at him and see he had his own.

I pulled out a chair, nodded at the one he'd dropped to the floor. He righted it and sank into it.

"It's going great, Gary," I said. "Nothing like getting up

in the middle of the night to come see your nephew in a police station."

"I'm . . ." He swallowed. "I'm sorry."

"What are you doing here, Gary?"

He shrugged, said, "They say I tried to rob this guy."

I waved my hand, showed him the walls. "Not here. We'll get to that. What are you doing in New York?"

He picked at a dirty fingernail, shrugged again.

"Your folks here too?"

"No." Almost too low to hear.

"They know where you are?"

"No." He looked up suddenly. "I need to get out of here, Uncle Bill."

I dragged on my cigarette. "Most people in here say that. You run away?"

"Not really."

"But Helen and Scott don't know where you are."

He shook his head.

"You still live in Sarasota?"

Another shake.

"Where?"

No answer.

"I can find out, Gary."

He leaned forward. His blue eyes began to fill. With an effort so desperate I could see it, he pulled himself back under control: boys don't cry. "Please, Uncle Bill. It's important."

"What do you want me to do?"

"Get me out of here. I didn't hurt that guy. I didn't even take anything off him."

"No?"

He spread his hands; a corner of his mouth twisted up. "He didn't have anything."

"Why are you here?"

"Something I got to do."

"What?"

"Something important."

"What?"

He dropped his gaze to the table and was silent.

I sat with him until my cigarette was done. Once he looked up hopefully, like a kid wondering if you'd stopped being mad at him and were ready to play catch. His eyes found mine; he looked quickly down again.

Wordlessly I mashed out the cigarette, got up, opened the door. Hagstrom stepped out of the observation room at the same time, and I knew he'd been listening to what we'd said.

Back at his desk in the squad room, Hagstrom brought us both coffee in blue PBA mugs. "I checked you out," he said.

I drank coffee.

"Your sheet: five arrests, one conviction, misdemeanor; interference with an officer in the performance of his duties."

"You want to hear the story?"

"No. That officer was kicked off the Department the next year for excessive use of force. You also did six months twelve years ago on a misdemeanor in Nebraska." He shook his head. "Nebraska, for Christ's sake. Where is that?"

"In the middle."

"You think your sister still lives in Sarasota?"

"Even though the kid says no? Maybe. Helen and Scott Russell. Street has a strange name . . . Littlejohn. Littlejohn Trail."

Eyes on me, Hagstrom picked up his desk phone, dialed Florida information. I worked on the coffee. After a while he put down the phone again. "No Helen Russell, no Scott, no Gary, anywhere in the Sarasota area."

"They move around a lot."

"You got any ideas?"

I shook my head. "Sorry."

"This is your sister?"

I didn't answer.

"Christ," Hagstrom said. "My brother's an asshole, but I know where he lives." He finished his coffee. "I wondered why the kid wasn't afraid you'd call his folks."

I had nothing to say to that, so I just drank coffee.

"Mike Dougherty, lieutenant, Sixth Precinct?" Hagstrom said. "Says hello. Says he's a friend of yours."

"That's true."

"In fact, you seem to have a lot of friends on this Department. Especially for a guy who's been picked up half a dozen times."

"Five."

"Whatever. You're Captain Maguire's kid."

I took out another cigarette, lit it, dropped the match in a Coke can Hagstrom fished from his trash. I made myself meet Hagstrom's eyes. "That's true too."

"I never met him. Leopold did." He tipped his head toward the man who'd been typing when I first came in and was typing still. Leopold looked up, surveyed me silently, went back to work.

"What I'm saying, Smith, I hear you're okay."

I finished my coffee. "I never heard that."

That got a snort from Leopold. The third guy, off the phone now, looked up from the sports page of the *Post*, went back to it.

"This kid," Hagstrom said. "Your nephew. He's fifteen?"

"That's right."

"If I put him in the system now, he'll have a hell of a time getting out."

I nodded; I knew that was true.

"We'll find your sister, but Child Services will have to check them out. Wherever they live now, they'll contact the child protection agency there. There'll be an investigation. He'll be here, in Spofford, while that happens. Even if they send him home, they'll start keeping records. He have brothers or sisters?"

"Two sisters. Younger."

"Your sister and her husband—they abuse these kids? That why you don't speak to them, maybe?"

The question was asked with no change of manner. Hagstrom sipped his coffee and waited for the answer.

"No," I said.

"That the truth, Smith?"

"Yes."

"So why'd the kid run away?"

"You heard him. He says he's got something important to do. He also says he didn't run away."

"When I was his age, 'something important' only meant a girl. Or a football game."

"Could mean the same to him."

"Does he do drugs?"

"I haven't seen him in a while. But he doesn't look it."

"True."

Hagstrom studied me, making no effort to hide it. I finished my cigarette and shoved it in the Coke can. The cop with the paper flipped the pages. The other kept typing. Somewhere else a phone rang.

"I'll release him to you if you want him."

"All right."

"I never did the paperwork. What he said, he didn't take anything from that wino? It's true. I got no reason to hold him, except he's a green, underage kid who doesn't even know how to pick his targets. A wino on Thirty-third Street, jeez. Will he tell you where his parents are?"

"I don't know. But I can find them."

I took Gary in a cab to my place downtown. He slipped me worried sideways glances as we moved along near-empty streets. For most of the ride he said nothing, and I gave that to him. Then, as the cab made a left off the avenue, he shifted his large frame to face me on the vinyl seat. "Uncle Bill? Who's Captain Maguire?"

I looked out the window at streets I knew. "Dave Maguire. He was an NYPD captain. My uncle."

"My mom's uncle too?"

I nodded.

"I never heard about him. All these cops, it seemed like he was a big deal."

"He was." That was about as short an answer as I could give, but he didn't drop it.

"I heard them say you were Captain Maguire's kid. What does that mean?"

I turned to him, turned back to the window, wished for a cigarette. "When I was just about your age I moved in with Dave. For the next couple of years I kept getting in trouble and he kept getting me out. It got to be a joke around the NYPD. Dave was the only one who didn't think it was funny."

Gary gave a thoughtful, companionable nod; this was something he understood. After a moment he asked, "Did you?"

"Think it was funny?" I asked. "No, I didn't."

He was quiet for a while. As we turned onto my block he said, "You moved in with him, like you mean, instead of living with your folks?"

"That's right."

"Did my mom too?"

The cab pulled to a stop. "No," I said.

I paid the cabbie, unlocked the street door, had Gary go ahead of me up the two flights to my place. At this hour, on this street, there was no one else. Even Shorty's was closed, everyone home, sleeping it off, getting ready for another day.

Upstairs, I showed Gary where the shower was, gave him jeans and a tee shirt for when he was done. The kid in him had stared around a little as the cab stopped and he realized this street of warehouses and factory buildings was where I lived. He gave the same wide eyes to my apartment above the bar, and especially to the piano, but he said nothing, so I didn't either.

I made a pot of coffee and scrambled four eggs, all I had in the house. When he came out of the bathroom, dirt and grease scrubbed off, he looked younger than before. He was wiry, long-legged, and he didn't quite fill out my clothes, but he came close. His shoulders were broad and the muscles in his arms had the sharp, cut look lifting weights will give you.

I watched him as he crossed the living room. The circles

under his eyes seemed to have darkened; they looked as though they'd be painful to the touch. He'd found Band-Aids for his knuckles. I saw a bruise on his jaw.

"Hey," he said, his face lighting up at the smell of scrambled eggs and buttered toast. "I didn't know you could cook, Uncle Bill."

"Sit down. You drink coffee?"

He shook his head. "Uh-uh. Coach doesn't like it."

I poured a cup of coffee for myself, asked, "Football?"

"Yeah." He dropped into a chair, shoveled half the eggs onto a plate.

"What position?"

"Wide receiver," he said, his mouth already full. Then he added, "I don't start yet," to be honest with me. "I'm just a sophomore, and I'm new. This school, they're pretty serious about football."

I looked at his broad shoulders, his muscled arms. "Next year you'll start."

"Yeah, I guess. If we stay," he said, as if reminding himself not to get too sure of things, reminding himself how many times he'd started over and how many times he'd have to. I had done that too.

"You used to play football, Uncle Bill?" he asked, reaching for a piece of toast.

"No."

He glanced up, clearly surprised; this was probably heresy, a big American man who hadn't played football.

"We left the U.S. when I was nine and didn't come back until I was fifteen," I said. "Your mom must have told you that?"

"Yeah, sure," he said offhandedly, but a brief pause before he said it made me wonder how much he did know about the childhood Helen and I had shared.

"The rest of the world plays soccer," I said. "Not football. I played some soccer, basketball when we came back, and I ran track."

"Track's cool," he said, seeming relieved to be back on familiar ground. "I run track in the spring. What events?"

"Longer distances. I started slow but I could last."

"Track's cool," he repeated. "But except when you're running relay—I mean, it's a team but it's not really a team. You know?"

"I think that was why I liked it." I brought a quart of milk and the coffee I was working on over to the table. "Take the rest," I said, pointing at the eggs. "It's all yours."

"You sure?"

"I don't eat breakfast at four in the morning. You look like you didn't get supper."

He ate like someone who hadn't eaten in a week; but he was fifteen, it might have been two hours. Between bites, he said, "Thanks, Uncle Bill. For getting me out of there."

"I've been in there myself," I said.

"Yeah." He started to grin then stopped. He flushed, as though he'd said something he shouldn't. He bit into a piece of toast. "How come you don't come see us?" he suddenly asked.

"Hard when I don't know where you are."

He poured a glass of milk. "You and my mom . . ."

He didn't finish his sentence and I didn't finish it for him. I said, "It happens, Gary."

After that I waited until he was done: all the eggs, four pieces of toast, two glasses of milk, a banana.

"Feel better?" I asked when the action had subsided.

He sat back in his chair, smiled for the first time. "You got anything left?"

"You serious? I could dig up a can of tuna."

"Nah, just kidding. I'm good. Thanks, Uncle Bill. That was great."

"Okay, so now tell me. What's going on, Gary?"

The smile faded. He shook his head. "I can't."

"Don't bullshit me, Gary. A kid like you doesn't come to New York and start rolling drunks for no reason. Something wrong at home?"

"No," he said. "What, you mean Mom and Dad?"

"Or Jennifer? Paula?"

"They're kids," he said, seeming a little mystified at the

question, as though nothing could be wrong with kids.

"Are you in trouble?" I kept pushing. "Drugs? You get some girl pregnant?"

His eyes widened. "Hell, no." He sounded shocked.

"Is it Scott?"

"Dad?" Under the pallor, he colored. "What do you mean?"

"I told Hagstrom it wasn't. That you wouldn't run away to get away from Scott. But guys like Scott can be tough to live with."

He didn't so much pause as seem caught up, blocked by the confusion of words. His shoulders moved, his hands twitched, as though they were trying to take over, to tell me something in the language he was used to using. "It's not like that, Uncle Bill," he said, his hands moving apart, coming back together. "I told you, I need to do something. Dad, he gets on my case sometimes, I guess. Whatever. But he's cool." His hands were still working, so I waited. "I mean," he said, "this would be, like, cool with him. If he knew."

"Then let's call and tell him."

I hadn't expected anything from that, and all I got was another shrug.

"He gets on your mom's case, too, am I right?" I asked. "And your sisters'? That can be hard to take."

"I—" He shook his head, not looking at me. "This isn't that. That's not what it is."

"Then what?"

"I can't tell you."

"Christ, Gary." I put down my coffee. "How long since you left home?"

"Day before yesterday."

"Your mother must be worried."

"I left a note."

A note. "Saying what?"

"I said I had something to do and I'd be back as soon as I could. I said not to worry."

"I'm sure that helped." I was sorry about the sarcasm

when I saw his eyes, but it was too late to take it back. "We have to call them, Gary."

He shook his head. "We can't."

"Why?"

Nothing.

"Where are you guys living now?"

"Uncle Bill. Uncle Bill, please." He was leaning forward the way he had in the police station, and his eyes looked the same. "You got to lend me a few bucks, let me go do what I got to do. I'll pay you back. Real soon. Please—"

"You left home without any money?"

He glanced away. "I had some when I got here. But some guys . . ."

I looked at the skinned knuckles, the bruise. "You got mugged."

"Three of them," he said quickly, making sure I knew. "If it was just one—"

"They don't play fair in that game, Gary."

"Yeah," he said, deflating. "Yeah, I know. Look, Uncle Bill." I waited, but all he said was, "Please."

"No," I said. "Not a chance. Not if I don't know what's going on."

He shrugged miserably, said nothing.

"Gary?" He looked up at me. I asked, "Did you know I had a daughter?"

He nodded. "She . . . she died, right?"

"In an accident, when she was nine. She'd be a little older than you are now, if she'd lived." I looked into my cup, drank coffee. "Her name was Annie," I said. "I never talk about her to anyone."

He said, "That's . . . I get that."

"Do you know why I'm telling you about her?"

"Yeah. But . . ."

"Why?"

"Because, like, you're telling me something important, so I'll tell you. But I can't."

"It's partly that," I said. "And it's partly, I want you to know kids are important to me." I spoke quietly. "Maybe I can help."

A quick light flashed in his eyes, a man who'd seen water in the desert. Then his eyes dulled again: the water was a mirage, everything as bad as before.

I waited, but I didn't think he'd answer me, and he didn't.

"All right," I said, getting up. "You look like you haven't slept in a long time. I have people who can find your folks, but I'm not going to wake them now. Take the back bedroom. I'm not going to sleep, Gary, we're three floors up, and I have an alarm system here, so don't even think about it. Just get some sleep."

"I—"

"You can sleep, or you can sit around here with me. Or you can tell me what's going on. That's it."

His eyes were desperate, trapped; they searched my face for a way out. What they found was not what he wanted. His shoulders slumped. "Okay," he said, and his voice was a small boy's, not a man's. "Where should I go?"

I showed him the bedroom in back, unused for so long. I brought him sheets for the bed, offered to help him make it up. "No, it's okay," he said, and he looked like someone who wanted to be alone, so I started out.

"Uncle Bill?" he said. I turned back. "Thanks. I'm sorry." He shut the door.

I cleaned up the dishes, put the milk away. I went through the clothes Gary had left neatly in the laundry basket, picked up the jacket—the word arched across the back was WARRIORS—from off my couch. I was hoping for something, a label, some scrap of paper, that could get me closer to finding where he'd come from, but there wasn't anything. Back in the living room, I put a CD on, kept the volume low. Gould playing Bach: complex construction, perfectly understood. I kicked off my shoes, lit a cigarette, stretched out on the couch, wondering how early I could call Vélez, the guy who does my skip traces. Wondering what it was that was so important to Gary, so impossible to talk about. Wondering where my sister lived now, whether everything was all right there, the way Gary had said.

The searing crash of breaking glass came a second before the alarm started howling. I yanked myself off the couch, raced to the back, but I wasn't in time. When I threw the door open I saw the shards, saw the pillow on the sill and the chair lying on the floor, and knew what had happened. Gary was a smart kid. He'd been afraid to mess with the catches, afraid the alarm would go off before he got the window open. So he smashed it. Held a pillow on the broken glass in the frame, lowered himself out, dropped to the alley. And was gone.

I charged down the stairs and around the block to where the alley came out, because I had to, but it was useless. I chose a direction, ran a couple more blocks calling Gary's name. A dog barked; a drunk in a doorway lifted his head, held out his hand. Nothing else. Finally I stopped, just stood, gazing around, like a man in a foreign place. Then I turned, headed back to the alley. I checked under my window, where the streetlights glittered off the broken glass. No sign of blood: I let out a breath. I straightened, looked up at the window. Light glowed into the empty alley and the alarm was still ringing.

I'm sorry, Gary had said, before he closed the door.